BRISTLING WITH

THORNS.

"JIST CHALK WHAT I TELL YER—THEY'LL FITE."

A STORY OF WAR AND RECONSTRUCTION.

BRISTLING WITH

THORNS.

By O. T. BEARD.

THE GREGG PRESS / RIDGEWOOD, N. J.

First published in 1884 by Laird & Lee, Publishers
Republished in 1968 by
The Gregg Press Incorporated
171 East Ridgewood Avenue
Ridgewood, New Jersey, U.S.A.

Copyright© 1968 by
The Gregg Press, Inc.

Library of Congress Catalog Card Number: 68-20006

Printed in United States of America

AMERICANS IN FICTION

In the domain of literature the play may once have been the chief abstract and chronicle of the times, but during the nineteenth and twentieth centuries the novel has usurped the chief place in holding the mirror up to the homely face of society. On this account, if for no other, the Gregg Press series of reprints of American fiction merits the attention of all students of Americana and of librarians interested in building up adequate collections dealing with the social and literary history of the United States. Most of the three score and ten novels or volumes of short stories included in the series enjoyed considerable fame in their day but have been so long out of print as to be virtually unobtainable in the original editions.

Included in the list are works by writers not presently fashionable in critical circles—but nevertheless well known to literary historians—among them Joel Chandler Harris, Harriet Beecher Stowe, Thomas Bailey Aldrich, and William Gilmore Simms. A substantial element in the list consists of authors who are known especially for their graphic portrayal of a particular American setting, such as Gertrude Atherton (California), Arlo Bates (Boston), Alice Brown (New England), Edward Eggleston (Indiana), Mary Wilkins Freeman (New England), Henry B. Fuller (Chicago), Richard M. Johnston (Georgia), James Lane Allen (Kentucky), Mary N. Murfree (Tennessee), and Thomas Nelson Page (Virginia). There is even a novel by Frederic Remington, one of the most popular painters of the Western cowboy and Indian—and another, and impressive minor classic on the early mining region of Colorado, from the pen of Mary Hallock Foote. The professional student of American literature will rejoice in the opportunity afforded by the collection to extend his reading of fiction belonging to what is called the "local-color movement"—a major current in the development of the national belles-lettres.

Among the titles in the series are also a number of famous historical novels. Silas Weir Mitchell's *Hugh Wynne* is one of the very best fictional treatments of the American Revolution. John Esten Cooke is the foremost Southern writer of his day who dealt with the Civil War. The two books by Thomas Dixon are among the most famous novels on the Reconstruction Era, with sensational disclosures of the original Ku Klux Klan in action. They supplied the grist for the first great movie "spectacular"—*The Birth of a Nation* (1915).

Paul Leicester Ford's *The Honorable Peter Stirling* is justly ranked among the top American novels which portray American politics in action—a subject illuminated by other novelists in the Gregg list—A. H. Lewis, Frances H. Burnett, and Alice Brown, for example. Economic problems are forcefully put before the reader in works by Aldrich, Mrs. Freeman, and John Hay, whose novels illustrate the ominous concern over the early battles between labor and capital. From the sweatshops of Eastern cities in which newly arrived immigrants toiled for pittances, to the Western mining camps where the laborers packed revolvers, the working class of the times enters into various other stories in the Gregg list. The capitalist class, also, comes in for attention, with an account of a struggle for the ownership of a railroad in Samuel Merwin's *The Short-Line War* and with the devastating documentation of the foibles of the newly rici and their wives in the narratives of David Graham Phillips. It was Phillips whose annoying talent for the exposure of abuses led Theodore Roosevelt to put the term "muck-raker" into currency.

While it is apparent that local-color stories, the historical novel, and the economic novel have all been borne in mind in choosing the titles for this important series of reprints, it is evident that careful consideration has also been given to treatments of various minority elements in the American population. The Negro, especially, but also the Indian, the half-breed, Creoles, Cajuns—and even the West Coast Japanese—appear as characters in various of these novels or volumes of short stories and sketches. Joel Chandler Harris's *Free Joe* will open the eyes of readers who know that author solely as the creator of humorous old Uncle Remus. And there is a revelatory volume of dialect tales, written by a Negro author, *The Conjure Woman* by Charles W. Chesnutt.

In literary conventions and the dominating attitudes toward life, the works in the Gregg series range from the adventurous romance illustrated so well by Mayne Reid or the polite urbanity of Owen Wister to the mordant irony of Kate Chopin and the grimmer realism of Joseph Kirkland's own experiences on bloody Civil War battlefields or the depressing display of New York farm life by Harold Frederic. In short, the series admirably illustrates the general qualities of the fiction produced in the United States during the era covered, just as it generously mirrors the geographical regions, the people, and the problems of the times.

PROFESSOR CLARENCE GOHDES
Duke University
Durham, North Carolina

December, 1967

CONTENTS.

BRISTLING WITH THORNS.

CHAPTER I.

THE IMPRESS OF THE DIE.

The Confederacy was organized. A passionate protest styled itself a nation. Mississippi furnished it a head. Fire-eating Mississippians were enraptured. They hailed it as the dawn of a revolution that would fling the "mudsill" and the slave in the wallow, sceptre the master class with a lash, and place "gentlemen" in command of the world. Such was their dream of a golden era. Among all Mississippians none were more enthusiastic than Walter Trenhom.

Trenhom was an impression, the society about him the stamp.

Begun before he could remember, continued without intermission, the imprint was strong and deep; the work of a clear cut, purposeful die.

For more than a year past every public gathering, every drawing room of this State was a mouth of reviling and denunciations, flinging its venom of utterance at everything northern or national. It was a torrid atmosphere of hate and delusions, deepening the imprint of Southern thought on the mind of Walter Trenhom.

The voices penetrated his ear.

He became a cavern of echo. He sneered at the Yankee, despised the laborer, worshipped "king cotton," propugned State's rights, and glibly asserted the omnipotence of the South. Trenhom belonged to a fighting family. His grandfather was a distinguished soldier of the revolution. His

father sustained a heroic part at Chepultepec and Cheru-
busco.

With two generations of fame inviting him to emulation,
and an inheritance of hot blood to push him on, it was impossible that he would remain inactive in the midst of conflict.

He was at Slimpton when the first note of battle reached
him.

During the preceding six months there had been warm
contestation as to the relative merits of Stanmore's three-year-
old filly and Oglehope's half Arabian colt, and it was to be
settled on the mile of straight away road ending at Sol. Burty's grocery.

The neighboring planters all gathered to see the sport and
look through the bottom of Burty's glasses. Burty's bottles
were in demand; the planters' loose change flowed in a prodi-
gal stream over his counter; bottle turners became exhilarated;
eyes flamed, tongues loosened, and Burty was happy. The
contending racers were sent up the road to the starting point.
Half way up a horseman, hat in hand, dashed by them at mad
gallop. The crowd in the store, hearing the heavy beating of
the horse's hoofs and the frantic bellowing of the excited
driver, ran out into the road. The horse paused. The rider
was off. It was half a tumble, half a leap; but he stood on
his feet in the midst of the wondering crowd, screaming with
the lustiness of a sturdy pair of lungs.

"Sumter! Sumter! Sumter! Huy-y-y-agh!"

"What is it, colonel?" asked Col. Bartdale.

"Hoop! Hoop! Hoop!" shouted Col. Crabtree — for it
was he who did the riding and shouting. "Sumter, huy
y-a-y-h!"

"Took!" cried a dozen voices.

"Captured!" cried a dozen more.

"Keflumexed!"

"Wallopped!"

"Took! Burned!" shouted Crabtree. "Hoop! Hoop!
Ho-oya-a-h—!" Then he paused for breath.

"H-o-o-y-a-a-h!" screamed the excited crowd in mad
chorus. They flung their hats in the air; they embraced in

couples, in threes, in fours; they yelled; they grasped hands, slapped each other on the back, threw their arms about one another's necks; they danced; they leaped; they shouted until exhaustion brought their delirium of joy to a pause.

In front of Burty's bar the crowd pressed about Crabtree for details.

The questioning of the crowd and Crabtree's answers ran like this :

"An' hit surrendered fo' shoa?"

"True's shootin'."

"Yer say it was burned?"

"To a cracklin'."

"Burn the Yanks?"

"No!"

"Dad fetch'd ef 'tain't a pity."

"Dog gawn'd shackelty coots! they'd ort to jest flung 'em in an' burnt 'em up."

"Did they make much of a fight?"

"Yanks fight?"

"Bah; they ain't a chick-a-dee's fight in the whole bilin' of 'em."

"And you say they let 'em go nawth?"

"Yes!"

"Ratted shame; ort to put chains on 'em an' toted 'em round for a circus."

"What do the Yanks say?"

"They talk of war!" Crabtree replied. At this the crowd laughed uproariously.

"The idea of a sniveling, canting, clock-peddling Yankee fighting! 'Tain't in 'em," exclaimed one of the group.

"But they will," spoke up a voice at the end of the counter. It was "Uncle Jack" Backfole who spoke.

"Uncle Jack" was a character. The owner of twenty negroes. Tall, gaunt, strong as an ox, with a seamed face the color of tobacco juice, and the best rough and tumble fighter in the county until after he had passed his first half century.

"Pshaw!" "Fudge!" "Fight!" "Boo!"

"I fout with 'em in Mexico 'n seed 'em," Jack persisted.

"That's when they had Southern gentlemen with them and to lead them."

"Mout be! But jist chalk what I tell yer — they'll fite."

"Whip 'em with rotten pawpaws!"

"Yaas, but they uns don't fite that way!"

"You Uncle Jack! Drat it! You ain't agin yer country, be ye?"

"No, I hain't. I'm for Massisip agin the world. But don't you go to foolin' yuself on soft hoein'."

"Hole 'em like coons. Shoa."

"Yaas; but when ye go fer the hole jist look out fer wile cats." Uncle Jack poured his "dryso" down his throat, laid the glass on the counter, placed his back against it, and looked over the crowd. Crabtree was nettled. He turned on Uncle Jack.

"Wild cats?"

"Yaas, that's what I called 'em."

"I'd whip a dozen of 'em."

Uncle Jack bit a huge morsel from his plug of twist, rolled it into the side of his jaw, and replied:

"Mout be; but dad fetched ef yer innards don't bother ye when ye gets through with one."

"Gentlemen," snorted Crabtree, "do yeh heah Uncle Jack? The idee of a weasen-faced, skulkin', shrinkin' Yank fightin'!"

"Yaas, I say they'll fite," retorted Jack, steadfastly.

"So will any cowardly animal when cornered," interrupted Col. Bartdale. "But, sah, you will find the resistance of the Yankee to be the kicking of a toad, sah! The squirming of a sarpent, sah, after youa heel is on them, sah."

"Yaas," retorted Jack; "but look out for his snap and bite afore ye gets yer heel thar!"

Bartdale turned upon the speaker. "Uncle Jack, I am surprised at you. Surprised at you, sah! The Southern gentleman is invincible, sah! Invincible! A half-dozen Southern regiments can stride over the North at will, sah! Yes, at will, sah! From the Potomac to the Passamaquoddy, sah! To the Passamaquoddy, sah!"

"Hoo-y-a-a-h!" shouted the excited crowd.

"Mebby, colonel, mebby!" retorted Uncle Jack; "but if they do, they'll go as prisoners. Shoa!"

Bartdale was amazed and excited. "Heavens, Uncle Jack! You astound me. Astound me, sah! The men of the South are accustomed to arms and to horses, sah! They are the best marksmen and the most expert horsemen in the world, sah! They have martial ardor, sah! And they are daring and brave, sah! Daring and brave, sah! The most patriotic people in the world, sah! They will sweep the Yankee scum. Yes, sah, sweep the Yankee scum before them. Yes, gentlemen, before them."

"Hoo-y-a-a-h!"

"This glorious victory" —

"Hoo-y-a-a-h!"

"Is only a foretaste, a nibble, sahs!"

"Hoo-y-a-a-h!"

"We'll march to Boston, to Boston, gentlemen, and eat the whole apple there."

"Hoo-y-a-a-h!"

"Yes, gentlemen; we'll eat the apple there. We will dictate terms to them there, sahs!"

"Hoo-y-a-a-h!"

"With the Yankees at our feet, sahs!"

"Hoo-y-a-a-h! Hoo-y-a-a-h!" again screamed the news-excited, whisky-maddened crowd.

Uncle Jack shook his head. "I'me with yer, boys! I'me for Massisip every time, you bet! But I ain't no dawg awn fool. You fellahs think ther ain't goin' to be no showah" —

"Not much!"

"You jist wait till them Yanks shakes therselves and gits ready to rain; drat my skin ef you don't think the Arctic Oshun's bruck loose an' peltin' on ye with icebergs!"

"Oh!"

"Jist look out fo' tall scratchin', that's all."

The horse race was abandoned. To pump Crabtree of Charleston news was more exciting. At last he had told all he knew and all he surmised. And the crowd learned, as far

as Crabtree knew them, all the details of the bombardment
and surrender of Fort Sumter.

The younger planters resolved on instant action   They
would raise companies and without delay.   They would haste,
else all the harvest of glory would be reaped.   Time and
place for future meeting were quickly arranged.   Bottles
were paraded and emptied, many wild cheers for Mississippi,
Jeff Davis and the Confederacy disturbed the sultry air, and
the enthused crowd mounted their horses and dispersed.

On his way home Trenhom thought only of his company,
and who would compose it.

Man after man stood up before him.

" Yes ! Yes ! Jim Slocum, Si Coe, Burney, Joe Ratley "—
the long list paraded in his brain.   Tall and short, fat and
lean, swarthy and fever blanched.   But, singular to say, without exception they were all " pore whites."   Not one of them
a slave-holder.

To these poor whites slavery was a petrifying curse.   It
robbed them of manhood; it sifted out their vitality; it
chained them to ignorance; it beat them down in the wallow;
it housed them like beasts; it herded them with dogs; it made
of them its scavengers and hounds; yet of these Walter Trenhom would make his company.

Sarcasm of the century.

When slavery needed an iron hand, it turned to its
sludge.

It would make its buttress of its silt.

Full of ardor, Trenhom galloped homeward.   One after
another of the neighboring planters dropped out on the way,
and at last there was no sound on the road but the swift beating hoofs that hurried him on.

He was within the circle from which he hoped to gather
his recruits.

The dream of glory took possession of him.

He saw himself at the head of his company, garmented in
the bedazzlements of war, drums bravely beating, colors gaily
flaunting, bright steel shimmering, and wild huzzas following.

He traced his pathway.   Marches through cities carpeted

with flowers and adulation; tents pitched on the fragrant bosom of clover; battles that were to be routs; rapid promotion; a return homeward; a crown of laurels. Then father and grandfather would be repeated; he, too, would be enshrined in affection and honor.

When he had reached the height, and stood on its summit in the broad sunlight, crowned with victory, he saw before him a cabin, perched on the hill side, a little way removed from the road.

Between the cabin and the road there had long ago been a fence; so long ago that the remnant of it was rotted and lay sprawling on the ground. Half way up from the road the open space was overgrown with weeds, thistles and brambles, through which here and there was to be seen the frowsy head of a decaying stump. Nearer the cabin the earth was naked and parched. This, too, was dotted with stumps, some of them caverns of rottenness and nests of vermin, while others were begrimed and smutted by fire. In a wallow near one of these, and not more than thirty feet from the door, a large, razor-backed sow lay grunting, her litter running over her and mouthing her teats out of the filth. The cabin was not more than twelve feet square, constructed of small, unbarked pine logs, notched at the ends, to hold them in their place and bring them nearer together. The roof was made of rived clapboards held in position by pine poles laid transverse and bound with withes to the logs below. At one end of this building was a chimney, broad at the base, tapering, and also constructed of logs. This had been daubed inside and outside with mud, and the chinks between the logs of the cabin had been filled in the same way, with moistened clay. Logs split, smoothed with an ax and jointed at the sides, formed the floor within. Of ceiling there was none, the broad spaces between the rafters and the clapboard roof was surrendered to dust, cobwebs and bugs. To this pen there was one rude door with leather hinges, and a glassless window opening, shuttered like the doorway.

The cabin was a blot on the landscape. It was an uncouth and startling exclamation of mendicancy made by the slave system. And yet, cramped, pinched and forbidding as it was, it was a home. It gave shelter to a man and his wife and family. Here lived Joe Ratley, "Red Joe." Seeing the cabin and "Red Joe" perched on a log in front of it, Trenhom drew reins and turned his horse into the beaten path through the weeds to secure his first recruit.

CHAPTER II.

A CRACKER COURTSHIP.

In the year 1855, a duplicate of the Ratley hovel stood near Peeky Run, two miles north of Ratley's as the crow flies. The cabin was a little removed from the run, looking down on its shimmering surface as it rolled on, glittering like silver dots through the dense overhanging foliage. It was the home of one Zeek Buggs and his overflowing nest of little Buggs. It would have been worse than the Ratley place, if possible. But it was not.

There is an impassible in filth, discomfort and degradation. In either place the impassible was reached.

The pit of nastiness has a bottom; both hovels stood upon it.

The road to Slimpton, in front of the cabin, follows Peeky Run, and a few hundred yards eastward bends to the south around the base of an oak-clad hill and is lost to view.

On an early May morning of that year, a boy of twenty summers approached the curve from the south and paused in the middle of the road as his eyes lit on the cabin. He stood a few moments, nervously moving his left shoulder up and down, his eyes following the movement of his bare toes, stroking the pliant clay dust beneath him. After a few moments he moved on twenty or thirty yards in the direction of the cabin, and halted again. Several times this movement was repeated; at last he reached the point where the road approached nearest the cabin. There he stuck fast; then drew himself back among the glabrous, shining leaves of the holly bushes, and the white flowers that made a frame-work about his long, flaming red hair. In this setting its bright color was intensified. He was a boy with a purpose, half inclined to draw back. His resolution was heroic up to the bend of the road.   One half fled when the test was in view; the other half nearly ran him through the holly bushes and across the run when he stood fronting the door of the cabin.

Weak minds are inconstant, blossoming with resolves, barren of execution.

They stride out without estimating.

Approaching the end, they overweigh difficulties and turn.

Ignorant of their capacities and blind to obstacles, they rush to the performance of a purpose; then they shuffle and hesitate before shadows or build insurmountable barriers where none exist, and fly from the *chevaux de frise* their terrors have created.

Such was the boy down before the Buggs cabin.

He was a beast overburdened.   He had drawn steadily on the level.

At the turn of the road the hill began.

From there on was heavy dragging, with many pauses for wind.

The front of the cabin was a chuck hole.

There the overladen beast stuck fast.

Having drawn back, half concealed by the bushes, he stood.

For a time he was motionless.   A bright yellow-plumed Mississippi warbler lit on a low hanging bough over his head, shook his wood-brown tail, ruffled the olive tints of his back, and burst into full-throated song.

An olive-crowned thrush hopped from branch to branch of an adjoining holly bush, turning its white neck first one side then the other, crying "peche! peche! peche!" with shrill, energetic twitter.

The cry of the bird aroused the boy.

He plucked a white holly flower, the startled thrush spread its wings, and the boy listlessly pulled and tore the white leaves, while the toes of his right foot toyed with the rank grass that clung about his ankles.

At last a voice reached him.

"Ho, Joe!"

How long he would have stayed, whether he would have advanced or retreated it is impossible to say.

If the boy's mind was filled with a riddle, or if he was trying to solve it, the voice dispersed the effort.

It is possible the boy was not thinking.

He had reached a certain point in his purpose; it deserted him, and he sank into lethargy.

The voice pricked and roused him. He answered back "Hi!" and at once advanced towards the Buggs cabin.

It was Zeek Buggs who probed him into activity.

Zeek was seated on the ground facing his cabin, his back resting against a stump, his knees drawn up to his chin, indulging in "bacca fro' a cawn cob." He had not observed Joe advancing and halting. But his daughter "Lissy" was not so blind. She saw Joe at the bend of the road, and through a broad chink in the cabin had noted his every wavering movement until he shrank into the holly-bushes. Seeing that Joe halted, she called out through the chink, "Dad, ther's Joe!" Dad looked, saw Joe, and hailed. When Joe approached the stump the younger members of the family gathered in and about the door. Three little ones outside, without even the covering of a fig-leaf, were tumbling with a litter of dogs. "Lissy," "Lindy Yan" and "Nervey" were half concealed behind the door, "peeking out." A girl of five or six, perfectly nude, stood full in the doorway, and behind her the prolific mother of the flock, with a snuff dip in her mouth, looking over the child's head. Joe grew embarrassed under the battery of eyes, and resorted to a child's panacea: he pushed the forefinger of his right hand into his mouth as he paused, voiceless, by the stump that sustained Zeek Buggs' lazy back. The boy was attired in his Sunday best, and on a mission.

He was shoeless, his brown jeans pantaloons, which halted half-way between his knees and his heels, were laced over his shoulders by two blue cotton suspenders, but his clothes were clean and evidently fresh from the wash run; his white cotton shirt opened in front, and, fastened by one button at the throat, exposed his sun-browned breast, and its broad, unstarched and unironed collar reached well down to the points of his angular shoulders.

Of coat and vest he was as innocent as he was of foot-covering.

The boy was Joe Ratley.

As Joe stood by the stump, Buggs, without removing his pipe, spoke: "How'd Joe."

Joe mumbled "How'd," and stood silent.

Buggs looked up, "What be, Joe?"

An idiotic grin spread over Joe's freckled and sallow face.

"Want suthin?" continued Buggs.

"Maum done sent I."

"Maum did?"

"Yaas."

"Maum got ager?"

"No! He! He!"

"Got 'nother brat?"

"No! He! He!"

"Don't you see him's fixt?" interposed shrewd Mrs. Buggs. Buggs removed the pipe from his mouth and looked Joe over, from his brown felt hat to his bare toes.

"Yaas, him be!"

Then a nude child and a pup rolled over against Buggs' long legs.

"Drat yer!" snorted Buggs, as he kicked them away. The child limped round the corner of the cabin howling, the pup biting at its heels.

"Cavortin' arter gals, bein't yu, Joe?" It was wise Mrs. Buggs who asked it.

"Reckon?" said Buggs.

"Shoa!" replied the Bugg in calico.

"Maum done tolt I," whined Joe.

"Ding my buttons!" ejaculated Buggs.

"Maum done tolt I," sniveled Joe again.

"That's hit, be it?" asked Buggs, looking up at Joe.

"Maum done tolt I."

"To com fo' one o' ther gals?"

"Yaas, maum done tolt I."

"Which pup yer want?"

"Hech?"

"Which gal yer want?"

"He! He!" Joe giggled. His idiocy was deepening.

"They's a bilin' o' them," continued Buggs.

"Yaas!"

The maternal Buggs again removed from her mouth the frayed end of the stick with which she was snuff saturating her gums, and spoke:

"Reckon hit be Lissy!"

"You shet!" snorted Buggs. "Dad fetched ef he's fool nuff ter want that brick-top."

"Reckon it be," replied the undaunted mother Buggs.

"Shet yer gabblement, yo' heah!" Then Buggs burst into an uncontrollable fit of laughter. "Dad ratted! They all two red heads 'u'd set yan neck o' woods afiah!"

Joe's finger plunged farther into his wide mouth. Melissa's red head disappeared behind the door and the snuff dip returned to "Maum" Buggs' gums.

"Be hit bricktop?" queried Buggs.

"Don't keer. Maum done tolt I," replied Joe, with his eyes fixed on the sun-baked earth.

"There's Lindy Yan!"

"Yaas!"

"Lindy!" shouted Buggs: "yere!"

No answer.

"Drat yer shackelty hide! Yer heah?"

At that moment the vigorous hand of "Lissy" was applied to the rear of "Melinda Ann" and she pitched out of the doorway snapping "Y e-u!"

As she turned to go back to the door Buggs paternal called her.

"Yeu gal!"

Melinda paused and faced about.

"Joe's artah yer!"

Melinda imitated Joe.

Her finger ran to her mouth. Her face and his were two caverns, at which a finger, half concealed, stood sentinel.

Motionless she confronted Joe with her body, her head bowed. If she saw anything of him it was only his toes.

This was Melinda, a girl of sixteen, tall and straight as an arrow, nut brown, unkempt hair, flowing in tangled waves over her back, shoulders and face, pale blue eyes, and a face which but for dirt and ague blanch would have been pretty; hands small and sun-browned, long finger-nails black with filth, well-shaped bare feet, dirtier than either her hands or face. Her one visible garment was a faded and soiled calico gown, which fell far short of her ankles, exposing the lower half of her beautifully rounded legs. That she wore no under garments was made evident by the exhibition of her body and limbs through the many rents in her dress. Covering it was not.

It filled no requirements of decency.

Seen through all the gaps, the exhibition was shameful.

It was a barbarous want of attire. And yet she was shameless.

She had no better; she never had better; she knew no better. With no experience beyond filthy poverty; chained all her days to foulest ignorance; breathed upon only by bestial instincts; nurtured in a hot-bed of groveling desires; she was degraded without knowing it; indecent, and blind to it.

She was the inscription of her life-long surroundings.

A result of the slave system.

Scoria of the slave furnace.

At once an exfoliation, and a tattered protest against slavery.

Receiving no reply from his daughter, Buggs spoke again.

"Git wi' um—there's more pups heiar nor there's bones."

"Maum done tolt I she'd give we 'uns a skillet," added Joe, in his most persuasive tones.

"Yaas, reckon sh'll go."

"An' a quilt kiver," added Joe.

"Yaas."

"An' a bushel o' grits," continued Joe, enthusiastically parading his riches.

"Wher yer gwine, Joe?" asked Buggs paternal.

" Ter Scroon's clearin'."

" Wher's Scroon? "

" Done gone ter Arkasaw."

" When 'd he git? "

" Dun'o.   He's lit fo' sho'."

" T'ain't no loss ! "

" No ! "

" He's allus a low down, triflin' cuss ! "

" Yaas ! "

" A poa shackelty coot."

" Yaas ! "

" The ignorantest crittah ! "

" Yaas ! "

" Turn up him snout at cawn juice."

" Yaas ! "

" Nevah drink'd a drap in him bawn days."

" No ! "

" Scraped cotton ovah yan like a niggah."

" Yaas ! "

" No scratch of a gent'aman on him."

" No ! "

" Poa, shacklin cuss ! "

" Yaas ! "

" An' him streak't ? "

" Yaas, done gitted."

" Drat ef I ain't glad."

" Yaas."

" An' yer gwine theer? "

" Yaas, maum done tolt I."

" All right, Joe, take the gal."

" Hech ! "

" 'Lindy's gwine."

Joe pushed the finger back in his mouth, giggled idiotic-
ally, " He! he! he!" looked down on the ground, then turned
one vacant eye on Melinda, and Melinda neither blushed nor
paled nor simpered; she simply stood with her finger between
her teeth looking at Joe.

At this juncture the mother and sister joined the group

about the stump, and seeing that neither Joe nor Melinda were likely voluntarily to lessen the distance between them, Mrs. Buggs gave Melinda a violent push between the shoulders that fairly threw her into Joe's arms.

Joe continued his imbecile "He-he-he!" and threw his arms about Melinda, who seemed no way averse to his rugged embracing.

"Yere, Manzy, git a broom, an' they two uns 'll jump over hit."

This was the suggestion of prudent papa.

" Ther hain't nairy broom," replied mamma **Manzy.**

"Git down theer an' cut a holly stick **an' let 'em uns** jump thet."

The stick was brought.

Joe and Melinda, hand in hand, jumped over it, and — they were married.

Melinda entered the cabin, and in a few moments appeared with a piece of discolored calico formed in the shape of a sun-bonnet, and rejoined Joe.

The bonnet and dress were her entire wardrobe.

As soon as Melinda came to his side, Joe turned and walked down the path, Melinda following a few feet behind him.

Without a kiss, without a tear, without a prayer, without a farewell, without a " God bless you," uttered or thought, this girl, unregretted and unregretting, walked away after Joe— walked away in rags and filth — down through the path, out into the dusty road, and passed out of sight around the bend without once turning her head, away from the only home she had ever known — forever.

CHAPTER III.

THE TWO TOADS.

A mile away from Buggs' cabin Joe turned into a foot-path leading over the hills, and steadily marched on until he reached Scroon's abandoned clearing, passed through it and stood before the open door of the cabin. There he paused, looked in and turned. Then for the first time he seemed to be aware that Melinda stood behind him.

All along the clay road and the tortuous path over the hills they had been dumb.

Not one word passed between them.

She kept pace with him, lagged when he loitered and increased her speed when he hurried.

She was his; a dog with a new master.

And like a pliant dog she nosed his heels and conformed her pace to the speed or drivel of his legs.

When Joe's eyes fell on Melinda, an idiotic leer spread over his face.

Then he laughed, "He! he! he!"

Melinda stood looking vacantly on the few feet of bare earth intervening between her and her new - found hus-band.

"Pooty, hain't ye?"

Melinda was dumb.

"Drat ef ye hain't pooty; hain't ye?"

Melinda nervously wound one of the strings of her calico head covering about her fingers, then swung the bonnet to and fro, with the swaying motion of her body.

"Come yeer."

Melinda advanced.

"Set."

Melinda silently looked to know where.

Joe was seated on a squared log that served for a doorstep. He pointed to a place beside him — " Yeer." Melinda
sat down.

Joe's milky eyes were close to her face.

He raised his right hand quickly and chucked her under
the chin.

" He! he! he! "

" He! he! he! " chorused Melinda.

" Drat ef ye hain't pooty."

" He! he! " simpered Melinda.

" Pooty! "

" He! he! "

" Maum don't tolt I."

" He! he! "

" Maum 'lowed you's a peert heifer."

" Yees."

" An' dinged pooty."

" He! he! "

Then they sat in silence.

Two great toads. They had croaked, now they gaped.

A quarter, a half hour sped away, then Joe stood up and
walked into the cabin.

A cotton bed tick filled with straw, as it had been abandoned by the former occupant of the place, lay on a rude bed-
stead of pine poles in one corner of the cabin; a birch broom
leaned against the wall in another corner; a few broken dishes
lay scattered on the floor. This was the cabin and its furnish-
ing. After Melinda had felt the bed, looked into the broad,
open fireplace and up the chimney, Joe spoke again.

" 'Lindy! "

" Eh? "

" Gwan ovah to maum's an' git the skillet an' grits."

" An' the kiver? "

" Yaas, maum done tolt I we uns mout hev 'em."

Melinda turned to go.

Joe called again.

" 'Lindy! "

" Eh? "

" Dad fetched if yer ain't pooty."

"He ! he !"

And Melinda trudged away under the burning sun with this little joy trickling in her heart. Some one had told her she was pretty. She had heard it for the first time in her life. As she crossed Peeky Run on her way to " Maum " Ratley's cabin, seeing the reflection of herself on its glossy surface, she paused and looked. She sat down by the stream and looked again. Her little feet dropped into the current. She leaned forward, her fingers dallying with her glowing limbs where the rippling waters rolled about them. Unconsciously she passed her hands upward, downward, and the loosened dirt and dust flowed away in the branch. She saw how her limbs glistened fresh from the lavatory. Perhaps she noticed how much prettier they looked. She made a cup of her hands and washed her face and her neck. She moistened her tangled mass of hair and pushed it back from her brow and face. Then she looked again in the stream. A contented smile stole into her young face, and she trudged on. In front of the Ratley cabin she paused, and found relief from embarrassment by introducing her forefinger between her rosy lips. Maum Ratley saw her and spoke :

"How de?"

Melinda devoured the earth with her eyes.

" Seen Joe?"

" He ! he !"

" Marrit ter Joe?"

" He ! he !"

" Wher's Joe?"

" Yan! " whispered Melinda, pointing over her shoulder in the direction she came.

" Joe told yer to ter come?"

"Yees, told I ter come."

" Marrit."

"He! he !"

" Marrit be yer?"

"Yees ! he! he!" murmured 'Lindy, still devouring the earth with her eyes.

The mother-in-law pointed to the decayed door sill and uttered one word, " Set."

Melinda sat down, twining the bonnet strings nervously about her fingers. Mrs. Ratley entered the cabin and brought out an iron skillet, a tin pan, a gourd, two battered knives, and a sack containing about a half bushel of grits, and laid them down at the girl's feet.

Melinda looked at them, inventoried them in her mind, ran them over again and again. There seemed to be something missing. At last her wandering thoughts grasped it.

" Kiver," she whispered, without looking up.

" Eh? "

" Kiver ! "   A little louder.

Mrs. Ratley removed the corn-cob pipe long enough to say, " Quilt kiver? "

" Yees ! "

" I done tolt Joe tu git yer ! "

" Ther kiver " murmured Melinda.

" Eh? "

" Joe done tolt I."

" Him did? "

" En he done tolt dad."

" Him did? "

" Yees ! "

" Him hain't no bug eatah, ain't Joe."

" He ! he ! "

" He-um a peart un, him be! " snorted the exultant mother.

" He ! he ! "

" An' him tolt Zeek? "

" Yees, he-um tolt dad."

Mrs. Ratley ran her fingers into her frowsy hair, rubbed a few minutes vigorously. The sought idea touched her dirty finger tips, she strode past Melinda into the cabin, and returned in a few moments with a faded, tattered and filthy bed cover, which she added to Melinda's store of riches. As soon as the cover was laid down, the girl stood up, threw the quilt over her shoulder, opened the sack, thrust the tin pan, gourd and knives into the grits, gave the neck of the sack a twist, landed it on her shoulder on top of the quilt, seized the skillet in the vacant hand, and without a word walked away.

When Melinda returned to her new home, thereafter to be known as the Ratley cabin, Joe was seated on the door log, his clasped hands holding his long legs up to his chin. A vacant grin illuminated his face as Melinda trudged past through the cabin door and laid her burden in the center of the floor.

" Git 'em."

" Ther be."

" Seen maum? "

" Yees."

" Powful good."

" Yees."

" She-um tolt I ter git yer."

" Yees."

" Git kiver? "

" Ther be."

" Maum yowl."

" No! "

" Powful good maum."

Having reached this point Joe noticed Melinda. With his left hand against the side of his head, the ends of his fingers began a violent rooting for a thought. Slowly it came to him. Melinda was washed. Flushed with the walk and the load, her purified skin looked beautiful. It dawned on Joe.

" Lindy! dad fetched you's pooty."

"He! he! "

"Pooty ez a spotted hoss, yo' be."

" He! he! "

" Ther's the ax."

Melinda looked, saw the ax, took it in her hand, went out, chopped an armful of wood, and, by the aid of the flint which Joe carried, a glowing fire was soon streaming up the soot-coated chimney.

While Melinda was building the fire Joe cleaned two squirrels. These he had shot while Melinda procured their

household treasures of his mother. The ax he had fished
out of a hollow tree, where he had hidden it long ago. He
found it in the road, where it had probably been dropped
from a passing wagon, and concealed it for use when he
might need it. That and a gun, with which Joe was an expert, were his only treasures. The gun was drawn from the
loft of the cabin, where he hid it when on his hunt for a wife.
The tree was disemboweled of the ax, and Joe, with his gun
and ax, with the stores from " Maum " Ratley, and a wife,
was rich.

Thus they began life.

Deer, bears and squirrels were numerous in the surrounding forests, and the occasions were rare when there was any
lack of an abundant supply of meat in the cabin.

The peltries of deer, wolves, cougar and wild cats which
frequently fell victims of Joe's unerring aim, supplied him
with powder, whisky, which he called " cawn juice," the scant
clothing they both used, and the scantier store goods which
at rare intervals entered their hovel.

As they began they continued.

Such manual labor as was performed Melinda did.

She planted sweet potatoes, corn and tobacco, and tended
them.

Wood-chopping, digging, planting and hoeing was her
work.

The women did that work at the home of her childhood.

Melinda came to her new home with this training strong
upon her.

It was the only life she knew.

It was ingrained by years, by practice, by observation.

She was penetrated by no thoughts of hardship.

Resistance never occurred to her.

" Women folks is made to hev chillun, tote wood and
scratch taters."

That she had heard and remembered, and in her new
home she practiced.

She carried wood from the beginning; hoeing potatoes
and mothering children came after.

Of love there were no words or thoughts.

Melinda knew hunger and cold, and pain, and squalor, and filth.

Her life had been a prolonged submission to them all.

She was in their grip. She was riveted to the inexorable.

Their severe pressure was on her.

She suffered; she knew that; but she never thought of escape. There was no hope of better to urge her to writhe, or struggle, or protest.

With her mouth in the dust she crawled.

There was no room for love in her groveling surroundings.

Animalism there was.

Love there was not.

Love is a product of mind.

Nature does not plant it.

To love there must be thought and tenderness, and capacity to feel. Melinda had neither.

She was a human toad.

Joe was another.

Joe was one too many in an over-crowded nest, and was pushed out to make a nest of his own.

Melinda was pushed out after him.

There was no feeling in the matter.

The boy needed some one to make fires, bake corn pone, fry squirrel, and be a mother to his children, and the girl was pushed away from a table where there were too many mouths for the "taters," upon the first person who was willing to take her.

That Melinda might have grown to love a better man is possible.

That she did not then or ever afterward love Joe is certain.

He gave her little opportunity.

Married, the owner of a woman, he felt himself to be a man.

He had been the companion of boys.

He turned at once from the beardless to the bearded, and

3

to their ways, and, the second night after his wooing, came home—drunk.

Was Melinda shocked?

Not at all.

She had seen it too frequently.

She had shivered too many nights, perfectly nude, in the open fields, concealed from the fury and heavy hand of a drunken father, to be shocked by a drunken husband.

As Joe staggered through the door, loading the still, dark air with obscene oaths, but one thought entered her mind, "Will him wallop?" and when in drunken stupor he fell prone and helpless upon the floor, she turned her face to the wall and went calmly to sleep.

Before the first infant came, at the end of a year, these scenes had been repeated many times.

She made no protest.

It was possibly useless.

She had never heard of a woman protesting.

It never penetrated her mind that she had a duty in that direction.

Even if it had, she knew no words in which to protest.

She lived on in passive subjection, in hushed endurance, thankful that she escaped the heavy hand, and wondering how soon it would come.

The first child came.

Maternity is a double birth—a creation and a re-creation.

A child born into the world; a woman born into knowledge.

It is an upheaval.

Then if there is any good in the depths of a woman's nature it is thrown to the surface and fused in the thought of motherhood.

Melinda drew her babe to her breast—that was the mother instinct.

She looked about the desolate cabin and pressed the child tighter to her bosom, and said, "Poor chile!"

For the first time she saw her nakedness.

Her vacant mind was filling; dispersion vanished.

She began to think of the child, the misery before it, then, what would she do to remedy it — for the child.

She was groping in a rayless abyss.

With help she might have reached the light.

When the child was born, Joe was absent.

The night following and the next day Joe was gone.

The second night he came to the door, stumbled in and lay on the floor in a drunken stupor until late in the morning.

When he awoke he saw there was no fire, nothing to eat, and Melinda was in bed.

He raised up, walked over to the bed, and with an oath struck her full in the face.

The child mother saw the hand descending, saw it raise and fall the second time.

She set her white teeth together, but she neither spoke nor flinched from the blows.

Then she staggered, painfully, uncomplainingly, to the floor, lighted a fire and cooked breakfast for the beast.

The babe lay wailing in the bed.

The brute looked wonderingly at it until his corn bread and venison were cooked.

Then he went out and Melinda went back to bed.

The upheaval was useless.

The groping was abandoned.

The vacant mind was filling with something else.

It took form.

Two weeks after, when Melinda was entirely recovered, it bore fruits.

Joe came home in the night intoxicated. When he awoke in the morning he filled the room with profanity.

He was bound hand and foot with thongs, and helpless.

When he stirred, Melinda sat up in bed and looked at him. Looked steadily, calmly, silently; then lay down again and nursed the child.

Joe's threats were multiplied; his oaths horrible.

Melinda was silent and irresponsive.

When the child was nursed, Melinda raised from the bed,

walked past Joe to the fire, baked a corn-cake, sat on the hearth and ate it.

Then she stood up, walked to the door, went out and returned with a heavy hickory rod.

Joe looked at her in amazement.

The oaths died away on his lips.

" 'Lindy, onlash me."

" I'm gwine ter lick yer, Joe."

" 'Lindy?"

" Yaas."

" Yer hain't gwine ter."

" Yaas, Joe."

" What fer yer gwine ter?"

" Fer wollopin' I."

" 'Lindy!"

" Yaas, Joe."

" Yo-um best git yer gone."

" I hearn yer, Joe."

" Ding blast yer corn-shuckin' hide!"

" Yer kickin' 'fore yer spurred, Joe."

" Ef yer tech me, ding my buttons ef I doan larrup an larrup yer!"

" Joe!"

She sat down on the floor facing him, not one ray of emotion in her face.

" Jess shet yer gabblement an' onlash these yere!"

" Joe!"

" Shet an' onlash!"

" Joe!"

" Dog awn — drat — "

" Ef yer teches me agin — "

" Yaas — ding me — yer'll see!"

" Make shoa wuck, Joe."

" Eh?"

" Make shoa, Joe."

" Eh?"

" Shoa!"

" For what, shoa?"

"I'ZE GWINE TER LARRUP YER."

"I'ze boun' ter kill yer ef yer does." Her face looked
infantile when she said it.

"Eh?"

"Ef yer don't kill I next wallopin', I'ze boun' ter kill yer,
Joe. Boun' ter." Still the infantile look was upon her.
Then she stood up.

Joe looked on the girl surprised.

For the first time in his worthless life he was awed.

If Melinda had wept or blustered. If she had been a
scream cat, ruffling her back, Joe could have understood it.
But to sit there beside him with a heavy rod in her hand and
speak to him so softly, without a trace of passion or anger,
that was beyond his feeble comprehension.

Then Melinda spoke to him again.

He was lying on the floor, face up.

"I'ze a gwine ter turn yer."

"Fer what?"

"I'ze gwine ter larrup yer."

Then she turned him over and rained blows upon him while
he whined like a whipped cur.

Hearing the child cry, Melinda paused in her work, went
over to the child, took it in her arms, nursed it, soothed it,
laid it down in bed, then again raised the rod and returned to
Joe, who during all the time she was nursing had begged and
entreated to be released.

The girl was deaf.

She was immovable.

She was destiny.

Again she showered vigorous blows upon the quivering
back, and hips, and limbs, until the oaths died away in tears
and prayers; until she had given him the full measure of her
resolve.

Then she turned away from him to the child.

During all the long day Joe lay prostrate on the floor without either food or drink.

To all his entreaties for release or sustenance Melinda returned only silence.

Not one syllable passed her lips. As the sun was dropping down behind the trees in the valley Melinda stooped over him and commenced to undo the thongs that held him. As she did she said:

"Joe, ef yer beats me, make shoa—mind yer, make shoa."

She asked no assurances, made no bargains, but lapsed into silence and unbound the thongs. Joe attempted to rise, but his cramped limbs refused their office. He sat up, and asked for a drink of water; this Melinda brought him.

For an instant a malignant light came into his blood-shot, milky eyes, but under the calm, unflinching gaze of the girl who stood before him it faded, faded slowly away—died out, never to return.

He was conquered and cowed. If the girl had then known her power—then known what use to have made of it, how different it would have been.

Joe never attempted to beat Melinda after that.

Otherwise there was no change in their lives.

The cabin grew filthier; the clay chinking frayed out from between the logs; the rain and storm beat in.

Melinda effortless and her children helpless, were in the abyss.

The abyss was a cesspool.

It was to the door of this house of misery that Walter Trenhom rode to secure a "Confederate hero."

CHAPTER IV.

IN SEARCH OF A RECRUIT.

When Trenhom rode up to the door Ratley was sitting near it, on the ground, with his back against the logs of the cabin. A drab slouch hat was pulled over his eyes to shut out the rays of the setting sun; his long legs, ending in dirty bare feet were stretched at full length upon the parched and unswarded earth. Hearing the horse's hoof beat, he looked up and saw Trenhom. Then Trenhom spoke:

"How d'e, Joe?"

"Peert eend up."

"Beautiful evening."

"Yaas."

"Pleasant lately."

"Yaas, sence hit fair'd up."

"How are you getting on?"

"Waal, hit's sorter 'twixt hay and grass."

"Game plenty?"

"They's owdacious scace."

"How's the children?"

"Scrawny."

"Sick?"

"Dogawned ef I don't disremembah. They's a powful harryment, chillen is."

Hearing the voices outside, Melinda stood in the door. Trenhom had never seen her before. He saw her now at disadvantage. She wore but one garment, a faded calico gown, longer than the one in which she was married, but fully as foul and tattered. If it had been constructed to display her supple form it served the purpose admirably. It outlined every curve of her body. Six years had changed Melinda but little.

At twenty-two most of the women of her class were sallow, wrinkled and old.

Snuff dipping and " cawn juice " grind quickly.

In such a mill youth, beauty and roundness vanish rapidly.

But Melinda neither used tobacco nor whisky. She was the one "low down" woman in that whole region who did not.

The rosiness of sixteen was on her cheeks, the same roundness in her face, and her wealth of tangled nut brown hair yet flowed over her back and shoulders.

A child was nursing at her breasts when she heard the voices. Laying it down, she appeared in the doorway as the child left her when it abandoned its life-giving food.

Trenhom looked upon her exposed bosom, on her lithe, supple form, on her rounded cheeks, on her tangled web of hair, and he thought, " what a picture of filthy beauty." He touched his hat and addressed her :

" Good evening."

" Even," she responded.   Not a muscle of her body moved. She stood with wide open eyes. Her mouth was closed and there was an imperceptible motion of her lips; that was all. And this was the first white gentleman that ever stood before her cabin door, or ever addressed her.

" Children well ? "

" Yees."

" Any ague ? "

" No."

" I see you've some corn in."

" Yees."

" Doing well ? "

" No great scratches."

" It looks well."

" Hit's mighty nigger'd out lan'."

" It looks as if it might make a fair crop."

" Hit do once an' agin."

" I came to see Joe."

" Yees; ther him."

" I see; I want him to join my company."

" Yees."

" I suppose you have no objections."

" Eh !"

" I suppose you don't care."

" No."

Still she stood motionless.

Joe had risen to his feet and stood leaning against the cabin.

" You'll join, Joe ?"

" What ?"

" My company."

" What com'ny ?"

" My cavalry company.*

" Critter company ?"

" Yes."

" What fer ?"

" The war."

" What waah ?"

" Haven't you heard ?"

" Heern ?"

" Yes."

" A waah ! Fouten ?"

" Yes."

" Hier ?"

" No, not here; in the Carolinas and Virginia."

" Whah's 'um ?"

" Way off east and north."

" Fer ?"

" Yes, hundreds of miles away."

" Who's um wid ?"

" With the abolitionists."

" Who's um ?"

" The Yankies."

" Dad rat the Yanks."

" Miserable abolition creatures."

" Yaas."

" Their tyranny has become unsupportable."

" Eh ! "

" They are putting on too many airs."

" Yaas ; rot their corn shuckin' hides."

" You know they have elected Lincoln president ? "

" Yaas ! I heern he'um a dratted mulatter. "

" And they are determined to abolitionize the country an emancipate our slaves."

" Eh ? "

" They are going to free the niggers."

" Make niggah uns free ? "

" Yes."

" No mastahs ? "

" No."

" No dawgs to houn' um ? "

" No."

" No lickin' ? "

" No."

" Ding my buttons, an' ther gwine ter do that ? "

" Yes, sure."

" Great snakes an' gawl ! Make 'um triflin' niggah uns free, an' no lickin, no mastahs, an' no houn's ? "

" Yes, that's what they are after."

" An' let niggah uns gwan loose roun' ? ' "

" Yes."

" Like we uns ? "

" Yes."

" An' not boun' to git outen er road an' tech 'im hat to we all white gen'lmen ? "

" Exactly.   That is what they'll do."

" Great snakes an' gawl ! "

" You know we have captured Sumter ? "

" No-o-o ! "

" Yes we have ! "

" Shoa ? "

" Yes, sure."

" By gawl ! " Joe brought his broad red hand down with emphasis on his thigh.   " Yee'd ort to fotch 'um up to Burty's, gi'um a hundred on his bar back, an' burn 'um wi' a slow fiah.

Dratted bug eatin' coot, thet hain't none too seveigrous fer 'um."

"And you'll join my company?" Trenholm smiled and replied interrogatively.

"For roun' hier?"

"No, for the seat of war."

"Off ther in 'Jinny."

"Somewhere there. The opinion is that the real seat of war will be in Virginia."

"And there'll be rail fouten?"

"The opinion is that Yankees will never dare face Southern gentlemen."

"Yaas they uns 'ull squall like houn's."

"Many of our wisest people think that. But there may be fighting."

"Down airnest rail fouten?"

"Yes. It may be that the spirit of the revolution has not been devoured by their greed of gain ; that it may survive ; that they may prove foemen worthy of our steel, of whom we shall win our laurels only by superlative heroism. It may be that the conflict now begun may prove the most desperate and deadly cut and thrust, with cannon, rifle and sabre, of the century. But I do not think so. Our leading people do not think so."

Joe stood looking at Trenhom in open-mouthed wonder. One-half of this flow of words was beyond his comprehension. But he gathered this much out of it, there might be real shooting, man against man.

When Trenhom paused Joe's dirty finger tips sought his scalp, and, after a moment's scratching, he said :

"Kunnell, ter bleege you, I don't mine jinin', hif ther critter com'ny is ter liter roun' hier."

"But it is not ; it's to go east and north."

Joe shook his head.

"The pay will be good and certain?"

"Yaas."

"And you will join?"

"Don't see as how I kin."

"You are surely not afraid ?"

"I haint the skeery sort o' a cracklin'."

"Why not join then ?"

"Waal, yer see hi'm shackelty like, an' ther's the woman an' chillun."

Trenhom's gaze was riveted on "the woman," standing silent and statuesque in the doorway, the soft evening breeze sweeping her light calico covering close about her shapely limbs, flinging them out in bold relief for the admiration of his wondering eyes. Trenhom was not ignorant of "low down life" around him. He had never penetrated one of the outcast homes, but he had seen the men, lazy, loutish, idle and shiftless, and he had, in passing along the roads, seen the women drawing the water, cutting and carrying the wood, plowing, seeding, hoeing, harvesting—however little or much was done—while the men roamed the forest with a gun on their shoulders and a dog at their heels, or lay in drunken stupor about the cross-roads groceries; and he had seen enough of Joe to know that he was neither better nor worse than his class. He was a "low down," "a cracker," a "sandhiller," "pore white trash," with all their beastly instincts, degraded habits, discrowning of women, and disregard for their families.

When Joe.appealed to his family Trenhom would have turned away.

An anomaly had crept into his life.

In all his experience the slave and the poor white lay prostrate in the dust grovelling—a lash on the back of one, a heel on the neck of the other—both equally cringing, fawning and submissive.

Now he had been refused by a "low down."

A toad eater had dared to think.

A parasite had found audacity to say no.

He would have turned away in anger and disgust, but he remained.

He was in the power of the grotesque.

A paradox held him.

Joe's mummery for refusal was so absurd Trenhom would

"WISH'T I WERE A SLABE."

have laughed. He only smiled, and turned to the statue in the doorway. He had resolved that Joe should be his first recruit.

"I have been asking Joe to join my cavalry company."

"Yees!" Her voice was soft, low and musical, and but for its atrocious *patois*, would have been delicious.

"And go away to the war?"

"Yees!"

"Are you willing that he should go?"

"Yees!"

"He says he must stay here to take care of you and the children."

"Him needn't ter."

"You will get along very well with him gone?"

"Yees."

"And you are quite willing to have him go?"

"Yees."

"That's patriotic."

"Eh?"

"You are looking at the matter in the proper light."

"Reckon."

"I'll speak to Mrs. Trenhom about you."

"Who be she-um?"

"My wife."

"Yer don't needn't ter."

"She will see that you want for nothing."

"Reckon I kin scrape."

"If all the women of the South are like you, we will preserve the institution of slavery from the Northern vandals."

"Eh?"

"I say if all our women are like you, we will preserve our country from the oppressions of Northern tyrants and save our slaves."

"Wish't I wer a slabe."

"What?"

"Wish't I was a niggah slabe."

"You?" exclaimed Trenhom in a tone of surprise.

"Yees."

" You have children ? "

" Yees."

" And them slaves ? "

" Yees."

She spoke deliberately, calmly, without motion of hand or body, with no tinge of passion or emotion in her voice.   Her words were a dead level of soft notes.

Trenhom looked at her in amazement, then exclaimed :

" Great heavens ! "

He believed that slavery was of Divine origin.   That it was the highest plane on which the subordinate class could be planted.   And yet when a woman, whose life was lower than that of the slaves, whose comforts were less, whose degradation was deeper, deliberately announced that she envied the slaves, he was shocked.   Again the impulse was on him to ride away, but he turned to Joe.

" Well, Joe, you hear what your wife says."

" Yaas."

" She is willing for you to go."

" I heern."

" You'll go, of course."

" Women's pizen critters; they-um don't never know nuthin'."

" I think yours knows what she is about."

" Mout be."

" I shall put your name down."

" I'm shackelty, kunnel.   Shackelty."

" You'll do."

" Hain't worth a chitterling when I'ze ther shakes."

" You haven't the ague 'now ? "

" They-um be snaglin long ter-morer."

" Then you will not go."

" I'd like ter 'bleege yer, kunnel."

" But you will not go ? "

" I'd like ter 'bleege yer like all wrath.   I wud."

Trenhom, in disgust, turned his horse and rode away in the dim twilight.   His mind at first was full of disgust at the evident cowardice of Joe.   Then rose up before him the phantom of the woman who wished she was a slave. What must her life have been ? What horrors had she endured ? What storms of abasement and suffering had beat upon her that she would in those calm, low, musical tones, wish that she, too, and her children, were chattels to be owned and bought and sold ?

When he had thought of the words his mind became pervaded with the woman, with her perfect figure, and her face that had not yet been seared by the scorching iron passed over it.

Privation is a sharp graver.

It carves deep and strong.

But here was a face of resistance.

For twenty-two years the graver had harrowed the surface and not made a scratch.

When the ensemble of the woman—her life and appearance—occurred to him, he was startled. If Melinda had been homely, then and there she would have stepped out of his mind forever.

The autocracy of beauty held her there.

When Trenhom had departed, Joe returned to his pipe and lounge against the logs. For a few moments wandering thoughts of " Lindy " flitted through his vacant brain. " She wanted fer me ter gwan ; " yes, she " wanted fer me ter gwan ; " but before bedtime this had disappeared ; without inquiry as to why or wherefore, without regret or thought of regret, without feeling, or self-condemnation, disappeared, was forgotten, and his dull brain lapsed again to vacancy. When he shouldered his rifle in the morning, even Trenhom and his proposal and the war had slipped out of his mind. All about him, on the highways and bye-ways, men were whispering, muttering, gathering. Joe sauntered listlessly off into the forest, a gun on his shoulder, a dog at his heels, gazed into the trees as he loitered along, pausing and listening for " game sounds," then sank down between the gnarled, uplifted roots of a huge tree, drew out his corn-cob and rested until rest passed into slumber. On the highways, and at the country cross-road, trees blossomed with placards ; every blossom a proclamation, enrollments here, enlistments there. Infantry, artillery, and cavalry.

The cross-road groceries overflowed with men brave and determined ; with blusterers strutting and swaggering ; the air fetid with vaporing, gasconade and profanity.   " Vandals," " assassins, " " nigger-lovers," ·" miscegenationists." Billingsgate turned against the nation.

Where populations were dense companies filled instantly ; but in districts where it required one-third or more of all the arms-bearing people to fill a company, there was more delay.

Enlistments were rapid until all the martial, adventurous and reckless were enrolled ; then dragged at snail pace.   The country gathered each day to witness the parade of gleaming arms, the tramp and evolutions of " Tigers," of " Alligators," of " Yankee Exterminators."

The novelty was exciting.

The fife and drum were exhilarating.

The " cawn-juice " was abundant.

They hurrahed for the " Exterminators ; " cheered for " Mass-si-sip," for the confederacy, for " Jeff," cursed all "Yanks" and their " mulatter president," and returned to their homes drunk.

It was so much easier to hoot and get fuddled than it was to sustain the fatigues of a campaign, the restraints of military rule, or the brunt of battle.

The first " rat-tat-tat " reached Joe's ears.   He went with the others.

With hands in pockets he stood and gaped.

When tired of standing he lay lounging against a tree and gaped wider.

" Licker ! "

" Yaas."

He never refused.

He swallowed, drew the back of his red hand across his face, and lounged for the next invitation.

Drums, bugles and banners ; declamations and decanters ; pulpits and petticoats did their work but slowly in Joe's neighborhood.

It drawled.

The "fire-eaters" were amazed, then indignant.

They had expected the poor white population to flock en masse to their standards.

They did, but not under them. The glory crowd were enrolled ; all to whom patriotism, honor, love of adventure could appeal were already enlisted, but that was not enough.

Companies were yet hungry for men, their stomachs not half full.

With wide open insatiate mouths they pounced upon the gaping crowd.

They coaxed and punctured, taunted and lured.

Every device of cunning was applied to secure the full complement of men.

Joe was approached.

" Hed ter keer fer the woman."

He was plied with gibes and whisky, and he answered back :

" Hed ter keer fer the woman."

Drunk or sober there always remained with him sense enough to maunder that set phrase, until he sank in speechless stupor.

Joe detested the Yankee.

He said he did, and he did so far as he was capable of despising anything.

Even the most degraded despise something or somebody.

There is always a lower round to the ladder.

Joe looked upon the Yankee as the lower round.

But his contempt or hatred, for both at times took fitful shape in his feeble brain, were not strong enough to drag him to the mouth of Yankee rifles.

But Joe was a moth, a miller.

He would flit about the flame.

He was a chip, safe in slack water. Hung up by the shore in the dead he might have remained.

To appeals of honor he was deaf. To love of country irresponsive.

From glory he would have fled.

But the "grists o' fun," the "cawn juice," the "hi-low-Jack," "nigger equality," and the "Yank yaapin' and an' runnin' like a houn'" with "nary fight in a bilin' of 'em," which he heard in the camp, were things that appealed to his passions and desires.

Flung into the strong current, he was caught up and hurled away to the muster roll, where he made his mark.

On the long list every name except seven had over against it an X and "his mark."

Joe was enlisted. He was a soldier of the Confederacy.

The boys slapped him on the back, gave three cheers for Joe, three more and a tiger for the Confederacy, and—produced their flasks.

The fire burned low on the Ratley hearth—the little ones lay and breathed softly, lost to chill, discomfort and dirt.

Melinda sat watching the flame spirting, flinging up its golden tongues from behind the green back log, then hiding away in the gloom; watched until the flame and flare died out, then she covered the glowing coals in the hot ashes, lay down beside the children and—calmly slept.

The morrow dawned—and the morrow after—day followed day, and Joe came not.

A camp was formed when Joe enlisted.

He joined it at once.

He ate and slept and drank and carded.

At the end of ten days there was bustle, confusion, hurry, partings, cheers and tears.

An hundred men stood in the road.

A drum and fife, a flag—tramp! tramp! tramp!

Some beat back the rising lumps in their throats, turned their faces over their shoulders and looked—looked eagerly—longingly, for the last time.

Others looked steadily or indifferently ahead.

Among them was Joe.

From the day he enlisted he had neither seen, heard from or sent word to Melinda.

Without a message, without a tear, without a thought, he marched on, tramp, tramp, tramp.

A cloud of dust rose up behind him, the grocery, the camp—all familiar scenes disappeared.

He was swallowed up in the gray passion-crested sea that lashed against the Union.

CHAPTER V.

"I WAS A DALTON; I AM A TRENHOM."

The sun had already passed from sight, leaving its trail of soft twilight, when Walter Trenhom turned from the road and rode under the shadows of the slender shafted tulip poplars, crowned with gorgeous, flame-colored, bell-shaped flowers, that lined the broad carriage-way through his expansive grounds, up to his door. Before he had passed half the distance an aged colored man stood in the roadway a few yards in advance of the steps leading up to the porch, and called:

"Hi, dah, you Pete!"

"Yi-i."

"Dat de way t' ansah youm bettahs!"

No response from Pete.

"Owdashus, sassy, lazy niggah! Spry you'seff up dah!"

"He I is."

Pete turned a hand-spring, landing on his feet, the crown of his uncovered kinky head grazing the rotund stomach of Uncle Awk. Uncle Awk cuffed Pete, pronounced him a lazy, "no 'count, triflin' monkey niggah," and wound up by notifying him to "'spect his bettahs," and "mine youm mannahs foah Mawst Walt."

Awk started in life with a better name. Originally he was Plutarch. His earliest teeth cut out the first three letters. The next letter was dropped among the cotton bolls before he found his first pair of breeches. Thus he had blossomed into "Ark," broadened by the southern tongue into "Awk." Pete was yet rubbing his ears when his master rode up; then he sprang to the bridle. Awk, who was hatless, touched the grizzled locks over his forehead, looked the warm beast over, and asked:

"How um git?"

"Very free," replied his master.

"Dats um, fine crittah dat—fine crittah dat."

"I rode from Burty's—"

"What dat, Maws Walt? Youm bin ter Burty with dis yere cole!"

"Why yes, I rode him there, and as he is back, I rather think I rode him back."

Awk was standing with his legs wide apart, his head set well back, his hands raised.

"Foa de Lawd, Maws Walt, you ruin yoursef widout Awk. Yes, sah."

Trenhom laughed.

"Youm doan know nuffin 'bout hoss crittah, sah. No, sah."

"What hurt will it do him?"

"Hurt, sah! Hurt, sah. Dat cole got no mo leg dan a baby, sah. No, sah."

"He did very well."

"Cole like dat good fo' shawt, sah; dat's it, sah, good fo' shawt. Heah, you done bin ride him ten mile, sah."

"That isn't much."

"How you tawk, sah. Youm doan kno' no mo' 'bout hoss crittah dan de yan leel baby o' you'n, sah; no, sah."

Walter laughed again at the zeal of the old man.

"Ride dat cole ten mile—san' road at dat. Who ebbah heah sich foolishness; I nebbah done heah de like."

"Look at him, Uncle Awk; see how fresh he is. He isn't injured in the least."

"Injah! He done roonationed, dat cole is. I can't hab dat no mo', sah."

"All right, Uncle. I won't do so any more."

"Dat you shan', sah! no, sah! Clah ter goodness, ten mile in de san' road. Dah, you, Pete. Go keeaful wid 'im—lazy, no 'count, niggah. Hab Jack bine 'im leg wid flannen; bine um tite, yer heah? Ten mile in a san' road," and he stood watching the colt disappear around the corner of the house, muttering, "ten mile in de san' road, clah ter goodness." When the horse had passed from view he turned to his master, who was being dusted by a colored boy. Here was a fresh trial for Awk.

"'Clar," he exclaimed, "ef dese yah growin niggahs ain't mo' igranteh dan muels. Dat dey is. Yeah you Sam. What youm doin' wid dat yeeh wiss. Bushin youm mawstah up an' down like a hoss. Doan you know mo' an dat. Heah (taking the broom), dis yeah way. You see you Uncle Awk. Mine now dis yeeh! see dat! Doun, dat's it! Saff, dats de way; not hawd as ef yez scurrin' de bun cruss from cawn pone. Saff! like dis yeer. Yer see dat? Wid de grain—so! yer see dat. Den yer hain't done pushin' de dirt into de nap. 'Clar ter goodness ef I can lawn dese yeeh ignoramus niggahs nuffin; muss do eberyting myseff tell I'ze 'clar done use up."

Mrs. Walter Trenhom, hearing the footfalls of the horse, and the voice of uncle Awk in front of the house, came out from the parlor, and stood in the doorway, an amused spectator of a scene repeated every time Master Walter rode out and returned.

Mrs. Walter was a Southern woman, born in Mississippi. A daughter of one of the oldest, best known and most influential families in the state. Her father had represented his district several times in congress and died full of years and honors. At eighteen Louise Dalton was a wife. At twenty she stood in the doorway of her luxurious home watching uncle Awk teach the art of dusting. She was a grand looking woman standing there, her face wreathed with smiles, her large, moist, violet blue eyes sparkling with light. Mrs. Walter was a blonde, of medium height, broad, low forehead, straight, firm nose, an honest, liberal mouth, beautiful white teeth, and a form cast in a generous mold without a superfluous particle of flesh about her. She was a healthy, wholesouled looking woman. If there was anything small, or mean, or selfish in her nature, there was nothing in her outward appearance to betray it. As Walter placed his foot on the lower step of the stoop to go up, his wife advanced to the foot of the veranda to meet him. Throwing her arm about him and cooing in his ear, they crossed the veranda, passed through

the door, and entered the broad hall that ran from front to
rear of their home.

Awk, watching his master's receding form, muttered:

"Sumpshus niggah; good enough to clean tatah fo' pore
white trash — idee he wiss gen'l'man like Maws Walt,
clah!"

After Walter had changed his clothes and they were
seated at the tea table, he spoke of the news at Burty's—
the "fall of Sumter."

"Can it be possible?" said his wife in a voice that betrayed her deep agitation.

"Not a doubt of it."

He looked up, and to his surprise saw that her eyes were
filled with tears.

"Why, Lou!" he exclaimed.

"Let us not speak of it now, dear. After tea—all too soon
then." She had heard none of the details; only Sumter had
fallen. But that was more than enough.

The conversation drifted to the state of the weather, the
roads, the illness in "servants' quarters," and finally to Awk
and that abused colt.

After tea they retired to the library, Walter lighted a cigar,
threw himself back in his easy chair, and Mrs. Walter, after a
visit to her babe, came and sat on a low stool by his side.
Then Walter told his wife all he had heard of the bombardment and fall of Sumter as it came to him at Burty's. The
wife listened in silence; she wondered at the enthusiasm with
which he told it, and the transparent delight the narration
gave him. Her clasped hands grew closer together, the warm
glow fled away from her cheeks, and the glad light stole out
of her eyes. Walter failed to notice it. He was enveloped
in the smoke of burning Sumter, saw nothing, heard nothing,
thought of nothing but that and the glowing words in which
he was painting the scene on the mind of his listening wife.

When he concluded he blew a fresh cloud from his fragrant
Havana, the blue aromatic wreath circled his head. Then his
wife spoke, slowly, pathetically.

"I am grieved and—surprised."

"You know, Lou, that our people were building assailing batteries."

"Yes, dear."

"And that the assault had been threatened for some time."

"But I did not think it would proceed so far. I believed in the power of that better judgment which sometimes springs out of delay."

"Then you thought the Yankees would run away in the night without fighting. So did I."

"No, Walter, that was not it."

"Didn't think they would run away? You thought they would surrender when they were convinced of the determination of our gallant friends ? "

"Not that either."

"I give it up, Lou. You who have always been the soul of transparency are wrapped in a mist too deep for poor me."

"Not intentionally, dear. My belief was that our Southern friends would not proceed to the extremity of violent resistance to the government."

Walter's legs were crossed, he was leaning, rather lying back in his chair. When his wife's full meaning penetrated his mind, his legs were uncrossed, he sat bolt upright and with wide open eyes, looked down in amazement at the woman who sat there telling him she did not believe South Carolina would hurl shot and shell at the Union. For an instant it appeared as if he doubted the evidence of his ears. Yet these were the words. She did not believe, and—this was his wife —a woman Southern born and bred, who did not believe that the South would cross arms with the Union.

"Surely you do not believe the gallant men of South Carolina are cowards ? "

"Indeed no, they are gallant and brave like all true Southern gentlemen."

"Well, Lou, I confess— "

"I know your opinions, dear, and the opinions of all our personal friends. I have heard them in our parlors, over our tables, over the tables of our friends, at all the social gatherings we have attended during the past year, and I do not concur in them or approve them."

"And you have remained silent all this time?"

"Yes, dear; I thought it was an entirely harmless ebullition of feeling, a sort of political spasm that needed but time for a physician, and I would not invite discussion and contention with my husband about a matter that I supposed to be of no consequence."

"Surely the right to secede and the right to resist are of some consequence."

"Perhaps! I am not a success, you know, at chopping words, but it occurred to me if secession and resistance were never put to the test, it made no difference whether the abstract right, I think that is what I have heard you call it, did or did not exist. And fully believing it never would be tested, I remained mute."

"You astonish me; indeed you do, Lou!"

"By having remained silent?"

"Something at that; but more that you do not detest the government of the United States."

She raised from her low cushioned seat, stood up beside him, placed her soft, white hand on his shoulder, and, looking calmly into his face, said in words that were almost reverential in their tone:

"My dear husband, we have never known the government of the United States except through its blessing."

"That is the past, Lou! The past. When the government was controlled by the Southerners—when the South was the government—when the South ruled it, as it did for sixty out of seventy years of its existence."*

"I do not know enough of politics, Walter, to know who ruled it. But the blessing my grandfather and my father knew, and I and you know."

"I don't deny, Lou, the blessings of the past. It is the future we are looking to and guarding."

"When these blessings are threatened it will be time enough."

*Reply of Senator Hammond to Senator Seward in the United States senate.

"They are threatened, and now."

"How, dear?"

"Don't you know that the North has elected the President? That the election is purely geographical? That the South will have no voice in the government. That the government will be the North, and they will control it and control it in their own interests?"

"I see no great danger in that."

' Sit down, dear." His wife dropped back to her low seat.

"Let us talk of this. I confess you greatly surprise me."

"In what respect?"

"You see no wrong and danger in the North controlling the government?"

"Certainly not. If the South, as you say, has controlled the government sixty out of seventy years, it seems but fair the North should have opportunity to control it four out of seventy-four years."

"I declare, Lou, you make me doubt the evidences of my senses."

"It does seem to me," continued Mrs. Trenhom, "if the North submitted to us sixty years we can safely submit to them four, and if that government was a blessing to them as well as to us during all that time, we have no reason or right to apprehend they will use their power to make it worse for us in the years to come than we did for them in the past."

"And you, a Dalton, speak thus?"

"No, dear, not a Dalton; I was a Dalton; I am a Trenhom."

"Thank you!"

Walter drew the pure, white forehead to him and imprinted a kiss upon it.

"And true to my husband and his interests and happiness," continued this noble wife, "let it carry me where it will. Let the consequences be what they may."

Walter's hand was resting upon the arm of the easy chair in which he sat. She laid her hand in his as she spoke.

He remembered it long afterwards.

The time came when these words, " Let the consequences be what they may," were stamped on his soul.

When she walked through the furnace to illuminate them to his dying eyes.

It was very pleasant to hear the sweet words of this beautiful woman assuring him of undying devotion. It was grateful incense in his proud young nostrils, and a loving light came into his eyes as he drew her golden crowned head to him. But the delirium of secession was on him. He could not remain silent.

" The two sections," he said, " differ in many essential things. The North has no peculiar institutions, and we have."

" Unfortunately," interposed his wife.

" Yes, unfortunately," he added, " but it is here, and while the rule of the South has done, and would do, the North no injury, the rule of the North and the election of a sectional president is a blow at that institution. It is a compacting of the anti-slavery North to make war on slavery. In effect, the election of Mr. Lincoln is a Northern declaration of a war of extermination against slavery."

" I hope so! I earnestly hope it is ! I shall thank God if it is." Mrs. Trenhom's voice was soft, calm and low at first. It was fervid and solemn at the last.

" Lou !" exclaimed her surprised husband.

" Yes, dear, I shall thank the good Father in Heaven if they will put an end to slavery by peaceable means."

" My dear, you speak like an Abolitionist."

" I am one. So are you, darling."

" I ! "

" You ! "

" An Abolitionist ? "

" Yes, my dear, good husband."

" Oh, no ! "

" If one of our servants escaped to the North, would you put any hounds on his track ! "

" No. God forbid."

" Would you invoke any fugitive slave law to bring him back ? "

"Indeed I would not."

"If all our servants should flee away to the North, what would you do ? "

"Probably help them to start in life in a new land."

"Not 'probably,' Walter. There is no doubt of it."

"It can never be tested, so it is impossible to say with certainty."

"Why not tested ? "

"Our servants could not be induced to leave."

A questioning smile flashed up into his wife's face.

Walter noticed it, and added : "You do not agree with me ? "

"No, dear. I am certain you are mistaken as to some of them, and I am quite confident there is little or no difference of feeling among them all on the subject."

"You think they would leave us if they could ? "

"I am confident of it."

"We have always treated them kindly ? "

"Yes."

"No whip has ever been used upon the plantation since you became its mistress."

"No, dear."

"And they know you will not permit families to be broken or any of them to be sold."

"They are grateful for it. Deeply grateful that it is so. And I am so glad." There was no exultation in her voice. It was simply joy. She repeated it again : "I am so glad and so thankful to you."

It sounded like a hymn of praise.

"And yet you think they would leave us if they could."

"I do."

"Who, Lou ? "

"Aunt Chloe, to begin with."

"Dear mother's old servant ? "

"Yes."

"Ungrateful ! "

"Not ungrateful, Walter."

For the first time this woman looked reproachfully at her husband.

"Why, Lou, did I not at your request purchase her husband, who was about being sold to a trader."

"You did, indeed, Walter, and it was good of you, very good of you."

"And now Chloe——"

"Blesses you for it every day, Walter."

"And would leave us if she could."

"Not if she could remain, and be free, but freedom is more precious to her than even we are."

"What has she to complain of ?"

"Nothing but the future."

"The future ?"

"Yes ; she cannot know what may happen in the future, or who may own her."

"Does she think I would permit her to be sold ?"

"Oh, no ! But when we are gone."

"She is old, and we are young."

He spoke with the confidence of youth and strength in his voice.

"But life is uncertain, dear, and poor Chloe often wonders, with tears in her eyes and a great ache in her heart, what will become of her, her husband and her children, if anything should happen to us."

"Poor old Chloe."

"Yes, I feel for her deeply."

"She was my nurse."

"And she loves you like a mother."

"And she thinks I would permit harm to come to her ?"

"No, Walter, not that. But she dreads the evil days that may come, when you may be unable to protect her."

Walter had ceased smoking, he was standing, leaning against the end of a grand piano, lost in thought. His wife came and stood beside him, her clasped hands folded across his shoulder and looking lovingly into his face.

Mrs. Trenhom's mother was a North Carolinian and a Quaker. In the mind of her daughter, her only child, she had

5

early instilled her own detestation of man-owning, and her dying request to that daughter was, if she ever became the owner of slaves in her own right she would free them at the earliest possible moment.

Mrs. Trenhom's father was dead, and the slaves and other property which she inherited remained in the hands of trustees until her twenty-first year, then they would be hers.

Her course was then long ago determined.

When she was married she exacted of her husband but one condition as to her property.

When the trusteeship would expire and the servants would become hers to control, they must be freed, sent North, and furnished with money enough to start in life, and this agreement was reduced to writing. Thus she had purified her own skirts of the sin. She cheerfully awaited the year that was to yet elapse; waited until her own servants were in the North, free and succeeding. Then she hoped the persuasive force of results would lead to the emancipation of her husband's servants. But she had said nothing.

She was patient.

She was not a woman to press seed until she destroyed its life.

She waited.

Abhorrence of slavery was in her heart.

Her mind was full of devising.

She was educating her husband by slow and easy lessons.

She found him a believer in the lash and the auction block, and that slavery was the natural and rightful condition of all colored people, his own included.

Without his marking the progress, he had grown in knowledge.

The whip was expelled from his plantation.

He saw the cruelty of the sale and separation of families.

He had grown to know his own servants, take an interest in them, and sometimes to wish they were all free. Not because it was their right or his duty. But because of his knowledge of them, his interest in them, his affections for them.

As to other people's servants, his opinion was unchanged. He believed in slavery.

It was a divine institution, a burden perhaps to the white men, but a burden that ought to be borne for the sake of its blessing to the slave. Standing there by the piano, his wife's soft hands resting on his shoulder, her tender, honest eyes fixed upon his face, Walter was troubled. Chloe had been his nurse. In childhood he drew life from her breast. She was his second mother. The past grew up before him. A thousand tender acts clustered around Chloe like a halo Then followed the scene when he purchased her husband. His black, loving nurse prostrate upon the earth, devouring his hands, calling his mother and father in glory to witness it, calling down Heaven's blessings upon his head. He thought of Chloe; Chloe, on whose breast he had lain as an infant; Chloe, on whose bosom the head of his dying mother rested; thought of her owned by another; thought of her as she pictured herself, if by any fatal mischance she should pass into other hands, and he shivered.

His wife observed his emotions.

"What is it, dear?"

"I was thinking of Chloe."

"Poor Chloe!"

"Poor, faithful Chloe; and she desires to be free."

"Oh! Walter, would you?"

"Would I?"

"If you were a slave, would you?"

"How absurd!"

"No, dear, not absurd. As a child you never had a joy or a sorrow but was shared by Chloe. Your every pain touched her; your every joy lifted her up. How, then, can you say her feeling differs from you?"

"But she is a negro."

"And, Walter, there is one God and Father for us all."

Her soft words, deliberately uttered, sank down into his soul.

She was graving in deep, strong lines.

CHAPTER VI.

"I CANNOT WISH YOU SUCCESS."

The conversation had taken a turn not contemplated by Walter Trenhom.

He had returned home full of Sumter, of the "Tapier battery," of the "iron battery," Fort Moultrie, Fort Johnson, the floating battery in the cove of Sullivan's island, the girdle of storm encompassing Fort Sumter; the first signal shell from Fort Johnson at half-past four on the morning of April 12; the smoke and curling flame rising from the burning quarters in the fort at eight o'clock in the morning of the next day; the flying shot; the bursting shells; the flagstaff torn away at half-past one of the afternoon of the 13th; the surrender; the pealing bells; the thundering cannon; the tumult of exultation.

All this was in his heart and—the resolve formed at Burty's to organize and beat back the "northern vandals."

When he entered his door he was eager to tell it all.

It seemed so easy.

Of Sumter and the carnival of joy at Charleston and elsewhere in the South he had told all he knew.

But the resolve at Burty's—the organization of military companies—how would he tell it.

They had been so peaceful and happy together.

Since their wedding they had never parted for a day.

She was bound up in him and he in her.

And now he was charged with a communication that must tear them asunder, perhaps forever.

For an instant there flitted through his mind a feeling of regret that he had gone to Burty's or that he had made any pledge to organize a company. But it was only for an instant. Walter Trenhom was a brave man. He was a stranger to fear. For himself he had no regrets. His duty was clear. It was his duty to serve his state.

A man may err; his ideas of duty may be false; but true or false, to follow the star of duty down into the depths, is an act of unsurpassable moral sublimity. This courage Walter Trenhom possessed. But how would he tell it to his wife?

Men who would charge a battery halt before a tear.

Trenhom halted.

His wife disapproved of armed resistance to the government.

That resistance had been resolved on.

It had commenced.

His state was in collision with the old Union.

He was a citizen of the state. He owed it allegiance and military service.

It required that service.

He must render it.

And yet he stumbled at the words which must break that fact to his wife.

After discussing Chloe he remained mute some minutes, all these thoughts coursing rapidly through his active brain. Then he sat on the piano stool, ran his fingers listlessly over the keys and said:

"Lou, it was not the South who began this contest."

"Was it not the South that fired the first gun?"

"Certainly."

"Was not that the beginning of actual contest; was not it the first blow?"

"By no means, dear." His fingers were still running softly over the keys. "The first blow was when Anderson removed from Moultrie to Sumter."

His wife looked at him, her violet eyes raised in inquiry.

"Yes," continued Walter, "the removal was the first act of hostility."

"I do not comprehend."

"Why, you see, Moultrie was untenable. Anderson was quite at the mercy of our friends."

"So I understood."

"Then he removed into the stronger fort."

" Was not that his duty ? "

" Duty ?   It was full of hostile significance."

" My dear, try to put yourself in Anderson's place.   An officer entrusted by your government with command, would you not feel it was a betrayal of your trust if you failed to place your command where they would be most secure."

The warm blood rushed to her husband's face for an instant, flickered and died out.

" I can't say what I would have done."

" I can.   You would have done what this Major Anderson did, and I honor him for it."

She was making it up-hill work for Walter.

" Suppose, dear, that it was his duty, and that I would have done the same in his place.   It was, nevertheless, a violation of faith on the part of the Washington government."

" My love, I do not profess to understand these matters, but it does seem to me it is the right and duty of the government to protect its property wherever it may be and to order its soldiers where they may be most secure."

" But that property was in South Carolina."

" And in the United States."

" Oh, no.   South Carolina has seceded and is out of the Union."

" Yes, I know; they have ordinanced—is not that it ?—out of the Union.   But the Union remains, and the right of the Union to the soil of South Carolina remains."

" Oh, Lou ! "

" Yes, I have frequently heard dear papa say that."

" What, dear ? "

" That nothing but successful revolution could destroy the ownership of the Union over the soil of South Carolina or its right to enforce its laws."

" That revolution has begun."

" But it will never succeed."   She stood up straight before him; her right hand slightly raised; its soft palm like a delicately tinted pink shell, open toward him; her beautiful face glowing, her fine eyes sparkling—" Never! never! God forbid!"

Walter stood up beside her; raised his hand in deprecation. " Don't say that, Lou! Don't say that!"

" It is the land of my fathers and yours!"

" I have no land but Mississippi."

She drew up to him, laid her white round arm across his neck. " Only poor Mississippi, Walter?"

" To Mississippi, and Mississippi alone, do I owe allegiance."

Tears gathered into the beautiful eyes that were looking into his. They rolled down her fair cheeks. She murmured in low broken tones:

" My poor husband, I fear we shall have sad times of it."

Then she laid her head on his breast.

Walter passed his hand over her tear-moistened cheeks, then over her flossy hair.

His task had accumulated difficulty.

" I do not think," he said, " there is cause for foreboding."

Mrs. Trenhom raised her head, smoothed back her disordered tresses, and sat on the piano-stool from which her husband had risen.

" Let us not," she answered, " deceive ourselves, Walter."

" In what respect, Lou?"

" That there is no cause for apprehension."

" I do not see any."

" Not with a great war impending?"

Walter laughed lightly, and stroked his mustache as he replied:

" Ah, Lou, you have borrowed the girls' habit of magnifying."

" It is preferable to the over-confidence in strength which underrates."

" Is that an impeachment?"

" Of you? oh, no."

" I do not see the application."

" I refer to our friends in the South."

" Do you think they underestimate?"

"Greatly."

"The strength of the North?"

"Yes, Walter."

"There will be no real trial of strength."

"There you underestimate their purpose."

"Our leading people are quite confident of this."

"They may know. But I cannot believe it."

"Nearly one-half of the North is with us, and they will prevent the extremists from making war upon us."

"Yes, I have heard there are such people in the North. But have we no Unionists here?"

"Oh, yes, a great many at one time; a few even yet."

"What has changed them?"

"Public opinion, Lou. An irresistible public opinion."

"And do you think, Walter, there is no such thing as public sentiment in the North?"

"Surely there is."

"Do you not imagine it will have the same effect there that it does here?"

"For us?"

"Against the South and this attempted secession?"

"Not at all. The majority of the Democratic party of the North is with us irrevokably. Our leading men are in correspondence with their prominent members and know it."

"They will discover their mistake."

"I am confident not. They have declared they will line the Ohio river with Democratic bayonets to prevent an invasion of the South."

"They are strong words. But I think I have heard quite as strong here on the other side."

"Perhaps. But injustice and oppression has changed all that."

"And the capture of Fort Sumter will be styled an oppression and injustice which will change all that in the North."

"My dear girl, you are drawing phantoms from your fears. There may be a battle, some minor affray or so brought on more by accident than design. But beyond that there will be nothing. I am confident of it. Secession will be peaceable."

" You do not think the people of the North are cowards ? "

" No, indeed."

" I am glad of that, at least."

" Why, Lou ? "

" I have heard of it so often that—well, I did not know."

" I never harbored that idea ; I know there are brave men there, a great many of them ; but the mass, the uncultured multitude, the mechanics and laborers and petty farmers— "

" Walter, you and I have travelled through the North. Did we anywhere see anything like the low, wretched, idle creatures we meet on every roadway here ? "

" I do not remember that we did."

" And these poor creatures form a considerable part of our white population."

" I regret to think that they do."

" And in event of a war you will have to rely on them to some extent ? "

" Yes, Lou, largely."

" Why do you think they will make better material for an army than the happy, intelligent looking laborers we saw in the North."

" I do not know that they will."

" I am not competent to judge, Walter, I admit that ; but it does appear to me that the North has great advantage over us, not only in numbers, but in the character of its fighting material. I believe that is what dear old Gen Oglevie calls it."

" The numbers they undoubtedly have, Lou, the intelligence and wealth also, but they are a sordid gain-loving people, courageous perhaps when in a fight, but preferring peace, plenty, and sacrifice, to the loss and hazard of battle."

" That was not their character in the days of our noble grandfathers."

" I do not mean that they are wanting in bravery."

" I hope not, Walter ; they are our countrymen."

" Were our countrymen."

" Were so, and are so, Walter."

" I will not dispute with you, dear."

" Nor I with you, Walter ; if I have done so, forgive me."

She looked up into his face and laid both of her hands on his, which were resting on the piano.

" There is nothing to forgive, dear ; you were but express-ing opinions."

" Yes."

" And what I meant was, that I did not doubt the courage of all those who would fight, or the whole of them, if they were drawn into a war; but that the number who see any cause for war are few, and the multitude prefer peaceable secession to conflict."

" And you think they have no love of country."

" Yes, as we have—love for their state."

" I think you misjudge them in that. They care less for their states than they do for the Union."

" Perhaps, but we have seceded, and the Union is a thing of the past."

" Yes, if they permit it to be so."

" Which they will."

" Time only can determine that, Walter."

" The capture of Sumter will produce an intense excite-ment throughout the South."

" And a corresponding excitement in the North."

" Of course, but it will not take shape there. It will, here. It will animate our people. It will unite the entire South, and in less than thirty days we will have a great army pre-pared for any emergency." Walter was warily approaching the communication he had to make. An hundred times it was on the point of his tongue, and yet he hesitated.

"If there is to be no war, Walter, why an army ? "

" Show of force, you know, is sometimes the surest conser-vator of peace."

" And do you believe, Walter, that is all ? "

"Perhaps not, quite. As I said, I think there may, probably will, be some minor fights ; possibly one great battle ; but it will not, cannot be protracted."

Mrs. Trenhom shook her head doubtingly.

" You will see, Lou. You will see one great battle, in which we will be victors ; then our Democratic friends in the

North will compel a truce ; compel a peace ; and the Southern Confederacy will be a recognized power on the face of the earth."

For an instant Mrs. Trenhom's fingers ran lightly over the keys ; without knowing it the notes took form ; it was but a whisper, but a breath, scarcely audible.

Walter Trenhom heard it, heard it for the last time in his own old home—a stanza of the Star Spangled Banner.

His wife was thinking ; thinking deeply ; her fingers were moving without guidance of her brain.

When she paused she said :

" Walter, you are aware I have but little means of knowing the temper of the North ; perhaps this love for the Union of their fathers may be dead ; they may underestimate its value ; but I have a feeling ; I cannot account for it ; perhaps I can give no sufficient reason for it ; but it is a belief that has grown on me since I have listened to you ; we have seen the opening of one of the most dreadful wars of history."

" You are an alarmist, Lou."

" I think not, dear."

" I cannot believe it."

" I feel it,—protracted, desperate and— " she shuddered and paused as a vision rose up before her of the sacrifice of human life entailed by a war such as her imagination pictured.

" Then," said Walter, " my duty is clear." If war was to be the holiday his ardent fancy first painted it, he might yet have retired. The warm love of his wife might possibly have chained him to the fragrant groves of his homestead. But if there was to be war, fierce, bloody, deadly war, his duty to his state was clear. No earthly consideration should restrain him.

Mrs. Trenhom heard him.

She looked up at him.

" Your duty, Walter? " she said.

" Yes, dear, my duty to my state is to serve her."

His wife stood in front of him. She threw her white arms about his neck. Her appealing eyes were riveted upon him.

"You would not go away and leave me."

"Lou, what is it you ask?"

"You would not leave me, dear?"

"Would you have me be a coward?"

"Oh, no!"

"I am the state's son; my sword is the state's."

"In such a cause?"

"Lou!"

"In such a cause!"

"No matter what the cause, my service is due to the state."

"And you will go?"

"I must!"

The fair head of his wife lay again upon his breast, his fingers were dallying with her silken locks; one, two, three minutes passed in profound silence.

Mrs. Trenhom raised her head. She withdrew her arms from his neck, and folded her hands before her.

"Walter," she said, "if you are determined to go I will not embarrass you with pleadings, repinings or regrets."

"Thank you, dear; you are a good, brave girl."

"I will pray—pray for your safety."

"Dear Lou!"

"But," and her voice, tremulous with emotion before, grew firm and clear, "I cannot wish you success."

"Lou! Lou!" cried her now thoroughly excited husband, "do you know what you say?"

"Yes, my dearest husband, I do."

"And you wish that our cause, my cause, may fail?"

"Walter, dear, dear Walter!" Her clasped hands were raised above her head. Her tearful eyes turned heavenward, "I shall pray God to guard and shield you and—to preserve the dear old Union of our fathers."

CHAPTER VII.

CATASTROPHE FROM A BISHOP'S BREAKFAST.

September 20, 1863, the second day of Chickamauga, was a dark day for the Union.   The rising sun was bloodshot and sullen.   The morning air was breathless as a grave.   An impenetrable mist lay like a fleecy mantle upon the bosom of the valley, which, long ago, was a home of the Cherokee, and scene of a fierce conflict, a rout, a war-dance, a torturing of captives.

Then the Cherokees christened it Chickamauga, which, translated, is "Valley of Death."

September, 1863, confirmed it.

The previous day two armies beat against each other like angry waves.   Hospitals overflowed into the forests   The farm houses were choked with mutilation.   The Dyer house had shelter and beds.   A surgeon stood at the door, behind him a train of blanched faces, parched lips and blood clots.

The inmate of the house, a woman, confronted them:

"What yer want?"

"Beds, shelter, comfort for the wounded."

"Fer Yanks?"

"For wounded Union soldiers."

"Durned ef eny dad fetched hurted Yanks hes 'um."

*Then the woman dragged the beds into the yard and burned them.**

Embruting of slavery.

The night was a prolonged moan, troubled with hypothesis, with devising, with generals coining plans, with the crash of falling trees for the morrow's barricades, and men chilled to the marrow, hurrying and wondering.   Bragg ordered Polk.   Polk was a mitred saber.   He was a copy of Bishop

* A fact.

de Beauvais, without his dash and crush. "Begin the battle early, as soon as there is light to see."

That was Bragg's order. This command was imperative.

The early hours came. Six—seven—eight—one after another sped away.

It was a respite.

Weary men were grateful. Rosecrans, Thomas and Garfield rejoiced. Bragg was a hurricane of wrath, sputtering profanity.

"Why in —— don't he begin?"

An aid is the distant tongue of a commander.

The tongue inquired of the mitred saber. The fighting bishop was breakfasting leisurely. The habits of the gown survived the girting of the sword. Polk answered the tongue:

"Do tell Gen. Bragg that my heart is overflowing with anxiety for the attack; overflowing with anxiety, sir." His soft white hands emphasized his eagerness; the continued clatter of dishes testified to it, and the attack halted for grace. Bragg cursed all bishops.

But the bishop's breakfast routed Rosecrans.

Twelve days before, Bragg lay by the rugged and precipitous edge of Cameron Hill, crowned with the menace of a single huge gun. The silvery Tennessee at his feet wound its way under the shadow of lofty hills carpeted with lichens and moss.

In his front mountains rolled away, fold over fold, until their pine-capped summits touched the clouds. This was Chattanooga — which is Cherokee for "hawk's nest." In this eyrie Bragg felt secure. He paraded his uniformed multitudes. He saluted the morning sun with drum beat and bugle blast. He thundered his defiance at the army of the Cumberland far away beyond the mountains. On the 20th of August there were strange rumblings among the Northern hills. The 21st unraveled it. Far up on the mountain side strange forms grew out of the dawn. There was a little cloud of smoke ; a crashing reverberation ; a splash in the river. It was a shell thrown from a Union battery. Bragg looked, wondered and hurled lusty imprecations at the hills.

The Confederate multitude looked and cried, "Yanks, be Gawl!" A brigade of blues had indeed scaled the mountains. A few days later a scout came to Bragg and reported. Yanks crossing the river below at Caperton's ; other scouts followed—

"Yanks crossing at Battle Creek and Shell Mound;" still others came reporting,

"Feds crossing above."

Chattanooga is a trap.

Its back door is the "valley of death."

When Rosecrans rushed at the door Bragg sped away.

Tullahoma was repeated.

The victors of Stone River were drunken with easy success and their commander was not an eagle.

Bragg fled, Rosecrans followed, stirruped in cheap triumph, a saddle of disaster.

Bragg's army was a ball rolling in snow.

The Union army was a snow ball rolling on the warm earth. The one grew as it retired.

The other lost fragments with every advance.

Bragg's lost opportunity was September 13th and 14th. The Union army was then spread out like a colossal dislocated crab. Thomas was the body, McCook was the right claw, four days' march southwest beyond rugged and tedious mountains. Crittenden was the left claw, equally far away to the east, separated from the main body by the sluggish, rocky-jawed Chickamauga. The victor of Montenotte would have crushed the left claw, then whirled and pulverized "the rock of Chickamauga," while the right claw was writhing upon the mountain tops.

Bragg was superior to either the body or claws. His superiority was overwhelming. Bragg needed bounce and velocity. He should have been a whirlwind.

He was a snail.

He halted, wriggled and crawled, until the southern mountains were scaled, the eastern river crossed and the claws were gathered into the body.

The army of the Cumberland was intact.

It was Bragg's leaden heels that preserved it.

Dawdling was its salvation. Behind dawdling was Infinite purpose. On Sunday morning, the 20th inst., Bragg was west of the Chickamauga. Rosecrans had been pushed away from the river That was the result of the fierce battle of the day before, and he stood with his back to the hills across the road to Chattanooga, behind him Mission Ridge and Lookout Mountain, a vast palisade of rocks. The Chattanooga road was his line of retreat. To lose it was destruction. The sun of the 19th looked down on the moans of the suffering ; on the prayers of the dying ; looked sadly down on the shattered wreck that lay in the valley; then dropped slowly behind the western curtain of hills. Darkness followed. Across the Chickamauga the camp fires of the Confederates flared out upon the chill night. Then a tumult of cheers rioted upon the calm air. It disturbed Rosecrans. It thrilled the wakeful army among the hills. It was a riddle ; Rosecrans tried his teeth on the nut, but failed to crack it. The cause of the cheers continued a mystery. A new problem had come into the fight—the unknown. And the unknown decides battles.

This was the riddle. Longstreet, lion of the Potomac, had joined Bragg, and with him a picked corps of trained fighters from the army of Virginia.

On the morrow they would untwist the night riddle of cheers with a deadly unraveling.

The Confederates were jubilant, and they were confident ; they were eager for the morrow, and when the morrow came, eager for the first notes of the tempest ; and Bragg raved and rapped out his oaths until nearly half-past eight, when the bishop's chops were wiped and his napkin folded.

Then the advance sounded.

Far up on the left of the Union line toward Chattanooga, the turbid air of the valley was full of motion.

Far over beyond the Chickamauga, Pigeon Mountain stood up above the mist, an island in a limitless sea.

The leafless tops of the sapless trees stood up stern, sullen and ghostly above the fog.

Dim forms clad in gray grew out of the ghastly " deadning."

A little spark flamed up in the haze and died out.

An instant later there was a sharp report.

It was the first muttering of the storm.

Another and another flash.

Then flame followed flame.

The zigzag edge of the forest was illuminated.

The fury of the tempest grew.

A sirocco smote the valley, belching upon the hills, and open fields, and forests a pitiless storm of lead.

It was a torturing showering; a remorseless pelting.

That is war as the rifle has made it.

Before gunpowder, a battle was a collision of human masses.

An army was a snow-ball hurled against a wall, crushed and dispersed into atoms; or it was an avalanche overwhelming its adversary. War was a trial of thews and sinews and lustihood. It was a horrible writhing of limbs. A gigantic wrestle, breast to breast. A crunching of skulls and stabbing of bodies. The hot breath of the destroyed burning the nostrils of the destroyer.

The sturdy crushed the weak.

The rifle dispersed the wrestle. It flung a gulf between armies, and equalized the dwarf and the giant. It revised the tactics of war. It spun the mass into threads, breathing smoke and flame from their sides. Chickamauga was war as the rifle made it; two hostile storm clouds prolonged; drawn out in fine lines; flashing lightning and hurling thunderbolts from their edges.

Cleburne and Breckenridge were Polk's right arm. They were a sturdy, truculent, pugnacious arm for a bishop. The arm reached out to clutch the Chattanooga road; to build a wall of fire across it. The wall built and maintained, Rosecrans must surrender or be lost in the mountains. Hence the struggle for the road and the wall. Another object. Fasten a rope at each end; press against its center and it resists. Unfasten one end and press against it with little force it coils back upon itself. The unprotected flank of an army is the

6

unfastened end of a rope. Turned and pressed it curls back. Pressed in force it crumbles and dissolves.

The arm that reached out for the road also reached out for the end of the Union thread ; to swing round it ; to press against it ; to curl it up ; to disorganize and crush it. Beatty was the end of the thread. The arm reached through the canopy of smoke ; through the forest ; across the plowed fields. Its track was luminous with lightning flashes. Its footsteps were preceded by a fateful sleet of lead. It was a horrible battering. A murderous buffeting. Beatty shrank from the storm. His brigade recoiled. The grays were jubi- lant. The battering and buffeting intensified. The eager arm felt the road and the end of the thread in its clutch. Then from the Union line there leaped a flame and a heat beyond mortal endurance. It scorched ; it withered ; it melted ; it extirpated ; it consumed. In dismay and agony the Confederates fled before the blast. The valley was full of smoke and flame.

Full of daring and madness ; full of anguish and death.

But the road and the end of the thread were safe.

Then came the catastrophe.

The thread snapped asunder in the center.

CHAPTER VIII.

"ROCK OF CHICKAMAUGA."

An army in line of battle is a dyke of arms and eyes and alertness.

The adversary is a flood, mousing for holes, probing for loose joints, thumping the line first here, then there, to find the weak spot.

The object of the dyke is resistance.

For this every fragment must maintain its position ; every section must joint with its neighbor.

A gap is the opportunity of the flood.

To find this it lashes, and probes, and pounds.

From half-past eight until one the flood pummeled and buffeted the dyke in vain.

It had no weakness.

It beat against it in wrath only to be hurled back in foam. Then, mystery of war, accident furnished what attrition and angry surging failed to create.

Wood was a rock in the dyke, cemented in between Brannan on his left and Davis on his right.

A horse advanced in mad gallop. His sides flecked with sweat ; his eyes and nostrils dilated.

He paused beside Wood.

" Orders from Rosecrans."

They were torn open.

" Close up on Gen. Reynolds as fast as possible, and support him."

Place four strips of paper before you in a line. The piece on your left hand is Reynolds ; the next Brannan ; next Wood ; then Davis on the right. Imagine each piece of paper from an eighth to a quarter mile long. This was the position. There are other pieces to the right and left of those, but that is the position of the center.

Wood was amazed. He turned to McCook: "Good heavens, Mac, what does this mean?"

McCook looked.

"Orders positive."

"But singular. See it is written by Rosecrans in person."

McCook looked again. "So it is! Can Garfield be dead?"

"Heaven grant not; but he never would have written this order."

"He wrote every order to-day but this."*

"Good heaven, if he were only with Rosecrans now! But what must I do?"

"Obey! There is nothing else for it. Be quick; and I'll fill up the gap with Davis."

It was a broad interval. A gap for the surging flood. If it could be filled by Davis, well. If the advancing tide struck it before Davis filled it, then disaster.

A crisis is the higher law of battle, it invites responsibility; it condones and rewards assumption.

But Wood was not a man to assume, or invite responsibility.

He was merely an arm—Rosecrans its motive nerve.

He obeyed.

He whirled about to retire behind Brannan.

The dyke was broken.

Col. Walter Trenhom was down before it. He was captain of the company in which Joe Ratley enlisted.

Since the day of home-parting, when, with his company, he disappeared in the cloud of dust, he had realized what was meant with secession on one side and love for the Union on the other.

At first Bull Run he gave his earliest command to fire at the old flag.

Since then he had participated in the triumph or disaster

---

*A fact. Gen. James A. Garfield, Rosecrans' chief of staff, wrote every order on that day except the fatal order which lost the battle.

of many a field of horror, and he had won the command of his
regiment by superlative bravery.

Now he was over against Rosecrans.

Three times he had dashed against the dyke further up,
and three times he had been pressed back foot by foot into
the edge of the forest.

Foiled but not disheartened, he edged away further to the
right of the Union line.

He stood over against Wood's front.

To the right and left of him Hood's other legions.

Col. Trenhom was already advancing.

But for the bishop's breakfast his advance would have been
two hours earlier.

Slowly, steadily forward.

His vigilant eyes witnessed Wood's movement.

" It is retreat !   Double-quick !   March ! "

There was a tremendous shout.

Hood's other regiments caught it up.

It was a roar.

A thunder of exultation.

Davis attempted to spread his thin line over the gap.

It was flinging handfuls of snow into a furnace.

Hood came on with a rush.

He was a flood, crested with flame, Trenhom its consuming point.

He struck Wood retiring ; struck Davis's thin line ; caught
it up like sand in the surf and beat it down with a deadly
thud.

Polk's breakfast conjoined the gap and the attack.

Accident of war.

The torrent burst through the interval ; overflowed beyond ; turned southward on the end of Davis's line, and rolled
it back like a thread.

A few brave men stood ; the maddened torrent gulped
them down.

The many were dismayed ; they dropped their arms ; flung
away knapsacks ; unbuckled their cartridge boxes.

They were panic stricken.

They ran.

The torrent pursued ; vomiting fire and whizzing rifle balls.

A panic is an enigma.

A panic is a furnace—melting armies in its fervid heat.

The panic infected the entire right wing of the Union army.

A few daring men hurled patriotism, entreaties and imprecations at the rushing crowd. They were deaf to everything but the roaring torrent.

They groped in the darkness of despair and rushed on

System was unclinched.

Divisions dropped asunder.

Regiments dislocated.

Companies atomized.

One-half the army was torn to tatters.

Unharnessed from command the incoherent and disheveled mass fled. A hatless officer dashed up from the rear.

"Why do you run ? "

The flying soldier turned his head over his shoulder and shouted, " Busted," and ran on.

A group rushed by.

" Halt ! "

" You be—— ! "

The hatless man hailed another.

The face was streaked with powder, smoke and dust and laced with perspiration.

" What regiment ? "

" Twenty-second ' Indiana.' "

" Where is it ? "

" Smashed ! "

" In the fight ? "

" You bet ! "

" Hot ? "

" Boiling."

" Where's the others ? "

" There's one ! " Then he rushed on.

The hatless man looked where the soldier pointed and saw a boy, his right leg roughly bandaged ; black clots of blood dropped from his knee. The boy was tremulous with agony. His face was blanched with despair. He stumbled, fell, rose, staggered, fell again, rose and staggered on.

The stream intensified.

Men, mules, horses, wagons, caissons rolled, tumbled, ran, crowding, jostling, surging, screaming, cursing.

Inexplicable chaos of wreck.

Rosecrans and Garfield, his chief of staff, hurrying to check the route were caught up in the mad current and whirled under its resistless impulse back through the gap that lies west and north of Mission Ridge.

The torrent paused from pursuit ; turned and dashed upon the " Rock of Chickamauga."

Col. Trenhom looked about him ; looked on the wreck behind him.

It was he who led the rush upon Thomas.

He was hatless, and—warm blood ran down upon his bridle rein.

Where Davis had stood the earth groaned under the cinders of war.

These were the cinders :

A dissevered hand with twitching fingers.

An arm—fair, round and white.

A leg, torn and mutilated.

A shred of flesh with a human eye glaring fiercely out of it.

Monstrosities of disfigurement and mutilation.

There a boy, a smile upon his lips, a little red spot on his forehead.

There a form ; a grand head upon it. The lower jaw torn away.

Horrible grimacing.

There another ; his hands clenched ; his legs drawn up ; a murderous light yet in his dead eye, and a writhing of agony on his set jaws.

A Confederate officer sat up, tightening a handkerchief about his lacerated thigh.

A few feet away was a Union soldier.

He moved.

He turned.

Then he, too, sat up and placed his hands upon his head.

He lay there when the Confederate officer fell.

He lay calm and stiff, apparently dead.

As he moved the Confederate spoke :

" Ah, alive ? "

" Yes, thank God ! "

" I thought you were done for."

" Was I so bad as that ?   Is there blood upon me ? "

" I don't see any."

" I don't feel any wound, only a great pain in the head."

" A cannon ball."

" It would have killed me."

" Yes, if it hit."

" How else could it do ? "

" Concussion of air, or grazed the scalp."

" Ah ! "—looking about him—" but where is the army ? "

" Skedaddled ! "

" Which ? "

" Yours."

" Good heavens !   And I ? "

" A prisoner, unless you git."

Then the Confederate slowly fell back upon the earth.

The blue (sympathetically)—" Are you hurt bad ? "

The gray (feebly)—" Yes."

The blue (anxiously)—" Can I help you ? "

The gray (generously) — " Yes ; but you'd best hurry away while you can."

The blue (devotedly)—" I'll take my chances, old fellow ; but I'll help you first."

The gray—" That's chivalrous."

"Christen it what you like, only tell me what I can do ? "

" Tighten the handkerchief about my thigh."

" I see.   You are bleeding."

" Yes ! "

The blue—Tightening the handkerchief and stopping the

flow of blood. "Poor fellow, you have lost a great deal. There, I guess it's all right now."

"Thank you ; you are kind."

"I'll watch it awhile."

"I am looking on you."

"Yes."

"Turn your face to me."

The blue—Turning his face, "There !"

The gray—"Ah !"

The blue—"Well ?"

The gray—"You were at Stone River ?"

The blue—"Yes."

The gray—"I thought so."

The blue—"Why ?"

The gray—"You saved my life there."

The blue—"I !"

The gray—"Yes. In the rush I fell. I was down ; a brute stood over me with musket clubbed. You turned it aside. But for you he would have murdered me. In the charge and melee that followed I escaped."

The blue—"Oh, I remember now, that was Jim Site with the musket. A good fellow, too."

The gray—"A fiend, if I ever saw one."

The blue—"Oh, no ! He was battle mad. Out of a fight Jim's as tender and gentle as a woman."

The gray—"What is your name ?"

The blue—"Halmer Huntley. And yours ?"

"Dale Cartier."

Huntley—"A major ?"

Cartier—"Yes ; with a chance to advance a grade if I survive. My lieutenant colonel lies over there : done for, I fear, poor fellow."

Huntley—"On the hill ?"

Cartier—"No ; off there in the valley. Your fellows did terrible execution three hundred to five hundred yards away."

There was a roar from Mission Ridge.

Cartier—"That's victory— "

Huntley—"Running— "

Cartier—" Who ? "

Huntley—" Johnnies !   Johnnies ! "

When the right wing was crushed, Thomas coiled the left wing about the lower spur of Mission Ridge. With one-half the Union army swept from the field, Bragg and Polk and Longstreet were confident.

It seemed but a question of moments. Successful resistance was impossible. They would destroy and capture the fragment that was unrouted. There were but five divisions in line against the whole rebel army inspired by success, strengthened and inflamed by a taste of victory. After the rout of the right wing there was a momentary lull in the storm. Thomas was in sore peril, but needed aid was hurrying down from the left. When Garfield was driven back through the western gap to Rossville with his commander Rosecrans and the routed right wing, Rosecrans was hopeless and pushed on to Chattanooga. But Garfield paused. The roar of Thomas's guns filled him with hope. He halted. He gave orders to organize the disheveled masses. Then he dashed down the Rossville road toward the dust cloud, the flame and the roar.

He met halting troops. " Forward to Thomas ! "

The thunder of a battery assailed him.

" Forward to Thomas ! "

The horse of his aid riding by his side sprang into the air : struck on its feet ; stumbled ; plunged forward ; fell. It attempted to struggle to its feet, and with a horrible scream fell again prone on the earth.

With violent effort it raised its head and turned its dilated eyes to its side. A shell had struck it and torn open its stomach ; its entrails were protruding on the ground. Slowly the neck fell back to the earth ; became rigid ; its mouth opened ; its lips were drawn up, and the sun shone down on its white gleaming teeth.

Garfield dashed on. " Forward to Thomas."

The roar grew louder. Forward, through smoke and the flame. Forward under the pelting of lead. Forward under crash of falling limbs. Before three in the afternoon he was

THE SHELL ROSE UP IN THE AIR,

beside Gordon Granger. He had made a circuit of the mountain. He was forward with Thomas ; he·stood in the jaw of the furnace ; and with him were heroic souls to gladden and strengthen the " rock of Chickamauga."

Where the fight raged hottest, where the smoke was deepest, where the roar was loudest ; in the face of the blinding leaden sleet, under the consuming rain of death ; in the parching nostrils of the battle storm he was there, " animating and cheering both officers and men."*

The lull was ended.

The storm had gathered power for a final blow.

A dark cloud rose above the trees on the left. Glittering with banners and arms flashing back the sunlight, shouting, volleying, thundering, the gray passion-crested wave, with impetuous fury, rolled out from the screening forests and dashed upon Thomas.

The advancing tide was a flame.

The five heroic divisions and their reinforcements were a furnace. The blue was a wall of explosion and detonation, loading the air with whiz and scream.

A shell flew over the advancing Confederates ; struck the hillside ; rolled to within a foot of Major Cartier and paused.

A fine thread of blue smoke issued from its nostril.

Cartier was weak and powerless.

He was unable to run or move from certain death.

" Adieu, hope and home."

He covered his face with his hands.

Huntley leaped to his side ; stooped ; lifted the shell ; swung his arms ; the shell rose up in the air ; curved downward ; struck the earth thirty feet away and exploded.

Cartier uncovered his eyes and looked.

The shell was gone. " And you did it," he said.

Huntley—" Yes ! "

Cartier—" Noble fellow ! "

Huntley—" I am sure—Ah— "

The echo of a volley reached the ears of Major Cartier.

*Report of Gen. Granger on Gen. James A. Garfield's heroic conduct at the battle of Chickamauga.

Sergeant Huntley threw up his arms. What he would have said was never completed. He fell forward on his face.

Red froth oozed from his mouth.

A stream of blood ran from his breast.

And over against the foot of Mission Ridge the storm beat on. Back from the barricades, close behind the uniformed divisions, an old man stood, shelterless, coatless and barefooted, his long silvery locks streaming over his shoulder.

His "butternut" pantaloons contrasted oddly with the blue uniforms about him.

An idle spectator ? No ! He held an old-fashioned hunting rifle in his nervous grasp, and he loaded and fired down into the valley with rapidity.

A soldier noticed him.

" What are you doing here ? "

" Gittin' a bead on secesh."

" Where do you come from ? "

" Ovah yandah." Pointing over his shoulder to the mountains. " Can see four states from thar."

" Lookout ? "

" Eggzackly."

" Among the crags ? "

" Top ov 'um."

" A Southren ? "

" Yas."

" And not a rebel ? "

" Nary." (Crack went the rifle.) " Nary ! "

" You're old for this work."

" Sixteen days arter Tennessee kem into ther Union I kem into the world to see arter 'er—and holp keep 'er thar."

" You're a good 'un."

" Dooty, boy, dooty. Fust chance to hit a lick fer the ole Union sence the Mexican wah."

Crack again went the rifle.

" Do the rebs bother you ? "

" Eggzackly. They've bin fer ole Fostah—thet's me."

" And you ? "

" I gin one a clamp, an' a hoss pistol with a buck load got tother. They'd barked up the wrong gum tree."

" Did they come again ? "

" They foun' 'tain't healthy up thar."

Through the long afternoon the " old man of the mountain " * hurled his messengers of death. " Thet's fer Tennessee," " Thet's fer Gineral Jackson," " Thet's fer the Union." And in front of him, from noon till night, the frenzied torrent beat against the " rock of Chickamauga ; " roared and lashed, and was hurled back in spray.

Day disappeared.

To the Army of the Cumberland the setting of the sun was an inexpressible relief. It was an uprising of hope.

The cold night air chilled weary fingers.

But cold night air is a pump.

It sucks the warm earth.

Draws streams from its fountains.

Each stream an invisible thread.

The threads put together in numberless multitude are impenetrable mist.

The pump worked.

The warm earth yielded.

The broad valley became a gray wrinkled sea.

Darkness, mist and repulsion laid their hand upon the turbulent waves.

Sullenly they receded back toward the river.

The storm subsided.

The brown and crimson autumn leaves dropped silently down on the white upturned faces below.

A woman came out from under the trees.

She bent down.

She looked into a blanched face.

She shuddered and passed on.

She looked again.

---

* Called so by Sherman and Hooker afterwards.

The eyes and nose were torn from the face she looked into. The revolting cavern yawned upon her. She cried out; pressed her clasped hands before her eyes, and walked on through the fog in the valley to the hillside. Face after face she bent over, searching them eagerly. Behind her was a trail of death, of suffering and one word, " w-a-t-e-r."

CHAPTER IX.

THE WOMAN ON THE BATTLE-FIELD.

Three years previous to the war there was genuine mourning on the estate of Gen. Chartrass. The general lay in the broad parlor of his great mansion. The colored servants, with tears of genuine sorrow rolling down their dusky faces, entered the wide hall with noiseless tread, passed through the parlor doors, looked down upon the white peaceful face, sobbed and passed out again. Gen. Chartrass had been an officer of the old army. On the death of his only brother he resigned; returned to his ancient estate in Mississippi and remained there until the Mexican war drew him to the field, to share the hardships, perils and glories of his old comrades. After the war he went abroad, making but rare and brief visits to his plantation, until his final return five years before. His absence had been regretted. His return was welcomed. He was the richest planter in the State, connected with its first families and a bachelor. With all that he was kind-hearted, educated, polished by long commingling with polite society, and generous. He told a good story, knew how to listen to and be amused by a dull one, and his house was continually full of all the best fellows in the country. Chartrass was a big man, and a big-hearted man. His many friends mourned him, and his relations—his cousins of the first and second and every other degree, of whom he had seen little and knew less —wondered which of them would inherit the estate. The general was an important figure in his life time. Important as he lay there dead, with the trail of a great estate behind him.

The cousins canvassed their kinship and their rights.

Dead men's estates sharpen the fangs of kin.

7

They turn smiles into snarls. The cousins were preparing to rend each other.

The servants and the many friends followed the coffin silently and sorrowfully out of the house. " Earth to earth." A clod fell down. It gave back a hollow echo. Dear friends wept audibly. From the servants came a long, low wail. He was a gentle and indulgent master. The cousins covered their dry eyes, inventoried the " niggahs " and thought of the estate. When the friends and relatives returned to the house the will was read. It was very brief. Houses, lands, servants ; all specified, inventoried, fully described ; everything to my dear ward, Erma Petillant, with the request only that she assume the name of Chartrass. The intimate friends of the general rejoiced. They knew and loved Erma. The cousins were dumfounded. They took their handkerchiefs from their eyes ; shook the dust of the Chartrass mansion from their feet ; and went away to consult the lawyers. If they could not have the estate, it was so much pleasanter to see the lawyers swallow it in big gulps than to have it pass into other hands. But the lawyers for five counties around would have nothing to do with it. They were friends of the dead general. They honored his memory ; they loved him in his grave ; and they loved his ward.

Who was the ward ? The cousins tore her to tatters. Shred after shred they pulled away from her.

She stood before them a girl, name Erma Petillant. Parentage unknown. Age seventeen.

When Gen. Chartrass returned from Europe he brought Erma with him, a girl of twelve. She was introduced as the daughter of a dear friend—his ward—brought from France. No living relatives known, competent to take care of her. She had stolen into his heart. " Yes, gentlemen," he frequently said to his friends, " riveted in there ; riveted fast. Anything wrong with Erma would kill the old boy."

Erma romped about him on the lawn ; filled his hatband and buttonholes with flower buds ; filled and lighted his pipes, and rode with him wherever he went.

They were inseparable. It was pleasant to look on

them. If he walked away from her, her loving eyes followed
him.

And he—his eyes never tired of lingering on her fawn-like
motions.

After her advent in the general's home she mingled freely
with his many friends. He delighted to parade her grace
and accomplishments.

All his dearest friends knew her. All honored and loved
her. She was so bright, beautiful and winsome, and she was
the ward of their friend.

When the general died these friends surrounded the
broken-hearted Erma with their esteem, their affection and
their protection.

The cousins were amazed. Chartrass was insane, so they
said ; they would find a remedy at law. "Law," snorted Col.
Valore. "Jim, hunt up them thah derrinjahs."

Judge Shootfast openly declared he would challenge "the
impecunious rascals." "Yes, sah, any dirty dog that says my
noble friend, Gen. Chartrass, wasn't right in his mind must
fight me." The cousins were hungry bears.

The honey was there, but so were the bees, in a swarm.
They knew Valore, and they knew Shootfast. Of course it
was "shotgun tyranny," "interferin' with justice," "outrage-
ous that a man can't git his rights;" but then, there was
Valore, Shootfast and a host more of the general's old friends,
just as quick on the trigger, and fully as pronounced in their
determination to defend the sanity of Chartrass and the rights
of his ward.

The cousins growled ; looked with hungering eyes on the
vast estate ; and retired. It was a compulsory settlement.

A little black spot in the mouth of a derringer being judge
and jury.

But it disposed of the contest finally and forever. The will
stood.

The ward inherited. At seventeen Erma Petillant Chartrass was the richest woman in Mississippi, and a thousand
tongues said the most beautiful. Erma knew nothing of this.

She was down in the valley of despair.

She saw nothing but the grave under the shadow of the trees from which she was carried away fainting. She thought of nothing but the dear old general. She remembered him far away back in childhood, as far as she could remember, .when she perched on his shoulder and plucked luscious grapes on the hill sides of France. And she remembered him then as the same dear old, generous, indulgent friend he had remained to the end, when the fading light in his eyes stole out to her and he whispered, " Kiss—me—Erma," and with a smile on his lips wandered away forever.

Erma was inconsolable. For weeks her life was despaired of. But youth and strength conquered. The tide turned. Erma recovered. During her sickness the General's old friends came every day in troops to inquire for her. When she was able to see them old gray-haired men, boyhood companions of her guardian, came to her bedside, full of kindly wishes and good cheer. Their wives came and their daughters. ' Later, when Erma was strong enough to leave her bedroom, they held a counsel. Erma was motherless and fatherless. Her guardian was gone. She would be visited by gentlemen. Some gentlewoman should reside with her. " Appearances, my dear," said Mrs. Shootfast. " Appearances, my dear," echoed her husband, the judge. Erma was in their hands. They were her friends. She told them she did not understand, " but you are the dear general's friends and my dear friends," and of course they knew what was the best. The judge and Col. Valore stood up and bowed. " So sweet," said Mrs. Shootfast. " So wise," said Mrs. Valore. " Sweet," " wise," echoed the gentlemen. And the companion was settled. Who ? Several names were suggested and canvassed.

For once these good ladies put all selfish, personal feelings aside. They thought for Erma, and they did it fairly. Erma listened in silence. " Have you no wish, dear ? " asked Mrs. Valore. " But one," replied Erma, " that the lady shall be kind, very kind and tender to the servants, and—have a gentle—voice. It—would—kill—me—to hear harsh tones where my dear, dear old Guardy has been so long."

Col. Valore brushed away the tears that gathered in the corners of his eyes and walked to the window to hide his emotion. He loved Chartrass; loved him living; loved his memory dead. It was a reasonable request. Chartrass was kind to his colored people and he had the softest voice in the world.

At last a name was agreed upon and a method of reaching her.

" Dear Mrs. Colature," was the lady. Erma would invite her for a visit as a "dear friend of the general's." If Erma was pleased with her the friends would arrange the rest.

The invitation was sent and accepted. Mrs. Colature came, was loved by Erma, proved to be all her friends believed, and without knowing why or how, she became head of the Chartrass place and chaperone of Erma.

A year passed. The general's old friends drew Erma from the seclusion in which she would have concealed herself. Mourning was no sham with her. The tint was on her heart. With her there was no measuring of months with colors and shadings. She mourned. The general's old friends came to see her, and she owed these dear friends so much she went to see them.

Gradually visits increased—society gathered about her.

Young people of whom she had known but little became her companions; young gentlemen laid their hearts and fortunes at her feet.

At last one came, he had no fortune.

His father had been rich, was generous, was asked to endorse the paper of a friend. It is so pleasant to oblige a friend, "only to sign your name there, you know," "great help," "everlasting obligation," and all that.

It seemed so easy and costless.

He endorsed, and found it the broad road to destruction. Wise men loan, fools endorse. Give your friend anything you have but your name. He gave his name and was ruined.

Erma was nearly nineteen. This suitor was five years older, a fine, manly looking fellow; he played and sang well, spoke French like a native, rode like a Mexican, shot like an

American, and, not the least of his attractions, he was the nephew of " dear Colonel " Valore.

Erma consulted Col. Valore, and, like an honorable gentleman, the colonel declined to advise. He said he believed the young man was not a gambler or a drunkard, two things Erma should avoid.

" Yes, dear, be sure to avoid them ; gamblers and drunkards have huge maws for devouring estates and happiness." Beyond that he would not say. " He is my nephew and is poor, and I cannot consent to influence your judgment. Don't decide hastily, dear. Consult your old friend Judge Shootfast and his wife. The result was, Erma accepted the colonel's nephew and at nineteen was his wife.

She had one year of unalloyed happiness, then came the war.

" The state calls me Erma. The state needs her sons."

So her husband said. What could she say ?

For months she had breathed an atmosphere of war. She thought and spoke as the women around her. She believed it was his duty.

It lacerated her heart. But better that than see her loved one sink under the impeachment of cowardice. She bade him go.

She poured out her wealth to equip his company, and he went away. He passed through a year of campaigning, then he woke one morning, shivering. He drew more blankets about him and shivered.

A high fever followed ; then a surgeon came.

" Ah! How d' ? "

" Bad."

" Sick ? "

" Yes."

" Let me see your tongue." The tongue was put out.

" H-u-m ! Feverish ? "

" Yes."

" Let me feel your pulse." The wrist was put up and the beats counted ; every throb of his heart that sent the blood in quick spurts through his veins.

"H-u-m! High."

"Is it?"

"Any pain?"

"Head aches dreadfully; bursting."

"H-u-m!"

"And my back—"

"Ah! Pain there?"

"Yes!"

"Much!"

"Intense!"

"Vomit?"

"Yes!"

"Much?"

"Yes!"

"H-u-m!"

"What is it, doctor?"

"Let me see your tongue again?" The tongue was put out.

"H-u-m!"

"What is it, doctor?"

"Fever! All right in a few days."

Three days later the skin was covered with eruptions. The doctor saw it; looked serious.

"What is it, doctor?" said the sick man.

"Small-pox!"

"Good heaven!"

The sad news reached Erma.

She drove rapidly to her friend, Judge Shootfast. There she had a will made. "Reasons" she had none to give. Her purpose was fixed. She would not pain her dear friends by listening to appeals and denying them. "Queer will; strange provisions. Sensible, though. Why should she make it now?" So the judge said to his wife. Next day he heard she was gone and why she was gone. "Grand girl! Grand girl! Always said so." The judge told it everywhere. "Grand girl." When the will was made Erma flew homeward; drew her child to her heart; rained tears upon it;

kissed it again and again ; her love burned itself on the babe's lips. Then she was gone.

Day and night she sped on, until she stood in camp. "I came to nurse my husband." To denials of surgeons, persuasions of friends, frightful pictures of consequence, she had but one answer, "He is my husband."

Immovable as heaven, irrestrainable as destiny, she persisted and triumphed. She bound the child-ache in her heart, chained her trembling fears and stood by her husband, in the putrid breath of the loathsome disease, pierced by its pungent, offensive, horrible fetor.

Her husband's face was turned from the door when she entered.

He did not notice. She stood by the bed, looking down on his fevered brow and erupted face. He felt the presence.

It was something. What was it ?

He looked up. Why ? Is there a magnetic current connecting loving hearts ? He looked and saw.

"Good heavens ; you, Erma ?" His voice was husky, almost unintelligible.

But the ears of love are acute, and love is an interpreter. Erma understood him.

"Yes, dear; do not excite yourself."

"Oh, Erma, how glad I am."

"Thank you, dear."

"But you must go, Erma.   Go at once."

"I have come to stay, dear."

"But, do you know ?"

"Yes !"

"That I have—"

"I know, dear."

"Small-pox ?"

"Yes, dear, I know."

"And you have come ?"

"Yes, knowing, I have come."

"Noble Erma !"

"Be calm now and quiet.

"But this disease is contagious."

"I know."

"Our child. Think of our child."

"She is well and God will care for it."

"Dear, noble Erma."

"Do not speak again, dear. Our house is in order. The rest is in the hands of the Lord. I have come to stay with you, and I will stay."

He said no more, and she began to set the room in order. The windows were closed. Her suffering patient was consuming under a mountain of blankets and covers, and the stench was oppressive. For an instant she felt its influence.

It was nauseating. Then she set her teeth together and subjected her nerves. It was the omnipotence of will. She walked up to the bed and touched the mountain. She felt its weight. She walked back towards the window, drew a large bottle from an ample pocket, bathed her face and hands and arms and neck. It was carbolic acid. Then she returned to the bed and drew off the topmost cover.

The door opened, and the colored man who served as nurse stood beside her.

"What dis yeer?"

"Taking these covers off."

"De Lawd!"

"Be quiet!"

"Dis yeer nebbah do, mistus."

"There is another one; put it in the corner."

"Goodness alive, what you doin'?"

"There is another."

"'Clah to goodness, ef I ebbah hearn de like."

"Be quiet, please." She removed all the covers but one light one.

"Are you more comfortable, dear?"

"Yes."

The miasma arising from his body pervaded the room. It was a sink intensified. It was stifling.

Erma went to the windows and opened them.

"Mistus, mistus, fo' heabin dat nebbah do! nebbah in de woale!"

" He must have air."

Then the surgeon came in. He noticed the bed and the windows.

" Who did this ? "

" I," replied Erma.

" This will never do, madam ! "

" He is more comfortable already.   See ! "

" You must close the windows again."

" There is no draft.   See, I have guarded against that."

" But the windows, you must close them; close them."

" Doctor, I have opened them and they shall stay open."

" Madam, I order it."

" I cannot help that."

" I am his surgeon, madam, his surgeon."

" And I am his wife, sir."

" Yes, yes !   But I am responsible."

" My dear doctor, I relieve you of responsibility."

The surgeon looked at his patient, shook his head and went away.   That night her husband rested better.

The third day after, the surgeon went away without prescribing.

The sick man's body was one universal ulcerous sore, pustulation everywhere, and purple black.   The foul odor was sharp as a sabre.   It penetrated like a knife.   The skin was parched.   It cracked and tore.   It was a frightful rending of the surface.   The intense pain of her husband penetrated Erma.   Her soul was bubbling with tears.   She put a stone over the fountain.   She would not trouble the sick man.   The only visible sign of her heartache was a smile.

More power of will.   She was thinking.

The male nurse was standing beside her.

Erma turned to him.

" Something must be done to allay the pain of that dreadful cracking and parching of the skin."

" Doan know nuffin'."   The nurse was hardened.   He had seen patients in that condition before, and knew its meaning.

" There must be something."

"Reckon d'aint nuffin'."

"Would warm sponging?"

"Lawd!"

"A warm bath?"

The colored man looked at her in amazement. There was a movement of the sick man's purple lips.

But they were soundless.

Erma had read the surgeon's signs.

She read the nurse.

She felt they had abandoned hope.

When she had cleansed her husband's hands she used warm sponging. The hands now were the only pliant and painless part of the body. She looked at the hands, looked at his neck and face and breast. She thought of the surgeon and his transparent hopelessness. Must she lose him? Why should he go in pain? If warm water had relieved the hands, why not the body? Thinking, the idea became fixed in her mind. He should have ease and comfort if it could be secured. He should have the bath.

She was resolved. Now as to means.

"Peter, I must have a bath-tub."

"D'aint none no whah!"

"Here, take all the money you wish, as much more for yourself, and have a long wooden box made that will hold water."

Peter took the money and looked wonderingly on the woman.

"Order hot water in the cook-room as you go out."

"Yas'm."

Pete ran away to the surgeon.

"Hot water?" said the surgeon. "Nevah heard the like."

"Tole she dat."

"Let her have it."

"Gib she de watah?" cried Pete, in astonishment.

"Yes, it will do no injury. He will die anyway."

"I knowes dem yah winnas kill um."

"It wasn't the windows, Pete. He was a dead man before she came."

Pete went away. In an hour a box six feet long, eighteen inches wide and deep, was in the sick room. Its seams were caulked and it was tight. The water was brought in, poured in the box and tempered down. Erma and Peter lifted the patient into it on a sheet. Five minutes passed. He was insensible. His eyes were closed. A writhing of pain on his face. The writhing vanished. The face smoothed. The eyes opened. Then the lips.

"Oh! This is heaven!"

Erma could have wept.

"Are you comfortable, dear?"

"This is heaven!" The fetor had completely disappeared.

"We will take you out now."

"Oh, Erma, no! I have no pain. Out of here is torment."

Then the surgeon came and stood beside the tub. He heard the last exclamation.

"Now that he is here, perhaps you had better let him remain."

"How long, doctor?"

"I don't know, madam; we will see."

He put his finger in the tub and felt the temperature of the water.

"How long has he been in?"

"Three to five minutes."

"H-u-m!" All looked silently at the man in the tub.

"How do you feel, dear?"

"All under the water is so comfortable."

"Shall we lower you?"

"If you can!"

The surgeon looked again, "Perhaps you had better lower him."

They placed a soft pillow under his head and pushed him down in the water. Nothing but his face appeared above it.

Five minutes passed away.

"Shall we take you out now?"

"Oh, Erma, I am so happy here."

The surgeon felt the water again.

"Let him remain."

"How long?"

"I don't know. Have some more water heated and keep the temperature where it is."

"Perhaps I had better cover the tub, all but his head."

"Perhaps."

The tub was covered. The patient's eyes and his mind were brightening. He murmured again, "This is heaven!"

"Is not the warm water debilitating," asked Erma anxiously.

"Yes!"

"Would not a stimulant aid him?"

"H-u-m!"

"Shall I give him brandy?"

"Yes; do."

The brandy was given. The surgeon noticed its effect.

"H-u-m! Singular! Shouldn't wonder—"

"H-u-m!"

"See how bright he looks?" Erma said this. Hope was rising up within her.

"Queer! Odd! Never heard of this before." The surgeon was muttering to himself. Then louder.

"Give him more brandy. A teaspoon at a time."

They kept him in the bath seven hours, giving a teaspoon of brandy at a time. Then they returned him to bed. His skin was soft. His sores moist. The next day Erma tried the bath again, seven hours more. When he was taken out the surface of his body was clear and soft. The sores healthy and white. The cracking and tearing of the skin was gone. That night he slept well. The next morning he awoke refreshed; his mind clear. He had turned the sharp corner. He improved steadily, with mild turnings he ran on into the straight, and was safe. Then Erma ran away with him to her home, and on its threshold—fainted. Mystery of womanhood; rending the beast that assails its love, and dying away at the sight of its retiring tracks.

A few weeks devoted to rest, recuperation and love-making, and the husband again buckled his sabre-belt. He was an ardent Confederate, and a brave one. The South needed its sons. Erma kissed him, dropped a tear where he had stood and turned back to her child. Valore, Shootfast and all the rest of them came. The surgeon had told; Col. Trenhom and others repeated. The story swelled. It rolled like an anthem about the Chartrass place.

When Erma went away it was "grand girl," when she returned, it was "grand woman," "magnificent," "wonderful," "heroic." The vocabulary of praise was exhausted.

Erma had friends before. She had worshipers now. In the fragrant breath of this adoration she lived until the autumn of 1863. Then a rumor came. Her husband's regiment was coming westward. Then a letter from her husband, brief and hasty. "Somewhere in the vicinity of Chattanooga." She hurried away to see him if but for a moment.

Chattanooga was in the hands of Rosecrans. She turned southward and reached Lafayette. Trenhom's regiment and her husband were beyond Pigeon Mountain toward Chickamauga. On again. It was Sunday morning. The shreds of an army were whirled past her, and she heard there was a fight "yesterday." Deep peals of thunder reached her ear. She looked up, the sky was cloudless. The thunder deepened. Fresh shreds whirled past her. She reached the Chickamauga. The roar ceased. The calm startled her more than the thunder.

The Trenhom regiment was found torn, mutilated, shattered.

"My husband, where?"

"God knows! Among the cinders!"

"When seen last?"

"About noon."

"And its track then?"

"Out through deadening, over the hill."

Erma rushed away. It was she that came out of the woods and looked down in the white faces. She stood on the hillside, above her the clear cloudless sky and bright moon. Behind her the valley lost in mist; the broad gray sea. From face to face. Would she never find him? The cry "w-a-t-e-r! w a-t-e-r!" ever wailing in her heart.

Far up on the hill, beyond the barricades, a man lay on his face. She turned him over, "not him! Oh, no! How blind. He is dressed in blue!" A few feet away she saw an up-turned face. Her heart stood still. She dropped on her knees, laid her hand on the forehead. It was cold. "Oh, God!" She tore open the coat, and the shirt, laid her hand on his heart. "Thank God!"

She felt a fluttering under her touch.

She drew her hand away. Pulled a flask from her pocket, opened it, drew the cold lips apart, and the teeth, turned the flask. Gurgle! gurgle!

The burning fluid ran into his throat.

There was a gulping. A shiver passed through the body. The eyes opened.

"Erma!"

"Dale!"

It was Dale Cartier.

Thus again had his devoted wife proved an angel of rescue.

CHAPTER X

NEWS FROM CHICKAMAUGA.

Major Munson was very content, sitting in his quarters at Fernandina. The order excluding females from the department had been relaxed, until it had been quite forgotten, and the provost marshal at Hilton Head if he remembered the old order, pushed it far away back in his head when pretty Mrs. Munson stood in the gangway of the Matanzas with her sister and asked permission to land and visit her husband at Fernandina. Provost marshals are men and human. It requires a woman to resist the tongue and eyes of her sex—a woman can say no to the sweetest lips and the loveliest complexion that ever were garmented in petticoats. In fact to be sweet and pretty is the one sin of appearance surest to win " no " from women who never sinned in that direction. But a man —even if he is old and ugly and clothed with the pomp of place, and a provost marshal at that—will be blind as a mole to orders that stand in the way of a pretty woman's wishes. So pretty Mrs. Munson, with her baby and her sister, were permitted to land and furnished transportation to her husband, who was assistant post surgeon at Fernandina.

Fernandina is on Amelia island, and the island is the belchings of the sea, the excrement of storms, its light, shifting sands eddying and whirling at the touch of every breeze, creeping in unwelcome intrusion through every crevice of the town.

Tea was over, and the major had settled down to his pipe and a magazine. His wife was seated beside him, the baby in her lap, looking down admiringly at the nude, plump legs, which stood up at right angles from its little body. She had disrobed it and was about putting on its night-dress. But the sight of those legs. How could she hide them—what mother can ? She stooped down and—adoringly kissed them and the toes. And the baby kicked and crowed, and the mother kissed again and again.

" Oh, John ! do look ! "

A cloud of smoke rolled lazily away from the major's lips, and through the wreaths his wife saw that his laughing eyes were yet fixed on the pages before him. He had heard that " do look ! " every night since baby arrived.

" Did you ever see such legs ? "

The major still looked straight ahead at the book.

" The pootiest—tootyest ! " more kissing.

Mrs. Munson's sister Kitty looked on from the opposite side of the table, a smile wreathing her rosy lips ; then the door was thrown open, and " Aunt Polly," their colored servant, stood in the doorway, her portly person nearly filling it, broad as it was. Then she passed into the room, exclaiming :

" Clah, ef dat Jupe hain't done got mo' lives dan a cat."

Hearing Polly, Kitty lifted her rosy face and asked, " How many is that, auntie ? "

" An' you doan know dat, honey ? "

" No, Polly, how many is it ? "

" Clar ef I doan hean you uns in de nawf knowed eberything."

" I don't know that."

" How many is it, Aunt Polly ? " asked the major.

" An' you doan know dat, Maws Majah ? "

" No, Polly ; do tell us. How many is it ? "

" Deed ef 'tain' perdic'lous. An' tain' in your books ? "

" No, Polly ; it isn't in the books."

" Den a man kin know all de books an' be mighty nigneramuses ? "

Kitty—" That's so, Polly ; a regular—what did you call it?"

Polly—" Nigneramuses."

Kitty—" That's it, Polly, a regular nigneramuses. But how many lives has a cat ? "

Polly—" Honey, he done got nine fo' sho' ! "

Major—" Oh, Polly—deduct one. Do ! "

8

Polly — " Duck one, Maws Majah, no, sah ; duckin' ain't no 'count. You kin duck an' duck, but till dey's kill nine time dey nebbah go dead, no, sah, nebbah."

" I think I could coax one to ' go dead ' the first time."

" Dat's much you know, sah ! You might jess so well try ter fool a runaway niggah from de mawsh wid a staach shirt."

"And a runaway slave would not leave his hiding in a swamp even for a clean shirt ?" queried Kitty.

Polly—" Deed no, honey."

" And a cat is never dead until he is killed nine times ? "

" Foh shoa ! "

" But how do you kill them the ninth time ? "

Polly—" Dis way, Miss Kitty : Yeh gits de cat by him bine laig "—

" Oh ! "

" Jess so, Miss Kitty. Den fine a crookt saplin with free branches."

" Only three ? "

Polly—" I'm tellin yer, Miss Kitty. Mine now, and wawk free timesrown it, wid you head obah you leff shouldah."

" Yes ! "

" Den buss him head clah off ginn a rock."

" Oh ! Oh ! "

Polly's recipe for cat killing was greeted with peals of laughter, out of which Major Munson asked:

" Wouldn't it do to bust its head clear off against a rock, without walking round a sapling?"

" 'Clar to de Lawd, majah, ef you doan know nuffin 'bout cats," replied Polly, as she stood with her broad black hands resting on the mound of flesh that concealed her hip bones, looking down on the major, pitying his ignorance of cats. Then she suddenly broke out, " Clar ef I ain't done dismembah'd."

" Forgot what?"

" Dat fool niggah Jupe."

" What about Jupe?"

" Him doun at de foat—done gone dead foh shoah dis time, and dey wants you down dah permejate."

"Immediately?"

"Dat's it, Maws Major, permejate."

"What good can I do if he's dead?"

"D'no, sah. De cunnel's orderer"—

"Orderly"—

"Yes, sah, de orderer, him done come an' say come permejate."

"And it is Jupe again?"

"Yaas, done come back dead wid some po' white trash, mo' fool he, get himsef kilt fo' no 'count, triflin' crackah."

The major drew on his boots and coat and went away down to the fort. In little more than an hour he returned While at the fort a gunboat from the North came in with Northern papers.

One of these he tossed to his wife's sister.

Instantly tearing it open, she began greedily devouring its contents.

As the major hung up his coat he heard a moan behind him.

Looking about, he saw Kate prone and rigid on the floor, the paper tightly clasped in her hand.

The major raised Kate, called his wife, applied restoratives. Kate opened her eyes and moaned.

Then the major looked at the paper. Great lines of huge type stared him in the face.

"Two days' battle at Chickamauga; Union troops defeated; Thomas saves the army; loss frightful."

His eyes turned to the list of killed.

Among the first was the name that brought the moan to Kitty's lips; and brought tears to the major's eyes.

It was Kitty's husband—HALMER HUNTLY.

CHAPTER XI.

DAT FOOL NIGGAH JUPE.

Jupe was a slave, born on the sea coast of Virginia, in Princess Anne county. Even when a child, paddling in the surf that rolled on the beach of Princess Anne, he knew that he had a master and that he was a slave. But, what is a slave? He had somehow learned it was the difference between himself and his master's sons. But that was not quite plain. To his young mind there was none. There is but one real republic—childhood. The master's sons and he, as children, had played, and fished, and fought together. As they grew up the fighting was abandoned, but the companionship continued. Jupe was black, they were sun-browned. Yet he had been told it too often not to know that they were free and he was a slave. They lived with their parents, he with his; they in a great house, he in a small, but what the distinction was beyond this he was too busy reveling in his wealth of youth to inquire.

His chains sat so lightly on him. There was no chafing or galling. And until he knew he was to be sold away from his home, he would not have changed his condition for any other on earth.

The slave hatchery knew the value of contented, well-conditioned slaves.

Wise people neither abuse nor overwork the cattle they are preparing for a market.

Virginia raised slaves for a market.

Georgia bought and worked them.

That was the difference between Virginia and Georgia.

Virginia was paternal.

Georgia was masterful.

Even when Jupe was first sold he felt his bondage only through his affections. There was no crying out, "Oh! that I am a slave." "Oh! that I were free." "He wept and pined?" Yes! But he wept for home and pined for his mother. He did not yet know that he was a slave. Until now it was merely a word. So far in his life it had only been a sound. It was yet to become a fact, branded into his soul. He only knew that he was taken away from Princess Anne, from the sight of the foam crested surf, from the home of his childhood, from his brothers, and sisters, and father and mother. He cried out, but it was the same word always: "Mammy! Mammy! Mammy!"

In the cotton fields of Georgia he learned that he was a slave, and he knew what it meant. There he passed the next twelve years of his life. In these years he often longed to be free. But as for hope, he had none. The heart of Georgia is far from the north star. Desperate slaves, even there, sometimes fled away. But it was to conceal themselves in morasses and caves; to hide away; no more. The idea of escaping to a land of freedom never penetrated these large interior plantations. "Where was there such a land?" The slave stolen from Africa knew of his native jungles; but that was far away over the sea. The others knew of nowhere on earth. They might hide away for a season, or they might elude shot-guns and bloodhounds and lay their bleached bones in the swamps, as others, goaded beyond endurance, had done before. They might die and be free. But to live and be free was beyond their hopes. It had never occurred, so far as they knew, and they were not dreamers. Densely ignorant people never are.

In 1861 there came to them a rumor. How it came no one knew.

There is war.

"What is war?"

To a child it is a sound without meaning.

The slaves on the large plantations of the far South were children.

To them "war" was a word, no more.

It must be something out of the ordinary course. Some

startling fact. Was it famine, or a distemper, or something threatening death to "king cotton?" This they did not know. They soon learned. "What is it about, and where?"

On the small plantations farther north, where masters vapored and house servants listened, where the house hands had tongues and the field hands had ears, they knew very early. But the large plantations of the cotton, rice and sugar belts were organized on a different basis. There they had no communication with house servants and their sources of information were cut off. But information came even to them. The war was in Virginia. That spread from plantation to plantation. Jupe knew where that was. It was a long, long way off. And what need he care? What need any of them care?

It was no concern of theirs.

If white men will fight, why let them fight.

The truth filtered slowly into their minds. First one fact, then another. Little by little.

There must be a first drop or there never will be a full cup.

The first drop was the war.

"Cursed Yankees!" said Col. Saltire to his overseer. Jupe heard his master. Here was another fact. The slave-owners were fighting the Yankee.

Jupe was putting two and two together.

He was learning the art of making four.

One day the overseer was persuading a poor white to join the army. Jupe heard the reply: "No! If the masters want ter keep thar niggahs let 'em fight for 'em."

His sum was complete.

The war was about the slave.

That night he prayed "Lord holp de Yonkee."

In the winter there came another rumor: "The Yankees have possession of the coast." It always was a marvel how these rumors found their way to the remotest plantations.

Jupe heard this too. "Where is the coast?" He knew the coast of Princess Anne all along down Cape Henry and as far as he could see. "Is there any other coast?"

He dare not ask.

He was ears without a mouth. The next Sunday after he heard this he was bathing in a brook that ran through the Saltire place. His mind was full of "the coast." The waters were running away softly over the pebbles. He felt the current washing the sand out from under his feet, and a garment which he had thrown in to wash floated away down the stream. He observed it. Then the thought came to him, Where would it go to ? Where does this water go to ? He was long thinking it out.

"To the coast ! To the sea ! It did in Princess Anne; it must here."

Accident was befriending him as it has the world from the beginning.

The swinging of a Pisa cathedral lamp was accidentally witnessed and observed. Result : The Pendulum. An alphabet, cut from moist bark to amuse children, chanced to be wrapped in parchment and leave an imprint ; hence type.

Chance is the lever of the Infinite under human device.

That is, God.

Crown chance with laurels ; its triumphs are as the sands of the sea.

Jupe wondered when the thought came to him. Afterward he wondered that he had not thought of it earlier. Up to this he was quiescent and hopeful. Now he became active and hopeful. Jupe's wife belonged to another owner, Mrs. Miranda Wither, five miles away over the hills. He would not see her until the following Sunday. Jupe tried to count the days on his fingers. How could he wait ? From Sunday to Sunday is eternity to an eager purpose. Without his wife he could not go. No! She would fly with him. He would wait and he could prepare. During every day of the week he hid away provisions. Sunday came. Never before was there a Sunday so welcome. The rising sun saw him on the hill tops striding forward to his wife. The larks that flitted in the bushes were not blither. The warblers caroling in the trees were not merrier than Jupiter, on the road for his wife and liberty. When he reached the Wither plantation his wife was engaged with Mrs. Miranda. It was hours before he could draw her out of ear-shot. Then he told her. His wife stood up before him when he spoke of liberty. As he went on her eyes opened wide—wider; her lips were set apart; then her teeth. She wept. "Bress de Lawd! Dey is fweedom." "Yes, bress de Lawd," whispered Jupe. "Come!"

Then Mansa—that was his wife's name—sat down by him on the ground, her hands folded on her knees, and looked straight down into the earth.

Puzzled people always look there, as if it would answer and solve for them. Freedom and her husband were on one side, her sense of duty on the other.

It was a bitter struggle.

The storm shook her strong frame.

"Mansa, we uns mus gwo dis night."

No answer.

"Does ye heah, Mansa?"

"Yaas!"

"Dis night."

"Juptah, I can't do dat."

"Not gwanter gwo!"

"No!"

"De Lawd!"

"Dah's mistus!"

"Dah's fweedom!"

"Fweedom'll lib; mistus gwan ter die."

"What we uns keah?"

"Juptah!" exclaimed Mansa in a tone of pain and surprise.

"What we uns keah!"

"Po' ole mistus."

"Heap mo' niggah—"

"I'ze allus done been mistus's nuss."

"Kin git mo' nuss."

"Ole mistus die widout I."

"Dars mo' nuss."

"No mo' nuss dat know Miss Randy."

In their crude way the matter was fully discussed in all its bearings. Mrs. Miranda was old and feeble. Her life depended on the presence and care of Mansa. So Mansa thought. It was Mansa's burden. "De Lawd" put it on her to care for "Miss Randy tell she done gone," and Mansa must bear the burden. She felt that she could not be happy even in freedom if she deserted the feeble woman. Then she owed something to Mrs. Miranda Wither. Mansa was to be sold South. "Miss Randy" had purchased her at Mansa's solicitation and prevented it. She would be patient and do her duty to "Miss Randy." When she was dead she would join Jupe. So Mansa had resolved. But Jupe would not go alone. He declared that again and again. Against this resolution Mansa earnestly protested. "De Lawd sabe we. Wat yer tawk. Gwo! Gwo! Gwo! Be fwee, mon! Be fwee!"

Then the determination was reached, he would go, and she, when night came, would walk over the hills and see him start.

Hand in hand they walked to the "Saltire branch." She lashed his provisions to his back, embraced him again and again, saw him enter the stream, saw him swallowed in the gloom—then hopefully—sorrowfully turned her face homeward.

So Jupe started for the coast and the sea. "How far is it?

The sea is at Princess Anne. That is so far. Is it only there? Does this water go there? Where else does it go?" These were questions he asked himself. He did not know how to answer them. He only knew that water ran away to the sea. This was the crude outline. Hope filled the gaps. He was in the stream. The water would guide him and it would blunt the nose of following hounds. At first, except here and there in pools, the water was barely over his ankle. When the growing light warned him of the coming of a new day it had grown half way to his knees. Then he took refuge high up among the branches of a tree that grew close to the stream bank, and waited for darkness to come again.

He lost count of the nights that followed. He tumbled into holes. He stumbled over stones. He journeyed slowly, painfully, but every step that he followed the receding waters brought him nearer to the sea.

Deeper and deeper the water grew.

It foamed about his hips. It rippled against his back. Walking in the stream was no longer possible.

Groping his way up the bank, he laid his hands upon a canoe. He was overjoyed. He thought it was Providence. Entering it hastily he pushed from the shore. Then it occurred to him, "Will not the canoe be missed? Will they not search for it down the stream?" A few days' freedom had given him the Providence of freemen—thinking. He was learning to put two and two together rapidly. He paddled back and replaced the canoe where he found it. Then he began to realize how great a peril he had escaped. Great beads of perspiration rolled from his head. He was smitten with terror. Sudden danger always has its after fright. It was a narrow escape. He hurried away keeping close to the stream, fearful to lose sight of it, pressing through the tangled underbrush and beating his head against low lying limbs. Suddenly he sprang toward the water. He was so near to it that one bound carried him in, up to his waist in the current. It was the impetus of a new alarm—the bloodhound. There was no deep baying in the woods, no rustling of the leaves. The hounds were far away. Their fierceness perhaps chained in slumber. But he knew that every step he made on the earth was an invitation to his capture. There is no denying a hound's snout when it once touches a trail. What would he do? He could no longer wade in the stream. He dare not walk through the forest. He dare not take the canoe. The land and the water were conspired against him.

CHAPTER XII.

THE TIDES ! THE TIDES !

Immediately before Jupe, where he plunged in the water, a log projected over the stream. He climbed upon this to think. Uneasily he crawled out under the deep shadows of the trees to the extreme end of the log as far as possible from the land. It was a huge two-pronged fork held over the stream by the superior weight of the end that lay on the shore. As he neared the end his weight destroyed the balance. The outer end bowed down into the water and partly slid into it. Then a new idea came to the fugitive. What if he could float on it. He would try. He hurried up the log to the shore. Jupiter was naturally strong, but there was a giant power in his arm that night. With a short stick which he found and used as a lever the two-pronged fork was soon in the stream. To follow and lie flat upon it was but the work of a moment after. The prongs of the fork prevented it from turning. It was his ark on which he glided down with the swift current. He had yet other difficulties. To guide his unwieldly craft to the stream bank before daylight and to secure it afterwards for a new night's journey. On this primitive raft Jupe glided into the Ockmulgee, past the confluence of the Oconee, into the broader waters of the Altamaha. One night in slak-ing his thirst he discovered a brackish taste in the water. At first he thought only of its bitterness. Where had he tasted the like before ? At Princess Anne. He almost shouted for joy. He understood it now. Brackish water comes from the sea. It did in Princess Anne. An old face. An old odor. An old taste. An old fact. How they do bring up the legends of long ago. Old memories rioted in his brain that night.

Jupe drifted on into the brackish water, past a bend in the river ; then, to his dismay he discovered he was drifting back again. What is this ? Have the waters conspired to suck him back into bondage ? Is flight, and endurance, and suffering, and contriving fruitless ? All the horrors from which he had fled rushed through his mind. He thought of the cotton fields ; of his mother from whose arms he was torn ; of Princess Anne ; of his old Virginia home. " The tide ! The tide ! " Thinking of his old home revealed him the truth. The sea has a pulse. That is the tide. And this pulse-beat is felt far up in rivers that flow into the sea. It was this incoming tide that was bearing the fugitive back. He had forgotten long ago. Now again he remembered the ebb and flood of the tide along the beach of Cape Henry. He paddled to the shore and plunged into his memory for knowledge of the tides.

Is it once a week ? Is it once a day ? At Batsham, in Tonquin, there is but one tide in each lunar day, and twice in each month when the moon is near the equinoctial, there is no tide at all. But Jupe did not know that. He had never heard of Batsham. He had never heard the tides discussed. He was gleaning his information from what he had seen. Slowly out of the past there arose up before him a vision of a schooner ashore on Cape Henry. That was long ago. It went ashore on a high tide, and he walked to it when the tide was out. That was early in the morning. Then the tide came in and went out again, and he walked out to the schooner in the evening. Impressive events burnish memory. This event was slowly removing the mold of years. A fragment of the truth had dawned on him. " The tide is twice a day, and it is low tide early in the morning and late in the evening." All discoverers are satisfied with the perfection of their first device. It is only testing and reasoning that leads them beyond it. For a moment Jupe was satisfied. Then it occurred to him—the tide is but now coming in and it is long past midnight. He was testing his recollection. " It can not be low tide every morning and evening." He was reasoning. When a man reasons with facts hid in his brain he can not

long escape the truth. If Jupe had been wiser he would
have known that the tide is the sea rising up to worship the
sun and the moon—that is attraction. But it is more a moon
worshiper than a sun worshiper. Hence it follows the moon,
and if it were not for the attraction of the earth it would all go
up to the moon. It rises as often as the moon passes the
meridian, and ebbs as often as it passes the horizon. Hence
as the moon passes two meridians, east and west, and two
horizons in a day there are two high and two low tides in
a day. But how shall we tell when these high and low tides
come ? There is no uniform law, every latitude and shore is
a law unto itself. Old books tell us to look for low tide when
the rising moon is one-quarter way up the heavens, and for
high tide when it has descended half way from the zenith to
the horizon. That rule would do for the coast of France and
some parts of England. There the tide chases the moon about
three hours behind. The sun's attraction curbs and holds it
that much back. But at the mouth of the Altamaha, near
where Jupe was, the stern chase of the tide is a long one,
there it follows seven and a half hours behind the moon, and
coming on at the rate of five hundred miles an hour. Hence
it follows when the full or new moon was directly over the
fugitive the tide would be going out, and would continue
ebbing about one hour and ten minutes, then it would flood and
would be at its highest seven and a half hours after the moon
had passed the meridian and about four hours later than that
it would be high tide at his old home on Cape Henry. So the
tide swells from the south to the north. But this tidal pulsa-
tion is not regular. It was this irregularity that puzzled Jupiter. When the moon is new or full the intervals between the
tides is but twelve hours and nineteen minutes. At times of
the moon's quadrature the intervals are eleven minutes
greater. Thus the tide pulse has a continued flux of about
six hours, then rests a few moments and retires back again.
But the mystified fugitive did not know this. He was waiting
for moldy facts to be spun from his memory. The fishing
boats at his old Virginia home were kept in a creek that ran
near the door. At low tide the creek was dry, yet sometimes

they went out in the boats early in the morning ; sometimes they were compelled to wait until late in the morning, and sometimes until nearly noon. Remembering these things he reached this conclusion—there are two tides a day ; they are changeable. He saw the tide flooding before him ; when would it go out ? Crouched there by the brink, concealed in the dense underbrush, he cast leaves and dry twigs into the water and watched their course. At last he learned, as all men will who try to know. Now he could travel but part of each night—the part during which the tide was running out to the se

After many days he drifted into an open sound—the Alta-maha. From out the light mist that lay upon the waters, there sprang a dark body and tall spars. It was years and years since Jupiter had seen the like, but he knew it at once. It was a vessel. He could have hailed it, so near was he to it. He had fled. He had walked ankle deep, knee deep, waist deep in water. He had floated on a log weary nights despairing, yet hoping for this. His food was exhausted. He was consuming with thirst. The refuge for which he had started, for which he had endured all, was there within hail, and he dare not raise his voice.

Men march to the battle-field with a song, then come doubt and trembling. Men prepare for great occasions, and when they arrive, fear withholds the effort that might make success. They estimate everything except their courage at the supreme moment.

Then, for the first time since hope of freedom entered his soul he thought, " freedom is only slave's rumor ; what if it is not true ? " Going to the vessel he would go into the arms of white men. All the white men he knew were slave owners or slave hunters. In all his limited knowledge of men there was nothing to justify him in believing there were any white men who were not foes to the negro.

A vision of a return in chains and a whipping-post arose up before him. He trembled. He groaned in spirit. He wished he had not fled. "Oh, if he were only back again." To add to his terrors, the day was breaking and he was pow-

HE DRIFTED INTO THE OPEN SOUND.

125

erless. In the short chopping sea of the sound his paddle was useless. It required all his efforts to prevent being swept into the waters of the bay. When the light of the new morning came into the sky an officer from the quarter-deck of the "Unadilla" swept the horizon and then the waters of the sound with his glass. He saw the log; then the man clinging to it. He ordered away a boat. Soon Jupiter was in it. Soon after he stood on the quarter-deck, a trembling and despairing criminal.

" Where are you from ? "

" Doan know, mawsa."

" Don't know where you came from ? "

" No, mawsa."

" Which way did you come ? "

" Doan know, mawsa."

" I found you yonder in the bay."

" Yaas, mawsa."

" And you don't know how you got there ? "

" No, mawsa."

Catechising was useless, and it was abandoned. There were other colored people on the boat. Jupiter was sent to mingle with them. The commander knew that the freemasonry of a common misfortune would draw out information sealed against white inquisition. Jupiter and the other escaped contrabands came together like drops of water, with a perfect commingling. He could trust a black man. From them he concealed nothing. The other colored men gave back to him all they knew ; their experience of freedom and their causes for confidence in the blue-coats. He heard them and the doubt fled from his eyes, the pressure was lifted from his heart ; content grew up in him. That night he listened to plantation stories and laughed. The next night he reached the point where he could tell his colored friends of his own flight and the amazement of his master at not finding him. " Dat Jupe, wha de debil him gwan. Him say dat." Then he laughed uproariously. " Guy, oh ! de Law ! Law ! Law ! Woan him eye snap ? Guy ! Hi ! Hi ! "

The next day the commander noticed Jupiter near the quar-

ter-deck. The commander was an observant man. He had
seen many fugitive contrabands before, he knew the effect of
a few days' mingling with their own race, and knew how it
oiled tongues and refreshed memories. The commander asked
him :

"My man, what's your name ?"

"Nawme Jupe, mawsa ! " He could talk.

"Jupiter ? "

"Reckon y'am, mawsa ! "

"Who was your master ? " This was touching on dangerous ground. The scared look again began to cloud Jupiter's
face. He hesitated an instant ; then he thought of the colored men for'ad, and answered:

"Maws Bob Sawtiah, mawsa ! "

"Sawtiah ? "

"Yaas, mawsa ! "

"Or is it Saltire ? "

"Yaas, mawsa. Dat same, mawsa ! "

"Then your name is Jupiter Saltire."

"Reckon y'am, mawsa ! "

"Where did you come from ? "

"Sawtiah place, mawsa."

"Where is that ? "

"Moas t'end de woal, mawsa ! "

To the ignorant the vast is very small.

"What county is it in ? "

"D'no um county, mawsa."

"What state is it in ? "

"D'no um state, mawsa."

"Is it in Florida ? "

"Nebbah done hear dat place, mawsa."

"Is it in Georgia ? "

"Dat's it mawsa. Sawtin ! Sawtin ! "

"Georgia ? "

"Sawtin, mawsa! Sawtiah place. Jawja fo' sawtin,
mawsa."

The officer drew a memorandum book from his pocket to
enter the name. "What for ? Why write about him ?"

Jupiter did not know. The act startled him. There was so many reasons why he should distrust the white man. There was a horrible clanking of chains in his soul. A blood stained whipping-post rose up before his eyes. The officer noticed his uneasiness.

"Are you alarmed at my writing your name."

Jupiter did not understand and was silent.

"I do this for the purpose of reporting to my superior officer."

Still Jupiter did not comprehend. He trembled with agitation. The kind-hearted officer pitied him and sought to allay his fears."

"This will help secure your freedom."

It was not exactly true, but Jupiter could understand it. The trembling ceased.

The bowed form straightened up.

"You need have no fear of your master in the future, he is done with you, now and forever."

Jupiter's eyes began to grow.

"You are a free man now."

Jupiter looked up and fell upon his knees.

"As free, my poor friend," continued the officer, "as I am."

The heavens were aflame.

It was an angel of light, a Providence that stood before him filling his ears with a seraphic music he never expected to hear from a white man on earth.

Tears ran down his cheeks.

"Free ! Free ! Bress de Lawd ! Bress de Lawd !"

He bowed his face down to the deck and pressed his lips to the officer's feet.

CHAPTER XII.

THE CONFEDERATE DESERTER.

Jupiter Saltire ran away on his master's legs. He was at Hilton Head, about him was a uniformed multitude, more people than he had ever seen, more than he believed there was on earth. He stared in wonder at the parades, the rush of horses and the tramp of men. He sat on the bluff skirting the shore, watching the tides ebbing, flowing and rippling on the beach. He was free and his first use of freedom was to lounge, gape and eat. He had planned a battle, a struggle for freedom, and he won. What would he do with his victory? He had never thought of that and he did nothing. His mind had worked out a purpose and rested. As a slave it was not labor that galled him; it was not labor from which he fled. It was mastership, and as a freeman he was idle, not because he was lazy, not because he hated labor, not because he believed that indolence and freedom were synonymous, but because he did not think at all, and there was no one to direct him. Sitting on the beach listening to the soft beating of waters on the shifting sands, watching the black wall of fog marching over the bar into the bay, he thought of his old home and his wife. When would he see her again and how, and "where will we go," "where will we live," and "how live." Affection plows and harrows, suggests and energizes. Jupiter's rude affection for Mansa was harrowing his brain, seeding him with manhood. He had nothing. He lived on charity. Some one fed him, he did not know who. Other colored people had money. They earned it. Why should not he. It was long and laborious reasoning. Affection had seized the reins. When the fog had mounted the bay, and thrown its pall over the tall spars and great hulls

that swung in the swift tide, Jupiter had reached this point.
"How?" That night he asked, "Where do the colored people
get money?" "Work for the quartermaster." The next morning Jupiter applied to the quartermaster. "Work?" "Yes."
Jupiter began labor as a freeman. Soon after there was a
rumor, "Colored men were to be armed." Jupiter pricked
up his ears. A little later a soldier approached him. He
had a book and pencil in his hand.

"Do you think you could carry a musket ?"

"Could dat, boss !"

"Would you like to ?"

"Deed den, I would, sah !"

"Will I put your name down ?"

"Fo' sojah ?"

"Yes !"

"Deed yo' kin dat !"

"You will be paid as a laborer in the quartermaster's
department."

"Yaas, sah."

"The government has not yet reached the point of accepting the services of colored men as soldiers."

"Why dat, boss ?"

"Afraid of prejudice in the minds of the people. The
government fears it would lose many of its supporters if arms
should be placed in the hands of the negroes."

"If a niggah kill a sesher woan he go dead sho as ef a
white man done kill 'im ?"

"Of course he will. But the prejudice is there."

"Yaas, boss !"

"And some people think a regiment of contrabands would
lope like deer before a Southern man with a whip in his hand."

"Dey fool deysef sho !"

"You think the contrabands will fight ?"

"Sawtin, sah !"

"Many of our soldiers here say the negroes will not stand
under a pattering of bullets."

"Ef niggahs kin stan de lash and de houns, an de tum
screw an de ine collah, reckon dey stan a lee'le lead."

"You think so."

"Laws, boss ; a chunk o' lead in de innards ain't nuffin ter a hunder laid on wid hickry, an brine rub in de soahs."

"And you will go ?"

"Sawtin, boss, sawtin ! an tank de Lawd fo' de chance, sah. I'ze got a woman dah ! "

Jupiter's name was enrolled. He was a soldier in the first colored company organized during the war. Ten days later Jupiter was on the "Darlington," bound south, in search of a fight along the coast. It was found at St. Mary's, in Florida. North of St. Mary's the Confederates had erected extensive salt works. The object of the expedition was to destroy the works. War is a compound—pounding and starving. To cut off the salt supply was to help starve. The colored troops landed. The enemy fled. The blacks followed through the dense woods. The Confederates made a stand. Their rifles flashed in the faces of their pursuers. The colored troops dashed on ; the Confederates in dismay fled again. The salt works were captured and destroyed. When the pickets were called in Jupiter made no response. They sought for him. They found him, his back set against a tree, his feet braced apart, the barrel of his musket grasped firmly in his right hand, but he was voiceless and helpless. They carried him to the boat, a stream of blood flowing from his breast and oozing from his lips. He was shot through the lungs. Jupiter's wounds was severe, his recovery tedious. At length he was well. Then the commandant at Fernandina desired information. Jupiter volunteered as scout. Three times he penetrated Georgia and Florida, bringing back valuable military gleanings. The third time his boat was swamped in Cumberland Sound, two escaping contrabands who were with him were drowned, and Jupiter had a narrow escape. These experiences made their impress on Jupiter. He was growing. In the summer of 1863 he resolved to penetrate Georgia to his old home and deliver Mansa. He was a favorite with the commandant of the post. The officer aided him. A light duck-boat and passage on a steamer to Altamaha Sound were furnished him. Jupiter needed no more. It was weary and

THE CONFEDERATE DESERTER.

wary journeying. Pickets on the Altamaha. Scouts, spies and
hounds everywhere. But Jupiter eluded them all. Conceal-
ing his boat when he reached shoal water, he pressed on to the
old plantation and over the hills to the home of his wife. She
was gone. Mrs. Miranda Wither was dead, and Mansa—was
sold.

"Who bought her?" "Marmaduke Titefist!" "Where?"
"Obah at Andasonville." "Where's that?" No one knew.
"How far?" No one could say. Slaves had no idea of distances.
"Which direction?" No one could tell that, whether north,
south, east or west, it was a "lang way." The slaves were
glad to see Jupiter. They would have been glad to help him.
But ignorance is a soundless pit. They could do nothing but
look on him, a hero who had escaped and returned—and drink
his tales into their wondering souls. Jupiter remained a week
about his old home, hoping that some of the slaves would be
able to learn "where is Andersonville."

It was a vain hope. Fear of betrayal he had none. He
knew that any slave in that region would have died before be-
traying him. So he came and stayed, his presence unsuspected by the whites, then he turned his sad face toward the
coast. One night resting on the banks of the Ockmulgee,
waiting for the moon to disappear, he heard voices. He stole
out from his hiding and looked. Not fifty yards away from
him was a camp fire. Three men were sitting about it, cooking. Beyond the fire Jupiter saw a fourth. Then he noticed
the fourth was bound to a sapling and that his hands were
tied. This set Jupiter to thinking. Who is the fourth? An
escaped Union soldier? The man wore a uniform. It was
not blue. But he had seen no prisoners, and he did not know
but that prisoners were probably clothed that way. Yes, it
must be a Union soldier escaped from prison, else why should
they capture and guard and bind him? For a long time
Jupiter watched them, wondering if there were any more. He
crawled stealthily toward them. There were but three and
the prisoner. He could hear them distinctly. After supper
and rest they would move on. Such was their purpose as
Jupiter gleaned it from their conversation. Their evening

meal was devoured. The captors ate. The prisoner hungered. Then the captors lighted their pipes, and Jupiter lay extended at full length in the tangled web of forest grass, watching, listening and thinking. The moon had already disappeared. The-duck boat would hold two. One of the captors stood up.

"Let's git," he exclaimed.

Jupiter was not twenty feet away. A revolver was cocked in his hand. He sprang to his feet, rushed at the group and fired. The man who had spoken threw up his arms and fell. A second man was on his feet with rifle raised. Jupiter fired again. The revolver ball crashed through the hand upholding the rifle. The rifle fell, and discharged as it reached the ground. Its holder fled. There was but the third man and the prisoner. The third man was unarmed ; his gun was resting against a tree beyond his reach. Seeing Jupiter and alone he rushed upon him. Jupiter's pistol refused to revolve. It was man against man. The escaped slave and the brawny white were locked in deadly embrace. For an instant there was a writhing and interlocking of strong limbs. The white cursed the " —— niggah;" "eat him up;" "skin him alive." The black was silent. The white man's jaws were against the side of Jupiter's head. The jaws open. Jupiter's ear disappeared in the cavern. The strong teeth closed upon it. Jupiter's right hand was disengaged. It still clasped the butt of the revolver. The hand raised, came down with a thud upon the head of the white. The jaws relaxed. Again the pistol rose and fell. The white dropped upon his knees.

"Spar me !   Spar me ! "

The third time the heavy iron of the pistol rose and with remorseless energy fell upon the bare head. There was a dull mashing of flesh, a hollow crunching of bones, a sputtering of blood clots, and the white man lay with his sightless eyes turned up to the sombre sky. For Jupiter to draw his knife, cut the leashes of the prisoner, and rush away with him to the river bank was but the work of an instant. The boat was drawn from its hiding, Jupiter and the prisoner were in it. They had glided down the bank fift f yards under the shadow of the trees. Then a little spark flamed out of a bush. An instant after a sharp report echoed through the forest, followed by a scream, "Ther's even!" and all was still. Jupiter pulled the boat steadily away from the shore until it was lost in the gloom of mid-stream. Then he gave the paddle to the rescued man and placed his hands upon his side. Immediately they were warm and moist. When he heard the shot he felt a slight sensation like the pricking of a pin, or the sudden touch of an icy point against his side. Now he knew he was shot. The man who escaped had concealed himself under a bush by the river and punctured him with a pistol ball. Jupiter felt no present pain, but the flow of blood continued. Would it continue? Was this the end? A year of freedom had given Jupiter forethought. He gave the fugitive directions. Concealment in bushes. Journey dark nights; middle of the stream; on to the broad water. The warm red stream was welling from his side. Jupiter lay down in the boat.

"Membah dat, dead o' alibe, you takes me."

"Yaas."

"Is you Union sojah?"

"No!"

"What den?"

"Confed, I reckon?"

"Sojah?"

"Yaas!"

"What yer prisnah fo'?"

"D'zartah, reckon!"

When the duck-boat reached the sound and Jupiter and the fugitive were picked up by a gunboat, the fugitive was nearly starved and Jupiter's life was suspended on a slender thread. But Jupiter was saved from the jaws of secession and with him Lindey's husband, the Confederate deserter, Joe Ratley.

CHAPTER XIV.

"HE STOOD BEFORE ME AND CALLED."

In the spring of 1864 a "blockader," on the way from Fortress Monroe to Fernandina, picked up a boat off the coast of North Carolina. The boat contained six fugitive slaves and a Union soldier. The soldier had been a prisoner of war, confined in Salisbury. He had escaped. Pushed for the coast. Slept in trees, jungles and marshes. He hungered and thirsted. Barefooted, ragged, emaciated, fevered, covered with sores, he reached a tide-water stream. Slaves aided him ; secured a boat for him, and fled with him, out through the fog, without chart or compass, into the broad bosom of the ocean. The sea was more merciful than secession, it tossed the soldier and his aids into the arms of a blockader, and he was carried to Fernandina. He was a battered and shattered hulk. He sadly needed repairs. They put him in that human dry dock—the hospital. Surgeon Munson had witnessed misery and suffering. With gashing, cutting, pustulation and pain he was familiar. Here was something new, a strong human form passed through the slow devouring of hunger; ground to a skeleton; and worn to the last stage of feebleness. It was a pitiful sight. A painful sound was in his appeal, " A little more, doctor, I'm so hungry. Oh! I was so hungry, then, so hungry. I will always be hungry, doctor, always be hungry ! " The doctor told his wife and told his widowed sister-in-law. Suffering Kate Huntley listened to the story with profound agitation.

" Poor fellow ! Can I do anything for him ? "

To Surgeon Munson it was a suggestive question. Since the fateful news from Chickamauga Mrs. Kate Huntley surrendered interest in life. She loved Sergeant Halmer Hunt-

ley deeply, devotedly. They had been children together—
lovers as far back as they could remember. She had launched
all her hopes and thoughts of life in him. When he fell she
was bankrupt in affection and in all life interest. If she would
only have wept and moaned the surgeon and his wife could
have comforted her ; they could have looked forward to the
time when the stream would be exhausted. But she did
neither. She sank into imperturbable apathy. It was a
paralysis of emotions more pathetic than any prodigality of
tears and exclamations. For months this bereaved woman,
with the flower-crowned monument in her heart, had moved
on, calm, silent and listless, the roses dropping from her
cheeks and the sparkle slowly fading from her eyes. She was
grievous to look on. Now for the first time she was touched.
A suffering penetrated the fountain and she wept, not for herself but for the misery of another. The cruel, barbarous
wickedness that denied helpless prisoners food aroused her
indignation.

Surgeon Munson quickly caught up Kitty Huntey's suggestion. "Here is something," he thought. "The salve of
another's suffering. Who can tell its potency ?" Then he
said aloud,—

"My dear, he needs a nurse sadly."

"May I nurse him ?" said Kate, eagerly   Mrs. Munson's
eyes were moist. How glad she was to hear the eager ring
come again into sister Kate's voice. She was on the point of
saying, "Kate, it will do you good ; " but happily she noticed
that her husband said nothing about Kate, and its possible
good to her, and she refrained. Kate was not thinking of herself, she was only thinking "Poor fellow, he's somebody's
husband, somebody's lover, somebody's son ; and so worn and
thin and hungry ; and the dreadful, dreadful, cruel war
brought him to this."

Surgeon Munson was heartily glad that she offered her
services. It was good of Kate, and he knew it would do her
good. "Come Kate," he said, "If you will be so good, come
to him. He needs soft words and tenderness and watch-
fulness "

"Oh, then, let me go at once."

"Certainly, if you will."

"Oh, John, how can you ask that?"

In less than five minutes she was prepared and went away with her brother-in-law to the hospital. Day after day she remained with her patient, from early in the morning until he passed into fitful slumber at night. He was so feeble. She moistened his lips; she softened the bed and turned and returned the pillows; she fanned him; she kept him cool and comfortable; his eyes followed her, she was so tender and her touch it was so gentle; she read to him—how sweet her voice sounded. One day he said to her "will you kiss me here?" and he laid his attenuated finger on his hollow cheek. "Dear old mother kissed me there when—I—went—a-way—to—the —war."

She pressed her lips to his worn cheeks, and her tears dropped down and baptised the spot.

"Dear—old—mother."

A smile wreathed his lips. His eyes slowly closed and he dropped into a soft, peaceful slumber. The next day Mrs. Huntley knew her patient had turned the corner. Then she sang to him. A little ballad.

The soldier listened and murmured "poor puss cat."

The next day Mrs. Huntley sang the same ballad, and again the patient murmured "poor puss cat."

Mrs. Huntley looked at him. He had said the same yesterday. Was there anything the matter with the man's mind? He talked and acted rationally. Why should he repeat "poor puss cat" to that song?

The third day the song was repeated and again the patient murmured "poor puss cat."

Mrs. Huntley was perplexed. After a moment's pause she asked, "Why do you say 'poor puss cat?'"

"Because that song reminds me of 'poor puss cat.'"

"What is there about the song to remind you of a cat?"

"Oh, not a cat!"

"Not a cat?"

"No, a man."

" Oh, a man."

"Yes, at Salisbury."

" Indeed.   A Union soldier? "

" Yes, I think so."

" What was his name?"

" Puss Cat."

" A man? "

" Yes ! "

" And named Puss Cat? "

" Yes ! "

" Why, what a funny name for a man.   And was that his real name? "

" I don't know

" Oh ! "

The riddle was deepening.

" He was in Salisbury when I was captured."

" Where did he belong? "

" Indeed I don't know, nor did any one there."

" That is singular.   Would he not tell? "

" I don't think he knew."

" Not know where he came from? "

" Well you see he was not exactly right."

" Not right?   How do you mean."

" Not exactly right in his mind."

" Oh, poor fellow ! "

" Poor fellow.   I found him there alone and chummed to him."

"That was good of you."

" Well, you see, he couldn't take of himself and he had no one take care of him.   Poor boys ! when hunger's on them, they get awful selfish.   You can't blame them.   It's a terrible sensation, hunger is.   It just grinds humanity out of a man."

" Poor boys."

" Yes, a fellow may feel, ' well I'll give a bit to another fellow hungrier than I ; ' but when the bit comes into your hand, your mouth lays right hold of it.   I tell you hunger just burns the heart out of a man."

" Poor hungry boys. And Puss Cat ? "

"Poor Puss was going down, down, every day."

"Poor fellow. Poor fellow ! "

" Yes ! Poor fellow ! And he never said a word only
'Kit ! Kit ! Kit !'"

" Kit !"

" Yes, Kit; only that and sing that same song you sang
yesterday and to-day."

" Kit !"

" Yes, that and the song. That was all I ever heard him
say, and I slept with him and took care of him, drew his rations
and cooked for him. I'd have brought him with me, or
stayed, only they sent him away with others to Andersonville."

" It was good of you."

" Oh, dear Mrs. Huntley, he was somebody's son."

" Perhaps they called him Puss Cat, because he was always
repeating ' Kit ! Kit ! Kit !'"

" Yes. I often thought that. But I learned he was
enrolled under that name, and that no one knew any other for
him."

" And this poor boy without mind was sent away to Andersonville."

" Yes !"

".It was cruel ; dreadfully cruel."

" Dear Mrs. Huntley, you don't know the rebellion. Its
soldiers are brave. Many of them are noble, generous and
humane adversaries, but many of its home emissaries are
inexorably marble-hearted, brutal and malevolent."

" You are very severe !"

" I have writhed in their clutch. I have seen their stony
eyes glaring in triumph over our sufferings."

" Poor sufferer."

" And I am penetrated with its rancor when I think of
poor Puss Cat, helpless and shorn of his mind, condemned to
the misery of Andersonville prison pen."

That night piercing screams disturbed the quiet of Surgeon Munson's quarters. He was aroused from slumber. The
screams continued. He sprang from bed. His agitated wife

followed. The screams intensified. They guided the surgeon and his wife to Mrs. Huntley's room. Hurriedly they opened the door and entered. A full flood of moonlight illuminated the apartment. Mrs. Huntley was in bed, lying at full length, her eyes wide open, her arms outstretched and fingers distended. The cries continued.

"Puss Cat! Puss Cat! Hal! Hal!"

Surgeon Munson spoke—"Kitty!"

"Puss Cat! Puss Cat!"

"Kate!"

"Hal! Hal!"

The surgeon's agitated wife called to her sister. The only answer was:

"Puss Cat! Puss Cat! Hal! Hal!

Surgeon Munson advanced to the bedside and took hold of her arms. They were rigid as bars of steel. He was powerless to move them. His wife moved to join him. He motioned her back and himself stepped away from the side of the bed. "Let her alone for a few moments. She is in a trance condition,—a sort of magnetic sleep." The screams gradually died down to a wail. Then the arms suddenly drew back under the covers. The head nestled down in the pillows. The wailing subsided into sobbing. Fainter. Then fainter. Then ceased. Quiet reigned again in the house. Surgeon Munson and his wife sat nearly an hour by the bedside, then seeing that Kate had fallen into soft and dreamless slumber they retired. Both were profoundly agitated and at a loss to account for the phenomenal occurrence. Each had the same fears. "Mental disease." But neither spoke of it. The next morning at the breakfast table both watched Kate anxiously and narrowly. If changed at all, it was apparently for the better. Both seemed to detect a new sprightliness in her voice. A fresher tinge on her cheek. They would have put away the night terror entirely but for the frequent pauses Kate made in her breakfast, and the puzzled, far-away look that came into her eyes. After breakfast Kate walked to the window, looked out upon the bay, drummed listlessly a few moments on the glass, then turning to her sister said:

"Sue, I saw Hal last night."

"Oh, Kate."

Sue looked at the surgeon. The surgeon looked back at his wife.

"I did, Sue! I saw him as plainly as I now see you and John."

"A dream, Kate."

"No, Sue. It was no dream. I saw him alive and in the body, worn and emaciated."

"Oh, Kate!"

"Yes, I did; I saw him and heard him—heard him call me Kit! Kit! Kit! just as distinctly as I hear you say 'Oh, Kate!'"

Anxious Mrs. Munson trembled. She was confident that brooding upon her bereavement had robbed her sister of mental balance.

Seeing the surgeon and her sister gazing upon her with distended, troubled eyes, Kate continued:

"You think it was a dream?"

"Yes, dear, that was all. Don't permit it to disturb you."

Mrs. Huntley had approached her sister's husband, taking him gently by the arm she drew him to a lounge and sat down by him.

"Let me tell you. Come sit here, Sue," pointing to a footstool beside the lounge.

Then she went on and narrated the story of the sick man in the hospital, and she concluded:

"I tell you, John, that is Hal. I know it, and he is alive in Andersonville."

"Did you think of it yesterday when you heard the story."

"It never occurred to me until last night. Then he stood before me and called. Oh, John, Sue! It was so pitiful. It would break your heart to hear him call, Kit, Kit, Kit!"

"Did your patient describe the man?"

"No. I never thought to ask his description. But," and she sprang to her feet, "I'll go this instant."

"Sit down, dear." John drew her gently back to the

lounge. In her present state of mind he feared a description of 'Puss Cat' that would be fatal to her hopes.

"You have no other reasons than your patient's story ?"

"I saw him !"

"Not until after you had heard the patient's story ?"

"No; it was after, of course. But that song. You remember he sings that. And Hal used to sing it."

"Yes, dear ; but it is a very common ballad."

"Yes !"

"Familiar to thousands."

"True !"

"It is not as if it was a composition of his own or yours, known only to you two."

"You forget his calling. His repetition of Kit! Kit! and so mournful. He always called me that. Puss and Kit. Wasn't it, Sue ? Always Kit !"

"It is the commonest of names, my dear."

"Oh, John," appealingly.

"Yes, dear; nearly every man in the army has a wife or a sister or a cousin or a sweetheart called Kit."

"Oh, dear !"

"And even men are called so. Christopher is curtailed into Kit. There was Kit Carson, and a host of others."

Kate looked from her sister to her brother, then lay back on the lounge, her hands folded over her eyes. One, two, three minutes passed. Then she sat up, with her clasped hands in her lap.

"Don't be annoyed with me, dears, and don't think that I am silly or dreaming, or addle-headed, but I tell you my dear husband is alive !"

"God grant it !"

"And that he is in Andersonville."

"Dear Kate !" John and his wife both exclaimed it.

"And that his name is Puss Cat."

Much more was said. Many arguments were offered to dispossess Kate of her belief, but she remained unshaken. The surgeon stood up.

"You will not go out, dear, until I return."

10

"I must go to my patient."

"You will please not go until I return. You will do that for me, dear."

Kate acquiesced without understanding. The doctor understood and hurried away to the hospital. He was resolved to remove the patient beyond Kate's inquiries if the description of 'Puss Cat' varied glaringly from that of Sergeant Halmer Huntley. He dreaded a shock of sudden disappointment. The sick man repeated the story as he had told it to Kate.

"Is he tall or short?"

"Medium height. Should say about five feet seven or eight, present appearance somewhat deceptive as to that, considerably bowed with infirmity."

"The color of his hair?"

"Brown, bleached a good deal in the sun. Has been hatless most of the time."

"His build?"

"Can't say, so worn with hunger and past sickness."

"And the color of his eyes?"

"Indeed"—he paused a moment. "No, I can not say; certainly blue or gray. I can not say positively which. You may know a fellow fifty years and not be able to name the color of his eyes unless your attention had been specially called to it, and hunger changes expressions so much."

"Any dimple on his chin?"

"If there is it is hidden by his beard."

"His complexion. Is it dark or fair?"

"Ah, doctor, the sallow blanching of fever and foul air blots out complexions."

Surgeon Munson learned no more than this. There was nothing in it at all to destroy or confirm Kate's belief. Sergeant Huntley was of medium height, had brown hair and blue eyes, but so had a million men. The height and the hair were the only two points on which there was positive agreement with Huntley. On the other points there was no positive disagreement. It was all so vague and indefinite. The same language might be used in describing any one of a million people. Soon after Surgeon Munson went away Kate

stood in the hospital bubbling over with anxiety. Her questions were a torrent Little details of manner and speech, of
teeth, a multitude of trifles that the surgeon would not know.
The questioning was, Munson repeated, multiplied by a
devoted wife's affection. But the sick man had told all he
knew. He could tell Kate no more. And when he learned
what hopes his words had planted he lamented. To the surgeon he afterwards said:

"Thoughtless words are the fruitful seed of misery. I
would rather have bit my tongue off than spoken of 'Poor
Puss Cat,' if I had known. She is such a noble woman, and
she has suffered so much ; and it is all so hopeless and fruitless—hopeless and fruitless, doctor. It is not her husband. I
am sure of it. There were no Chickamauga men with him. I
could not tell her that. She seems to-day to live in her belief.
Poor suffering woman ! It will be a cause of bitterness to me
forever that I have reopened the wounds of her grief."

The doctor was convinced. Kate was not. Day by day
her belief grew. It increased into certainty. It gave her a
new interest in life. She grew stronger. She would say to
her sister, "I am thinking, Sue, thinking. Something must
be done. Wait. I will get it fixed in my mind."

Four days afterwards Aunt Polly came into the breakfast
room.

"Clah, Maws Majah, ef dat Jupe ain' de biggest bawn
fool."

"What's the matter now? "

"Dat niggah ain't nebbah sass'fite 'less some one feedin'
him wid lead."

"Shot again ? "

"No, not dat yet. Heem gwan 'mong de seshahs tu git
he'seff shot."

"Where? "

"Ahtah dat fool woman o' heem."

Mrs. Huntley ceased eating. From that moment to the
end of the breakfast her eyes were riveted on the center of
the table. When Munson and his wife rose she followed
them into the sitting room. As they walked across the room

she stood between them. She threw her arms over their
shoulders, then about their necks.

"John," she said, " when Jupiter returned, wounded in
the fall, did he not say that his wife had gone to Andersonville?"

"Yes," replied John, thoroughly startled.

"And he is going there for her?"

John turned his face to the questioner. Her wide-open,
earnest eyes were fixed upon him. A firmness had come
about Kate's mouth that gave a new and strange expression to
her face. He paused a moment. Then he answered:

"Yes, I suppose so."

"I am so glad. It is the opening! the way, John! I am
going with him."

"Kate!" cried her sister.

"Good heavens!" exclaimed her sister's husband.

She drew the loved faces down to her and kissed them.

"John, Sue, dears! God being my helper I am going to
Hal—to Andersonville."

CHAPTER XV.

"HALT! HALT THERE!"

Mrs. Huntley's announcement astonished her hearers. They battered her with entreaties, prayers and tears; with representations of peril, of its uselessness and folly. It was hurling egg shells against an iron-clad. Kate's purpose was invulnerable to persuasions ; steeled against doubts and fears. Having decided, she remained inexorably steadfast. "If you will not aid me," she said, "I will go north and penetrate Georgia from Tennessee. Oh, Sue ! John ! I see Hal's outstretched hands. So thin ! thin and worn ! I see them day and night ! His voice is ringing in my heart. A helpless wail ! It tears my soul to listen to it, dears."

There was no resisting her will. No heart could be hardened against her plaintive, melting appeals. Jupiter was sent for and came. " Did he intend to go ? " " Yes." What had he learned about Andersonville ? " " Little." It was somewhere west of the Ockmulgee river. No more than that. Then he was told of Mrs. Huntley's purpose.

" Laws, Miss Kate, doan do dat ? "

Kate poured her story, her belief, and her hopes into his tender ears. He sobbed aloud.

" Po' chile. Miss Kate, I'll gwan to de-eend ob de wole wid ye."

She threw her arms about his neck. Then Jupiter and the family sat in council. It was agreed that Jupiter would speak no more about going himself, and that the few friends to whom he had imparted his purpose would be led to understand it was abandoned, and Mrs. Huntley's name was not to be mentioned under any circumstances. They would have another conference that night. In the meantime Surgeon

Munson would learn all that was to be learned about the location of Andersonville.

In the evening they met again, with doors and windows closed. Munson had secured several maps. From these it appeared that the Ockmulgee was navigable to Macon ; that a railroad ran nearly south from Macon to Albany on the Flint river, and that Andersonville was about two-thirds of the way down the road from Macon. The maps showed Hawkinsville on the Ockmulgee to be nearly west of Andersonville. Jupiter expressed confidence in his ability to penetrate the Altamaha and Ockmulgee, the only question was how far, and the course to pursue afterward. The only attainable guides were the maps. From these the route was planned. They would go up the Ockmulgee to or near Hawkinsville, and then strike across the country to the railroad, and go north or south as they happened to strike it above or below Andersonville. The next question was the method of reaching the Altamaha, into which the Ockmulgee pours its flood, Jupiter yet had his small duck-boat. But Munson would not trust Kate in this, crossing the broad sounds. A steamer was suggested, to take them to a point near Darien. Jupiter thought this was not safe ; it might attract attention from the shore. A small sail boat would be better ; he could make night journeys in this, towing the duck-boat to St. Simon's Island. Then wait for a fog and favorable wind, and dash across Altamaha Sound to near the shore, sink the large boat and take to the duck-boat. This plan seemed feasible and was adopted. Munson stood up. " Wait a bit, sah." Then the surgeon found there was much more to be thought of—" clothing."

" Have an abundance," answered Kate.

" Dat ain't gwan to do. Ef you gwo youze a po' low down wite, mine dat, an' you mus hab crackah clowfin."

Jupiter entered into details. As he talked, the confidence of Kate's sister and her husband grew. This man was so provident. He pointed out so many little details that escaped their observation. A year's freedom had improved his language and self-dependence had broadened his vision. He saw beyond the end of his nose. Kate was eager to set out the next night; but it was determined to wait until the end of the third day. That would give time for preparations and for valuable suggestions, overlooked in the hurry of their consultation.

Mrs. Munson was in a maze of doubts. "Oh, Kate," she said, when Jupiter retired, "are you not afraid to go away alone with that powerful black man?"

"Afraid! Of a man who will peril his life to bring his wife out of slavery. No, dear; a man who is devoted to his own wife will honor the wives of other people."

Objections ended there.

At midnight of the third day four persons stood on the beach of Amelia Island, between Fernandina and Fort Clinch. They were Jupiter, Kate Huntley, Surgeon Munson and his wife. Before them was a small sail boat; fastened at its stern was Jupiter's duck-boat. Surgeon Munson and his wife shook hands with Jupiter, and he walked down the beach. Kate's sister looked after him a moment, then hurried after. She threw her arms about his neck and whispered in his ear.

"Oh, be good to her, be good to her!"

"I'd die for she! As I hope fo' hebin!"

"God bless you! Good-bye!"

And she turned away. A few moments later Kate was in the boat beside Jupiter. There had been a tender parting. The sail was raised. It filled in the soft breeze. Slowly at first, as if drifting, it dropped away from the beach. Then the wind caught it. The waters rippled around its bow. The forms within it grew indistinct from the shore. Then faded out. Before John Munson and his wife there was only a broad expanse of water. No sound but the soft ripple of the tide upon the shore. Then they turned and walked silently homeward. In the minds of both of them the same thought:

"What a mad, fruitless pilgrimage."

The boat sped on. Kate watched the shore until it was lost in the thin veil of mist, then resolutely turned her face forward.

"Now, Jupiter, we are comrades."

"Youze capin and I'ze deck han'."

"No, Jupiter, we are comrades."

"Dat's a right pleasan' way o' tawkin', Miss Kate."

"Now, can I help you?"

"No, honey."

"But you must tell me when I can do anything. I must do my full share, remember that."

"Den stop tawkin'."

"Be silent?"

"Yes, honey; de win's hab eahs!"

During the remainder of the night there was no sound in the boat except the foaming of the waters about its bow. Hours sped away. Kate had been dozing in the stern of the boat. Jupiter touched her and whispered, "Can you tell what time it is?"

"Yes, I have a watch that strikes the time." She touched a spring and it ticked out one—two—three.

"An' day breaks in a half hour. We must put to de shoa."

They reached the beach of Cumberland Island and concealed the boats. Jupiter crawled on the beach and lay down in the bushes, the rope of the boat fastened about his arm. Kate lay in the boat and slept. When Jupiter awoke he cooked breakfast, being careful to make a small fire, surrounding it with logs for concealment. After dark they started again. During the night of the third day they reached St. Simon's Island, opposite the mouth of the Altamaha. A huge live oak, with its wide-spreading branches festooned with a dense growth of Spanish moss, grew close by the shore. At its feet was a narrow inlet completely curtained by the pendant moss. Jupiter had explored it before. Reaching it, he pushed aside the curtain and drew in his boat. So much of the journey had been passed in safety and they were secure from observation.

But the real peril was to come.

Up to this point no danger had been expected. They had only to avoid watchful eyes, and this they had done. The apprehended danger lay in the first twenty miles of the Altamaha. Its mouth was bristling with teeth. Booms stretched across the river and there were picket boats in its jaws and patrols on its lips. On St. Simon's Island there was no cooking. The fire might be seen and the smoke attract attention. But this had been foreseen. When the fog lifted from the Sound, Jupiter peered out through the curtain of live oak moss. He looked long and anxiously. Half way over toward Darien one of the blockading squadron lay anchored, floating lazily on the bosom of the unruffled waters. Far off on the lower delta of the Altamaha a faint column of smoke rose above the impenetrable tree tops. Jupiter could see nothing else but the shore and the trees. When he turned away from the curtain he said to Kate : "It look like de same."

Then they ate. After breakfast there was a consultation. All tell-tale papers and everything pertaining to Yankee land were destroyed. Kate wanted to cling to a pocket map she had brought with her.

" No. You must jist git it in youm head. Crackah womans doan go roun wid lan' picturs like dat."

Kate studied the map for hours, the rivers, their courses, the railroads, the towns, their populations, everything that was on the map until she could reproduce it from memory. Then she tore it to shreds.

" Now, Jupiter, what else ? "

" Dem eah 'ings."

" Goodness, can't I wear earrings ? "

" Coon don't wah sheep tail."

The earrings came out.

" Dah's dat fingah ring."

" Oh ! my wedding ring ! "

" Can't help dat."

" Oh, Jupiter. I can't take that off. Dear Hal placed it there."

" I'ze powful mis'able bout dat, honey ; but yo can't play clay-eatah in marryin' rings. Dey uns doan hab um."

Kate cried a little, pressed the ring to her lips and removed it. Then she sewed the rings in her dress.

The night they started from Fernandina Jupiter began a lesson on hair. It was necessary to shake it out, let the sun

get into it, put away brushes. In a word, it must "git frowsy."
But Kate begged so hard: "Oh, do let it remain as long
as possible." Pride of appearance was nearly as strong as
affection. But on St. Simon's Island, in sight of the Altamaha,
affection conquered. The pins were taken out. The hair
was unbound. When it came down part of it came off.
Jupiter shook his head. "Mo' lamb tail on coon. Dat nebbah do. No crackah ebbah seed de like." Kate shivered
a little and dropped the chignon into the sand. Affection was
very powerful at that moment. Jupiter gave Kate a lesson
in tying hair "po' white" fashion. Then it was unbound
again and remained all day bleaching in the sun. When
evening came Jupiter made no preparations for a start.

Kate was devoured with anxiety.

"What is it?"

"Won't do to gwo. Mus' wait fo' a fog ter come arly.
Got twenty mile ob de ribbah to gwo de fuss night."

The next day was no better. The third day was intensely
warm until mid afternoon. Then a sudden chill came into
the air. By four o'clock the opposite shore grew dim. By
five it had wholly vanished. An impenetrable wall of fog lay
on the bosom of Altamaha Sound. When Kate saw the film
gathering over the waters she turned to Jupiter. She could
tell from the set of his jaws and the stern look in his eyes that
the supreme moment was coming. He watched the other
shore as long as it was discernible. He caused Kate to take
the bearings again and again with a pocket compass. They
each had a compass. His was the first he had ever seen. He
looked in wonder, at the needle pointing to the magnetic
pole. But he could not learn to understand it. He watched
the water rising on the beach and saw that it had passed the
ebb and was slowly flowing in. He cast dry sticks out into
the current and watched the direction in which they floated
away. He noted that they set straight away for the opposite
inlet. At eight o'clock on the evening of the seventh day of
June Jupiter drew the boats from the inlet, lifted the sail,
looked carefully over every article in the little boat, helped
Kate in and turned his face toward Secessia. Slowly at first,

then rapidly, the boats plowed the bay, Kate with compass and watch on her lap answering Jupiter's directions.

"Not an' howah yit! Clah to massy it feel like two."

"It's an hour now," answered Kate.

"De win' ain't berry fass. Reckon we gib 'em 'nuddah quatah."

Fifteen minutes more passed. Jupiter stood up in his bare feet. His shoes were fastened to cords about his neck. He drew the sail in, unshipped the mast, rolled the sail about it, laid it on the seats of the boat, lashed it fast, then drew up the little boat beside the great one. Kate stood up. She too was in her bare feet, her shoes being safely stowed away in a great pocket. Kate protested against the shoeless, stockingless feet. It was pardonable pride. But Jupiter was firm. "Jawja po' white doan wear no stockin'." So the stockings that shaped up her pretty ankles were abandoned. The shoes might make a noise in the boat. So they, too, were removed. Jupiter held the duck-boat firmly until the little pink and white feet were dropped into it and Kate was safely seated. Then he pulled a number of plugs from the bottom of the sail-boat, which was laden with stone. They watched the water spurt in, watched the boat sink lower and lower and then disappear.

"Now, Miss Kate, whahs de coase?"

Kate looked at the compass and pointed it out. Jupiter seized the paddle and the light duck-boat leaped forward into the gloom. Kate was giving whispered directions, a little to the right, a little to the left, on and on. An hour passed, and then Jupiter paused. They could see nothing. So intense was the darkness that the bow of the little boat was not discernible from its stern. For the next hour progress was slower. Little spurts of speed. Then pausing and listening. The next half hour was the same. Jupiter knew he was in the river, but where? He did not know. He listened for sounds to guide him. He leaned forward and whispered:

"Ef ye heahs nise, tech my foot."

A few moments after Kate's little pink toes touched Jupiter's ankle. He held his paddle suspended in the air and bent his head down to the water. Then he touched her. She leaned forward and he whispered :

" What way?"

" Over to the left of us."

" Doan undastan dat."

Jupiter bent his ears down to the water again. He was troubled. If Kate could have seen his face and read his thoughts she would have been in agony. Then a faint sound came over the water. Jupiter's face cleared up.

" Dat's all right, Miss Kate. Dat soun' am on de right. Dis yeah fog mighty deceibin'. Dahs picket obah dah."

He paddled on a few moments, then touched Kate. She leaned forward and heard him whisper :

" Keep yeh han' in de watah ahead o' de boat an' look out foh log. Tech me when ye feels it."

Kate put her hand down. It was a cut-water of beautiful flesh. Jupiter paddled on slowly, the boat scarcely moving. Five, ten minutes passed. Then Jupiter felt a pressure on his ankle. 'He gave the paddle a turn in the water and the boat lay along side of a boom anchored across the river. Then Jupiter whispered again :

" Must git out, honey."

" On that log ? "

" Sho, honey."

" Couldn't stand on it a second."

" Git on you han's and knees."

He got out and sat on the boom, astride of it. Then he helped Kate out. She tried to cling to it. Then for safety she imitated Jupiter. She, too, dropped astride of it. Jupiter lifted the light boat over, and helped Kate, drenched with water, back into it.

" I'ze powful misa'ble 'bout dat wet, honey, 'deed I is, but it can't be help."

Kate shivered with cold, but she whispered back, " Don't be uneasy, good friend."

She wrung the water out and drew a blanket about her lower limbs.

After paddling a few moments, she felt Jupiter again touching her foot and leaned forward.

"Keep mighty sharp eahs fo' de pat'ole in de ribbah. De rail pinch am right heah."

Kate strained her ears listening. She could hear her heart thump against her sides. Minutes seemed ages. She could feel the boat rippling slowly through the water; but she could neither see Jupiter nor hear the strokes of his paddle. Suddenly she touched him, it was but a faint pressure, but he felt it like the blow of a sledge hammer. He dropped his paddle into the water and held it suspended. He listened and heard. It was the steady thud of muffled oars in the row-locks. The sounds became more distinct. The boat was evidently crossing the river from the right. Again Kate touched him, this time violently. From out of the shroud of fog came human voices to the left. The row-locks were crossing near the duck-boat. The voices were above. Kate's hand was in the water, her wide open eyes were trying to shape Jupiter out of the dark. She could tell from the water moving against her hand that she was receding down the stream. All else was mystery. Five minutes later the wash of water on her hand ceased. She could hear the boats above her, then a hail; an answer; a conversation, and the dip of oars retiring from the center of the river. Jupiter chuckled in her ear:

"Nizey huntahs dey is. Yer can't cotch coon wid gabble."

Then she could feel the boat spring up the river.

The night passed its center.

Youth will sleep on the skirt of battle.

Kate grew drowsy in the monotonous silence.

She would have slept, but Jupiter roused her into action. He whispered:

"Must be gittin neah de foat."

"A fort here; mercy!"

"Fort Bawington, and deys mo' blockadin o' de ribbah."

In a little time this too was reached and passed as

the other, though it was a broader and firmer obstruction.
When Kate was in the boat again Jupiter warned her to be
alert for patrol boats. But she heard none until they had
gone on so long that Jupiter notified her they must be passed.
A half hour glided away. Suddenly the little boat grated
against a large object in the stream. There was a voice,
then oaths, and a hoarse, loud cry—" Halt ! Halt ! Halt
there ! "

CHAPTER XVI.

POTATOES AND ONIONS SOMETIMES BETTER THAN PREACHING.

The duck-boat in its flight up the river had grazed the end of a guard-boat lying motionless and headed across the current. The two boats were dimly visible to each other at the point of contact. Before "Halt" was uttered both were fused in obscuration. Jupiter gave his hand a turn. The little boat had been heading up the river. Now it shot like an arrow toward the south shore.

"Halt! Halt! Halt!" Then a volley. The report was heard. The flashes were invisible. There is no punctuation to a fog. It blends itself with the river. It gulps down objects.

The river, the fog and objects within it are one.

In this intense merging, the guard-boat groped and its inmates fired. Kate and Jupiter could hear the oars, the oaths and the straggling shots receding down the river. The men in the guard-boat had not seen the direction from which they were touched. Jupiter paused. He could feel Kate trembling in the boat. Voices reached him from the shore.

Sound is the lighthouse of a fog. Guided by this Jupiter headed up stream.

Under his vigorous strokes the litttle duck-boat leaped through the water. The sounds below grew fainter and finally died away. Then Jupiter whispered, "Bress de Lawd, de las' pat'ole boat am done pass," and Kate, too, thanked God and blessed the beneficence of obscuration. Miles were placed between the duck-boat and the last great peril before Jupiter whispered again.

"What houah am it?" Kate touched the little spring and the watch ticked one—two—three—four.

Jupiter heard it. "Clah! de night am done gone. Ef dis yeah fog gits, it's day," and he turned the head of the boat to the south shore.

He groped along the bank. An immense trunked liquid amber stood on the shore. Near it was an indentation, a little mouth for a swamp to spit out its ooze and slime into the great river, a mouth thick-toothed with tall, slender canes and strong grass. When Jupiter became sure that it was the place he sought, he spoke above a whisper for the first time during the night, "Bress de Lawd, honey, dis yeah de place." Then he pushed the boat far into the reeds, drove his paddle down into the mud and made the boat fast. Kate had been in a tremor of excitement since she was aroused from the doze into which she had dropped, and now that she had passed the first great peril and had fairly broken through the jaws of Secessia and stood within its body, she wept. After this Jupiter wrapped her in blankets. He told her he would watch while she slept, then she could watch while he slept. She urged that he was tired, needed rest most and should sleep first. But Jupiter insisted. It was easier to watch in day time. "Nothing to fear but 'gaters' an' varmin, an' they ain't gwine to 'noy yeh. Sleep, Miss Kate! Sleep, honey, an' I'll watch an' think o' Mansa."

Journeying nights, resting and sleeping days, their progress until the night of the 11th of June was uneventful. The morning of the 12th, when Kate woke she was shivering. After that came a slight fever. Jupiter saw it and shook his head.

"Dat's pow'ful bad." Kate's finger-nails were blue.

When Jupiter saw it and saw her shivering he told her that was swamp ague. Kate, under the advice of Surgeon Munson, had brought with her several pages torn from medical works. At the tops of the pages were such words as these: "Diarrhœa," "Scurvy," "Intermittent Fever." Kate drew them out, read one of them, took a bottle from her pocket and took a pill. It was ague medicine. She restored the bottle to the pocket. The capacity of a woman's pocket is wonderful. This one was a little peripatetic drug store. On this morning, through the curtaining of reeds, tall grass and brambles that concealed them from the river, they could see steamers passing up and down. About noon Jupiter was sleeping. Kate was awake and watchful. She heard a noise. It startled her. Looking up, she saw a black head peering through the bushes on the firm ground that fringed their concealment. She touched Jupiter. He sat up and looked. He saw it was a negro, and placed his finger on his lips. His signs were eloquent of silence and caution. The colored man entered the fringe. Before him was a novelty—a colored man with a white woman, and hiding.

" Wha's y'uns fro' ? "

" Down de ribbah."

" Wha's gwine ? "

" Up ribbah."

" Wha's hidin' fo' ? "

" Ain't hidin'."

The colored man looked for some minutes without speaking, then he said :

" Ef ain't hidin' why don't y'uns stay in de open ribbah ?"

There was much more conversation, then the colored man went away, agreeing to come back after dark. They had no fear of colored people.

This man left seed behind him.

It sprung into root, stalk and fruit with great rapidity.

The seed was his question.

" If you are not hiding why not stay in the open river ?"

Steamboats and small boats were on the river constantly. They were undoubtedly moving unquestioned as they did in the North. They were far beyond the people watching the mouth of the river. Again and again Kate asked herself this question : " What is there about us to excite suspicion. Why not go boldly into the river and travel by day ? " When she had thought it all out she stated her views to Jupiter. For a few moments he looked at Kate with open-mouthed wonder. Then he said, " Clah to goodness. You is right 'bout dat. Ef de white mens see a niggah pullen a white woman in de

11

ribbah dey jis go lang 'bout dey biz'ness. Dey fine we here dey say we's hidin', sho'."

"Then let us go into the river at once."

Jupiter pulled his paddle half way out of the mud. Then he paused, pushed it down again and turned to Kate.

"Dey's no boats like dis yer in de ribbah."

"What kind have they?"

"De skiff boat, all flat. Dey'd notice dis, sho."

Here was another quandary. Then it was agreed to wait until night, and see if a skiff could not be procured through the slave acquaintance of the morning. During the afternoon Kate saw a boat pulled from the opposite shore to mid stream and pause. Soon after a steamer came along and took a passenger from the small boat. This event suggested a new train of thoughts. Why not go boldly out to a steamer and take passage up the river? She spoke to Jupiter about it. At first he shook his head. "Nebbah do! Feared o' dat."

"Afraid of seeing your old master?"

"Law miss, dey such heap we niggah dat ole maws wouldn't know Jupe ef he done rub agin him. Ain't 'fraid o' dat."

"Is it singular for a white woman to travel with a colored man on the steamers?"

"Doan 'o, Reckon not. Nebbah on one o' dem."

They agreed to wait for the night interview with the slave of the bushes. After dark he came. Kate questioned him. The result of his answering was this: There is much travel on the river. White men and their slaves. White women and their slaves. They often go off in a skiff from a point above. A free negro lives on the point and carries them off. After learning this much Jupiter and Kate held a whispered consultation. The result was, the slave escorted them to the cabin of the free negro on the point. Kate would have paid the slave for his services, but he would receive nothing.

"No, mistus," he said, "I d' no what I'ze holpin', but I'ze knows I'ze holpin'. De good Mawst 1h'll kear fo' yer."

Reaching the cabin they entered.

"Could they be taken off to the first boat up the river?"

" Yes."

" Could they stay in the cabin till the boat came; willing to pay for it ? "

" Yes."

No questions were asked. Why should the old negro and his wife ask? What was there to ask about? He saw before him a poor white woman, clad in a coarse faded gown of antiquated model, coarse shoes, calico sun bonnet and dishevelled hair, who spoke the dialect of the country. Jupiter had schooled her in this. " Tell you, Miss Kate, wha' d'aint no grunt, dey ain't no hog. Min' dat, an' keep up the crackah gabble." It was not by any means new to Kate. She and her husband had lived a year before the war in Tennessee, from which they were compelled to flee for the crime of loyalty. The other part of the picture was a black man, having on his head the tattered crown of what had once been a felt hat. He was barefooted and wore a coarse plantation shirt. Coat, he had none. His shoes, coat, and a few articles belonging to Kate, were tied in a bundle, which was slung from the end of a stick that Jupiter carried across his shoulder. Couples like these were to be seen anywhere in the country. Their appearance excited no inquiry in the minds of the old people. A supper was furnished them. Fish and corn-bread. Kate relished it immensely. She had not eaten freshly cooked food for several days. After tea Kate asked about the boats. When would they go ? She learned that the Macon boat ought to be along early the next day. The old man said he had taken a lady and her two "niggahs " off to the Macon boat last week. This started a fresh train of thought in Kate's mind. When opportunity offered she gave its result to Jupiter. Instead of crossing the country they would go to Macon and take the railroad down to Andersonville. Jupiter immediately assented. The next day the Macon boat came up. The old negro carried them to midstream. The steamer paused. Took them aboard. Without further incident they passed up the river under the shadow of Brown's mount, a ridge of shell stone, towering seven hundred feet above the river, the trace of ocean lashing yet visible almost to its summit ; past the great Indian mound, crowned with oaks and hickories, on the east side of the river ; then into the rocky, precipitous jaws shaded with beech and giant poplars, back of which lay Macon, on both sides of the Ock-mulgee, a bridge rewedding what nature had divorced. When the landing was reached Kate walked straight up into the town. Jupiter followed a respectable distance behind. After they had proceeded to the outskirts of the town Kate paused. When Jupiter stood beside her she asked what they would do for lodgings until she could learn about the cars. Jupiter told her to walk on slowly until he could inquire of negroes. Soon he caught up to her and she turned back with him to a negro cabin. Its occupant was an aged negress.

This woman was a slave and paid her mistress one hundred dollars a year for the privilege of earning her bread.

The mistress levied a toll on God and lived by it.

The slave paid the toll, washed, sewed, waited on parties and prospered.

During the evening the toll-payer said she had done wash-ing for Yankee prisoners in the hospital.

Kate was sitting, plunged in an abyss of thought, the word " prisoner " roused her.

"Here, in Macon?" she asked in surprise. She did not know there was a prison pen for officers at Macon.

" Yis'm, heah! "

" I thought they were at Andersonville?" The moment she said it regret pricked her into misery.

" Dey is a pen at Andahson'—dey say it 'm misable awful dah; jist heaps an' heaps o' po' critters, an' dyin' like pizen'd rats."

Kate shivered.

" Po' creeturs! " she exclaimed. Throughout she imitated " po' whites " as nearly as she could.

"Dat dey is, mistus. Dat dey is. I'ze mighty glad to heah you say dat. Dey's such heaps o' de white ladies heah goes down to see 'um an' make fun o' dey mis'ry."

Tears were in Kate's eyes. The colored woman noticed it. She looked again; then walked quickly to the door and shut it. When the door was closed she came over and laid her wrinkled hands on Kate's head.

"Deah mistus, cry way down in you hawt, but you'll git inter mistrouble sho' if dey sees teahs for de po' Yanks. Dat yo' will, honey."

Kate took the hands in her own, pressed them closely, laid her lips against them, laid her head on them and wept, and she thought, "Oh, how I would like to tell this good creature."

The knowledge that Macon ladies visited Andersonville set Kate to thinking. The Macon papers of the next morning contained a lengthy report of the capture of escaped prisoners from Andersonville. They had reached the mountains almost in sight of safety. There was also an assurance to the Southern people that the mountains and passes were so thoroughly guarded that escape was next to impossible. Then for the first time Kate was agitated with the riddle, after Andersonville, what? No question of her husband's living and being in Andersonville entered her mind.

Between dawn and mid-day there is interregnum.

Kate was passing through this interval.

The safe passage on the boat was A. Ladies visiting Andersonville and impassable mountains were more letters. The alphabet of knowledge was filling. Suddenly there came to her this thought:

"We were safer in the crowd of the boat than in the solitude of marsh and forest."

The fruit of her thinking was this aphorism: "A crowd is a desert." Kate was approaching the mid-day. She was growing wise. When opportunity came she conveyed her thoughts to Jupiter. It was this: "Why not lose ourselves in the crowd of Macon? Why not effect the rescue from here?"

Rap the flint and steel of two thinking heads together— the result is light.

Truth is words in percussion.

Discovery is brains in collision.

The conclusion of the consultation was this: Kate would hire a little house in the suburb of Macon and operate from there. The house hired, she would leave Jupiter, go to

Andersonville on the cars, ascertain where Mansa lived, learn all that was possible about the prison, and on her return they would agree upon a plan of rescue. When the colored woman returned at noon Kate spoke of the house.

Yes, that was easy enough. One vacant right in the rear on the next street. Looks poor outside; very good order within. It was pointed out. The rear of it not an hundred feet from the cabin they were in, and there was a tumble-down stable on the back end of the lot. The owner of it she also knew, and would guide her to him.

"You'ze money to pay!"

"Oh, yes!"

Kate had several thousand dollars in Confederate money, procured for almost nothing by Surgeon Munson, and she was liberally supplied with gold, besides having more than a thousand dollars in greenbacks sewed in her garments.

Before Kate went to the house-owner, the colored woman said to her:

"Honey, I doan' know, an' don' want ter, on'y dem hans is too saff and white fo' po' low down."

Kate was visibly perturbed. If this woman could penetrate, why not others? But the woman had not penetrated. The very soft hands, clean finger nails, little attempts at "fixin' up," as the old woman afterwards called it, all satisfied her that Kate was playing a part. But what part? Of that she was ignorant and unsuspicious.

She observed the fever that came into Kate's face—and the paleness that followed.

"Doan be askeer, honey; I'ze had a pow'ful lang time fo' lookin' on ye. Jess dirt yer hans an' g'lang. Dirt hides de white an' de saft."

Kate accepted the lesson. That afternoon the house was hired, a month's rent paid in advance, and with the aid of their hostess, the necessary articles for cooking, eating and temporary comfort were procured, and that night Kate was a housekeeper in the heart of Georgia.

Rest, shelter and medicine had already expelled the incipient attack of fever. The next day, the 16th of June, 1864,

Kate was in the cars, a ticket in her hand for Americus, a station on the road below Andersonville.   The cars, nearly full on the start, rapidly filled on the road.   At Montezuma an elderly lady entered and occupied the seat immediately in front of Kate.   An instant after several young ladies romped in, and with much clatter occupied the vacant seats about the elderly lady on both sides of the aisle.   A clerical-looking gentleman passed down between them.   From their conversation Kate learned it was the Rev. Sniggins " going to visit the nasty Yanks."

The cars started and the young ladies opened their mouths.

" Nasty wretches."

" Snivelling."

" Canting."

" Miserable."

" Thieving."

" Cowardly."

" Yankee hirelings."

" Invaders."

" Hope they'll die, every one of them."

The utterer of this atrocious sentiment was the youngest of the cluster—not over sixteen.

" My dear, it grieves me to hear you."

Kate looked up.   It was the elderly lady who spoke.   Kate noticed her.   It was a benevolent face, with a kindly mouth and tender eyes.

" Oh, Mrs. Spleenless, haven't you enough of the Yanks yet."

It was one of the older of the girls who flung this stone.

" I don't understand you, my dear."

" Haven't most of your friends closed their doors against you for trying to take food to these miserable wretches?"

" I regret to say they have, dear."

" Nasty, vile wretches.   I wonldn't give one a grain of corn to save his cowardly life."   This was from the youngest.

" Don't, dear," responded tender eyes.   " My dear boy was

a prisoner North, and treated with much kindness. He was wounded and sick, and they cared for him with great tenderness. Under the dear Father in heaven, I owe his life to the people of the North."

"And his wounds."

"And his sickness."

"And his captivity."

"Oh, yes; but those were cruel accidents of war."

"Yankee war."

"To steal niggahs."

"Whatever it is about, I cannot forget how they cared for him."

"Oh, but that is different."

"He is a Southerner."

"And a gentleman."

"A Southern gentleman has a right to demand proper treatment, that these miserable Yankees cannot expect."

"So different from these nasty Yankees."

"They are somebody's sons and brothers," responded the old lady. "And I would help them if I could. Unfortunately I cannot. The prison commandant will not permit it."

"I am glad."

"So am I."

The mouths of the misses were all moving at once.

The saintly Sniggins approached during the storm of words. One of the misses spoke to him—

"Oh, dear, Mr. Sniggins, did you hear Mrs. Spleenless, she is defending her course towards those filthy Yankees."

"Yes, dear Miss Begrime, I heard her, and it pains me deeply, very deeply, indeed, that one of my flock; yes, one of my flock, with whom I have labored so long and so prayerfully to keep in the right way; in the right way, my dears, should so far forget her duty to God and the South."

"Doctor," said Mrs. Spleenless, looking over her spectacles, "do you not go to them."

"Yes, I do, madam, I do indeed. It is my duty."

"And for what, doctor?"

"To preach to them. To pray for them. To carry the bread of life to their hungry souls."

"You would bring unbelievers to Christianity much faster by carrying potatoes and onions—the bread of health—to their festering, scurvy-smitten bodies."

"Oh!"

"Oh, my!"

"Mrs. Spleenless!"

"Dear Mr. Sniggins!"

The mouths of the misses were in agitation. Sniggins rubbed his chin and turned away, muttering, "That woman ought to be seen to. Such sentiments are dangerous to the country."

The cars bumped together. Doors at both ends opened. Voices brawled "An-dah-sin," and the train halted. Kate went out with the crowd. There was a small platform; near it a long, rude building, like a storage house; about it several teams, a crowd of old men and boys in gray uniforms, and several others in blue. The gray Kate could comprehend. But the blue, what did that mean? As she walked toward the end of the warehouse she passed close to two blues loading a wagon with provisions. She heard their voices:

First voice: "There's more of them gabbling secesh petticoats come to mock at our calamity."

Second voice: "I hope God will blast the eyes of every woman who comes to laugh at the sufferings of our comrades."

Here were two men in blue uniforms, out of prison, unguarded, working for the rebels, and cursing secession. Kate was puzzled. She couldn't understand it. But she photographed the two faces on her memory. Then she turned the corner of the warehouse and followed the crowd slowly down the road. One of the wagons followed after. Kate dawdled. So did the wagon, but it caught up to her. Its driver was the owner of the first voice. As he came alongside of her, Kate spoke.

"I hear that some of the prisoners have queer names."

"Not near so much so as you secesh!"

"Isn't one of them named Puss Cat?"

"There is one of them called Puss Cat."

"Do you know him?" asked Kate.

When she heard his answer she seized him by the arm. It was the clutch of a vise. Her heart beat against her ribs like a trip hammer. This was what he said:

"Know him! Know him! Why ma'am, he is an old Chickamauga boy!"

CHAPTER XVII.

HER SOUL FROZE WITHIN HER.

The driver had seen hundreds of women about the prison dressed as Kate was; looking, so far as he could see, precisely as she did, all moved by the same curiosity to see the "Yanks" and gloat over their misery, and there was no restriction upon his conversation with them. When Kate seized his arm he was surprised. He had been marching along with his eyes bent on the road, beating the sand with his whip; now he turned his face full upon her. He saw her earnest eyes fixed upon him. She spoke:

"And his name," she said, "is Halmer Huntley."

Her voice was soft, musical and low, scarcely above her breath, but the driver heard it.

"How on earth did you know?"

Kate was too confident to be halted by doubts. She was so sure it was her husband that she never thought of hesitating lest her hopes would be answered with despair.

"And his name," she persisted, "is Halmer Huntley?"

"Yes, that is his name, ma'am, the grandest old sarge that ever wore chevrons."

Kate's hands were clasped together, and she was murmuring, in bird notes, to herself, "Oh, I knew! I knew! I knew! God is so good!"

At that moment her face was glorified.

Then she whispered to the driver, "Do you like him?"

"Like him! The old boys love Sarge Hal like a brother."

"Would you help him?"

"Give me a raw potato, or an onion—or—heavens, ma'am! if you want the boys to pray for you, just give me one lemon to smuggle into Sarge Hal."

"And you have done that?"

"Look here, madam, I'm not around answering secesh catechism."

"Would you help Hal yet, if you could?"

The driver turned upon her suddenly, perhaps to detect lurking evil, if there was such. But he saw nothing but a soiled face and gentle, loving, humane eyes. Kate could not hide these.

"I tell you, ma'am, you may be on giving me away to that Wirz fiend. If you are—pshaw! I don't know what you are on; betray me if you want to, but I won't throw away a chance to help Hal, or any of the boys."

"Oh, I am so glad." There was a genuine ring in the voice that the driver could not doubt.

"But," said he, "what interest have you in him?"

Kate drew close up by his side. They were moving at a snail pace through the deep, yellow, friable sand.

"I am," she whispered, "his wife."

"You! you! a sand hiller."

"I am not a sand hiller."

"Ah! ah! Heavens! Hal's wife!"

"Yes!"

"Kit?"

"Kate!"

"Kit! Kit! How often I have heard it. Kit! Kit! How he loved it! Kit! Kit! How happy he grew over it. Kit! Kit! When the lightning was flashing above us and the storm was beating down upon and drenching our uncovered bodies! Kit! Kit! And when the flashes lit up his face it looked so happy! Kit! Kit! To see his face in the blinding light and the pelting storm, it helped us all. Kit! Kit! You don't know the effect of a little leaven of happiness in a lump of misery! Kit! Kit!"

"I am beginning to know it now."

"And sometimes it was so piteous. Kit! Kit! So piteous! Kit! Kit!"

"Oh, Hal! Dear Hal!"

"And you are Kit?"

" Yes! "

" You are not a big woman? "

" No! "

" But you are the biggest woman I ever saw. "

" Oh! "

" And the bravest. "

" Oh, no! "

" Brave! You are heroic! With your eyes open you have deliberately walked into the jaws of hell. "

" Oh, poor Hal. Poor suffering prisoners. "

" Look here, Mrs.—— Kit. We are half way over now. You can walk on if you please. But it will be safer if you leave me here. Don't look about—after I tell you. This evening walk down the railroad until you come to Little Sweetwater creek. "

" Little Sweetwater? "

" A creek fifteen or twenty feet wide, just below the depot. Not the first little brook, remember. The large one. Follow the path up that till you come to the wood, and go along the road until you come to old Marmaduke Titefist's place. "

" Marmaduke Titefist! "

" Yes. "

" Oh, I am so glad! So glad! God is so good! "

" Do you know him? "

" No. But go on, please. "

" Well, you go there. It's the first place on the road. You can't miss it. Titefist went to Savannah to-day. I heard him say he wouldn't be back for two weeks. There is no one on the place but his bed-ridden wife, two old negroes and a young negro woman nurse. "

" Is her name Mansa? "

" Mansa! Yes! Yes! That is it. But—heavens! Where did you get to know so much about the country? "

" It is God who is guiding! Oh, how good! How wonderfully good is God! "

" Yes, God is good; He has saved us so far. But—but— sometimes I think He would be better if He would hurry Old

Wirz and the villainous imps about him here down into the hottest flames of——"

" Don't! Don't! Please!"

" Let's call it to the bottomless pit. Go now. Don't forget the Titefist place. The negroes will let you into a cabin and I will see you to-night. The chances are big, but I will take 'em for Hal. Go now! Kit!—Kit!—Kit!—"

" Till then, dear friend, good bye!"

The wagon pursued the road to the stockade gate. Kate followed the petticoated railers of the cars along a road leading southward up a hill. There she found them peering into the great guns surmounting a star-shaped fort. The moment she turned into the south road her nostrils were saluted with an odor. She did not observe it before. She was too intent with her purpose to observe anything. Now it assailed her. It was a stench so strong that it battled down and rose above the fragrant aroma that floated on the soft air from the pine forest north of the stockade which lay in the valley below the fort.

" Stink like pigs," puffed one of the chatterers.

" Nasty creatures," snuffed a second with a scent-bottle at the end of her upturned nose.

From the fort the chatterers turned to the officers' quarters. The officers were all bows and grins. The chattering mouths escorted by the bows and grins walked down to the palisade. Kate followed. She observed that the palisade was about twenty feet high and turreted. The turrets were little sentry boxes one hundred feet apart all around its top. Attached to each of these she saw small platforms on which armed sentries were walking. Within the stockade was a vast multitude of people. She could see that many of them were coatless, hatless and shoeless. Bare-headed men were walking about listlessly under the fierce sun. Others were reclining under blankets and coats propped up by sticks. Looking down into the ravine she could see but little more than that. But the breath of the valley was a loathsome, noxious effluvia; it was nauseating.

Near the palisade were a number of men in blue uniforms.

Kate soon learned that these were fresh arrivals who had not yet entered the prison stockade. They had already been standing four hours in the broiling sun. Kate noticed that one man near the end of the line was reclining on the sand.

Then Kate heard a harsh voice, " Git you Yank oop ! oop ! I'll plo' you head off ! " *

" I am unable to stand," responded a feeble voice.

" Oop ! oop ! you ! oop ! "

The man attempted to rise and fell again.

" Oop ! oop ! get ! "

Some comrades stooped and raised the man. The moment they released their grasp he fell again with a dull thud upon the sand.

Kate was burning with indignation. Her little hands were clenched, the nails penetrating her soft palms, her white teeth grinding together. She photographed the man for eternal hate. This was the photograph : A slender, weazened man, about five feet eight inches in height, with drooping shoulders, whitey gray, restless eyes, protruding brows, low, retreating forehead and small head. He wore a gray cap, a juvenile calico waist, to which his drab pants were buttoned, six year old boy style. A baby uniform on a beast. Bread and butter toggery on a murderous club. The face covered with frowsy hair with its ferret eyes and mouth protruding like a rat, was disagreeable to look upon. This was Wirz— the giant monster of the century, the fit instrument of the most pitiless, malevolent, diabolic conspiracy that ever smirched the pages of history.

As they approached the southwest corner of the stockade, the gate yawned and belched out a wagon. Kate saw it and shivered. Her soul froze within her. She turned away her face in horror. Miss Begrime and the other misses gave one look, exclaimed and ran on. The wagon was loaded with Union dead, uncoffined, unshrouded, many of them entirely naked, hideously bloated, slime oozing from their mouths and bodies, maggots squirming over them, and two of the bodies protruded over the wagon, the wheels, with every revolution,

* Affidavit of Augustus Swenson, Co. A, 13th Pennsylvania reserves.

grinding against and into the corrupting flesh,* and the torn flesh was clinging to the wagon tire.

Kate was horrified. She covered her ears and ran on after the girls of the Cass.

"Girls, where are you going?" shouted one blue-eyed miss.

"Oh, I don't know," replied another, who seemed to be the leader, "where we can see the most fun."

Kate was not sanguinary. She was a tender woman, gentle and loving. But she felt then that she could stab that girl. She would have turned away in loathing from them. Where? Where? That was the riddle. If she went where they went she knew that she would be in a beaten track.

The unusual was the rock on which she feared being dashed.

Love and hope led her on in the train of the abhorrent, under a pattering of words that stung and burned like molten lead.

Kate followed the chatterers.

She was walking barefooted on coals of fire.

She had only yet seen the outer garments of horror.

She passed on.

The stench penetrated her.

Again she would have fled. She would have cried out. She dared not.

She was bound to the rack of heartless chatterers. She followed on around the south end of the stockade to the hospital. The girls entered. There was no floor. Patients were stretched groaning upon the naked earth.

The train pushed on rapidly. Kate followed slowly, reverently, down between the moaning sufferers. The fourth figure shocked her. There were no teeth in his jaw; his knees were drawn up almost to his chest; slime was oozing from his mouth. A man was bending over him. Through the ooze she could hear the voice: "Ol! Ol! don't—tell—moth-er—dear—old—moth-er—that—I—die—this—hor-ri-ble—death

---

* Augustus Swenson, in his affidavit says, when the dead were carried away "Some of the dead bodies hung down over the wheels and the wheels ground off the flesh."

—don't—! It would—pain—her—so—don't. Oh! d-o-n-'t! Poor moth-er!"

Kate's soul was overflowing, but she dare not pause. She moved slowly on Near the middle of the pen a figure lay alone. It was almost nude and uncovered. Under it was no straw, no blanket, no quilt—nothing, but the bare, harsh sand. His eyes were wide open and staring. His hands were folded across his breast. He was a boy, seventeen or eighteen—a white-faced boy, and he was speaking: "Mother, take me home. Do mother! That's a good mother! Take-me home! I must go home, you know, if only for a day, mother—and— lie under the trees with sisters. Take me home. I knew you would—take me—home—home—mother." Poor Kate! how she did long to drop down in the sand beside him, to pour a flood of tears upon his face, to kiss his fevered lips and bear a message to the mother who would never take him home, nevermore. The hopelessness of the effort and her one great purpose restrained her. It needed barriers of steel to with- hold her then; but she refrained, and moved on after the girls she so heartily hated.

Outside the door was a crowd. Above the crowd the rat- face on the white horse; about the crowd a number of dogs, growling, looking fiercely into the crowd, and licking their chops. Their breasts and legs were covered with blood. The rat-face spoke.

"Dunner! ish dot Fret?"

"Yaas, Cap'n, dis year's Fred."

"You cotch him?"

"Yaas, ther dogs git 'im."

"I hopes dey pite him goot."

"Waul, they cotched 'im by ther leg, climin', an' I jis let 'em chaw to git ther jaws in."

"Dot's goot; dot's goot. Dey dares him goot?"

"Yaas; you look."

Rodent-face looked. "Hah! you run away bime by agin, I don't tink some dimes, hey? Dey don't dares him haf enough. No, not haf goot!"

Kate looked at the boy Fred and shuddered.

12

It was a harrowing, heart-rending sight.

His cheek was torn entirely away from the bone and hung down upon his neck a shredded, quivering mass of flesh.* The tongue and throat were visible through the gaping wound, and poor Fred's legs were tooth-mauled, lacerated and mangled, the calf of one leg torn entirely away; the cords hung in shreds and the white bones glared through the bloody flesh.*

Kate closed her eyes.

" Oh, God! "

Was she dreaming?

Had the everlasting pit of fiends and furies yawned and swallowed her? Was this Abaddon?

She heard a voice.

" This is horrible."

Kate opened her eyes.

Above her she saw the soft blue ether, the hills with their crowning of green-topped pines, and the sun with never a veil between its bright golden face and this maleficence, and before her she saw Mrs. Spleenless with hands upraised and tears filling her tender eyes.

" Oh, what a shame! What an outrage! What inhuman violation of the law." It was Mrs. Spleenless who spoke.

" Madam, such language will not be permitted in this camp or in the state."

Mrs. Spleenless turned upon the speaker, who had just entered the crowd. Kate also looked. She saw a steel face, with dead, icy-gray eyes pushed far back from flat cheeks, under shaggy, overhanging brows, a strong, protruding chin, compressed wafer lips with deep lines from their corners to the edge of the lower jawbone, a long, pointed nose, and long, white hair.

" And who," asked Mrs. Spleenless, " are you, sir? "

" I, madam, am General Winder."

" Ah! "

" And I repeat to you that such language will not be permitted in this state."

* A fact, as testified to in the Wirz investigation.

"And I repeat to you that this shocking brutality is a violation of the law of the state, and should be punished as such."

"To what do you refer, madam?"

"This hunting and rending off· poor humanity by dogs."

"Madam, you are misinformed."

"I am not."

"It is lawful."

"What is?"

"To hunt men with dogs."

"No! No! No!"

"It is!"

"Here?"

"Yes, here!"

"In Georgia?"

"Yes, madam, here in Georgia!"

"No! No! No! It cannot be."

"The supreme court has so decided."

"What! Here! Here in Georgia?"

"Yes, madam, in the case of Moran against Davis. Moran hired a negro boy owned by Davis. The boy ran away. Moran pursued him with dogs. To avoid being torn to pieces, the boy sprang into a river and was drowned. Davis sued Moran for the value of the boy, and the supreme court said: "It is lawful to track runaway negroes with dogs and follow them up until they are caught. A pursuit in this mode is justifiable.""

"Sir, I am ashamed of the state."

"And the state, madam, is ashamed of any of her children who do not uphold the means necessary to its success."

"Suppose, sir, that the North should pursue our escaped sons in the same way."

"Ah! hum! That is different. These are miserable Yankees. Invaders of our soil."

"But they are men."

"Mighty poor specimens of men."

"Poor or not, sir, they are suffering, dying men."

" Dair dreatment here is too goot for dem."* It was Wirz who spoke.

" These sufferers should be treated humanely."

" Madam," said Winder, "I will put a stop to this. The whole country seems turning to the Yankee."

" It is this brutality that drives us there."

" It will not be permitted. No! I will stop it. A sense of duty demands it.

" Save the lives of these men and you will have no trouble in that direction—"

" Save them ! Save them ! Turn them out healthy and strong to destroy our sons and brothers ! The noble, suffering sons of the South ! Madam, this pen was not built for that. Nature can work faster than the bullet. Here we can use them up faster than any general in the field."†

" Sir, God cannot bless a cause that uses such cruel, barbarous means."

" Ah, madam," returned Winder, " God's blessing is with the cause that wins." Then, turning to an officer, he said : " Escort this woman to the depot and see that she never enters the camp again. There has already been too much sympathy expended on these wretches."

Fred was removed to the hospital, where he died next morning.‡ Kate longed to kiss the hem of the brave woman's garments. But she dare not. She saw the train in which she was moving ; heard the laughter festering the already polluted air, and she followed on. They went over to the gate ; an officer passed them through to the inner palisade. They paused before the second sentry box from the south gate. One of the mouths suggested, " Let's go up and get a good look at the nasty creatures." Kate halted. The officer who passed them was a friend of the misses on the platform. Seeing Kate in their trail, he said nothing to her. In fact hardly noticed her, and after she passed forgot there was such a person in existence. Kate would have turned and left them.

---

* A fact.

  † Statement of R. W. Drake, 7th Indiana Cavalry.

  ‡ A fact.

But where should she go ? Would the sentry pass her without the officer, and what would the officer say seeing her without the others ? Above all things she desired to see and know without being observed. She could not say how, and why, or when the knowledge might be valuable, nor yet the purpose to which it could be used, but she felt that it was her duty—a task her purpose imposed upon her, to obtain the fullest possible information about all locations connected with the prison and its routine. All this had led her so far. But why should she join the grinning, babbling crowd on the platform by the sentry-box. Then it occurred to her that she was more open to observation thus alone, between the palisades, than she would be in the crowd on the platform. She was the center of two storms—attraction and repulsion Then—oh ! oh ! she nearly cried out, " I may see him ! I may see him ! He is there. .Oh, Hal ! Dear Hal ! " and she dashed at the ladder. Up ! up ! round after round. She thought of nothing lighted by the sun, nothing under the heavens but—" Hal ! " She reached the platform. The palisade top touched her waist ; and she stood there, the boy sentry by her side, the chattering mouths about her, looking down into the Andersonville Prison Pen. Looking down upon hunger-suffering and woe that should have melted a heart of stone. Looking down upon the helpless victims of a merciless brutishness that shocked the civilized world.

CHAPTER XVIII.

ANDERSONVILLE.

A railroad running north and south, between Macon and Americus; four or five straggling rough board structures resting drowsily on the yellow sand west of the road; twenty or thirty people as vapid and rickety as the buildings—such was Andersonville before the Confederacy made it synonymous with all that is cruel and brutal. West of the railroad, and but a few dozen yards removed from it, are two marshes in which spewings of toads and reptiles and swamp ooze, decaying wood, weeds and rank grass are distilled into poison. The marshes are fifteen hundred feet apart—one above and one below the town. From the marshes the poison runs off in two leafy brown, sluggish currents, across the railroad track, and unite fourteen hundred feet east of it. From this confluence of poisons the stream, in lethargic flow, runs nearly due east, between hills rising with gradual swell on either side until it is lost in the Little Sweetwater, less than a mile below.

Five hundred yards from the confluence of the two little streams that ooze out of the marshes there is another marsh. Around this marsh the Andersonville prison pen was constructed.

As finally completed, the pen is an oblong, seven hundred and eighty feet by sixteen hundred and twenty feet, the stream creeping through its narrowest part, about one hundred feet south of the center.

"Sid." Winder superintended the building of the pen. When he began, the marsh and the hills that rise on either side of it were clothed with heavy timber.

Early in December, 1863, Winder was at work, the people

of the surrounding country came to look on. The whole population of Americus, a little town a few miles below, were on tiptoe of excitement.

"Got so many Yanks don't know what to do with they 'uns all."

"Gwine ter build a prison at Andahsen."

"Let's gwo!"

They went.

Among those who went was Ambrose Spencer. When he arrived negroes were digging a long trench; other negroes were felling trees; others again were hewing their sides.

"What are these for?" said Spencer.

Winder looked. "What!"

"The trees hewed on two sides."

"We put one end in the ground in that trench, the hewed sides close together; then pack dirt about them. The result will be a close pen with walls twenty feet high!"

"Ah!"

"Reckon that'll hold 'em!"

"Going to erect barracks or shelter of any kind?"

"No! The dratted Yanks who will be put here will have no need of them!"

"Why, then, are you cutting down the trees? They will prove a shelter to the prisoners from the heat of the sun at least!"

"That is just why I am cutting them down; I am going to build a pen here that will kill more Yankees than can be destroyed in the front."*

"Sid" Winder turned away and Jim Scrogs removed his "cawn cob" long enough to suggest: "That air mawsh in the center o' the pin 'll help kill 'em mighty fass."

---

*Testimony of Ambrose Spencer of Americus, Ga., in the Wirz trial.

NOTE.—The author has produced the statement as it appears in the published report of the trial, omitting the oath that accompanied it. If such was the object in constructing the pen it fearfully served the murderous purpose. The total number of enlisted men killed in action on the field of battle or by the hands of guerillas during the four years' war was 44,238. The deaths in Andersonville, into which the first prisoners were taken February 24, 1864, were 13,412. Of these, 9,479 died in the six months between February 24 and September 21. If the "killed in action" were equally distributed over the last three and a half years of the war, then the threat of Winder was made good. Andersonville did kill more Union soldiers than were killed at the front.

"But why," said Spencer, "don't they put the pen below or above the marsh?"

"Don't want ter, I reckon."

"That water would kill a dog."

"Yaas."

"There's Little Sweetwater, five feet deep and twenty feet wide, not five hundred feet from where they are putting the pen, and not a marsh on it. Why don't they put the prison there?"*

"This 'll sarve bettah, reckon!"

"They could go below the marsh and take in both creeks, Little Sweetwater and this Double Branch run."

"Yaas, they uns could."

"Then they would have an abundance of water for cooking, bathing, every purpose, and good, healthy ground?"

"Yaas."

"Why in the world don't they put the pen there?"

"This yere sarve bettah, reckon."

"It looks like a purpose to kill!"

"Yaas; kill the mizable coots o' Yanks heah quick. Bettah thet nor gittin shot wi' um."

Spencer went away. The construction progressed. The pen was completed.

The marsh lay a festering sore in its center.

Then came the captives. Eight hundred first from New Hampshire, Connecticut and Michigan, weary, worn and hungry from prolonged travel, cooped like beasts in freight cars.

Down from the depot they marched, wearily on through the shifting sands, amid the jeers and taunts of a gaping crowd.

The gate opened.

The stockade swallowed them.

Then they saw walls of pine, a slimy brown creek, six feet wide and five inches deep, struggling through the soft mud,

* Little Sweetwater Creek is not located in any of the narratives of Andersonville prison life, but its position and character is truly described in the foregoing statement of Ambrose Spencer. It is a sweet, clear, abundant stream of water.—[The Author.

and a waste of yellow sand dotted with huge stumps. And there were no buildings, no sheds, no tents, no shelter, no concealment from pelting storms, no screen from the blazing sun.

That was the 15th day of February, 1864.

" A desert," cried one.

Wait! A desert is mercy to this.

The volume of captives swelled.

The heroic, plucked from the front of battle.

The daring, tricked by guerillas.

The devoted, who sacrificed liberty to save a brigade or a division of an army.

They rolled into the pen, a continuous stream of captive humanity.

The deadly dews drenched them. The lightning flashed in their unscreened faces.

Hungry, emaciated and torn with pain ; shelterless, tattered and naked, the pitiless storms beat down upon them and they froze.

The fierce rays of the tropical sun followed the storm and they consumed.

Human ingenuity exhausted itself. They made storm covers of blankets and of coats.

They burrowed in the ground.

The storm pursued them ; searched them out ; penetrated them.

The eight hundred became thirty thousand !

The Confederate guards camped on the stream that flowed through the stockade.

The water flowed from the wolves to the lambs.

It was morbific at first.

The Confederates camped on it and it became virulently septic.

The soil was saturated with their garbage, their offal and their filth.

The storm is a scavenger and a creek is a sewer.

The scavenger swept the excrement, the washings of rottenness, of carrion, of compost. down through the stockade.

It was bilge water nastified.

Hideous spume !

The creek was a serpent breathing death.   Its mouth full of corrosive poison.

The earth and the air—boundless creation—was full of life-giving water and thirty thousand Union prisoners were condemned to drink of Double Branch.

Double Branch was a Confederate executioner.

Then came the morass.

A morass is an infinity of craters ejecting pestilent vapors.

Slime and green scum were already upon the morass in the stockade.

The scavenger—the storm—carried down upon it the sewage of the pen.

It fermented.

It became a mass of putrefaction.

Out of putridity came a loathsome life—maggots.

And the hot sun was upon it all.

The earth abhors nastiness.

It flings it off in effluvium.

The subtle, noisome exhalations loaded the air.

Then came scurvy.

That is born out of storm and exposure and want of proper food.

Faces puffed.

Syncope from slight exertions followed, with weak vision, blindness and inability to sleep; then dysentery.

Old sores opened.

Broken bones that had united came apart and grated together within the body.

Horrible music!

Mouths and throats and bodies ulcerated.

Teeth loosened and fell out.

Gums, nostrils, bronchial tubes and intestines poured out streams of offensive blood.

Limbs rotted off.

Worms devoured living bodies.

The fetid breath of disease aggravated the noisome exhalations from the creek and the morass.

Poisoned by the earth; poisoned by the air; poisoned by the water; tormented with vermin; irritated by gnats, mosquitoes and winged ants; devoured by maggots; blackened with smoke; befouled by mud; with matted hair, shelterless in the midst of mills and lumber piles; thirsting for water with limpid streams but a few yards away; perishing for fuel while boundless forests nodded to them from the surrounding hills; rotting for vegetables while potatoes blossomed and corn tasseled before their eyes; goaded to madness by brutality; writhing in helpless impotence under taunts and jeers and murderings; perishing by hundreds, by thousands; with death marching by their side—a putrid horror; living and dying these martyrs stood firm, and to the end the shattered fragment of the wreck never faltered in their devotion to the American Union.

CHAPTER XIX.

A DAY OF HORRORS!

When Kate stood upon the sentry platform she saw clouds of vaporous stench floating in the rarified atmosphere low down over the inmates of the pen. The pungent gases assailed her nostrils. They were foul and sickening. She was oppressed, but she had no active sense except sight. Her eyes penetrated the multitude; man after man they devoured from head to foot. She saw their matted hair, their dirt and smoke-begrimed persons, their rags. She saw them sitting, standing, walking, reclining. She saw the fierce sun beating down upon them. But, in the shifting multitude she nowhere saw the one man she sought. An ague assailed her. Her eyes grew dim. "O-u! o-u!" she murmured, and shivered. It was an awful sight. Longing, suffering, agony, hunger, thirst and despair.

The chatterers looked over the palisade a few moments and turned away. Kate too looked with eagerness of love to discover one form.

From the platform through the gate, across between the palisades, through the outer gate, jabbering and clacking, the girls went, Kate at their heels. At the gate an officer took them in escort.

Between the gate and the corner of the palisade a crowd of men approached.

The clanking of iron rose above the loquacious din.

The crowd drew nearer.

The girls paused and laughed.

Kate saw and congealed.

She saw a huge iron ball and six men on each side of it.

Six on the right, six on the left.

The six on the right had each an iron band riveted to his left ankle.

To the iron band there was riveted one end of a heavy iron chain.

The other end of the chain was riveted to iron bands about the ball.

The six on the left were fastened in the same way, only the band about the ankle of these was on the right leg.

She saw that they were all barefooted, many of them without coats, and that the garments of all were torn and frayed.

There were five hats and caps among the dozen men— and—

Then she saw that a broad iron band was riveted about the neck of every one of them and that these bands were connected by heavy chains from one to the other.

Thus the twelve men were linked in a double circle of iron.*

One of the chains touched Kate's ankle.

The iron, heated in the sun, burned her like a half dead coal.

Day and night—through heat and cold—these men were bound.

The tropical sun, through the long summer days, flamed down upon the iron.

The iron absorbed the heat.

The bands grew tepid, then lukewarm, then blood hot, then burning.

These hot bands chafed, they blistered, they cauterized, they roasted.

And when night came, and the dews fell, and the storm descended, the iron bands were turned into avalanches of ice upon their tender flesh.

Kate was blinded by pity and indignation.

Then she saw that one of the twelve was carried by some of the others.

"Where are they going?" asked Jule of the escorting officer.

* A fact, testified to by numerous witnesses.

"To the blacksmith shop."

"What for?"

"To cut the bands off one of them."

"Which one ? "

"The one they are carrying."

"Why don't they make him walk ? "

"He's got a parole. He's dead! "

Wirz on his gray horse was beside the officer and heard his remark.

"Yes, dot's de way to barole dem."*

"What have they been doing ? " asked Miss Begrime.

"Some of them grumbled about their food."

"Ought to give them pound cake."

Luce asked if the chained men were all grumblers.

"No," responded Escort. "Some of them are chained for trying to escape."

Luce opened her eyes ; "Why, I didn't see any of them torn much."

"No, you see they were caught tunneling."

"Tunneling ! "

"Yes, the rascals in there pretend to dig wells. They say the water is not good enough for them. Then they dig ! dig ! dig ! "

"But how does that help them ? "

"Why, when they get the wells down a ways, they open a hole in the side and burrow under the stockade."

"Don't the guards see the dirt ? "

"Ha ! ha ! ha ! The cunning scoundrels work at the burrow in the night and drop the dirt into the well."

"Then ! then ! "

"Then in the day time they lift out the dirt they have dropped in during the night—making believe all the time they are going deeper with their wells. "

"How mean it is to give our dear boys so much trouble ! "

"Do they get away ? "

---

*Beverly C. Benham, 1st sergeant Co. A, 9th Minnesota, testifies that a man in the stockade asked Wirz for a parole. Wirz struck him on the head with a revolver and killed him, and remarked to a Confederate officer, "That's the way to parole them."

"Ha! ha! Not frequently, I can tell you."

"How do you prevent it?"

"Oh, we discover them before they get out."

"How do you do it?"

"We have men in there—Southern men."

"Make believe prisoners?"

"Yes! and they tell us all about it. We let them work themselves tired. Build up their hopes of Yankee land. Then, just as they think they are going to bid us good-bye, and—"

"You catch 'em."

"Yes!"

"Oh, how nice! And it's so smart of our dear boys, isn't it? Do they try it often?"

"Burrowing all the time."

"Oh! Oh! How funny!"

The exclamation was made by little Blue eyes.

They had reached the guard-house and were standing before it.

Kate's eyes had been riveted on the glowing sand. Her mind was confused and dead to all surroundings. The atrocities she had witnessed rained like blows of a hammer upon her brain.

Her head ached.

Her heart ached.

Her limbs were growing numb.

She was following blindly.

The exclamation roused her.

She raised her eyes and saw two men sitting on the earth bent forward and nearly double.

Then she saw two posts in the ground, a few inches apart, strongly connected at the top and bottom. Between the two was a space, a slot.

Several feet distant were two other posts, similarly planted and with a slot between.

The two slots faced and grimaced at each other.

A board had been dropped in the slots, the lower edge

rested on the ground. On the upper edge four notches were cut.

These notches were half circles.

Each half circle was half the size of a human ankle.

Another board was placed on top of this with notches cut on the lower side to match the notches in the first board.

On the top of this second board were notches half the size of a wrist.

Then came a third board, with notches on the lower side to match the notches on the upper edge of the second board.

On the upper edge of this third board notches were cut half the size of a human neck.

Over these a fourth board fitted to match.

In this frame of torture two men were riveted.

Their ankles were placed in the notches of the first board, and the second board placed on top of them.

Their wrists were then fixed in the notches on the top edge of the second board and the third board fitted over them.

Their necks were then placed in the larger notches on the upper edge of the third board then the fourth board was placed on top and bolted down.

In this torturing position the two men sat.* Their ankles, wrists and necks immovably fixed.

Their heads were uncovered and the flame of the sun was beating upon them.

The sun was a fire.

Their skulls were pans.

Their brains in the pans were sizzling.

One poor sufferer wore no shirt or coat.

The other was coatless and his shirt was sadly rent.

Their faces and bodies were covered with dirt.

Great green flies stabbed their quivering backs.

Winged ants and flies swarmed about their heads ; marched into their nostrils and filled their ears. The flies and ants pricked.

They punctured.

They stung.

* A fact.

They stabbed.

They tortured.

The victims were powerless to drive them away.

They writhed in impotent helplessness.

The girls seeing the men and the flies, laughed, and Miss Luce asked Escort, "What are they in here for?"

"One for trying to escape. The other for buying vegetables."

"Oh! oh! Look!" said Miss Luce; "see that big green fly right on the end of his nose! See! See! He's trying to stick his tongue out at it! He! he! he! oh! His tongue cannot reach it! See him wriggle his face! See him squirm! He! he! oh! Isn't it funny?"

The prisoner's face was writhing under the torture.

Kate could endure no more.

She walked up to the tortured face and brushed away the flies.

"Hiah, yeu!" shouted the sentry; "git away from ther!"

Kate moved back, and Miss Begrime, who stood nearest to one of them, spat fairly on his naked back.*

Kate's hands were clenched; her nails were cutting into her flesh; her soul was a torrent of indignant words. She felt that she could smite that girl; could rend her; could trample her under her feet.

The girls were there and the escort and the sentry, and Kate had been warned away from the prisoner. She had witnessed in silence and inaction, but this was the drop that overflowed.

She could not endure and live.

She marched straight up to the slime-covered back, and, heedless of the "Git, yeu! Git, y-e-u!" of the sentry, she raised her dress and wiped it carefully off.

She would have done it if the path had bristled with death.

Then she turned and walked away up the road to the depot.

At the depot she passed within a foot of the Union teamster, but he made no sign.

---

* Joseph Powell, an East Tennesseean, who was a prisoner at Andersonville, testified that the women there surpassed the men in bitterness, and that a Mrs. Jones spat down on the helpless prisoners.

13

On the platform she saw a thermometer and it marked 102 degrees, in the shade, burning heat for the stocks and chain gang.

There, too, she saw Mrs. Spleenless under guard, and she heard her voice.

She was pointing to a wagon in which meal was being loosely shoveled.

"Is not that the wagon that carried out the dead ? "

"Yes."

"And you have not cleansed it ? "

"No ! "

"And you shovel meal into it after it has carried human bodies in the condition that those were, and feed that meal to the prisoners ?"*

"Yes, what of it ? "

"That of itself would kill them. It is monstrous ! monstrous ! "

"It's good enough for the Yanks ! "

"Merciful heavens ! "

How Kate loved that woman. How she would have loved to press her lips to her aged hands, to have said one word to her. But she dare not.

She walked slowly across the track.

She found a path.

With tottering steps she followed it, down across a small creek—the south branch of the prison stream—on over the knoll ; down until she came to a larger stream. Here the path turned to the right, up the stream and through the pine forest, where it opened into a broader road. Then came a clearing and fences. At last houses.

Kate paused.

She fixed the scene in her mind : A broad, sandy road ; a large house ; a few scattered barns ; a collection of negro cabins ; a setting of heavy pines ; and the fading light of the sun over all.

She found a path leading along the skirt of the forest to the rear of the cabins. Following this, she soon stood at the

*A fact.

SHE RAISED HER DRESS AND WIPED IT CAREFULLY OFF.

end of the southernmost cabin. Twilight was rapidly fading into night. Kate was waiting. She heard a footstep. It approached. It was passing close by her. Kate whispered, "Please!"

It was a woman, and colored, she addressed.

The woman paused.

"Are you Mansa?"

"Yaas, mistus."

Kate laid her hands on the woman's shoulders, placed her lips close to her ear and whispered:

"Are you Jupiter's wife?"

She could feel the strong form trembling under her hands. The girl looked suddenly about the corners of the cabin. Brought her face back close to Kate and whispered, "Yaas, mistus."

"Saltire's Jupiter."

"Yaas, mistus."

Kate threw her arms about the black neck and whispered in her ear: "Mansa, I bring you good news from Jupiter!"

Mansa threw up her hands. "Bress de good Mawstah in heaben!"

It was only a whisper, but if it had been the thunder of a cannon Kate would have never heard it. Nature was exhausted. The agonies of the day had beaten the life out of her. Her arms relaxed from Mansa's neck, and she dropped senseless to the earth.

13

CHAPTER XX.

"I KNOWED YER BY THE PRISON SMELL."

"Oh! oh! I tinks yo wur an angel an' ye'd done flow'd 'way."

These were the first words that greeted Kate when she opened her eyes. There was a dim light in the room and a volume of resinous smoke. The light, the smoke, and the aroma were from a little torch of pitch pine. By the light Kate saw she was in a cabin, reclining on a bed, and that a colored woman was bending over her. The woman was Mansa. Kate looked at the face and was strengthened. Then the scenes of the day, like a hideous phantom, rose up before her and she trembled.

"Is ye cold, honey?" whispered Mansa.

"Oh, no!"

"Don't be askeer hiar!"

"Oh, no!—but I have seen—oh! oh! what I have seen!" And she clasped her hands over her eyes to shut out the vision.

"Been obah ter de pen, honey?"

"Yes! and—oh! oh!"

"Pow'ful bad dah, honey! Pow'ful bad dah! Now doan' yer say nudder wud, honey, till me come baak."

Mansa smoothed Kate's hair, bathed her forehead with cool water, drew a cover over her, and went out of the cabin, In a few minutes she returned with a steaming cup of tea. Kate looked surprised. Mansa observed it.

"De mistus mighty po', honey; mighty po'—an' old maws git dis year at Sabanah."

Kate drank the grateful stimulant quickly. It refreshed her. She lay a few moments with her eyes closed. Then she sprang up. "Oh, dear! Poor Mansa! How cruel of me! How thoughtless! And you want to know so bad. Forgive me, Mansa!"

"Po' chile, I done know'd yo' was baad. An' I done wait so lang, mistus, so lang. Leel mo' no 'count, mistus! no 'count, mistus. I'ze oany a niggah, mistus; oany a po' niggah, mistus, and niggahs mus hole dey self, mistus, and wait; wait, mistus, de comin' ob de Lawd! An' yo's so tiad, honey—so tiad. I kin wait, mistus!"

Kate held one of Mansa's black hands in her own. She heard Mansa's words, calm and patient. They touched her heart more than any impatient eagerness. But in the black hand she held there was an eloquence of anxiety. It trembled in her grasp. Kate drew it to her, touched her lips against it, laid her burning cheek upon it. And Mansa bent over her and whispered in her ear:

"Mistus, Lawd love yo'! Youze no po' white, honey! No po' low down, honey! dey uns nebbah doan keer fo' we uns dat way. No, mistus, nebbah!"

Then Kate drew Mansa down beside her on the bed, and in whispered words told her the story.

Mansa sat there shaking like a leaf.

When she heard of Jupiter going to the old home she sobbed aloud:

"Po' Jupe! Po' Jupe! How misapint him be!"

Before Kate had half finished Mansa had dropped on her knees before her. Her strong hands were clasped over Kate's lap and her great eyes riveted on her face.

When Kate finished Mansa stared at her—one—two— three minutes in mute wonder. Then she found tongue:

"Mistus," she said, in soft, reverent tones, "De Lawd Him will sho' bress yo'. Sho', honey! Sho'!"

Not a word about Jupiter. Her admiration for this brave woman swallowed up every other thought.

Kate's hands dropped on her lap. Mansa stroked them, patted them softly, laid her black cheeks against them, patted them again.

"Deah honey! Deah honey! An' yo'm a Yonkee."

"Yes, I am Northern born. They call us all Yankees."

"An' do de deah Lawd make yo'uns all dis yeah way like?"

"Mansa, you know it is for my husband."

"Fo' true, mistus, but I'ze done tink dat no one gits de l awt fo' dat resk."

"Didn't Jupiter take a greater risk for you when he went to the old home for you? Isn't he taking as great, perhaps a greater, risk now in coming for you again?"

Then the full flood of Mansa's thoughts turned away from Kate to Jupiter.

"How does him look?" "Where did Kate see him first?" "How long does she know him?" "Do him tawk o' Mansa?" "What has he been doing?" "Is him happy?" The questions "How does him look?" "Do him talk of Mansa?" "Is him happy?" she repeated over and over again. And Kate poured into her eager, thirsting heart a volume of information, that was balm for the waiting years.

Then Kate told Mansa of the soldier who was to come. This roused Mansa to action. She said that the master was absent, that the mistress was bed-ridden and she must make instant arrangements to have an aged colored woman go in and watch by the sick woman while she guarded the road and brought the soldier to the cabin.

"Can you arrange it? Will not your mistress suspect?"

"Deed, honey, I kin dat. I'ze pow'ful misable! pow'ful misable I is. It done bin comin' dis yeah lang time, lang time." And Mansa's chin and eyelids dropped, the light faded out of her eyes. She raised her hand to her cheek and her head fell over on it. It was a transformation, sudden and laughable. Kate laughed.

Mansa looked out of the corner of her eyes, saw Kate laughing; her lower jaw lifted; her mouth spread across her face.

"K-i-i-yah! so—pow'—ful mis'—ble, I is—pow—ful! I tell mistus dat! and she marched out of the cabin door, closing it behind her.

An hour passed—two—three. Kate was in despair.

"He will never come! Oh! why did I trust him!"

Without was profound silence.

It was oppressive.

Waiting became unbearable.

Kate stood up. She must go out.

She searched for her bonnet.

She found it.

She turned toward the door.

The door was open, and in the doorway stood a man.

It was the teamster.

Kate was startled. She nearly cried out in surprise.

The soldier raised his finger.

There is mute eloquence in a finger.

The exclamation died out on Kate's lips.

The door was closed and the soldier stood beside her.

"Read that," he said, "and then put out the light."

He handed Kate a little chip.

She held it to the light and read—

"DEAR KATE, GOD BLESS YOU! GOD BLESS YOU! HAL.

That was all. Again Kate read it. She pressed it to her lips. She pressed it to her breast.

"Oh! Thank God!" she whispered, "Thank God!"

Then the soldier spoke.

"You have read it?"

"Yes—and—oh! oh! I do thank you! I do thank you! Long as I live I will bless you! bless you! bless you!"

"And you don't despise me?"

"You! You!"

The soldier had extinguished the light.

"Yes, you don't."

"Why, why, should I despise you—you of all men in the world?"

"For accepting a parole and working for the infernal rebs."

"Oh, I didn't know. I never thought of it. I supposed you were compelled to."

"Well, not exactly. I might have refused. To tell the truth I sought the parole."

" Oh ! "

" Dear Mrs. Huntley, don't think hard of me! Don't, please don't."

" Dear friend, I do not. I can never think ill of a friend of my precious Hal—and—least of all, of you."

" Thank you. You will permit me to tell you."

" Certainly, if you wish it. But it is not necessary. If you are satisfied, it is all right, dear friend. I am sure it must be so. I know it must be so."

" I do wish to speak of it. My term of service—three years—has expired. Just before the battle in which I was captured I heard of the death of my wife—"

" Dear friend ! "

" My wife is dead—and I have three motherless children."

" Poor orphans ! "

" They have no relatives ; no one to care for them but me. Not one in the world."

" The government, dear friend, and all patriots."

"Governments, dear Mrs. Huntley, have short memories and are near sighted."

" But they cannot forget the soldiers' children."

" They have done it and will do it again. While we serve the Government it sees us. When we cease to serve it, it becomes deaf and blind and parsimonious."

" Oh ! "

" Governments are soulless—and children need soul, which government is incapable of supplying if it would. For this reason I have sought to preserve my life for my children."

" Poor sufferer! "

" It is not aiding the Confederacy. They could have the same work done by negroes who are not subject to military duty."

" Surely! "

" I saw my comrades dying by hundreds every day, and I knew if I remained in the pen I could not survive."

" Oh, how awful it is."

" Awful! That is a faint word. All words are faint to express the horrors of that pen. It cannot be pictured.

Without living in it, it is more unintelligible than the bottom-less pit. There are things that cannot be described. This is one of them. It never will be! Never! It is easier to picture a stench to a man without a nose, or a sound to a man without ears."

"Oh! oh! and this you have lived through, and—and—dear Hal has lived."

"Yes! until I knew that I would be carried out a mass of corruption like the others. Then I took a parole—for my children."

"How I do pity you."

"And you do not blame me?"

"No! God knows I do not, and your countrymen will not."

"It does me good to hear that. And it has given me opportunity to save many of the boys."

"Save them!"

"Thousands have perished there who could have been saved by a few lemons, or by potatoes or onions—by any vegetables."

"I have seen abundance of them all about."

"Abundance! I have heard scores of rebels say this part of Georgia never raised so many vegetables. I have seen them rotting at the store and about the depot."

"And they would not give them to you?"

"They would not even permit those who had money to buy them."

"What inexpressible cruelty?"

"I tell you it was done with a deliberate purpose to kill us—that we should perish with the indescribable tortures of scurvy; that we should rot to death."

"Can men be so wicked?"

"Wicked! The embruting of slavery and the madness of rebellion has consumed the humanity of the South."

"Oh, not all—I saw one woman to-day"—

"Yes, I know who you mean. She is a good woman. There are many such, and many tender-hearted men even among our guards who would help us if they dare. But they are only chips in a malignant, overwhelming torrent. Even the preachers. There is one—he was on the cars to-day—Sniggins"—

"Yes! I saw him!"

"He comes and preaches and prays"—

"Is not that good?"

"His real purpose is to persuade the foreigners among us to desert and enlist in the Confederate army."

"Oh, shame!"

"It is a fact.

"In view of these things, what could I do? I knew if I had a parole I would have a chance of saving myself, and I could occasionally smuggle in vegetables to the boys."

"And you did?"

"Ask Hal when you see him."

"Noble friend! What is your name?"

"John Mason."

"John Mason, your name is stamped on my heart for eternal remembrance." She said it slowly and solemnly.

"Thank you! Thank you!"

"And you saw Hal to-day. How does he look?"

After a few moments' pause, Mason said: "You saw that Sniggins to-day?"

"Yes, and I hate him."

"Well, if Hal's hair and whiskers were trimmed the same way, he would look like Sniggins."

"Oh, no!"

"He would indeed."

"How changed he must be."

"Hunger thins. Exposure and bad food sallows, and bad air corrupts the blood. Yes, he is changed. But he is the same old Sarge Hal."

"Dear Hal! Dear Hal!"

"Noble old Sarge. That's what he is."

"I have come to get him out if possible."

"I supposed so."

"If he only had his mind—"

"Mind! Mind! Oh, yes! There was something the matter with his head."

In the darkness Mason could feel Kate's clutch on his knees. He had been sitting on a low bench; she on another little bench close by him. He could hear her quick, spasmodic breathing.

"But," continued Mason, "he's all right now."

"Thank God! Thank Heaven!" It was an anthem of praise that burst forth from her overflowing heart.

Mason rapidly told the story:

"I don't know how he got to Salisbury. He got separated from we Chickamauga boys. But a few days after we came here Sarge Hal came in a crowd from Salisbury. It was an awful night. We heard the whistle on the road and the roll of the cars mingling with the roar of the tempest. We knew what that meant. It was an addition to our sufferers. Brilliant streams of electricity flashed across the heavens. The clouds burst in quick, sharp crashes. The gate of the stockade opened. There were pitch-pine stumps there then. They were blazing and sending up volumes of smoke. Through the smoke, through the chilling rain that poured down in a deluge, we saw a long human thread pushed in through the gate over on to the west hill-side. They were Union soldiers. Soon they gathered about the lurid light of the stumps. They sought warmth. They were frozen to the marrow. But it was a vain seeking. The storm was a giant mocking the efforts of pigmy fires. As the lightning illuminated the pen one of our boys noticed a man sitting alone, upon the hillside, near the dead line. Jasper—he was a sergeant in your husband's company—he walked up the hillside to the lone man. He stood beside him. We could hear his voice in an interval of the storm. 'My God, boys! it's Sarge Hal.' We left him at Chickamauga. We thought he was dead. That night he was resurrected out of the storm. We saw them come down the hillside. We drew him to the fire. We saw the old form, the old face. But oh! how thin and worn. We clasped his hands; we embraced him; we danced about him; we shouted; we laughed. We forgot the lightning, and the pealing thunder, and the chilling rain. Joy was a giant stronger than the storm. Then we listened. We heard his voice: 'Kit! Kit! Kit!' We spoke again. He looked upon us; a vacant smile played about his mouth. He murmured, 'Kit! Kit!' He looked into the face of the glowing heavens, lifted up his arms and repeated, 'Kit! Kit! Kit!' Some of the old boys sat down on the drenched earth, buried their faces between their knees and sobbed like children. The storm was again the conqueror. They had borne up, too brave, too strong, too passionate to weep. But Hal was good to the boys. They looked on him as a father, and they loved him. This sight broke their hearts. The boys drew Hal to the earth, as near to the burning stump as possible—and during the live-long night he sat looking at the flame, repeating, 'Kit! Kit! Kit'—in the driving rain murmuring, 'Kit! Kit! Kit!' Oh! it was a mournful plaint, 'Kit! Kit! Kit!' The Salisbury boys said it had been going on for weeks. They didn't know his name. They called him 'Puss Cat,' and by that name we afterward learned he was enrolled on the prison register of this place."

Mason's head was bent low over Kate, his voice not audible beyond the door. He could feel her quivering under his word lances; could hear low moans and sobs, and he finished his story.

"I think, though, that it saved him. Yes, I think the impairment of his mind saved him. He couldn't see, couldn't know the horrors that surrounded him. It is the seeing and knowing—the phantom of the inexorable—it is despair that kills."

"Poor! poor, hopeless sufferers!"

"He didn't know. Despair wasn't grinding the soul out of him. And the boys, why, we all took care of Hal. Yes, all the old boys—all took care of Sarge Hal."

"Dear, noble self-sacrificing sufferers. God will reward—"

"God only can reward many of them now," answered John Mason, solemnly; then he added: "Two weeks ago Hal had a severe fall."

"A fall! Oh!"

"It was a lucky fall."

"Lucky!"

"Wait! There was a rush from the dead line. Hal was in the way of it. He was overthrown. He fell with great violence, striking the side of his head. Some of the boys ran to pick him up. They thought he was dead. I happened to be in the stockade at the moment, and near him. They lifted him up. I was standing in front of him. He opened his eyes. —'Why, Jack, old boy.' Those were his first words. 'Why, Jack, old boy.' Remember, ma'am, he spoke to me first—me first—'Why, Jack, old boy.' You see, he saw me first. That was it—'Why, Jack, old boy.' Maybe I didn't holler. Lord! Lord! wasn't I happy. 'Jack, old boy.'"

"Jack, old boy, dear friend, I shall love you. Oh, how I shall love you, forever and ever. Jack, old boy. And it was you first, dear Jack, old boy."

"Thank you! Thank you! Say it again, please."

"Dear, dear Jack, old boy."

"Oh, that pays, even if I am a parole."

"Don't! don't Jack, old boy. Remember the dear children."

"I do remember, and have remembered, and that sustains me. Well, Hal has been all right ever since. Whatever was crooked in his head was straightened by that shock."

"Wonderful are thy ways, O Lord!"

"Wonderful! But he has gone down faster bodily in the last two weeks than he did in all the time of his imprisonment."

"Poor Hal! Poor Hal!"

"Now, Mrs. Huntley, let us talk of ways."

"Dear Jack, old boy, you are familiar with the ways of the prison. What do you suggest?"

Kate then told how she came, who was with her, and about the house in Macon. And Mason gave a brief description of the ways of the prison. They talked nearly two hours. Many plans were suggested, discussed and rejected. Finally a plan was agreed upon, a day fixed, and John Mason, with a kiss on his cheek, $200 in greenbacks, and $2,000 in Confederate money in his pocket, and a "God bless you, dear Jack, old boy," stole out into the darkness.

The first morning train conveyed Kate to Macon.

Jupiter rejoiced when he saw her.

When he heard of Mansa he was overwhelmed with delight. He was a willing servant before. He was a devoted
friend now. They put their heads together. Kate unfolded
the plan. Some things were needed. A horse and wagon
were indispensable. Jupiter suggested counsel with the colored woman. Kate was alarmed.

"I tells yer, honey, dese yer culled uns, dey knows. Dey
igno'ance am on'y puttend. Dey's possuming. Dey is! dey's
fo' de Nawf, and de Yonkees, an' yo kin truss 'um to de deff!
to de deff!"

Kate was persuaded. The old lady was taken into counsel. She listened in silent wonder, expressing her amazement
with her hands and her eyes, and the lights and shadows that
flitted over her wrinkled face.

"Now, auntie, will you help?"

"Mistus, I'ze bin prayin' fo' freedom dis fifty long yeah
gone; fifty long yeah. An' sometimes I'ze fear it nebbah
come. It so long, honey, so long. Now um moas at de doah.
I knows dat. Moas done come. I see de glory in de hebbins.
I see it, moas, openin'. May be I'll go fo' it comes. But de
chillun, dey's gwine ter be free. Bless de Lawd. I knows
dat, de po' chillun! An' ef de Lawd hab suthin fo' po' ole
mammy ter do in de wuck, I'ze gwine ter do it, sho! Sho!
Honey! Sho! I'ze gwine ter help the Lawd whah I kin."

Then Kate narrated the proposed plan of escape and the
necessity of buying a horse and wagon.

When Kate concluded there was a silence of several minutes.

The old woman's brain was busy.

She was thinking.

It resulted in this: She knew a free colored man. He
owned a good horse and a suitable wagon. She could procure
that.

She went away, and soon returned with assurance that the
horse and wagon was procured. Auntie then suggested that
she had a son. A slave. He hired his time, and worked a

little farm midway between Francesville and Parchelaga ; and to the best of her belief that was about half way to Andersonville. It might be best to use the Macon horse to her son's, and her son's horse the other part of the journey.

This was a sensible suggestion, and was immediately adopted. Other arrangements were speedily made. On the night of Tuesday, June 21, 1864, Kate started, Jupiter driving. The old auntie insisted on going with them to her son's and guiding them on the road. Westward they journeyed, through Warrior, Echaconnee and Knoxville. On, still, five miles farther ; then south through Francesville to the cabin of the son. The cabin was reached long before daylight. The son cheerfully loaned his horse to continue the journey The old lady immediately turned about and walked home to Macon. Kate and Jupiter rested during the day. After dark they set out again with the new horse, and before morning Mansa was in Jupiter's arms. The horse and wagon were taken to a barn in the skirt of the woods, where Mansa assured them no one ever entered, and Kate lay down to rest. Sleep she could not. A few hours would land her in Heaven or plunge her in a gulf of eternal despair.

At nine o'clock on the morning of Thursday, June 23, a gray-headed, humpbacked negro crossed the track in front of the Andersonville depot, and shuffled slowly along to the end of the warehouse. A white string hung over his lower jaw, he was apparently chewing one end of it. A very close observer might have seen a slight protuberance on his breast.

At the end of the shed he paused, and leaned idly against it.

A half hour later a team drove up from the stockade.

The driver dismounted.

It was a morning of strings.

This one had a string tied about his right ear.

Humpback shuffled toward the man with the stringed ear, brushed against him, passed him, crossed the track and disappeared.

The protuberance on humpback's breast was contagious In passing, it left the stringed mouth, and infected the stringed ear.

The protuberance contained a pair of shoes with the counters cut out to press them in a smaller compass. There was also a scissors, a comb, a small piece of soap, a towel and a pair of spectacles.

Four hours later the train came in from the North.

As the train whistled a mulatto woman, barefooted, wearing a coarse, soiled plantation dress and calico hood, crossed the track from the west.

She stood at the end of the platform when the passengers alighted, and followed them down along the road to the commandant's office.

Her eyes seemed to be riveted on but one of the group. That one was a man. Not the first man followed by a woman's eyes.

When the man entered the door of the commandant's office, the woman stood by the window, looking in.

When the man came out the mulatto girl stepped up to him.

" Mawstah, mistus done say, please yo' come permegiate."

" Who is your mistress?"

" Mistus Titefiss. She 'um berry sick."

" Can't she wait till I come out of the prison?"

" No, mawstah, she 'um berry baad—she say please come. It pow'ful pawtent. Yes, sah, pow'ful pawtent. She say she know de good bruur come."

" Has Brother Titefist left his brandy unlocked?"

" Yaas, mawstah, an' it's pow'ful savin' dat brandy am, fo' yo' go in dah!"

" Very well, I'll go with you." And he turned about and followed her up to the depot and along the road.

Before reaching the house, the girl turned into a path leading past the cabins.

" Diss de bess way, mawstah." The man followed her. Reaching the third cabin, the girl paused and pointed to the cabin door.

" In dah, mawstah."

" But sister Titefist is not in there!"

" Dat de place. Go in dah, mawstah."

The man hesitated. He was about to speak. Then a broad hand passed from behind his head and closed over his mouth.

A strong arm from behind clutched his body and bore him rapidly into the cabin. The mulatto woman followed instantly and closed the door.

The broad hand and strong arm belonged to the hunchback negro of the string.

To gag and bind the captive was the work of an instant.

Then the woman stepped into a closet and the humpback stripped the prisoner of his clothing, even to his shirt, substituting coarse negro garments in their stead.

After the stripping, and the prisoner was firmly rebound, the woman came from the closet and searched his pockets. Then the garments, including the slouch hat and shirt, were pressed into the smallest possible compass, placed in the humpback's bosom, and he went out.

The woman bolted the door and stood guard over the bound and gagged prisoner.

A half-hour later Humpback again stood at the depot; he passed by the wagon driven by the stringed ear; as he did so the contents of his bosom were vomited into the tail end of the wagon, and Humpback crossed the track westward, never again to recross it. He was seen about Andersonville no more.

The sun crept slowly toward the horizon.

Anxiety is a fearful protractor of time.

It was the longest afternoon the mulatto or the hunchback ever saw.

A few minutes before sunset a man stood on the inside of the inner palisade gate. He felt in his right vest pocket, "Hum!" then in his left vest pocket, "Hum!" Then he thrust his right hand into an inner pocket in the left side of his coat and drew out a small book. The book was a New Testament. He opened the book. There between the lid and first leaf lay a little slip of paper. "Haw!"

Without looking at it, the sentry said, "All right, sah," and the man with the book and the ticket, and the "Hum! Hum! Haw!" passed out.

"Haw!"cried the sentry to his mate, "I reckon ef ole Snig wur to cum hier ten yeah he'd go through the same motions."

The man who had thus passed the inner gate walked slowly on, with head bowed down, to the outer gates. Then he delivered up the ticket to the guard and passed on. The ticket read:

HEADQUARTERS CONFEDERATE STATES MILITARY PRISON,
CAMP SUMTER, GEORGIA, *June* 23, 1864.

GUARDS PASS *Rev. Jirobath Sniggins.*

H. WIRZ,
Captain Commanding Prison.

GOOD FOR THIS DAY.

Slowly the man walked up the road to the depot and across the track.

Then the sun had disappeared.

Slowly he moved on down the path to the Sweetwater, on and on to the great road.

How sweet was the breath of the pines !

He drank it down in immense draughts.

He was in the great road.

He saw the cabins. He was among the cabins.

He passed the first, the second, the third.

He stood before the fourth.

He pushed open the door.

He entered.

He cried out from the fullness of his heart, "Thank God ! Thank God ! free at last ! "

At that instant a gray arm was thrust through the door.

The arm clutched a pistol.

By the feeble light of the burning pine splint the man of the "Hum ! Hum ! Haw !" saw the arm and saw the pistol. And then he heard a voice from the owner of the arm and pistol—a voice that froze his heart within him.

"Free be ye ! Throw up yer hans ! Dawg ye ! I knowd yer by the prison smell ! "

CHAPTER XXI.

"UNCLE BILLY DONE COME WID THE UNION."

When the man of the gray arm and the pistol spoke, Sergeant Huntley—it was he at whom the pistol was pointed—threw up his hands and dropped on a bench as if he was shot.

"Gawl," snorted the man with the gray arm, "when I passed yer in the road I thought it was Sniggins, sho'! Sho'! Dawgd if yer ain't well got up! But yer couldn't fool Sim Byle's nose; not much! I'd know that prisin' smell anywher! anywher! Thort to play ole Snig, did yer, an' with that smell on yer! Youse a cute un! Dad rat if yer haint! But that smell; gawl, how't sticks." While he was speaking he was covering Sergeant Huntley with his pistol, and the fugitive, standing on the brink of escape, was plunged into the depths of night.

The scheme of rescue had been simple and perfect. Hal Huntley resembled Parson Jirobath Sniggins. On Thursday he was captured and his clothing and his pass secured.

John Mason was master of instruction of the parson's manner and habits, and Hal had learned his lesson perfectly.

Through the gates of perdition, through the people that lined the road to the depot he had passed in safety. Not two hundred yards from the cabins he passed the Confederate Sergeant Sim Byles, better known as "Crookneck," in the road. "Crookneck" touched his hat and went on, and Hal congratulated himself that the last breaker was passed. Then came the gray arm and the pistol.

Before a dozen yards separated Huntley from the Confederate guard "old Crookneck" paused; began to rub his long nose · turned his head; looked after the retreating figure;

14

rubbed his nose again ; then sprang into the timber skirting the road and faced backward.

From tree to tree he dogged Hal's footsteps.

"Crookneck," however, failed to observe that when he paused, a figure further in the timber also paused, and as he moved on, the figure moved on, when he stood before the cabin door with his pistol covering Hal Huntley and boasted of his smell, the figure of the deeper forest shambled round the corner of the cabin. It was the Hunchback. Then from the other side of the cabin came the mulatto woman. She, too, had been watching in the road.

When "Crookneck" saw the colored man he called to him.

"Heiah boy ! git me some lashin' to tie this year drat Yank."

"Yis, mawstah ! in dah some !" pointing inside the cabin.

"Crookneck" entered.

The Hunchback and the mulatto instantly followed him, and the mulatto closed the door.

Hunchback shuffled past "Crookneck's" pistol hand ; as he did, with one hand he seized the pistol, his forefinger thrust under the hammer ; with the other hand he struck "Crookneck" square between the eyes.

It was a blow from a pile driver. It drove "Crookneck" to the floor stunned. Instantly Hunchback and the mulatto were upon him and he was bound hand and foot and gagged. It was a quick victory. When it was over Mulatto extinguished the light and passed out of the door ; without there was quiet and darkness. Being satisfied she returned and reported and the Hunchback lifted the bound man and bore him away to the third cabin, leaving Hal and the mulatto to themselves.

When Hunchback returned he called the mulatto out. They walked together to the end of the third cabin in which the parson and Confederate sergeant lay bound and gagged. Then this conversation took place :

"How soon we gwine to stawt ?"

"Bout half houah."

"When de man gwine ter meet we at Flint Ribbah ?"

"Hush, don't yer tawk bout de ribbah."

"Dey cawn't heah we."

The words were very low.

"Doan know what heahs."

"D'ain't no winnow dis yeah side de cabin."

"Doan yer whispah whah we's gwine."

"When mus we git dah ?"

"He say mus be at de Coe place fo' daylight."

When this was said they paused and shuffled away.

There were no windows at the side of the cabin, but there was a small opening between the logs. A close observer might have seen that it was freshly made, and if the parson and sergeant, who heard every word of it, could have been outside, they would have noticed that the mouths of each of the speakers was close up against the opening.

Acting ?

Yes, every day, every hour, there is acting away from the footlights, to which even Sellers and Dundreary are but poor pinchbeck.

From the little speaking tube the mulatto and Hunchback hurried back to the fourth cabin. There was a light in it, and Huntley was drinking a cup of strong tea, the first for many months. Once in the cabin the mulatto began to peel like an onion under a knife. First the plantation dress.

Before a negro man ! oh !

Certainly ; why not ?

Women will cut their dresses off in the middle of their backs, expose their shoulders and arms and—under their arms —during long hours of ball-room hug and whirl ; and afterwards, if seen by one of those same huggers of the ball-room, in a night-dress or under garments, not half so much exposed, they will throw up their hands, cry oh ! my ! and run and squat like pretty pink and white toads. But this mulatto had no mock modesty to make a fool of her. She exposed her arms and shoulders, and Mansa assailed them with soft soap and hot water. First came a little white spot, then more, then all white

Kate Huntley was resurrected out of the suds. There was embracing, a whispered "Hal," "Kate," a kiss, a dozen kisses. Then Kate dropped her feet into another pan of water and began scouring her legs.

Words and explanations were interdicted : there was no time, and fright and peril coin ears out of forest trees. Hunchback stood in a corner and removed his shirt. Kate Huntley was a modest woman. But she was not shocked. Why should she be ? In a crisis of life and death it is only your prurient prudes who know whether a man wears a shirt or not.

The hunchback's shirt was off and Mansa stood beside him a scissors in her hand. Snip, snip, snip. The hump fell to the ground. It was quick and painless surgery. A gray wig followed the hump—and Jupiter stood chuckling and restoring his shirt. Jupiter tore open the hump, drew the cotton from it and threw it in the loft ; then tore the covering to tatters. While he was at this Mansa was scouring Kate from her toes to her knees with soft soap and sand. The color from neck, face and arms had been easily removed. A more permanent dye was placed on her feet and ankles, lest it should scour off in the sand.

When the scouring was done the party hurried to the barn. Mansa hitched the horse to the wagon. A huge bag of cotton lay in the wagon. Snip-snip again. The end of the bag dropped down on a hinge of thread. It was a sham bag after all. Inside was a box, padded heavily on the outside with cotton, and baling drawn round it to resemble a bag. On the bottom of the box, inside, were bed springs. On these were boards. On the boards two heavy quilts. The bottom boards were removed from the middle of the wagon and over the opening the box was perforated with holes and the cotton pushed away toward either end of the bag. This was to secure air to the inside of the box. Sergeant Huntley crawled into the box and lay on the quilts. Jupiter, with a huge needle, sewed a cotton padded end into the bag. Kate first, then Jupiter, embraced Mansa. Jupiter would not take her along. It would increase the load and add to the perils. Mansa sorrowfully acquiesced. Her mistress was very old and very ill and her master absent. She thought it would not be right to abandon her mistress to two old and helpless field hands. She would stay. She knew the war was "Gwine to buss foah lang." She had heard her master say it. And this prudent master had taken all his slaves except Mansa, the nurse, and the two old worthless negroes away to Savannah and sold them. Mansa did wish to go; and Jupiter; he had come all this way; he had wagered his liberty and his life on the chance of rescue; yet unselfishly both buried their hopes and desires under their duty and sorrow.

Out of the barn; through the woods; slowly at first over the pine cones and long brown needles, under the shadow of the great trees, until they struck the Hamburg road. A looker on might have seen a bale of cotton, a white woman and a negro; that was all.

The road struck, the negro chirped to the horse, "Git." The horse struck a long, sweeping trot. On and on they went through the night.

While the horse was creeping through the forest, Mansa was busy. The wig and shreds of the hump were buried deep in the sand of the stable. Then the traces left by the horse were buried and the tracks raked over. From the stable Mansa went to the spring, a bucket in her hand. She filled it, walked to the cabin door, began there and poured water all over the path to the barn, in the barn, and about the barn. Wherever Kate, Hal, or Jupiter had stood she deluged with the spring. All the time she was whispering.

"Hi! dis yeah niggah too smaat fo' houns."

Then she went to the great house and sat on the doorstep listening to the deep breathing of her sleeping mistress and looking out into the night. Heavy clouds swept up from the south, a faint glow suffused the sky and died away. Then again the blush swept across the gloom. A deep, rumbling murmur rose above the creaking of the pines; a little drop of water fell down on Mansa's head, then a quick, bright light, a crash—and the rain fell down in a driving storm.

The tempest beat upon the wagon on the road. Above, the lightning flashed; the thunders roared; the winds moaned through the forest; the heavy limbs grated and crashed against each other; and the rain pelted down in a deluging torrent. Kate and Jupiter bowed their heads to the storm, and chirped to the horse. In three hours the first stage of the journey was passed. The fresh horse was awaiting them. On again, in the storm. Before daylight they reached Macon; drove slowly through the streets to the barn in the rear of Kate's cottage, and entered. The door was closed. Kate was penetrated with chill. In her anxiety she forgot it. How was Hal? How had he endured the night and the ride? A little string had been passed through the front end of the bale. The man within had one end about his wrist. Kate without held the other end. She pulled one-two, "How are you?" Answer one-two, "All right." It was a string telegraph. Once in the night there was no answer. Kate was fearfully alarmed. Wanted to cut open the bag.

"Sleep, reckon," suggested Jupiter.

One, two—vigorously.

One twitch, two twitches, on Kate's finger. "All right." Now she wanted to see. Jupiter watched the door. Kate drew a scissors from her pocket, snip, snip, snip. The end of the bag loosened, fell down; a pair of feet appeared, a pair of legs, a body, a head, and—Kate and Hal were devouring each other with kisses.

Jupiter drew out a knife and began at the bag. He ripped it to pieces. He drew out the box, pulled it apart. He stored the boards in different parts of the barn. Then he pushed the cotton in a corner. While he was at that, Kate and her husband were engaged in some mysterious operation behind the wagon. Soon Kate walked out, up the path to the house. A few minutes later a man with a wooden leg hobbled up the same path; and a little later, Jupiter. When they were all in the house they found breakfast ready, meat and vegetables and steaming hot coffee. The man of the wooden leg smacked his lips and rubbed his chest and stomach.

"Oh, how good it is."

The eyes of the others were bright with joy and dimmed with tears.

"To think that a man should be brought to this."

The others could hardly sit at the table. They danced about him and waited on him, and Kate kissed him and put little bites in his mouth, as if he was unable to feed himself. They made a baby and a pet of him. One hour after breakfast a carriage stood before the door. Within there were many embracings. Auntie was nearly hugged and kissed to death. Then Kate and the wooden-legged man entered the carriage. Jupiter mounted with the driver. They drove along the street, across the bridge looking down on the Ockmulgee like a broad band of silver winding through the deep gorge, and up to the Savannah depot. Then the carriage halted and spilled out its contents. Kate bought tickets. The wooden leg went thump, thump, thump, across the platform.

A bell rang.

"All aboard!"

Jerk, jerk, jerk.

Puff, puff, puff.

The train rolled out from the town.

At night they were in Savannah.

This was Friday, and Kate's second visit to the city.

On the previous Monday she came first. She visited drug stores. That was for dye stuffs. Then she visited the suburbs. That was for a house. On this Friday night the party drove straight from the depot to the house that Kate had hired on Monday. No one gave them a thought. They were just like so many others, women, wooden legs, and negroes, who passed out of Macon and into Savannah every day. Why should anyone think of them? They realized that "a crowd is a desert."

It was a pretty little home that they entered, with broad, spreading magnolias behind, and a high fence and dense growth of shrubbery all about the rear of the lot. As soon as they entered the house the wooden leg came off in a hurry. Then followed a strap that bound an ankle to a thigh, and a foot fell down to the floor. "Tell you, it's just awful," said Hal, trying to rest his weight on the numb foot.

Kate rubbed the thin foot and kissed it.

"Don't believe I could have stood it another hour to save my life." Then he began to whistle "Yankee Doodle."

"Oh, for goodness sake," cried Kate, and the whistle was cut off short.

That night they all slept on the floor. The next day they had beds. In a week they were comfortable. Jupiter and Hal remained within during the day, and walked the grounds in the rear at night. Hal grew fat, and all would have been happy, but for Mansa. How often they all talked of her and her noble self-sacrifice. On the second Sunday night Kate said: "Now, boys, I tell you what I'm going to do."

"Well, Captain Kitty, what is it?"

"Kitty, indeed; as if I was a little kitten."

"And if it hadn't been Kitty—"

"Ah, dear boy! Poor Puss Cat!"

"Dear Kitty!"

"I'm going for Mansa."

"Oh!"

"Lawsee, Miss Kate."

"I am. If I'm captain, you high-privates must obey orders without protest."

"Mighty danjahsome, mistus! mighty danjahsome."

"You took greater risks for us, Jupiter, and I will not see you pining without one effort."

"Me pinin, honey!"

"Me pinin', honey! Just hear him. Do you think I'm a goose. I know the signs. Why, sir. I can read it in your eyes every day."

"Clah ter goodness, Miss Kate."

"You needn't 'clah to goodness,' nor 'clah' badness. I'm not to be deceived."

"But—"

"And you needn't 'but' either. I'm captain of this—this squad. Isn't that high military?"

"Oh, yes! Squad's good."

"Very well, then! Now, squad, 'tention! I am going; sure. 'But' or no 'but;' 'clah' or no 'clah;' I told Mansa I would come if I could. What is there to prevent it?

Women go and come there every day. There is nothing to
distinguish me from the crowd. The only difficulty I shall
have will be to see Mansa and get her away."

Hal assented to this.

Then Kate continued: "I told Mansa if I came it would
be on Tuesday, any Tuesday, and to watch for me in the
vicinity of the cabins. Now you boys have a week's supply
in the house, and to-morrow morning I start."

On the morrow she did start. On Tuesday she was at
Andersonville. The first person she saw at the depot was
John Mason. She passed close to him, slipped a note in his
hand and whispered, " Dear Jack, old boy." Then she sauntered leisurely down the railroad.

On the previous visit she went to the pen. But Hal was
there then. Now she would not look on its horrors for an
empire. She walked down the track out of sight of the pen
and the crowd. Then she turned into a screening of bushes.
It was a tireful day. All waiting is tireful. But night
came at last, and Kate walked back up the railroad until she
crossed the Sweetwater. Then she followed the path and the
road through the woods to the Titefist place. An hundred
yards east of the cabin there was a soft step in the road
behind her. A hand was laid on her shoulder. Kate almost
swooned from fright. Then a voice whispered in her ear: "I
know'd yo'd come! Know'd yo'd come!"

"Oh, dear Mansa!"

"Jupe, am he safe?"

In a few words Kate told her story and her plan. Then
the two turned their faces toward the north star and walked
on through the silent forest. Before daylight they reached a
station far up the railroad between Andersonville and Macon.
Having made sure of this fact they walked along the wagon
road eastward until they were secure from observation. Then
they turned from the road into the bushes and waited until
Kate's watch told her it was near train time. Then they
emerged from the bushes—a white woman, plainly dressed,
and—a negro man. A little too full about the bosom this man
was, if examined closely ; but a good enough man for any but

the closest scrutiny. They walked boldly up to the depot. The woman bought tickets to Macon. At Macon she bought tickets to Savannah, and the next day Kate and Hal, Mansa and Jupiter were happy. Then Mansa told what followed the escape.

Parson Sniggins had frequently stayed all night with the officers at the stockade. The first day his family thought nothing of his failure to return ; but on the second day they sent to inquire. One of the men at last remembered. " Saw a yaller woman talking to him." Heard her. Mrs. Titefist wanted him. They hurried over to the Titefist place. Mrs. Titefist didn't send for him. No yellow woman about.

Riddle.

More search.

Then more complication.

Sniggins's pass had been taken up at the gate.

Who used it ?

Search !

" Puss Cat" gone. No one knew how. Must have flown! Hounds were taken out.

No use ; it had rained heavily, and water knocks the snout off a dog.

Late on that day Mansa walked into the third cabin, very innocent like, and saw the captives.

" Clah to massy ! what you uns doin heah ! Tied ! Gags too ! Po' mans !"

She unlashed them. They were stiff and sore. Sniggins declared it was " awful cruelty ! Unhuman to leave men tied and gagged two days and nothing to eat. Tied by a humpback niggah an' a yallah gal. Cut 'em to pieces ! Yes, cut 'em to pieces ! Too good foh 'em." Then they inquired of Mansa :

" Where's the yallah gal ? "

" What fo' yallah gal ? "

" And the humpback niggah ? "

" Clah ef ebbah I know a humpback niggah ! "

" And the prisoner ! "

" Clah ter goodness ! What yer tawkin 'bout ? "

The questions were put in a hundred different forms. The

parson roared and the sergeant swore, but Mansa's face was a Hercynian wood.

People said "the slaves are fools."

Try to penetrate one.

They were the perfect masters of mask.

When they dropped the curtain there was no peep hole to the stage.

The released captives hurried away to the stockade. Thence with the dogs to Flint River. The parson wanted to see the "Humpback niggah cut to pieces. Yes, sah! cut to pieces. Brutal wretches to leave gentlemen two days, sah! yes, sah! two whole days, without food! monstus!" And Wirz would give "A tousan' tollar to dramp on de Yankee's pones!"

Days and days they searched. They tore Coe's house on Flint River inside out.

"Know they went that way," so Sniggins said. "Heard it through a chink in the cabin. Providence provided it! Yes, sah, Providence! Yes, sah, for the South, sah! Thought there was no window, but thar was the chink."

And Mansa, as she told it, would bring her great hands down on her knees with a tremendous thud to think "How we uns done fool um."

Months passed, August, September, October. They were undisturbed and very happy. They attracted no attention. No one thought of them in the bustling crowd. But there is nothing so dangerous as easy success. On the morning of November 23d, Kate went to market. Mansa insisted on going with her. Kate protested. Mansa persisted. "I'ze shame fo' you to carry de big bask't. Dey done forget we dis lang time." So Mansa went. Their purchases were made. Mansa placed the basket on her head and trudged on behind Kate. Half way home they turned a corner. At the corner they almost ran up against a man.

"Dawgd, Mansa!"

"Ki, dat you! How'de! how'de! Clah! Clah! How'de mistus? Clah! Clah! ef I ebbah so glad sence I done bawn! An' dat yo'; yo' sho nuff seff—my good old maws

Duke! How'de! how'de!" And Mansa seized one of the man's hands and shook it while she danced about him, her tongue keeping pace with her feet. "Missey Jone, dis my good ole sho nuff maws. Yo' Chloe done fool yo', Missey Jone. I'ze no free gal."

"An' yeu told the lady thet?" It was the first sentence Marmaduke Titefist—for it was he they ran against—could interject in the storm of words.

"I'ze did dat, Maws Duke."

"I thought she was free," said Kate. The words came trembling from her lips.

"Clah! Clah!" continued Mansa, as she seized a small satchel that Titefist held in his hand and placed it on her head; "take I wid yo', Maws Duke; dat's good maws. Clah, I'ze de mizablest gal. An' how's de ole missy? How de ole missy? Yo' look gran', Maws Duke. An' how de ole place?" Her back was turned to Kate. She never looked at her.

"What did yer run away fer?"

"I done gits de megrims fer lonsome widout de uddah niggahs."

"An' how yer git heah?"

"I'ze done wawk."

"Well, dad-rat yer impudence! I'm on my way home now. Will yer go in quiet."

"De Laws, Maws Duke. I'ze pow'ful glad ter git back teu de ole place. Pow'ful glad. Pow'ful glad."

Then she turned to Kate. "Good-bye, Missey Jone! I'ze gwine with good ole maws. Gib my lub to de chillun."

Then again she turned her back on Kate. There was not a tremor in her voice, or a shade of sadness in her eye. She stood beside her master with his satchel on her head, chattering about her mistress and the old place. Kate was dumbfounded. But the mask and the lies opened the way for safe retreat. She drew ten dollars from her purse and reached it toward Mansa. "Well, Chloe, I'm sorry to part with you, but here's your month's wages." "Tankee, Miss Molly;" and she reached her hand for the money. But Marmaduke Titefist's arm was the longest. He took the money and put it in his pocket.

"So you infernal nig, you had to change yer name too, eh!"

"Ki! coase Maws Duke, coase! Golly, but I'ze gwine home, dat I is, to good ole missy."

Then she danced again.

Titefist drew out his watch. "Come, there's no time for talk." And he hurried away with Mansa to the train, and Mansa never looked back. She knew that to run was useless, and it would bring ruin upon the others. Kate was alone with her basket and misery, and she was full of wonder at the cunning and repression of the slave's misery.

Many doleful days followed. Then they heard that Sherman had cut the Macon railroad. "Oh! if he had only intercepted Mansa." They did not know. On the day that Titefist and Mansa left Savannah, Howard tapped the Macon road at Gordon. As the train with Titefist on it neared Gordon there was a danger signal.

Toot! Toot! Toot!

Shrill screams from the engine.

Down brakes!

Windows opened.

Heads out.

Gray uniforms all around.

"Out! Out! Out! Everybody out!"

"What's the matter?"

"Been a fight ahead. Need the train for wounded."

Passengers scrambled out. Looked about. Everybody for himself. Titefist was caught in the hurly-burly. Then he looked.

"Whar's my she niggah! Dad-rot that she-niggah! Her infernal jy wur all possum!"

News from up the road.

Yanks cummin'!

Git!

Helter skelter! Right and left. away they went.

The grays went eastward.

The others ran wherever they could go.

Then the blues came. Tearing up the rails, turning, twisting, curling them.

Hurrah for the Bummers!

Then a curly black blossom rose on the tops of the bushes.

"Ki! Glad to see yer, is I, Maws Duke! Halleluyah! dey's de ones I'ze glad ter see."

Then she ran out to the blues. There were other colored people.

Hundreds of them.

Thousands of them.

They were at the rails.

Mansa went too.

She tore at the rails all along down the road.

Mansa was a "bummer!"

In Savannah there was dismay.

Sherman coming!

The news filtered slowly into the seclusion of Kate's home.

On the night of December 20th the city was a bedlam. Men, women, children, hurrying, running, wringing hands, cursing, screaming, bawling; horses, mules, wagons, carts, drays, hogs, cattle, furniture, rush, creak, crash and rattle. Confusion everywhere!

And outside the city, all through the afternoon and evening, there was boom! boom! boom!

The little cottage was sealed. Its inmates lay down undressed.

At three o'clock in the morning of the 21st, the boom! boom! boom! was hushed. The clatter in the streets was subsiding. The first flush of day was gilding the eastern horizon. Kate sat up suddenly in bed. Put her hand to her ear.

Leaped to the floor.

"Hal! Hal! Jupe! Jupe! Listen! Listen!"

It was she who was making the noise. She rushed to the door, opened it a little, and peeped out. She heard a sound that thrilled her soul.

It was Yankee Doodle.

"Hal! Jupe! Oh! Oh! If Mansa was only here now. Come. Come."

"UNCLE BILLY DONE COME WID DE UNION."

She rushed down the path to the street. Hal and Jupe, bareheaded, stood beside her. Up the street they heard a measured tramp, tramp, tramp. They saw a crowd in blue— a flag at its head ; before it drums and fifes, and "Yankee Doodle ! "

"Hurrah ! "

" Oh, if Mansa was only here now ! "

" Oh, look at that woman ! " Kate pointed her out.

The woman was marching ahead of the drum corps.

One hand was reaching behind her, beckoning on.

One hand grasping the tattered remnants of a soldier's hat, stretched out before her, was pointing ahead, she grew distinct in the growing light.

It was Mansa. They could hear her voice.

" Dis yeah de way ! Dis yeah de way ! Fastah ! Fastah ! Dis yeah de way ! Dah dey is ! Dah dey is ! Glory to God ! Miss Kate ! Maws Hal ! Jupe ! Jupe ! Hallelujah ! Unckle Billy done come wid de Union ! " *

---

* During the march to the sea the boys would say, " Uncle Billy is here ! " " Uncle Billy is here ! " " Uncle Billy says this ! " " Uncle Billy says that ! " Nothing for Gen. Sherman, but " Uncle Billy ! "

CHAPTER XXII.

THE WRECK OF WAR.

The war was over. The wreck of the Confederate army drifted slowly over the South. Early in June, 1865, a horseman appeared on the road above the Ratley cabin. He wore a gray uniform   It was rusty, dusty and travel stained. His horse was walking. Even that seemed painful to the jaded beast. In front of the cabin the rider drew rein. When he did the horse halted and spread his legs wide apart, as fagged horses will   Many minutes the horseman looked upon the cabin. Once he turned the horse's head as if he would ride to it.   Then he faced about and pursued his journey, under branches covered with translucent, pearly berries ; past untilled fields, crested with the foam of green, rustling leaves. Then he struck a track of desolation. An army had passed there, devouring like locusts. Fences were gone, forests had disappeared. It was a track of ruin. In the center of the track he turned into an unfenced field, along a road grass-grown and fringed with poplars. At first the trees were green. As he went on foliage disappeared. At the end of the avenue the trees were lifeless and charred. Under the dead limbs the rider halted and looked. Before him two chimneys stood, scorched and blackened monuments of habitations. Between was a waste of ashes. The rider dismounted, and standing by the horse, one hand resting on the saddle, he gazed in silence upon all that was left of a once beautiful and happy home.

An aged negro, with the aid of a heavy stick, shambled up the path, from a collection of cabins across the field in the rear of the house. Behind one of the chimneys he too paused; then moved on and paused again, looking down at the ashes.

As he turned he observed the horseman and approached him.

"How'de mawstah ?"

The rider answered, " How'de ?"

The negro picked up his ears. His old eyes brightened. He rubbed them, and shambled rapidly toward the man and the horse. "I know'd ye! I knowd ye! Dat voice! Heabens, Maws Walt! an' dat yo'! Yo' sho' noff sef. Bress de Lawd, dese ole eyes done seed yer agin fo' I gwos!"

The rider was deeply affected. "Yes, Awk, it's me ; what there's left of me, sure enough !"

" My po' chile, po' chile. How yo' mus' hab done suffah'd 'n den you come home to dis. An' de mistus. Goodness ! Goodness alibe !"

"Where is she ?"

"Yan," pointing across the field ; "in de big cabin."

"And well ?"

"Yis, bress de Lawd ! an' won't she jump. Ki, an' dis yo' sho' nuff, clah, it jess take my breff way fo' glad." He had dropped his cane and stood with uncovered head and hands raised towards the heavens.

"And how are you, Awk ?"

" Oh, Maws Walt !"

"Not Master Walt any more ?"

"Dat you is. Dat you is. You'ze my Maws Walt all your bawn days, sho, sho. Bress you, honey. Who else hab. No, sah. I'ze been Awk an' youze bin Maws Walt, and I'ze gwan to be Awk an' yo' own sef Maws Walt ter the eend— an' I'ze nigh dah—moas nigh dah."

"Thank you, Awk, and you are well ?"

"Yas, sah, wid the rheumatiz, an' de new freedom, an' wid dis and wid dat, I'ze gettin on tolable, sah, tolable."

As they talked they were walking together across the field. Half way over a woman stood in the door of the great cabin. She saw the men in the field. She shaded her eyes with her hands and took one look. "Oh, Oh !" Then she ran out. In the field she flung her arms about the man. She kissed him ; she hung about his neck. She wept ; she laughed ; she exclaimed, and she hugged again ; and as they walked on towards the cabin she would laugh and talk and whirl about and hug him again. From out of the little cabins came a black swarm. The old hobbling ; the young running. They gathered about the horseman, they seized him, they clasped his body, they clung to his legs ; they danced, they laughed, and they hurrahed. Thus after four years of war Walter Trenhom was welcomed to his home.

From the day when he disappeared in the cloud of dust he had never returned. He knew that his house lay in the track of an army ; that guerillas had made a shelter there to shoot stragglers, and that it had been burned. Thus the desolation that lay about him was no surprise. Walter and his wife talked long into the night. At least the woman did, and she thought it was very nice. If you wish to be thought the nicest fellow in the world just say "yes" and "no" and appear to be immensely interested while a chatty woman lets her tongue run.

Why shouldn't Mrs. Lou Trenhom be happy? The dreadful war was over. She had her husband home and safe, and she was telling him how she had heard of him here and heard of him there, and what everybody said, how good and kind and brave he was, and how nobly all the colored people behaved. She had an immense deal to tell, and while she talked, squeezing his hands, toying with his whiskers, and passing her soft hands over his hair, he was sitting, submitting and thinking. This is what he thought, " She is wonderful and so good. Not one word about all the ruin I have helped bring upon her. Not once does she say, ' I told you so.' " She did tell him so at the beginning, before the war. But she did not thrust it as a thorn in his side now. So many do that. The " I told you so " family is immense. A puncturing tribe. Pricking and lancing. Lou Trenhom was not one of them. Neither then or ever after did she allude to it. When speaking of the old servants and telling how they all remained and how good they had been, she did say, ' Walter, one great good has come out of it all—slavery is gone. I am so glad."

"So am I," replied the soldier, "heartily glad—heartily glad!"

When Mrs. Lou heard it she was very happy. She knew that defeat had left no seed of bitterness behind it.

Two weeks after this another figure approached Slimpton. As he neared the town he turned into the forest and pushed on until the town was passed ; then he took the road again and walked on with a lazy, shiftless gait until he reached the front of the Ratley cabin. There he paused. A fence had grown up along the road. The intervening weeds, brush, stumps and hog wallow had disappeared. Near the cabin were flower-beds, brilliant with pink, carnation and violet. Lower down toward the road were beds of lettuce, young onions, radishes and peas. The man stuffed his hands in his breeches pockets and opened his eyes. Then he saw that the openings between the logs had been filled, that the window was occupied by a sash and glass. The man whistled. Then he sputtered, "Dawgawn ! wonder whah Lindy's gone."

By the roadside near the man was a huge log. He sat down on the log and drank in the scene. It was an amazing transformation. As he said after, he was "clar upsot." The man took off his hat and rubbed his head with the ends of his fingers. Then he muttered, "Reckon I kin ask wher she'um !" With this idea he stood up, walked over to the gate and up through the path to the cabin. As he approached it a woman stood in the doorway. Seeing her the man paused. He was riveted to the ground. His mouth and eyes were both wide open. He was looking with both. It was what they call open-mouthed wonder. The woman who stood in the door wore a cheap dress, neatly made, and it was whole and clean. Her brown hair was brushed back from her forehead and bound in a great coil behind. The pure pink and white, unwrinkled face, was voluble of good health, content and sweet temper. When the man had fully devoured the scene his tongue started : "G-a-w-l — Y-e-u-u — Lin-d y-Yan ! Dawgawn ! How'de ! "

For a full minute the woman stood looking at him in silence. Some children came to the doorway. She pushed them gently back, drew the door close, and walked down behind the carnations to the man. Then she spoke. Her voice was very soft, and without a trace of emotion : " Joe Ratley, I thought you were dead ! "

" Yer did ! "

" I did ! "

" Ha ! Ha ! Yer see I hain't ! "

" I am sorry, Joe ! "

" Sorry I hain't dead ! Yer be. Yer a good wife, hain't yer ? Sorry I hain't dead ! "

" I think I am, Joe."

" Think ! Gawl ! Think ! "

" Yes, Joe, I heard it or dreamt it, one or t'other, and I never thought of you since, that I remember, Joe."

" Never thort o' yer husband ! Gawl ! "

" Joe ! "

There was something in the tone that made Joe prick up his ears.

" Eh ! "

" Joe, if you swear here again you must walk off the way you came. Yes, Joe, swearing is not allowed here."

" Not swar on my own place ! "

" It is not your place, Joe. I don't know whose it is. I live here. My chil'un live here. They haven't heard swearing, and they shan't, Joe. Joe, they shall not hear swearing."

If this woman had been the least little bit excited he would have been in clover. He could understand that. But to plunge a threat at him on such a dead level of calmness, without an extra flush on her cheek or an extra flash in her eyes, that was too much for Joe. His was not a retentive memory, but somehow a vision of that long ago, when he lay bound on the cabin floor writhing under Lindy's blows, rose up before him. Then he said :

" Well, ef I kan't, I hain't gwanter. Wher's the chillun ? "

Melinda pointed to the cabin. Joe moved toward it. Then Melinda spoke again :

" Joe, you can't go in there. Not there, Joe."

" Can't ? Ain't you my woman ? "

"I don't know, Joe.

"Waal! Dod—"

"Stop, Joe!"

Joe became dumb. Melinda stood facing him with unruffled face. Then she said:

"Joe, you come here to-morrow. I'll see Mrs. Trenhom first. Then I'll tell you what's to be. To-morrow."

This was Joe Ratley's welcome home, and he was forced to be content with it. On the morrow he returned. Melinda met him at the gate.

"Joe," she said, "Mrs. Trenhom says our marrying was no marrying at all, and we must be married over before you comes here. I'm set against it, Joe. Yes, set against it. But she thinks it best for the children, Joe, and I'll do as she says."

That afternoon they went before a minister and were married. Melinda doubted its wisdom then and afterward. But she believed in Mrs. Trenhom, she had been so good to her. When her husband went away Mrs. Trenhom remembered what he had said about this woman of the filthy cabin. With many misgivings she drove there. Lindy met her at the door. Mrs. Trenhom's first impulse was to turn away in disgust. Lindy was standing tattered and barefooted on the sun-b ked earth in front of the .cabin. A little nude girl was clinging to her faded dress. As the child peeped out from behind she drew her mother's torn garments against her limbs, thrusting one soiled knee and part of the rounded limb through the rent. The only attraction about Lindy and the child were their faces and their poverty. Mrs. Trenhom admired the children, nude, ragged and dirty as they were. It was honest admiration and it was cunning. If a woman has a heart anywhere about her the way to reach it is to admire her children. Cunning? Yes; the cunningest thing in the world is honesty. Melinda was caught in the net of Mrs. Trenhom's admiration. She was so nice. So thought Melinda; and she was the first educated woman, the first lady who had ever spoken to her. Mrs. Trenhom persuaded the mother to accept dresses for the "sweet children," and they were very pretty when they were dressed. Then she took them to her own home. There a colored servant, after many protests against " low-downs," washed them, combed and brushed their hair, primped them up, gave them a good dinner and took them home again. Melinda noticed the change. That was the beginning of washing and brushing. From that out she continued it. Then came the house. One of Mrs. Trenhom's servants dropped along with a broom. She entered the cabin as if by chance and sat awhile. "Sun so hot." That's what she said. " Clah, honey, youze gibbin me a roof fro' de sun, an' watah ; jis a little watah, honey." One of the children brought the water. Then the colored woman said: " Clah, sweet honey, now I'ze gwine tu help yer wash up to pay fo't," and without a word the woman soused the floor, and soused and scrubbed until everything within looked like a new pin. Melinda looked on in wonder. She never knew it was part of a cunning plot. Then came Mrs. Trenhom, very innocent like, as if she had not prompted the colored woman with the broom. " Oh ! how nice this is. Now, if the walls were whitewashed and a window there." You see she was cunningly working without offending.

So one improvement followed another. Lindy was a child in mind. She was incapable of devising. But being shown she learned. One day Mrs. Trenhom proposed to hire a colored man to Lindy.

Lindy couldn't pay.

"Never mind, dear ; you'll see he will earn enough to pay."

The man came ; with him fences, a garden and flowers. The cabin and its surroundings were rising out of the mud

The children were delighted with their dresses, with their new life, with the flowers, with everything, and in the light of their joy Lindy blossomed into a new being.

Then Mrs. Trenhom proposed education. If the children would come to her house for an hour every day. They went. They mastered A, B, C, and marched on into the mystery of combining letters. As the little ones learned they taught mother. Thus they all marched on together. Reading opened a new world to Melinda. She began to grasp the idea of a

God. She had never heard it before except in profanation. Within and without she was purified. She buried the "cracker" with her ignorance and filth. It was this new woman that Joe married.

All the way from the minister to the gate Joe's tongue was on hinges. Melinda was silent. At the gate she turned.

"Joe," she said, "I have heard you. I married you because Mrs. Trenhom thinks it's best for the children. For them I would do anything. For them, Joe, I have married you, and I think it is the hardest of all. Yes, I think it is. I don't like you, Joe. I never did since you struck me, Joe! And, Joe, I'd be glad if you'd go away. I think 'twould be best for the children!"

"Lindy! now look year!"

"You're the same, Joe. Yes, I know that from what you've been saying, Joe."

"You're gittin' awdacious peart."

"Peart enough by the help of a good woman to get out of the ignorance and nastiness where you left me, Joe."

"Yaas, mighty peart."

"And I tell you, Joe, we're not to be dragged down again. No, Joe, not down again."

"Whose draggin' on ye?"

Melinda stood with her back to the gate. A minute or two passed in silence. Then she said:

"Joe, before you go in here, you must promise you won't swear before the children."

"Whose gwin' ter?"

"That won't do, Joe. You've got to promise, Joe."

"Well, I promise."

"And that you won't beat them."

"Ain't I their dad?"

"I'm sorry to say you are, Joe."

"Waal."

"But you shall not beat them. No, Joe. They are good children. Yes, good children. Better than any dream I ever had of them, and they shan't be dogged backward. No, Joe, not backward."

"Wall, I shan't tech 'em."

"And you must not come there drunk."

"Ef a fellar gits a little too much he won't think."

"I reckon you'd best remember. I reckon you'd best, Joe."

He opened his great mouth again and looked—the vision of the thongs was before him—then he said : "Yaas, reckon I'd best. I ain't gwan to forgit."

After this warning, Joe walked up to the cabin. When they first walked up to this cabin years ago, Lindy followed Joe. Now Joe followed Lindy.

The war ruined many, but it was a Providence to Lindy Ratley and her children, and it was an inestimable benefit to many poor whites. It broadened their visions and seeded them with thought. It lifted them up. Many staid up. Others no leverage could elevate. What they were before the war they remained. A rock can be rolled to the height and it will stay. Sludge must be carried and then it washes and slides back to the depths. Melinda owed her new life to Mrs. Trenhom. She began it ; she continued it. But once begun Dale Cartier's wife became an efficient assistant. These two women, Erma Cartier and Louise Trenhom, were fast friends. Before the war they were intimates. Their husbands were boys together, then officers in the same regiment, encountering the same privations. Then the common danger of their husbands knit them firmer together. When the Trenhom place was burned, Cartier's home escaped. When Erma saw the red sky the night of the fire, she knew it must be her friend's house or cabins, and with a single negro attendant drove at once to the scene of ruin. She found Mrs. Trenhom, heard how the fire occurred and begun to rail at "the vandalism." But Mrs. Trenholm quickly bridled the friendly tongue.

"I don't blame them at all—not at all. Guerrillas used it against my protest, to shoot stragglers. That was simply murder. The Union troops have respected all other property, and when they learned of my protest against the guerrillas they would have quenched the flames. But that was impossible. You see they have saved a large part of my furniture."

" The Yankees do that ? "

" Yes, the Union troops, aided by, the servants."

" Insult you ! "

" Not at all.   They expressed only regret at the necessity.
They have been everything that is kind and courteous."

When the building fell and they were gazing on the smol-
dering ruins, Erma urged Mrs. Trenhom to accompany and
make a home at her house.

No.   Her duty lay with her people.   She would live in the
large cabin.   And she did.

Then Erma inquired if any of the servants followed the
troops.

" Not one."

Why should they?   Mrs. Trenhom had already freed every
one of them.   She did this the day she came into possession
of her property, and promised work and wages to all who remained, and they all remained.

When Col, Trenhom came home Major Cartier came with
him to Slimpton.   There their roads parted.   The summer was
devoted, by both Trenhom and Cartier, to reorganizing their
plantations.   In the fall Cartier was called North on business.
When he returned one of the first things he said was:

" Oh, Erma, I saw that sergeant ! "

"Alive ! "

" Alive !   Bless you, yes.   Did you think I was hunting
through graveyards ? "

" How glad I am.   I thought he was dead ! "

" Dead ; I was sure of it.   I never was so startled."

"Are you sure it was he ? "

" Sure.   I spoke to him for hours ; visited his home, and
saw his wife."

" Pretty ? "

You see how women's heads will jump even on the gravest
occasions.

" Pretty !   You wouldn't call her a beauty.   She is fresh
looking.   A good, honest, motherly little body.   A woman to
win you to her from the first word, and the bravest little soul
in the world."   Then a thought of the small-pox horror came

to him, and he added, "Except you, dear, always except you."

"Thank you ! "

Then Dale Cartier went on and told the story of " Puss Cat" and the rescue from Andersonville. Erma was an eager auditor. Her admiration was unbounded. Her exclamations a multitude. When he concluded Erma clapped her hands with delight.

"What a noble, brave woman."

"It was brave, dear. But no bravery ever equalled yours in facing that dreadful sick room."

Erma shivered. "Poor Dale ! " Then she added, "Oh, how I would like to see that woman, Kitty ? "

"You may, dear ! "

"I may ! Oh, how ? Will you take me there ? "

"She may possibly come here ! "

"Here? To us? To visit us? "

"Will it please you ? "

"Oh, Dale ! How can you ask it ? "

"They may come for more than that. To stay ! "

"I shall be delighted."

Then Cartier told how he met Halmer Huntley ; that he was yet suffering from his wound and imprisonment; that his wife dreaded the rigor of a Northern winter; how he had suggested a removal to Mississippi, and that he had given them assurance of a cordial welcome. After this Dale and Erma agreed they would visit some of their friends on the morrow and talk the matter over with them. The result was a letter:

"BROAD OAKS (near Slimpton), Miss. ⎱
        "October 14, 1865. ⎰

"DEAR MR. AND MRS. HUNTLEY.—I have spoken to many of my friends of my suggestion to you and of your fears as to the reception a Northern soldier would receive. You know how earnestly I assured you those fears were groundless. My friends concur with me. The war is over. We have put it behind us. In the final surrender we were treated with magnanimity. We did hope to succeed. We failed, and the unexpected kindness of the victors leaves no room for bitterness. There is none here, not a particle. Northern soldiers can come and do here as they can come and go and do among their own friends in the North, and there are, as you know, special reasons why you will be welcomed with open arms by myself and my friends. My dear friends, put away all doubts and come. Come at all events and visit us, and if our soil and our climate and the warm hearts of our people do not wed you to us then set me down as no prophet. The visit you more than half promised I will not be denied.

" Your ever grateful friend,

"DALE CARTIER."

To this was added a postscript :

" Dear Mr. Huntley, you must not say no. I do want to see you. I do want to thank you, and I want to see 'Kitty.' Pardon the familiarity; but I will see 'Kitty' and you if I have to go to the north pole to do it, and when you come you must make our house your home. I have been out among my friends, and you will see from the enclosure, signed by the first people of our county, how gladly you will be welcomed at Broad Oaks and Slimpton. Kiss your dear wife for me, and come! come! come! I owe you the dearest husband in the world, and I do want to say how grateful I am. Again I repeat, come! come! do come!

" Yours affectionately and gratefully,

"ERMA CHARTRASS CARTIER."

This was the enclosure :

" We have learned from Major and Mrs. Dale Cartier of the generosity and gallantry of Mr. Halmer Huntley, a federal soldier, and we beg to assure him that if he will honor Slimpton by a visit or residence, he will be received and welcomed by all the people with open arms and hearts.

Signed,   " WALTER TRENHOM,
                           " GERSHAM VALORE,
                           " MRS. GERSHAM VALORE,
                           "OGLETHORPE SHOOTFAST,
                           "MRS. CLARINDA SHOOTFAST,
                           "PRESTON BARTDALE."

After these followed some twenty other names of lesser note. When Hal Huntley and his wife received the letters, they wondered why they had misjudged the South. " Noble people, but misguided. All right now. Slavery was the brutalizer; that gone, they are kind and generous and humane, like the rest of the civilized world."

The last doubt was removed, and gladly they turned their faces toward the South. Erma and Dale and their friends overflowed with kindness. There was no end to their hospitality. The visitors were charmed ; the charm made them residents. Before spring they were the owners of a small plantation near Slimpton and settled on it. Then they wrote to Jupiter and Mansa, and in less than a month they came. Nothing suited Mansa better, and they bought a few acres on Peeky Run, a mile away from the Ratley cabin. During the following autumn there was to be a change in the Slimpton postoffice. Jared Sparling wanted the place. It was said he was sure of it. Sparling was a small planter, a thing half way between the bottom silt and the crust, and during the war a Union man. The mention of Sparling's name for the post-office was fuel under the pot. It began to boil with fervor. The vapor it threw off was like this : " Low down fellow. No 'count critter. Agin his friends in the wah! Insult to all of us. Ought to have a gentleman there. Rather it would be a Yankee than a Southern traitor.' This suggested Huntley's name. One and another said, " The government can't object to him. He was a Union soldier and a good fellow. Why not have him appointed? " Huntley was approached. " No. Wouldn't take it under any circumstances." But these people with a purpose never took "no" for an answer. A little " no " is but a pebble in the path of persistence and hate, and they hated Sparling heartily.

" Gentlemen," said Judge Shootfast, " let us have him appointed; then we'll compel him to take it." The Sparling haters were shrewd and potential ; they secured the appointment of Huntley. The first intimation he had of it was from an editorial in the " Slimpton Weekly Buzzer."

" We are glad," said the Buzzer, " to stop our press to announce to the people that Mr. Halmer Huntley has been appointed postmaster at Slimpton. Many of our readers will recognize in Mr. Huntley the gallant federal soldier who saved the life of our distinguished fellow citizen, Major Dale Cartier, on the bloody field of Chickamauga."

When Mrs. Huntley read this, she began to tremble. " Hal," she said, " you will not accept this? "

" Of course not."

"I am so glad. I see only trouble, trouble, trouble, in it."

But if Kate talked, so did the men of persistence ; on his plantation, at their homes. At dinners and teas to which he was dragged ; talk, talk! buz, buz! "Such a kindness to us all. You ought; indeed, you ought. You intend to live here. You owe something to the community. Personal feeling must give way to the public good." This was from Shootfast, Bartdale and Valore, while their wives plied Kate with even greater volubility ; they saw that even if she wasn't the gray mare of the team, the team did not move without her. Then came Erma and Dale. The "Slimpton Buzzer" announced the result : "Reader, we congratulate you. We congratulate everybody. We are happy. We are in the seventh heaven and going up. At the earnest solicitation of our foremost citizens, Mr. Halmer Huntley has consented to withdraw his objections and accept the Slimpton postoffice. Victory number one, hurrah ! "

CHAPTER XXIII.

GATHERING OF THE CLOUDS.

A storm has portents.

Nods, winks, whisperings, mysterious gatherings and murmurings from the " Buzzer" were the presages of the storm that burst over Slimpton in the early summer of 1875.

There had been troubled elsewhere. Immediately following the war there had been some in Slimpton. But it was quickly repressed. The negroes outnumbered the whites in the county four to one, and they used their power discreetly.

When suffrage was conferred on the blacks, and they discovered they could control the selection of officers, they were jubilant. They had a meeting in Shiloh church. The colored pastor presided. The colored people were there in crowds. They came from the remotest points in the county and camped in the woods. No consideration of personal hardship could restrain them from that jubilee.

It was " kingdom come." Trumpets, white robes, and heavens opening.

The woods were melodious with their songs and reverent with their thanksgiving.

The meeting opened with prayer. All negro political meetings do.

The first thing was to propose negro candidates.

This brought Awk Trenhom to his feet, " Mr. President."

The president spoke : " Bruur Trenhom hab de floah ! Proceed sah."

Awk proceeded. He was opposed to nominating negroes.

" What dat?" came from a far away corner of the church " Doan want none we black uns in de awfis ! "

Awk turned his face to the sound.

"Dat's what I say, sah! we uns all am too igrunt fo' dat."

"Mr. Chee'man!"

"Mistah Chee'man!"

"Mistah Presiden'!"

Rap, rap, rap, from the cane of the president.

"Brudren, we mus hab ordah!"

"Dat's it, sah! dat's it, sah! I rises to a point ob ordah!"

Awk stood facing the crowd, bent forward on his cane.

"What you pint ob ordah? You 'sumes to perrupt a ole man! ole 'nuff to be you gran'fadah. Bruur, I'ze 'shamed fo' you! I is! Yes, sah, I is dat. I pity you, sah, I does, deed I does dat, sah. You mus' be po' cotton fiel' han', sah. De fuss mannahs, sah, am to hab 'spect fo' de ole! Membah dat, sah. I lubs you brudah. An' I pity yo' sah. Po' bruddah! Tain't yore fault youze rais' n de cotton fiel'. But look heah, good brudah, 'spect de ole! 'Spect de ole! Dat's de rail demencement ob larnin'. Begin right, good brudah. Den dey's a right smawt chance fo' you to gwan to de perflection ob larnin'!"

The mouth in the corner was plugged. Its owner slunk away out of sight.

In the silence that followed the president asked Awk what he proposed.

Awk soon told it. He advised they should select all the principal officers from among the whites, not because they were whites, but because, unfortunately, all the learning was among the whites. Some of the minor offices could be given to the most intelligent and trustworthy among the blacks; the more important places to whites.

The older negroes who controlled the caucus assented.

The younger ones grumbled and acquiesced.

The rock of stumbling was, who should be the white men.

Awk suggested, "Dah's my young mawstah."

"Mawstah! Mawstah!" exclaimed some.

"Hea'um! Hea'um!" exclaimed others excitedly.

"Law!"

"Mawstah!"

"Heaben!"

16

"Mawstah!"

"Yaas, brudren. I said dat—'Maws—tah!'"

The voice of a stout young colored man rose above the din. "I rise to a pint ob ordah! Dey ain't no mo' mawstahs."

Awk listened calmly to the pattering of words. When they had done he raised his voice, "Brudren, ef you had bettah mawstahs moas ob you would be bettah mans!"

"Oh! Oh! Oh!"

"I say dat! Ob couse you po' bruddahs dat had po' no count white trash fo' mawstahs am pow'ful glad to kick 'em off. Jess like mules wid shakley ridahs."

"Ha! Hah!"

"Hi! Hi! Ki!"

"Dat's so!"

"I knows youze 'shamed o' your mawstahs, ob couse you is. You couldn't help dat, an' I'ze 'shamed fo' you too. But bruden, Mawst Walt an' Miss Lou ain't none ob dat kind, dey ain't.

"Dat's so! Dat's so!"

"No, bruden, dey no low downs."

"Ki! Dat's true, sho! Dat's true!"

"Dey made all we slabes free. Ebry one, sahs, free! Yo' heah dat. Fo' de 'mancipation, we didn't hab to wait fo' no reclamation to get free. No, bruden. Yo' heah dat! De Lawd put it in de hawt ob good Miss Lou; blest Miss Lou, dat she am ; an' Mawst Walt ketch de fiah, an' dey made we free. Bress de Lawd! Does yo' heah what I tole yo'!"

"Hallelujah!"

"Glory to God!"

"Three cheers for Col. Trenhom?"

Cheers followed.

Awk straightened his bent form. Tears were rolling down his wrinkled cheeks. In a voice tremulous with emotion, he spoke :

"Bruden! bruden! Three cheers fo' bless'd Miss Lou and dear Mawst Walt!"

And the cheers were given with hearty good will.

The speech settled the question.

A committee was appointed to wait on Col. Trenhom. Awk was at its head. They urged him to accept the office of probate judge. Trenhom hesitated. His wife urged him to accept. It would do much to start fair on the new road.

Cartier, Valore, Bartdale and Shootfast sat in council on the question ; the result was this : The negroes were in the majority; they could elect whom they pleased. It is better for us all to have an honest gentleman like Trenhom in the important office of probate judge, than an ignorant negro. We will advise him to accept.

They did advise him.

Trenhom accepted and was elected. No question of politics was raised ; the negroes never asked, and the Southerners never doubted. Was not Trenhom a Confederate Colonel? What further guarantee did they desire? There were no questions on either side.

It was a fortunate choosing, and under the advice of Awk and other influential colored people, this policy of selection as to all other county offices was continued.

There was but one exception to it. Jupiter Saltire had been elected sheriff, and afterwards sent to the Legislature.

Elsewhere in the State was unending wrestling and cudgelling; a prolonged tooth and nail shindy. At Slimpton the atmosphere was tranquil ; that was the fruit of Awk Trenhom's tactics.

And Slimpton reaped its benefits.

Laborers flocked from the disturbed sections to the peaceful quarters.

Settlers came in from the North.

A dam was thrown across Peeky Run ; turbine wheels lashed its waters into foam and filled the air with the whir of spindles from the Yankee-built cotton mill that grew up on its banks.

Population swelled.

Land increased in value.

The laws were enforced.

Property was respected.

Life was secure.

Comfort and happiness expelled squalor and misery from a multitude of homes

Prosperity is a bantling of peace.

Slimpton was prosperous.

Then came the portents.

After Col. Trenhom had been in office a year, his neighbors discovered he was voting the Republican ticket. The raised their eye-brows, turned up their noses, and gabbled. Then they learned he had voted that ticket at every election since the war.

The irreconcilables were shocked.

"Trenhom, a Confederate Colonel, vote with the rads! What's the world comin' to?"

A few super-virulents in petticoats refused to be appeased. They drew their puny heads into their turtle-shells, and never recognized Trenhom or his wife after.

Cartier was loyal to his old colonel, and Barkdale, Valore and Shootfast, after many weeks of sackcloth, ashes and mumbling, concluded "the State and county is Republican anyhow. Trenhom is of good family; a gallant soldier; a true Confederate, and he is but one vote. One vote more or less makes no difference." And with wry faces they agreed to swallow the colonel, coated though he was with "the bitterness and nastiness of radicalism."

That was before the storm and its warnings.

The first murmuring came from the Slimpton Buzzer.

This was the muttering:

"Our sister States have kicked off the nigger riders. It can be done in Mississippi, and it must be done. Don't talk about majorities. Work and redeem the State. Work, be firm and wise; this time there is to be no fail. Remember that. 'Up, guards, and at 'em.'"

Three days afterward, Gen. Pontoon arrived from Jackson. During the day he was in close converse with Valore, Cartier, Shootfast, Bartdale and others.

The air was full of rumors.

"Pontoon! What is he here for?"

"Goin' to be fun, sho' as you bawn!"

That night there was a secret meeting. Windows blinded, doors closed and guarded.

Gen. Pontoon was a hammer.

The meeting was glowing iron under his blows.

There was no dissent.

White men ought to rule the State.

"But, General, how can it be done? We are in a minority. The Republicans outnumber us four to one in this county, and nearly two to one in the State; their majority is vast." Such was Col. Valore's query and suggestion.

Pontoon stood, a big, ruddy man with puffy cheeks, coarse, protruding lips, small, steel-gray eyes, and blotched nose. He stroked his fat chin. A cunning smile broadened his thick lips.

"Ah, gentlemen, I have looked for this question. Yes, sahs, I have expected it and I am prepaw'd for it, sahs. Yes, gentlemen, prepaw'd for it. I have come up heah. Yes, gentlemen, up heah to this beautiful county, the pride of Mississippi. Yes, sahs, the pride of the State, sahs, with the noblest, the most patriotic gentlemen and the most beautiful women, sahs. It is a pleasure and a great honah, sahs. And I have come prepaw'd. There must not be any Radical majority."

"But," said Col. Valore, "if their voters outnumber ours, there will be a majority."

Pontoon stood up again. "Ah, gentlemen, I am prepaw'd for that too. There must not be any Radical majority. No, sahs, no majority."

"But how will it be prevented."

"Gentlemen, I have expected that question. Yes, gentlemen, I came prepaw'd for it. It must be prevented. Yes, sahs, that's the way to stop it. Prevent it, sahs!"

"How prevent it?"

"Prevent it! My valiant friend you surprise me. Yes, sahs, I am amazed! Profoundly amazed. Don't let them have a majority. That's the way to prevent it. That's the way, my dear colonel. That's the way, gentlemen. You see I have come prepaw'd for all questions."

"But, general, have you any suggestions to make as to specific methods?"

The general stood up again. "Ah! hum! There are a great many people here, gentlemen."

"But all true. I vouch for every man of them," interjected Judge Shootfast.

"Yes. Certainly, my esteemed friend! Certainly. Quite a number! Quite a crowd! Perhaps you had better appoint a committee. You see, gentlemen, I have come here prepaw'd; quite prepaw'd for that too."

"How large a committee?"

"Hum! Hum! Yes! Committee. Say three!. Yes, three will do. Quite prepaw'd for that. Say three."

Cartier moved that Shootfast, Valore and Bartdale should be the committee. Pontoon was uneasy. He stroked his fat chin and elevated his eyebrows.

"Hum! Perhaps my distinguished friends are—are—. Hum! Well, gentlemen — you see—my distinguished and valiant friends may not have—time."

"Nothing to prevent, nothing to hinder," interrupted Bartdale. "Nothing to prevent us serving the State, no, sir; nothing, nothing!" added Shootfast.

"Hum! I am not quite prepaw'd—not quite prepaw'd for that committee."

Then the cunning light came back into Pontoon's eyes.

"My distinguished friends will agree with me. Yes, gentlemen, I know they will. I am prepaw'd for that. I am prepaw'd to have them agree with me. The State has other service for my learned and valiant friends. Yes, gentlemen, I am prepaw'd to assert that. I do it with confidence, gentlemen. Other important duties; you agree with me, do you not, Colonel Valore?"

Colonel Valore nodded "certainly."

"Ah! I knew you would! I was prepaw'd for that."

A voice in the rear of the room interrupted Pontoon.

"General, how shall we appoint the committee?"

"Hum! Yes! I am prepaw'd for that. Make out a list. Yes, sahs, a list of all the gentlemen present. All—remember all—gentlemen, and their positions in the Confederate army—and—pursuit before the waw."

The list was made out and handed to Pontoon. He drew out his pencil and erased all but three names near the bottom of the list. Then he delivered the list to the secretary, who read:

POSITION IN CONFEDERATE ARMY.	NAME.	OCCUPATION BEFORE WAR.
Captain	Hiram Pelter	Slave Driver.
Captain	Ezekiel Savage	Slave Trader.
Lieutenant	Sam. Boosy	Saloon Keeper

The gentlemen present looked in each other's faces.

A mysterious light flamed up in many eyes. And Pontoon complacently stroked his fat chops, while the meeting confirmed his selections.

Hi Pelter stood up. "General, when can the committee see you?"

"Me! Hum! I am not quite prepaw'd for that! Hum —a—yes! A distinguished patriot will call on you."

"What's his name?" asked Pelter.

"Name! Not quite prepaw'd. No. You will know him, gentlemen of the committee. Yes, gentlemen, you will know him when he comes. A distinguished patriot I assure you, gentlemen. You will know him."

Then the meeting broke up.

As they glided stealthily out in the dark Judge Shootfast whispered to Bartdale, "This means business. I can see that. Sure! Sure!"

It did mean business.

The next week's Buzzer was seething. "Thank God the hour of deliverance is nearer than we hoped. It is almost here. Throw up your hats. Shout. Get drunk. 'Tis the year of jubilee. In future none but white men of unquestioned fidelity to our social and political faith* will be permitted to hold office under any circumstances. None!" "Mark it! Mark what we tell you. We are going to shake off the crazy God-and-morality-negro-worshipping, black-and-

*Yazoo Herald.

white-blood-mixing, women crowing, baby-strangling, c-e-o-w-pronouncing New England-Yankee-clock-peddling, chicken-stealing, box ankled, bandy-shanked, round-shouldered, cant-ing, psalm-singing, cowardly, cut-throat, vulgar, slimy-mouthed, onion eating, sausage-stuffing scoundrels from the North."* We are going to drive them out of the Post-office. Chalk that down, Yankee Postmaster, and out of every office. Make a big score there all of you. Keep your eye on every Yank. Some are State and some are federal spies. All are thieves," † and " when these boot-licks of tyranny sneak back North, carpet-bag in hand, we ask them to think of us as a people.

" What hates the Cotton Mather and the Roger Williams stock,
  That dirty pile of hell's manure first dumped on Plymouth rock."‡

Kate Huntley saw the article and was amazed. Not an hour before the editor of the Buzzer was in the post-office, all smiles and affability. Kate was its postmistress. Her hus-band's Chickamauga wound incapacitated him for business. He insisted on resigning. Dalton Craft, of the Buzzer, was among the most zealous advocates of Mrs. Huntley to succeed her husband. The Huntleys' plantation experience had not been a success, and Mrs. Huntley could do the post-office work. The salary was needed ; that, with her husband's pension, which he could not draw while he was postmaster, placed them in comfortable circumstances. And now, to be assailed almost by name, and in such vile terms, it shocked Kate.

A little time after she read the article the Buzzer man came in again. Kate looked at him out of her troubled eyes. The same old smile was on the man's face. He was appar-ently unchanged. As he opened his mail drawer he spoke to her.

"Ah ! How de, Mrs. Huntley?"

The man's pleasant tones surprised her. He was goading her. Slashing her with thorns, and yet he stood there before her with a smile on his lips. She spoke to him.

*Iuka (Miss.) Gazette.   †Panola (Miss.) Star.
‡ Brandon (Miss.) Republican.

" Mr. Craft, I have been reading this week's Buzzer."

" Ah !   Quite a good number !   Going off like hot cakes."

" One article in it pains me very much."

" You mean the leader."

" The first article.   Perhaps you call it that."

Craft rubbed his hands.   " Sharp and strong, isn't it?   I've received a heap of congratulations on that."

" I am sorry to hear it."

" My dear Mrs. Huntley ! "

" Yes, I am surprised to hear that any of our people endorse such sentiments."

" Dear madam, these are the sentiments of all our people."

" Oh, no ! "

" Indeed, yes ! "

" And you all despise and hate me thus ! "

" You !   You, dear Mrs. Huntley !   You, as an individual, no.   As an individual—as Mrs. Huntley, we all admire and esteem you, and personally would do anything for you.   It is the Yankee postmistress that we hate."

" Did you not urge me to take the place ? "

" I did, indeed ; so did all our prominent people ; and so they also urged it upon your husband."

" Have I not been honest in office ? "

" No one has ever doubted it."

" Have I not been obliging ? "

" You have, indeed."

" And courteous to everyone ? "

" You could not be otherwise."

" Have not my husband and myself secured you more mails and prompter delivery than you ever had before ? "

" I'll testify to that everywhere.   The post-office never was managed so well."

" And yet you wish me to go out of it ? "

" Yes, dear madam; it is against the policy of the State to permit Northern people to hold office."

" If that is so, why did you solicit me to take it ? "

" We were not quite prepared to assert our rights then,

and it was either you, a Yankee, or a scallawag, and we pre-
ferred the Yankee. We would do the same again."

"Oh! Indeed! Then I and my husband were mere tools
of your spleen. Clubs to hit some Southern man who had
buried his war passions and given his support to the government."

"Dear Mrs. Huntley, you put it harshly. Indeed you do."
And Craft walked away, whistling "Dixie."

Only the day before this interview at the post-office, a
stranger glided up the stairs to the Buzzer office, and after
entering, carefully closed the door behind him.

Before him he saw a man at a desk writing. The
stranger's entrance had been noiseless. He was unnoticed
until he spoke.

"Mr. Craft?"

Craft looked up, surprised and startled. Seeing the
stranger, he answered "Yes."

"Editor of the Buzzer?"

"Yes. Whom have I the honah of addressing?"

The stranger hurriedly scrutinized the room, then he whispered:

"You may call me 1900."

"1900!"

"S-s-c-c-h-h! Yes! 1900."

Craft looked the man over. He was tall and slim. Bones
in breeches. A slouched hat covered his short gray hair. A
pair of huge ears curled down under the rim of the hat. A
great curved nose made a narrow bridge between eyes hidden
away under shaggy, overhanging eyebrows. A strongly protruding chin and thin lips, marking a mouth square across the
jaw and set like a vise. It was a slit in brown parchment.
This was the man.

Craft laid down his pen. "1900" drew a chair close beside him and sat down.

"I'm here on business. Partly with you. 1900 is enough
of a name. You were at a conference the other night. Pontoon was there."

Craft nodded.

"That's all right. I know you very well from description, and I am here on that business."

"I am not of the committee."

"I am aware of that. Quite aware of that."

"Have you seen any of the committee?"

"No, not yet."

"Shall I show them to you?"

"Quite unnecessary. I can pick them out in a crowd. My first business is with you."

' I am honored. What can I do?"

"Much, sah, much. Every great cause needs a John the Baptist."

"And I—"

"You can prepare the way."

"In what way?"

"Make it red hot for the Yanks and scallawags. Make the Buzzer a furnace to consume their reputations. Make it a volcano to bury them under its lava. You can do that?"

"I think so."

"I am sure of it. Our committee have watched your course and are aware of your abilities."

Craft bowed.

"Charge them boldly with every conceivable wrong and malignant purpose. Make them odious—odious. Fire the hearts of the people against them. Fire their hearts. There is nothing easier."

"That is undoubtedly true."

"After a time, when the people are prepared for it—you will hear rumors. We will arrange that. We will start them for you. Charge them and the negroes with arming and conniving. Charge the niggahs, Yanks and scallawags with incendiary and murderous purposes. A part of the people can be swayed by their hates. Another part by their fears. Between the two we will have a solid people with a pretext and apology for the measures that will be necessary to drive the Yankees and scallawags from power and subdue the niggahs."

"I see! I see!"

"We shall rely on your efficient aid."

"Mississippi and the South can rely on me to the death."

"Your country will be grateful."

"My dear 1900, watch the Buzzer. From this on it shall be a brazier for grilling Yankees, niggahs and scallawags. If my section needs that, it shall have it. For my country the Buzzer shall be made a bed of molten lava for them all."

With a profane and burning clincher of asseveration from Craft the conspirators parted.

CHAPTER XXIV.

THE 1900.

Late on the evening of the same day Hiram Pelter, ex-slave driver and ex-captain of the Confederate army, was on his way home. In the shadow of the trees a man stood beside him.

"Captain Pelter?"

"Yes, sah."

"One of the committee appointed the other night?"

"Yes, who be you?"

"1900!"

"1900?"

"Yes, 1900. I am the man."

"That was to come to us?"

"Yes. Where can we be perfectly secure from prying ears?"

"Come this way." And Pelter led him into safe shelter.

"Secure here?"

"Wait here an' I'll get the others."

"Savage and Boozy?"

"Yes."

"No. That won't do. Two is enough to any conference.

"But they are on the committee."

"I know. I'll see them."

"Why not altogether?"

"One at a time; one at a time, my friend. Three's witnesses. Two is only assertion and denial."

"And you distrust—"

"No, sir, not at all. Not by any means. I have a work to do, and I propose to do it, and do it securely for the good of the cause—for the country's sake."

" I see."

" Will you listen? "

"Sahtin."

" You are well acquainted in the county ? "

" Yes.   Know everybody."

" All prominent niggahs and Yankees? "

" Every one of them."

" And the low downs? "

" Know them all."

"Are they well affected toward the niggahs? "

" Friendly, you mean? "

" Yes, kindly disposed to them."

" Well, they're peaceable like, but powahful jealous."

" Yes."

" You see the niggahs are gittin' ahead a sight of 'em. Gittin' on right peert. Gittin' money and lands and comfutable like for niggahs."

" As they are doing generally through the State."

"An' the low downs mostly stick in the same old rut."

" Where they were before the wah? "

" Yes, and that makes them powahful jealous like."

" Would like to take the niggahs down a peg? "

" Indeed they would, shoa ! They're mad to see the niggahs gittin' on when they ain't."

" And they could be stirred up against the niggahs? "

" You bet ! A chip would stir and set them whirling."

" What about the Yankees ? "

" They're worse. Hate 'em worse. They go round puttin' on so many airs with their schools and churches and fine clothes and fancy plantin'."

" Exactly. Can't hide their success."

" Don't try, drat 'em. Don't try. Always grubbin' an' diggin' like niggahs, an' rubbin' their success under better people's noses."

" They are not smart."

" Smart ! Who ever saw a Yank peert at anythin' except makin' money. Ef they'd only cover their success up. Ef it didn't stick out so."

"Precisely. And this angers the low downs?"

"Angers all of us. One don't like it more than another."

"I am glad to hear it."

"You see a fellow don't like to be in the suds an' see another floppin' like pooty white linen in the sun."

"Of course not."

He did not suggest that the path out of the suds was the same for all; that was not his purpose. He came to bedraggle the clean, white linen, not to purify and rinse out the soiled. Then he added, "They can, of course, be united against the Yankees and niggahs."

"For that matter, they are united now. It's the doing is the question."

"Can they not be united to act against them?"

"To cuss and mouth at them; oh, yes! They do that now."

"But to use compulsion, force, violence?"

"That depends!"

"On what?"

"On the leading men—the kites. You see the low downs are only kite tails now, as they were before the wah."

"But they can not expect men like Judge Shootfast and Col. Valore to participate in any scenes of violence."

"No! Not that 'zacly. But they mustn't be fornenst it; they must stand by it."

"Oh, that's all right."

"When we satisfy the 'sand-hillers' that such men like the work, or wink at it, and that they will stand between them and hawm, we can get them to whip or hang every niggah and Yank in the county."

"Very good. That's as I expected. I give you that assurance. You may rely on it. You shall have the amplest proof of it."

"All right so far. But they mustn't give encouragement to leading Yanks and scallawags."

"Of course not."

"They mustn't visit 'em or have anything, in a social way, to do with them."

"That will be attended to. You may build upon that."

"Very good, then; the rest is easy canoeing. You have plans?"

"Yes, uniform throughout the State."

"Then what do you want us to do?"

"You will organize companies."

"How many?"

"That will be left to your own discretion. I would suggest not less than three, one for each of the committee. More if you think best afterward."

"And we shall command them?"

"Yes, and counsel together as to methods of attack and obnoxious men. They then should act in concert."

"I see."

"You should obtain full information as to all prominent and officious Republican niggahs and Yanks."

"And then?"

"Make it hot for them. Make it hot for them."

"Whipping?"

"That at first."

"And after?"

The man placed his thin lips against Hiram Pelter's ear and whispered, "Kill! Kill! Kill!" It was the hiss of a serpent. But Pelter heard it immovable.

· Reptiles are not startled by reptile hissing.

"If they appeal to the law?"

"There will be no law for them. If you make the judges and you and your friends are the jurors, you are the law."

Pelter rubbed his hands with delight. The plot was penetrating his skull.

"And the pretexts."

"If not ready made, make them."

"In what way?"

"Rumors! Rumors!"

"Of what?"

"You and your companies whisper it, then talk it openly. Niggahs are stealing. Niggahs and Yanks conspiring. Gathering secretly. Arming. Discover a plot; a host of plots to kill and burn and outrage. Spread it about. Get it on every tongue ; the more it is talked the more it will be believed. Force the thought into the minds of the timid. Iteration of words is water-drops on stone. It will wear into minds. People who repeat will speedily come to assurance. All you have to do is to accuse and accuse. Whisper it in confidence to A and to B. In confidence, mind you. Not to be repeated. You heard the niggahs say this and you heard them say that. And you saw the Yanks bearing arms to them here and there. Shudder and moan. Declare you are going to leave the country, can't stand it, afraid of your life. You and your command keep at it—a few days, a few weeks, and the work is done. There will be a multitude to swear they saw and heard all of it."

"Ah!" Pelter's eyes glistened in the dark.

"Yes! Call a poor worm a serpent and the many will swear it is so and go out of their way to club it."

"I see! I see! I see!" whispered Pelter, in ecstasy.

"But suppose, after all, they insist on coming to the polls and voting!"

"Announce in advance that you will regard any collection of negroes as a threat. Then, if they are too numerous to be driven from the polls, you must out-count them."

"Stuff the ballot boxes?"

"Certainly. Take possession of the polls. If we can not vo'e the negro down we can knock him down, and the result will be the same."*

"But if he gets in most votes and the registrar insists on counting them?"

"No difference how bold the fraud or how manifest it may be, hang the registrar.† Fill your ballot boxes, and see that they are counted, and hang the registrar that proposes to throw out a Democratic vote."‡

"Isn't that a little revolutionary?"

"Yes, undoubtedly.. The present contest is rather a revolution than a political campaign; it is the rebellion, if you see

---

* Article in Westville (Miss.) News.　　　† Jackson Clarion.
‡ Jackson Clarion.

17

fit to apply that term,* and no true man who wore the gray
should flinch from it. The man who would now throw a
Democratic vote out of the ballot box, no matter how it gets
there, ought to be killed. Shoot the man who does it on the
spot, and the public sentiment of the world will sustain you.
Such a man deserves to die the death of a dog."†

"That's true."

"It is true; and the men who secure the control of Mississippi to the white men will in the future be ranked among
the foremost patriots of the land. It is a noble purpose, a
noble purpose, to wrest our glorious State from the Yankees
and niggahs and scallawags."

Pelter's hand was resting on the other's knee as they sat
close together, whispering in the dark.

The fingers closed on the knee.

Each finger was an exclamation of approval.

"General, I'm your man."

"I knew it, knew it, sah, the moment I saw you. Patriotism, sah. Devotion to your country is written on your
face."

All that any person had ever seen before was hang-dog
brutality.

"I'd just like to lick a hundred free niggahs, just once all
round; ef I didn't make them know thar place I'd give a dollar
a head for all I failed on,‡ and you can bet on Savage and
Boozy every time."

"I know—I have seen them!"

"Have! Talked with them?"

"No! I will to-night. But I have seen enough of them to
know they are the right men for such noble work."

"You bet! They hain't no more use for Yanks than I
have. Them Yanks is low down triflin' coots anyway, an' as
for the niggahs, I swan I hates 'em as freemen."

"It is a pleasure to hear you, sir; a pleasure to hear you.
Your selection is another proof of the great sagacity of my
distinguished friend, Gen. Pontoon."

* Aberdeen (Miss.) Examiner.   † Yazoo Herald.
‡ A fact.

Pelter chuckled. It was the snarl of a cur with a smaller dog under his feet. After a moment's pause he said:

"There is one thing you forgot, colonel."

"What?"

"The name."

"No. I did not forget. I am coming to it."

"What is it to be?"

"1900!"

"1900?"

"Yes. That and no more. Here is a parcel of notices for meetings. You will put the number of your company on one side. You had best commence numbering at 20. Then the members will think there are a greater number of companies in the work. When you call a meeting post them up. The number of your company on the right, the date, omitting the month, on the left."

The man delivered Pelter the parcel, stood up, and before Pelter could speak, he was gone.

That night, as Capt. Hiram Pelter afterward learned, the strange man met Savage and Boozy and imparted to them the same instructions and left them with a similar package. When Pelter reached his home he opened the parcel and saw a number of small bills about four inches square; on them were printed words and figures like this:*

I DON'T KNOW.

1900!

In the morning Pelter, Savage and Boozy met and compared notes. Then they thought of the man of packages and

* See Report of Mississippi Election, 1876, page 192.

instructions. What was his name? 1900! That was all either knew. Then they went to the hotels. No such person was there. No such person had been seen there. Nor could they ever afterwards discover that any one had seen him except the editor and themselves. He came mysteriously, and mysteriously he disappeared, and Slimpton saw him no more until after the great tragedy. But he came with a whirlwind in his cunning brain, and he turned it loose.

CHAPTER XXV.

CLOUDS CHARGED WITH STORM.

Before the end of a week another visitor honored Slimpton with his presence. This one was a thing of adipose, urbanity and sleekness; white hands and watch chain, coming with flourish of trumpets. It was the distinguished General Hytoan; and he came as the guest of Judge Shootfast. There are men too vast for the average hotel. Hytoan was one of them. After dinner, over a smoke—even Hytoans do that— there was conversation—and on politics, of course. It was nuts and cheese. Both moaned over the fallen condition of the South and the country. "Ah! for the old—the good old time when gentlemen were presidents; when gentlemen controlled the Government; when the South gave it tone and character—all gone now, alas, and alas!" Then Mrs. Shootfast joined them, where they were seated on the broad veranda running across the front of the house.

" Ah, gentlemen; talking treason."

" Dear madam, there never was treason in the South, never, madam," replied Hytoan, bowing while he eyed the smoke curling up from the cigar held in his soft, white hand.

"I know, but these Washington people say so."

" My dear madam, they do not believe it; no, none of them. No, madam, the people of the North, ignorant as they are, never did believe that."

" They have said it, general."

" Ah, true ! But if they believed we were guilty of treason why did not they try some of us? There is a vulgarism, 'proof of the pudding.' You have doubtless heard it."

Mrs. Shootfast nodded.

" Exactly. There it is, madam, in a nut shell. If we were

traitors, why did they not indict and try some of us? It was, madam, because they knew we were not so."

"You are right, general," interrupted the judge; "crime indeed! Loyalty to the miserable Washington government is the only crime I know."

"And, my dear judge, there is too much of it in the South," replied Hytoan.

"Unfortunately, yes, deep-rooted and in some places, here especially, growing, growing."

"It is the new-fangled machines and the mills and what the people call prosperity that does it; as though prosperity was a blessing to poor trash. And " added Mrs. Shootfast— it was her tongue that was running—"how I do detest the clatter of those mills. Oh, dear! we will never see the good old quiet days again."

"And," said the judge, "the free schools established by the Radicals have carried away others of our people."

"Was there ever," responded Hytoan, "a greater humbug! Education should not be universal. All minds are no more capable of tuition than all lands are capable of cultivation. Public schools should be abolished. Education was never intended for any but gentlemen. Free schools are eleemosynary tributes to laziness and improvidence.* I agree with our Democratic friends in Choctaw. 'The free school law of the State meets my unqualified condemnation.' "†

'Yes, indeed," said Mrs. Shootfast, warmly. "It is better to let our children grow up in ignorance than to have Puritan ideas instilled into their young minds."‡

"But," added the judge, "they exercise a weighty influence upon the minds of the people. Rooting them in what they falsely term loyalty."

General Hytoan was a good listener. When the judge finished he asked in a reflective sort of a way as he with one little white finger dusted the ashes from the end of his cigar: "Do you not think we are responsible for some of it?"

* Forrest (Miss.) Register.
† Resolutions Choctaw (Miss.) County Convention.
‡ Brandon (Miss.) Republican.

"We! I! No! Indeed no! Heaven forbid."

There was a moment's silence, then Hytoan said:

"Over in Alabama—Marion, I think—a club adopted a resolution like this: '*Resolved*, that the members of this club in their social intercourse will not recognize any man as a gentleman or friend who may accept any appointment to office under any Republican Congress.'* Suppose we all tried that?"

The judge hesitated. But Mrs. Judge did not,

"It would be excellent."

"I quite agree with you, madam. Southern white men, and Northern men who come among us, if they vote the Republican ticket, should be made to feel that they are despicable outcasts, cut off from all human fellowship and sympathy. Between them and us there can be nothing but hostility, eternal and undying, and there is not a murderer or a thief in the world for whom we have not more respect than we have for the vagabonds who seek to impose negro rule upon the people of the South." †

The judge looked disquieted. He really was so, and he answered haltingly: "Perhaps — you — are — right. But—what—good—would—come—out—of—it ? "

"Because of the colored majority ?"

"Yes !"

"My dear judge. In Alabama they tried the policy of conciliation as we have tried it here. But they did not carry one single vote by it. Little by little they came to try the color line in municipal elections, then in county elections here and there, and finding it to succeed, they at last made the State canvass upon it and redeemed the State." ‡

"It has been suggested that suffrage founded on limited educational qualifications might aid us, but I do not believe it."

"Undoubtedly it would not. At first it would disfranchise fifteen thousand whites and probably two or three times

---

* Resolutions Democratic Club, Marion, Alabama.

† Vicksburg Times.

‡ Speech of Col. Taylor, Democrat, of Alabama, made in advising Mississippi to pursue the same policy.

that many negroes, but in ninety days every negro in the State would learn enough reading and writing to be a voter, and not one poor white in a thousand would attempt it. It would only place us in a more hopeless minority."

"That is my view of it, general. But to pursue a policy of social ostracism would embarrass some of us very much."

"In what way, judge?"

"We have a Yankee postmistress, a most estimable lady and a very efficient officer, and she accepted the office on our solicitation."

"Yes, doubtless."

"And there is Col. Trenhom —"

"I remember him, a gallant Confederate soldier. I knew his father before him. I had the honah to serve with him in Mexico."

"Yes, and the son is like the father, a gallant Southern gentleman. A gallant, whole-souled man, a noble fellow. And his wife is one of the sweetest women in the world; a special favorite of Mrs. Shootfast and myself; and yet the colonel is a Republican."

"A little pressure and he might abandon it."

"Not he, general. It is a matter of principle with him. He says the magnanimity of the North at the surrender, was unparalleled, and he can not be so ungrateful as to become their traducer or enemy."

"You think no pressure would move him?"

"None. He is wedded to public schools, to prosperity, to progress, and all the quackery of Republicanism."

"If you are correct, it is a pity."

"Yes, general, it is a pity."

"But we have a duty to our State and our beloved section. Should friendship stand between us and its performance?"

"It is a difficult problem."

"Undoubtedly," responded Hytoan, "and one which has confronted and puzzled most of our friends. I have suffered no little with the others. My friends are my weak point" (very sympathetic). "I cling to my friends. To part with

them is like parting with life" (the sympathies augmented).
"Yes, my dear judge, like parting with life; but—ah, me!
what have we Southern gentlemen not suffered for our States
and our section? I have done it. Not turned to hate them,
you know. I couldn't do that. No, sir. I could not do that
—not turn them out of my heart. That would be impossible"
(this in tremulous tones, very stagy); "but I did shut my doors
against them. I have done it, dear madam, sorrowfully; you
can understand it" (madam nodded). "I have done it for the
cause and the State, my dear judge, in full assurance that in a
little time—(slowly) a little time (soft and slow) it would be
all right again."

"If I could think that," said the judge, musingly.

"Ah, my dear sir, I speak with confidence on this point.
It is the experience of our friends in Alabama and Georgia."

"It is? If this alternative is but temporary, where is
its use?"

"It may have little effect on strong minds like our brave,
wayward friend Trenhom. But the weak crowd, the great
multitude of fainter men, are turned away from the Republicans and riveted to our cause. The Republicans are thus
reduced to a hopeless minority—none but blacks and Yankees
—and honorable gentlemen like our distinguished friend, turn
away from them in disgust. Then we open our arms to them
again."

"If I could only believe it would be so."

"My dear judge, is it not worth trying?"

"It would be a great cross to me. I value Trenhom's
friendship."

"'No cross, no crown,' you know, my dear judge."

Several minutes the judge sat in troubled silence, then the
general turned to Mrs. Shootfast.

"Do you not agree with me, madam?"

"Yes, general I do. I will never call on them again or
receive their calls; never."

"Until they reform, my dear madam, or we have redeemed
the State."

The general was softly angling for Shootfast.

"I don't know, general, when I forget I forget."

" Ah, my dear madam, you ladies have always been distinguished by self-sacrificing patriotism, deeper, far deeper than
ours."

" You are complimentary."

" No, madam," with his white hand over his heart and
bowing. " Truthful. But we poor gentlemen, when we remember—we remember. For the cause you ladies can bury
your feelings forever. We can only do it temporarily."

This was crafty angling.

The judge was listening.

Much as he hated the Yankees and Republicans, he would
have promptly scouted a proposition to turn his back upon
Trenhom forever. But as a temporary expedient it was less
offensive.

He was silent.

Then absorbing.

Then assenting.

He agreed to try it as a " temporary expedient."

General Hytoan was too wary to exult, too shrewd to continue the conversation. He had trapped his game, and he was
too good a hunter to play with the trap and permit it to
escape.

He knew the temporary would turn into the permanent.

Friendship lives in the light of smiles, of kindness, of reci-
procity, and of continuity.

Friendship is not a snake-skin to be shed and grow again.

Hytoan knew this; he knew that temporary alienation
between these men meant bitterness and afterward hate. It
is but a step from one to the other.

Shootfast was old and experienced, and should have
known, but there was Hytoan, distinguished, a social leader,
with his white hands and oily, hopeful words; and there was
the cause—" the glorious cause."

Shootfast fell, as wiser men than he have done.

Before leaving Slimpton, Hytoan met Valore. He assented, of course. " White men—Southern gentlemen—
ought to rule the State. Not, my dear general," he added

to Hytoan, "that there is anything special to complain of; there is not; but because it is their right. We were born to it. In this county we have no cause of complaint except that. The taxes are light, crimes are few, the laws are fairly administered, and the prosperity is without parallel. Of course, some who were up are now down, but as a whole the people were never so prosperous; never half so prosperous."

"Yes, colonel, I recognize the prosperity, but the seed is planted, and there are seeds that can never be destroyed."

"Except they be torn up by the roots."

"Some not even then."

"Unfortunately, they are mostly thistles, briars and noxious weeds."

"And prosperity, my dear colonel. It is a ball set in motion on a hill side—it rolls on of itself."

"I hope so."

"Our experience elsewhere justifies us in believing there is no doubt of it."

"Well, general, I shall hail our possession of the State with joy; but between you and I, it sometimes occurs to me that a three-bushel yield isn't worth the seed."

"Ah! true. But we'll have more than a three-bushel yield. Yes, my dear colonel, we never failed; never, sir, except when we appealed to force. That, sir, was the one great blunder of the South."

"Undoubtedly it was a mistake, or worse."

"But for that we might have controlled the Government continuously."

"Except, perhaps, during the Lincoln term."

"Even then, I thought you knew."

"Perhaps I did, but—I reckon I have forgotten."

"Why, sir, his election was of Southern devising. Secession had been determined upon, and the Democratic party was divided by our friends. It was done, purposely to elect Lincoln and afford us the pretext for the separation we desired."

"Hem! I remember now. I heard of it at the time and concurred in its wisdom."

"Yes, colonel, we all did, and it was the only piece of bungling work the South ever engaged in. People speak of us, the South, as hot and bold, and of the North as cool and cunning. There never was anything wider of the truth. It is we who have always been the astute, crafty, cunning section. By these qualities, with the majority of wealth and numbers against us, we controlled the country for half a century, and, if we never had laid them aside, would be in control to-day. Talk of the Yankee as shrewd and cunning, and artful— pshaw! he is and always was a child at the business. The South is the natural home of the subtle. Diplomacy, intrigue, and Machiavelism were born under Southern skies, kissed by Southern suns, nursed in Southern laps. They are our natural weapons, and we were supreme idiots when we abandoned them."

"I recognize the justice of your observations; but, after all, beyond controlling our own State, which we ought to do, what will we gain from it all?"

"We will control the country as we did before the war."

"Ah, my friend, you are sanguine."

"Look, colonel. See how little we need beyond a solid South Two Northern States will do it. And the Democrats of the North are as eager to kiss the dirt under our feet as they were twenty years ago. Give us the solid South and then be quiet, and they will quickly secure us the rest.

"All that may be possible, but, general, I confess, except for niggah suffrage I would prefer an alliance with the other party."

"With the Republicans?"

"Yes, with the Republicans. What would we say to a people in our midst who, in the crisis of a great war, acted as the Democratic party did in the North? What do we now call the very few men among us who were untrue to us?"

"Renegades and despicable traitors."

"Precisely. And were not the Northern Democrats that to their own people?"

" Undoubtedly they were; but, my dear colonel, during a
war we are compelled to use spies and dirty tools, and though
we may despise them, we can not afford, you know, to be too
nice in the selection of instruments. We must look to results
and close our eyes to the means."

" Possibly."

" And they were of great service to us."

" That I have doubted. Reliance on them protracted the
war. We all know that. It postponed the inevitable end and
added to the sum of expense and suffering. I tell you,
general, a party that has been false to the people among
which they live; false to their States; false to their country,
right or wrong, in the death grapple of war, is not to be
trusted. They will betray us, as they have betrayed their
countrymen of the North."

" Perhaps they would if it was not their interest to do
otherwise. They have no standing except with us, none whatever. They must succeed through us, and by fidelity to our
interests, or sink out of sight. It is their fidelity to their own
interest that is our main reliance. Through this we must succeed."

" But, suppose we do, what will we do with success? That
is the question. Tear out all the amendments to the constitu-
tion? I am not prepared for that."

" No, colonel; we will not tear them all out. If we can
secure pay for our war losses; pensions for our wounded; pay
for our slaves, and then can absolutely control the negro, I
prefer that he should be free. We can secure and compel his
labor at lower than the cost of slavery. There will be no
money invested in the man. That is one saving. We shall
not have to care for them in youth or old age. Neither their
burials nor deaths will be a charge or a loss to us. We will
have his labor and escape his burden. Then, sir, it will be
glorious. Glorious to see the Government, the Washington
we failed to capture, in the hands of our Davises, Johnsons,
Gordons and Hamptons. Glorious to feel that the blue must
supplicate the despised gray for the crumbs that fall from the

Government table.   Ah, colonel, my dear old friend.   If we can only see it before we go.   See the frayed old jackets of gray, and the bonnie blue at their heads, marching to peaceable possession of Washington.   When that day comes I shall be content to say, ' Lord, now lettest thou thy servant depart in peace.' "

The next day Hytoan departed.   Behind him the clouds were gathered and charged with storm.

CHAPTER XXVI.

THE STORM BURSTS OVER SLIMPTON.

During the two days succeeding the departure of General Hytoan, Mrs. Judge Shootfast was the busiest woman in Slimpton. Her carriage stood before the doors of all her old " true to the cause " friends. Not one of them, in a circuit of many miles, was omitted. On the third evening the greater part of them were gathered in her parlors. The Buzzer was there too, in the hands of every gentleman and many of the ladies. Its leader was a stunner.

"The time for action," so read the Buzzer, "has arrived. Friends, countrymen, to your posts. Bury feeling, bury friendships, bury love, bury everything but duty to your State and race. The niggers are organizing with intentions threatening the safety of the white people of the community. That is the fruit of Radicalism. And he who dallies with Radicalism in the State stands, torch in hand, beside a powder magazine, and puts to hazard the safety, honor and lives of those that it should be the pride of manhood to battle for, and, if needs be, die for.* We have men in our midst, Southern men, men who were Confederate soldiers, who are thus dallying, thus standing torch in hand. We blush for them. Shame ! Shame ! Shame ! These men are supporting the Republican ticket; acting in a manner totally offensive to the interests of the white men of our county and against the policy of the Democratic Conservative party. These men are traitors to their country and enemies to their neighbors. Henceforth the honorable ladies and gentlemen of this community should have no moral, social or political associations with them. They are beasts in men's clothing, and henceforth they should not be

* Aberdeen (Miss.) Examiner.

countenanced, nor should we countenance any man or woman
who condescends to associate socially with them.* Let unanimity of sentiment pervade the minds of our people. Let invincible determination be depicted on every countenance.
Drive them from society. Make them lepers and outcasts.
Send them to herd with niggers and Yankees and other dogs.
Rise, fathers! Rise, ladies! Rome demands your aid. Hit
them hip and thigh—everywhere, at all times. Then will woe,
irretrievable woe betide the Radical tatterdemalians." †

Valore and his wife, Bartdale, the nabobs, all were there
and read the Buzzer, and all chattered.

Craft of the Buzzer was there too.

"Noble sentiments—yes, sah, noble sentiments," said Bartdale. " I congratulate you, sah "—(this to the Buzzer editor)
—" yes, congratulate you! Doing glorious service! Yes,
sah ! glorious service to the State."

"And you agree with me, colonel," said the elated
Buzzer.

" Agree with you," replied Bartdale. " Sah, among honorable gentlemen there can be no dissent, no, sah, no dissent.
These renegades. Yes, sah, they are that, renegades and
traitahs, sah, ought to be put down, ought not to be encour-
aged, sah. The idea! The idea, sah. It is monstrous, yes,
monstrous, sah, to give them the ballot and political powah.
Think of it, sah, political powah in the hands of lazy, idle,
shiftless niggahs, sah. It is intolerable, sah, monstrous, sah.
Lazy, idle, ungrateful niggahs. They are free and don't know
what to do with it, sah. They are sinking, going down, yes,
after all we did for them in the good old days, sah. Lazy,
miserable crittahs, sah. Yes, sah, they need masters; need
'em more than evah, sah, and they, it is monstrous to think
of, sah; votahs, and making officers."

Bartdale had aged since the day he huzzahed over the fall
of Sumter at Bugby's, and fortune had dealt hardly with him.
On that day he was " an hundred niggah man," and in debt.
But the increase of negroes paid interest and held him up.

---

* Resolutions Noxumbee (Miss.) Democratic Club.
† Yazoo (Miss.) Democrat.

Emancipation swept away the negroes and the interest paying power of their increase.

Debts swept away the plantation, and Bartdale, in his old age, was a pauper. For a few months he lived on his friends.

But the attrition of bread and butter giving wears out friendship, and Bartdale began to suffer.

Then Jack Bartdale found him.

Jack had been the colonel's slave, and when emancipation came, Jack and his wife bolted.

They were gone for months.

Gone to test if they had the right to stay away. To know if freedom was a mouthing or a fact.

There was no way to know but to try the right to use it.

That tested, Jack returned and found his old master down in the dumps, on the verge of starvation, and talking of suicide.

"Too bad to see ole maws dis yeah way, like no 'count po' white trash."

That was what Jack said when he saw his old master's condition.

Chloe, that was his wife, assented.

After that they supported Bartdale. They labored early and late, denied themselves in a multitude of ways, amply paid when they saw the old colonel, in spotless linen and well brushed clothes, enjoying a laugh with any of his old comrades.

The night that Bartdale stood in the Shootfast parlors, denouncing "idle, worthless niggahs," he was an existence of negro charity; he owed his white shirt, its frills; the clothes on his back, the food within him, and the bloom on his aged cheeks, to the free-will offering of negroes who had been his slaves, to whom he never was either a kind or over indulgent master.

And to-day there are a multitude of Bartdales throughout the South.

Bartdale was not alone in his congratulations to the Buzzer. Its editor strutted in the incense of commendation.

18

Valore had his say. So had others. And Mrs. Shoot-fast was voluble. She did not say that she was part of the inspiration of the Buzzer article. Nevertheless it was a fact. During the Hytoan visit, she resolved on the parlor gathering.

The Buzzer editor was invited. "And an article, a few of your admirable words, you know. So charmingly pointed and piquant; they will lead us up to the point. So delight-fully, my dear Mr. Craft." That was Mrs. Shootfast's sugges-tion. And the words were uttered as we have seen.

With the hot Buzzer pills and the doctress Shootfast and other like minded enchantresses to sugar-coat and adminis-ter them, effects were quickly reached. The assemblage agreed, "hereafter there shall be no social recognition of the Yankee or scallawag, and no social intercourse with those who do recognize them."

Major Dale Cartier alone was gloomy and Erma Cartier tearful.

"Oh, Dale, how shall I ever give up dear Kitty Huntley? and her husband saved your life. Only for him! only for him! oh, Dale! how I shudder when I think of it." Thus Mrs. Cartier sobbed in the ears of her husband.

Dale made no response, only walked away in gloomy silence among the bitter-tongued throng.

The next day many rumors were in the air, and Slimpton was seething.

"The negroes were arming and rising."

So it was rumored, no one knew where, or by whom led, and no one could say who started the rumor.

But it was a fact, confidently asserted.

A and B had said it.

They had mysterious sources of information.

And — well, everybody knew it would come to that.

It was the long-predicted result of emancipation and suffrage.

"Yes, sah!" said one and another, "the ballot has turned the niggahs into demons."

Later in the day there came rumors that masked companies had been riding the night before.

The whites who heard it were jubilant. The negroes, who remembered their experiences immediately after the war, and who had heard of masked companies elsewhere, drew a long breath.

They were troubled. They saw the clouds gathering. They heard the mutterings of the storm.

Its breathings penetrated them with despair.

CHAPTER XXVII.

"IF A D— NIG VOTE AGIN US HE SHALL FOREVER DIE."

Pelter, Savage and Boozy were congenial spirits, and they had found employment that suited them.

Any work of brutality did that.

Of willing material there was no end.

The filthy cabins of the neighborhood were full of the idle, profligate and sinister.

It was but to ask and secure. They asked and enrolled twenty on the first day. Joe Ratley was among them.

Joe was delighted.

He would again hear the crack of the whip.

The crack of the lash was sweeter music in the ears of the Confederate deserter than the whiz of the Union bullets.

"Jine? dag awn, agin niggahs an' no count Yanks? Yaas, yeu bet yo' boots on't! Yaas, sah, put me down quicker'n scat. Dad rat ef it don't make me sick in the innards to see the airs them nigs and Yanks put on."

So Joe's name went down, and other Joe's with him, until Pelter, Savage and Boozy had each a sufficient number for immediate operations.

Then the committee applied to Shootfast for money.

Shootfast went out with one of those pests of moneyed people—a subscription paper.

Everybody hurrahed for the South.

They do elsewhere for railroads and bridges, and tunnels and churches, and for everything else. They are magnificent. Ought to succeed. Ought to be paid for—out of other people's pockets.

This paper was no exception.

The town overflowed with good wishes and words.

Good wishes and words don't deplete the purse—but cash —that was another thing.

Money was more difficult to secure.

Hearts were open and purses closed.

Shootfast found it a difficult task.

A dozen times he was inclined to abandon it.

Thrice a dozen times he roundly swore they were all stingier than Yankees and meaner than niggers.

At last, to his intense relief, he reached the point where he could prudently pay the deficit needed. Then he paused.

The day's work left him doubtful if a little Yankee leaven was not after all a good thing in the town.

"Certainly," he said to his wife after reaching home, " I could have secured three times the sum for any reasonable purpose from half a dozen Yankees in the place and had no words about it."

But the money was raised, turned over to Pelter, Savage and Boozy, and minus some crimping for " cawn juice " it was quickly applied to equipping the eager recruits.

The Pelter company was first on the road.

For half the first night they rode about aimless. Rode about negro cabins, shouting and blowing horns. On the way out some one travestied a sweet hymn, and as they rode they sang it:

> "' A charge to keep I have
> A God to glorify;
> If a d—— nig vote agin us,
> He shall forever die.''*

They liked that.

It suited their depraved natures.

They rolled it under their tongues as a sweet morsel.

It became the " My Maryland " of the new Dixie.

They bellowed it.

They roared it.

And the silent forests echoed back their profanity.

But riding and tooting and singing became monotonous, and like everything monotonous, tiresome.

* Testimony of John Longwood.

It was a bore.

They ought to do something, if only to get their hands in.

Action is the grindstone that sharpens men.

" But what will we do? "

It was past midnight, and they were halted in the road, clustered like a covey of partridges, in the deep shadow of the trees.

Various negro and Yankee names were suggested.

The Yankee was voted down.

" Too airly to tech Yanks. They're ugly customers to handle."

All agreed to that.

An idea dawned upon the dull brain of Joe Ratley.

" Let's give Nig Awk a shake. I don't keer how seveigrous. Ding him, I'd like ter take a squall outen the perked up niggah ! "

" Young Awk? " asked one.

"Gawl, no ! The nigs 'bout his place ur thicker ner bugs in a bed. Git, ole snaggle-tooth Awk. The ole nig's ole an' can't do nuffin."

" That's so," shouted half a dozen.

Pelter was delighted. "Yes, boys, that Awk's a mighty mean Yank nig. Allas hanging about the Yanks and Rads. Let's shuck him."

" Forward ! "

With this command the horses wheeled and dashed away after Pelter.

Two miles of a ride over the hills brought them to Plu-tarch Trenhom's cabin.

It was a pretty little place, embowered in roses and flowering shrubbery.

Reaching the cabin, the horsemen rode in through the gate and dashed up to the door.

Then tney made several circuits about it, racing, shouting, singing and horn-blowing.

Hearing the noise, Awk rose from his bed, and in his night clothes tottered to the door, and seeing tne men tearing through his cherished flower beds, he expostulated. The flowers were the gift of his loved mistress. That he told them. "Deah Miss Lou done gib de seed and plant ebry one o' dem wid her own blessed hans. Deed she did!"

Joe Ratley rode up before him.

"Shet, you drat niggah."

The old man, bent nearly double with age, stood in the doorway looking out at the masked crowd, listening, as if to detect the voice.

Ratley cried out again.

"See how neah I kin come to the nig's head."

Then he raised his pistol and fired.

Probably it was a mere bravado—an effort at intimidation. Awk was not hit.

The smoke lifted slowly up from the doorway, disclosing the old man standing immovable as he was before the shot was fired.

Brave men in the clutch of the inexorable never flinch, and Awk was a brave man.

"Good gen'lemen, I hain't nebber done nuffin to none ob yer."

Several of the maskers had already dismounted and approached the door.

Pelter, pistol in hand, was foremost among them.

"Let's have no niggah gab."

"Mawstah, I ain't gabbin."

"Jist you shet! does yer heah?" said Joe Ratley, plunging his clenched fist into the aged black's face. "Shet an' heah the capin, then yerl git a spell o' breathin'."

The others laughed at Joe's attempt at wit, and Pelter asked:

"Well, Awk, how do you like us?"

"Doan 'o, cap'in!"

"Captain who?" asked Pelter. He was evidently startled, thinking his disguise was penetrated, and having no desire to be discovered.

"Doan 'o. I'ze tryin' to make out."

Pelter breathed more freely.

"An' you can't make us out?"

" No, sah, not pe'tic'lah! "

" Do you know any of us! "

" I doan 'o as I mos'ly does, sah! "

" Well got up, hain't we? "

" You'ze mighty skeary."

" You'll be skeered a dawg'd sight wuss foah we uns gits through with yer," interjected Ratley.

" You just bet! " added another.

" He'll think a whirlicane's done struck him."

" What hez I bin doin', mawstahs? "

" Doin'! Doin'! You drat niggah," responded Pelter. " Hear him, boys. Innercent niggah, what nebbah stole a chicken."

" I nebbah stole nuffin, mawstah."

" No, but you've done a dawg'd sight wuss, hain't ye? "

" No, mawstah! "

" Yes, you have! "

" Infernal, lying niggah! "

" Choke him."

" Hain't you been voting the Radical ticket? "

A half dozen tongues were moving at once.

" I bin well sposed wid de 'Publicans, sah," replied Awk.

" And you voted with them? "

" Yes, sah! dat pawty's 'titled to my reward, sah! "

" Well, you've got to stop it."

" Yes, sah! "

" You hear? "

" Yes, sah! "

" And you've got to promise not to vote the Republican ticket any more? "

" I can't do dat, mawstah." Awk had straightened up as far as was possible for him. " No, mawstah; I can't do dat."

" You won't? "

" No, mawstah; dat pawty made de culled people free, sah, an' dey is 'titled to ouah reward, sah. 'Deed, sah, dey is 'titled to ouah reward in dis yeah world."

" And you are going to keep on voting with them? "

" So long as dey does de right, sah, an' de good Lawd gibs

me to sense de right sah. Yes, mawstah, I mus' do dat. Dey mus' hab ouah reward for de freedom."

"Now, look here, Awk, we don't want to hurt you, but dawg'd ef yo' hain't got to vote the Democratic ticket or die."

"Mawstah, I hain't got no ambition agin the Democrats, but I can't go trapousin' after dem. No, sah!"

"Heah him!"

"Pooty nig!"

"Ongrateful ole dawg!"

"Let's hang him."

"Let's skin him."

"Oh, yer can't, hey?"

"No, sah! When I done jine the 'Publicans I hearn de Democrat pawty were waw busted, an' I done hab nuffin ter do wid dem sense."

"Well, my colored angel, you've got ter reform. Does yer hear? Reform!"

Reform is the patent coating for every scoundrelism.

Hearing no response from Awk, Pelter asked him again.

"Awk, if we let up on you will you promise to vote the Democratic ticket?"

"No, sah!"

"Would you rather take a lickin'?"

"No, sah! Hain't I a free man? What right you got to lick me? My old mawstah didn't nebbah do dat."

"We'll give you a taste to see how it goes."

"I don't want none o' dat foolin'."

"There ain't goin' to be no foolin'. You've had too much meat an' too little cuttin' all yer'n born days, or yer wouldn't be such an audacious sassy niggah!"

"I ain't sassy, mawstah! Ef I is, I axes pawdon, sah. My old mawstah done fotch me up with mannahs, sah!"

"Hear the niggah!"

"Oh, ho!"

"Mannahs! 'Hoop! Mannahs!"

"Better nor the clown in a circus!"

"Ebo Shin scraping to the ladies!"

These are samples of exclamations that flowed from the group when the laugh ceased.

Pelter raised his voice above the din :

" Jest drop yer hoofs in the path and come 'long."

" What for, mawstah ? "

" We're gwan to lick yer."

" Oh, no, mawstah ! You haint de hawt to do dat, mawstah. Wid a po' ole man. Mo'an seventy, sah. Mo'an seventy yeahs—an' moas done gone."

" Ther' haint no use o' gabblement about it ; you've either got to vote the Democratic ticket or take a lickin'."

" Yes, sah ! "

" Will you vote the Democratic ticket ? "

" No, sah."

" You would rather be licked ? "

" I'd rader die fust, sah ! Yes, sah, I'd rader die fust ! "

At this point Joe Ratley threw his halter over the old man's neck, and mounted his horse.

In an instant the others were in the saddle, and trotted out· in the road, compelling their aged prisoner to run beside them.

Down the road into the edge of the neighboring forest.

There a halt.

Awk was stripped of his night clothes. Stripped to nudity. Two men seized his arms. They drew his breast against a tree. They clasped his arms about it ; and then tied his wrists.

Then they searched about among the low lying limbs for long lithe rods.

Deliberately they cut them off and trimmed them down, paring off the soft green leaves and young branches. This was but the work of a few moments. Then they turned to Plutarch. Joe Ratley stood first by his side. He bent the long, strong rod he held in his right hand, to test its litheness.

Under the soft, clear moonlight that stole down between the trees, jagged points, quite half an inch in length, were plainly discernible on his rod.

These were the stumps of the little branches cut off.

With every blow of his rod these points would puncture like daggers.

They would tear like harrows.

When the pliability of the rod was tested, Joe stepped away from Plutarch to the length of his rod.

He raised his right arm.

His right hand grasping the rod, was extended above and behind his head.

His left side was facing the left side of the man bound to the tree.

His breast was almost parallel with Plutarch's back.

Joe's body swung suddenly round toward Plutarch.

His hand and arm came down with a rush.

The rod whistled through the air.

It fell upon the center of Plutarch's back.

The keen edge of the rod cut.

Its sharp prongs stabbed.

The rod scorched.

It blistered.

It burned.

A long wheal sprang into being across Plutarch's back.

It was a fungus born of a rod.

The tree to which Plutarch was bound was small, and apart from the others.

The sky above was cloudless.

A luminous circle girdled the tree.

Within the circle there was an involuntary writhing of Plutarch's back.

Then purple drops spurted out.

Joe saw them.

He roared in glee:

" Fust blood, by dawg. I kin fetch it ev'ry lick."

He sprang back to striking position and raised his arm and hand again.

Pelter cried out, " Hold on Joe ! "

But it was too late.

Joe's eager arm fell.

A second time the rod whistled through the air.

A second wheal grew up beside the first.

Again Plutarch's back shivered as if he had been smitten with an iceberg.

That was the first effect of the blow.

It was a biting frost.

It chilled him to the marrow.

His flesh shivered under it.

Then the second long blister sprang into life beside the first.

The blister was a fagot.

It was a flame.

It was a consuming fire.

The rod was a bar of red hot, seething iron across his back.

It opened new fountains of blood.

Big drops trickled down to the ground.

Then Pelter spoke:

"Look heah, Awk; hain't yer had enough?"

"Yes, mawstah!"

The words trembled from his lips.

"You don't want no more harryment?"

"No mawstah!"

"Will you vote the Democratic ticket?"

"No, mawstah!"

His voice was strong and firm.

"You'd rather git moah lickin'?"

"I'd rather die, mawstah, dan go agin de pawty ob freedom."

His torn flesh ceased to quiver.

His voice burst out strong and clear.

It was a cry of exultation.

It quenched the ache and the burn, and the torture.

The words were scarcely uttered before the hissing serpent in Joe Ratley's hand, with its lacerating fangs, whistled through the air and fell upon the old man's back.

Again.

And again. With the passionate energy of ignorant hate.

Blood flowed every blow.

Little shreds of cuticle and flesh clung to the rod.

Blood trickled down in little streams.

Ten blows Joe Ratley struck.

Ten blows with all his brutal strength.

Then another of the gang interposed.

" Dawg it, Joe, ye'r gittin' all the fun."

Joe was pushed aside.

A fresh arm was raised.

" Now, boys, see me hit an old plantation lick, bitin' with the point."

The brute seemed to measure his distance from Awk with his eye.

He drew the rod quickly through his left hand.

He threw his right hand upward and backward.

The right arm fell with the velocity of a thunderbolt.

The rod whizzed through the air.

The point of the rod struck Plutarch's side.

It bit like a hound.

A shred of flesh flew before it.

It gashed like a knife.

A stream of blood spurted out after it.

The crowd ran to the side of the sufferer.

They examined the gash.

Then they exclaimed:

" Yo' did, by dawg! "

" Drat ef 'tain't a clean 'lick!' "

" Hain't forgot, hez yo'? "

The victim's back was alive with motion.

His lips were sealed.

His mouth was dead.

It was an emulous crowd.

The bite blow excited their admiration.

They tried to imitate.

They failed.

And the man who " hadn't forgot" was the hero of the night.

The shower of blows continued.

It was a storm of live coals.

When fifty blows had been struck Pelter spoke again.

" Awk, hain't yo' had all yo' want?"

It was nearly a minute before Awk's lips opened.

All his senses except feeling were numb.

Sound penetrated his soul, but slowly.

At last he spoke.

His voice was faint.

His words almost inaudible.

" Yaas, mawstah! "

" Will you vote the Democrat ticket?"

" I'd-rader-die-fust-mawstah! "

" Will you quit the dratted rads? "

" Dey's–de–pawty–ob–freedom–an'–'titled–to–ouah–reward –mawstaa! "

" You won't give them up, drat yo'! "

" I can't, mawstah; I can't do dat, mawstah! Dey's de pawty ob freedom, mawstah! "

His head was erect.

His voice rang out like a clarion on the calm night air.

Unflinchingly he faced laceration.

Unawed he endured rending.

He hung undaunted on the spit of wrath.

It was grand.

It was heroic.

He was a nineteenth century Huss.

Awk Trenhom was a martyr.

Again the scorching, blistering, tearing storm descended.

Whiz! whiz!

Thud! thud!

Blood spattered out.

Shreds of flesh followed every blow.

Awk's head dropped over against the tree.

Whiz! whiz!

Thud! thud!

A rain of blood followed every blow.

Awk's head hung limp over his shoulder.

His knees bent under him.

Whiz! whiz!

His knees gave way.

Whiz! whiz!

Thud! thud!

The weight of Awk's body rested on his bound hands and arms.

Whiz! whiz!

The arms slowly slid down the tree.

Whiz! whiz!

Pelter spoke.

"Will yo' give up the rads?"

There was no answer.

Whiz! whiz!

Again Pelter spoke.

"Will yo' give up the dratted rads?"

Awk was deaf and dumb.

He was a crouching, horribly mutilated heap, limp as a rag, at the roots of the tree.

The inquisitors and assassins thought he was dead. They wiped the clots and splotches of blood from their faces, brushed off the spray of human flesh from their persons, mounted their horses, and rode away singing:

> 'If you wants to be an angel,
> And with the angels stand,
> Bring niggahs to their senses,
> With a hick'ry in your hand."

CHAPTER XXVIII.

THE COAT DONE BRUSH'D.

On the day following the outrage by the Pelter gang upon Awk, Mrs. Trenhom and Mrs. Huntley, in a full glory of ribbons and spotless gloves, drove out to call on their friends.

First, on Mrs. Shootfast.

" Not at home."

Then, on Mrs. Valore.

" Not at home."

Then to a dozen other places.

" Not at home."   " Not at home."

These three little words, the most convenient and universal of society lies, became quite familiar to their ears.

What did it mean?

Then they remembered the Buzzer.

" Surely they can not have resolved to close their doors against us."

" Against me ! " said Mrs. Trenhom, with emphasis and some anger.

Even very gentle people will be angry under such circumstances.

Mrs. Huntley alighted at the post-office.   Mrs. Trenhom drove home.

She was distressed.

But as she entered the house she instantly saw a deeper distress stamped on the face of her husband.

" What is it, Walter ? " she said, as she walked across the room toward him.

Walter walked the floor, with set jaws and stern eyes, as men sometimes will who are too wrathful to turn their tongues loose.

There are men wise enough to know that an angry tongue is a wild beast which needs a cage. And like animals in a menagerie they pace off their wrath between bars.

"Surely," continued his wife, " you can not have heard of our calling already? That is nothing, dear."

She had taken his arm, and was walking to and fro by his side, looking up in his face.

Trenhom paused, lifted his eyebrows to their widest.

"Calling, Lou ! "

" Oh, dear ! I thought perhaps you knew."

Then he took both her hands in his own and drew her to the lounge beside him.

" What is it, Lou?"

" Nothing, dear, worthy your attention."

" But something has occurred?"

Mrs. Trenhom hesitated. Looking earnestly in her husband's eyes, then she put up her hands and passed them over his cheeks.

" I wouldn't ask, dear, to-day—not to-day—perhaps—perhaps there is a mistake—some mistake and—I fear you have trouble enough for one day."

Then a recollection of the Buzzer article came to Trenhom.

"Surely it can be nothing about the Buzzer vileness? "

" I don't know, dear."

" A-a-h ! Is it pos-si-ble ! They have refused to receive —you—you—my wife ! Your father's daughter ! Your own noble self ! Oh ! No ! That can not be ! "

Mrs. Trenhom sat silent, a slight flush came into her face, a moisture in her eyes, as her husband again clasped both of her hands in his.

" Tell me, Lou ! Tell me that it is not so ! "

" I fear that it is, Walter." Then she narrated the events of the afternoon. When her husband heard it he exclaimed in broken tones:

" Oh, Lou ! Lou ! That I should have caused you this pain ! "

" I do not think it pains me ! "

19

" This humiliation ! "

" It certainly is not that, Walter."

" This trouble, then ! "

" Yes, it is trouble. But they can not humiliate me, Walter. No one can do that for another. Our own acts are the only chariots on which we can ride into the valley of humiliation."

" Oh, Lou ! How sorry, sorry I am."

" Do not give it a second thought, Walter. We could be very happy alone on a desert island."

" But to be surrounded by life-long friends who refuse to recognize you."

" It is their fault, dear, not mine. I have only love for them. If they choose to return it with hate it will injure them more than either of us."

" It grieves me that I should be the cause of it."

" Put your grief away, Walter. So long as you are doing your duty, walking beside your conscience, there is nothing to grieve about."

" And you are satisfied? "

" Yes, dear, more than satisfied. If I were a man I would try to do as you are doing," and she drew his face down to her and kissed it.

" Thank you ! "

" I am happy in the belief that you are doing your duty to your country, and though you may fail, the work you have begun can not. It will result in a more perfect freedom and greater happiness to the people."

" Let us hope so."

" I am sure of it, Walter. The good God is marching the race forward. The ignorance and superstition of the past and the prejudices that grow out of them, may scatter thistles and sow thorns in the path, but neither, dear, are a permanent obstruction to the truth."

" Ah, Lou ! You were always hopeful."

" And you, Walter, always honest and doing your duty as you came to see it. That knowledge is better to me than all friendships, no matter how close."

"I am very glad."

"But did you not hear of it before I entered ?"

"No, Lou."

"I thought perhaps you did."

"No !"

"But you were troubled about something."

"Yes ! Greatly ! Deeply !"

"What is it, Walter ?"

"An outrage !"

"Outrage ?"

"A horrible outrage !"

"On whom ?"

"Poor old Awk !"

"No! No!" Mrs. Trenhom sprang to her feet. Her eyes blazed with excitement. "When ? Where ? How ? By whom, Walter ?"

"At his home, last night, by masked men."

"Ah !" She trembled from head to foot.

"Injured ?"

"Fearfully !"

"How ?"

"With rods !"

"Merciful heavens ! " Wringing her hands and weeping. "Where is he ? Dear old Awk !"

"Yes ! Dear old Awk !"

"To beat so aged a man !"

"It was barbarous !"

"And severely ?"

"It was a cruel, horrible laceration !"

"Where is he ? I must go to him !"

"I had him brought here. He is up-stairs. Wait a moment and we will go up."

"When did you hear of it ?"

"A few moments after you rode out. Some colored people discovered him bound to a tree, and knowing that he had been one of our servants, brought him here."

"And poor Awk, did he not desire to come ?"

"He was insensible !"

"Oh!" More hand-wringing.

"Has he yet come to?"

"No!"

Mrs. Trenhom started toward the door.

"Wait a little, Lou, until his wounds are dressed, and we will go to him; they are not fit for you to look at."

Mrs. Trenhom shuddered as she asked —

"Have you seen them?"

The strong man raised his hands before his eyes.

"Good heavens, yes! And I never want to look upon such a sight again. It was sickening! sickening! I have seen mutilation on the battle-field! I witnessed the disfigurements, the trunkation, the horrors of four years of bloody war, but I never saw anything so dreadful, dreadful at this."

"Oh! oh! Poor Awk! Dear, faithful old Awk! I must go to him!"

"As he is?"

"He is our dear, faithful old friend—faithful old Awk, and I must go to him."

"Can you endure it?"

"I must, Walter! I will! Dear! Dear, faithful old friend! He would not stay away from us one minute."

Followed by her husband, she hurried to the room where Plutarch Trenhom lay, suffering, moaning, and insensible.

The wounds on the lower part of his body were already dressed.

But Mrs. Trenhom saw the laceration from the center of his back to the neck.

When she first looked on the shocking mutilation, she shuddered and tottered.

Her husband reached out his arms.

Then she walked steadily up to the bed and gave assistance.

With soft and gentle touch she aided in applying lotions and bandages until the binding was complete.

Then she sat down by the bedside.

She was the first object that Awk looked on when he opened his eyes.

" Deah Miss Lou!"

" Yes, my poor old friend!"

" An' Maws Walt!"

" Here, Awk," said Walter, stepping to the bedside.

" I moas can't see you, mawstah."

Walter bended lower over him.

" Ah!" continued the old man. " Yis, dat's you, Maws Walt. I nussed you when a chile. An' yer ain't gwan ter forgit yo' old Awk."

" No, uncle, never in this world."

" An' Miss Lou! You'll remembah de ole man?"

She bent over him and pressed her lips against his black and wrinkled cheek.

" My poor old friend!"

The old man's eyes lighted up.

" You'ze allus good, honey. Allus good, honey! Dat's like de breff ob de angels!"

" Poor Awk, you'll be spared to us to take care of."

" No, honey; de ole man's moas done gone,—moas done gone. I'ze gittin' up to de lass' hill in de row, honey. Yes, moas dah, honey! De coat moas brush! moas done brush, honey." He paused a moment for breath. " Honey! Put yo' face down to de ole man once moa! One time moa, honey!"

Mrs. Trenhom's lips dropped down on his cheeks.

She kissed him.

The tears rained down upon his cheek.

A smile played upon the old man's lips.

" Dat's de breff ob heabin, honey. Heabin, honey. I'll tell yo' muddah, up dere! Dat I will, chile. Good chile— deah honey! I'll tell yo' angel muddah up dere! De—coat— done—brush!"

And Awk—slave and freeman—had left his seventy years of toil and suffering behind him.

While Walter Trenhom and his wife were looking tearfully down upon the lifeless remains of Plutarch, another scene was transpiring in the post-office.

Mrs. Erma Cartier entered it, heavily veiled, looked, discovered the front office vacant, and hurried through to the private room of Mrs. Kate Huntley, Yankee and postmistress.

Seeing her, Erma Cartier clasped her in her arms.

"Dear Kitty, you are not angry with me?"

"I!" replied Kate, rising and looking at her in wonder.

"It would break my heart, Kitty. Indeed it would."

"I don't understand, dear!"

"Oh! I was at home. Indeed I was."

Mrs. Huntley was surprised, and she looked it.

"But!" continued her excited visitor, "I couldn't help it. Indeed I couldn't. They have all resolved. It is so shameful. But I can't help myself, dear."

"I am sure of it," responded Mrs. Huntley, soothingly.

"Oh! please, Kitty, remember, no matter what comes, I shall love you always, always, dearly. I can never forget that your husband saved mine. But for his heroism my Dale would be dead! dead! and I with him."

"But your husband?"

"Oh, Kitty! He remembers, too. He does. Indeed he does! But what can he do? They are all set. All! All! And it is so shameful!"

"Yes, I think it is shameful."

"You won't blame me, dear. I shall never love you any the less. Nothing can change that. But I am so helpless. Dale says I must not come and I must not receive you in my home. Oh, dear! I have cried all night about it. And Hal saved his precious life. And I can't quarrel with Dale. It would kill me if he was angry with me."

"If your husband directs it, there is nothing for you, dear, but compliance," responds Kate, slowly.

"And you will not put me out of your heart?"

"No, dear!"

"And you will kiss me?"

Erma opened her arms.

The other woman entered them.

Erma clung to her, kissed her passionately, again and again, drew down her veil, and walked away.

The storm had burst over Slimpton.

CHAPTER XXIX.

POST OAKS AND HICKORIES.

The issue of the Slimpton Buzzer following the inhuman scourging and death of Plutarch Trenhom gave its version of it. It made use of the torture and tragedy as new fuel to the rising flame.

"We have warned our people," so read the Buzzer, "and there were many who thought our alarm unfounded. We have had most reliable information that the abolition radicals in the land of hickory hams and wooden nutmegs have raised a large sum of money to arm the niggers of the South. This means outrage and murder, and they intend it as such. We have proof that five hundred guns have already been sent to this county, and that more are coming. And their cut-throat emissaries are now here drilling the incendiary niggers and organizing them for masked maraudings against the lives and property of our peaceable citizens. Only three nights ago a band of these masked niggers attacked an old black man named Awk Trenhom. Many of our citizens will perhaps remember him. And what was his crime. Men of the South, think of it. Men who wore the gray, let it sink in your hearts. The old man had declared he was done with Radicalism. Yes! That was it! He was going to vote for reform; for law and order; for the Democratic ticket, and a lot of scoundrelly niggers dragged him from his home in the dead of night and beat him to death. But behind them—mark you it is only a whisper so far—we await proofs before asserting—it is alleged is one who by reason of the past ought to have stood by the old man, if necessary laid down his life for him, it is alleged that this man, learning that Awk was about to spurn Radicalism and all its kindred diabolism, prompted his taking off. Friends and countrymen, and comrades of the gray, how long shall we submit? To this complexion it has come at last. How long shall we submit? Post oaks and hickories are hung with mast that is good for hogs. A good crop of niggers, carpet-baggers and scallawags on post oaks and hickories would be good for buzzards and—Mississippi. How is that for high?" *

The Awk Trenhom tragedy removed a calm and commanding influence from the negro councils, and in the Buzzer setting it deepened the excitement of the public mind.

It was crafty.

And it prepared the people to hear of other outrages and to approve of any retaliatory measures.

Among the old Confederates it dispersed dissent.

If there was any hostility to the use of force it disappeared.

If there was any doubt of unanimity in favor of violence, it fled away.

The men who prepared for the lightning did it with skill.

A military company was openly organized, with Major Dale Cartier in command, to protect the people.

And the "1900" went forward with their work.

The first act of brutality was to them a mere whetting of appetite A "nip" before lunch.

Some men are born brutal.

As children they stick pins in bugs and worms, and gloat over their convulsions and witherings.

With the mass brutality is a growth.

At first it shocks.

Then they grow to it as medical students do to the loathsomeness of the dissecting room.

As men who work among rotting bones and villainous smells come to like the fetid vapors.

The lash and the bloodhound are not humanizers.

Those of the "1900" who grew up beside these adjuncts of Southern civilization were already hardened.

* A fact.

Their feelings were long ago annealed in the furnace of cruelty.

The younger—those who grew up since the war—were less savage.

But there was sure matriculation in lashing and looking on.

Brutality witnessed and assented to is a corrosive in the bowels of mercy.

Soon the younger had no more bowels than the older.

Night after night they rode the county, first this way then that.

Joe Ratley was always with this command.

Free whisky and wolloping niggahs were irresistible attractions to Joe.

After his second night's ride he carried home his disguise.

In the morning Lindy saw it.

She had already heard of poor old Awk.

She turned the black calico robe and mask with its peepholes over and over.

At length it dawned upon her what they were.

Then she rolled them up and walked toward the open fireplace.

Joe saw the movement.

"Heah! what yer at?"

Lindy held the parcel out before her with one hand.

Held it out as if it was some foul thing she disdained to touch.

With the other hand she raked the glowing coals and stirred the fire.

"Let be, yer heah! Let be!"

The fire was glowing, and Lindy dropped the parcel in its center.

Joe rushed toward the fire.

Lindy faced about and looked at him.

Joe paused, looked, then burst out.

"Them costs a heap."

The same soft, even tones that murmured to him when he lay bound on the floor, answered back:

"I reckon, but they ain't healthy here, Joe."

"Ain't a fellar to have no fun wi' the niggahs?"

"The best fun I know of would be to work honest as they do, and let them alone."

"Oh, drat it!"

"Best not swear, Joe!"

"I don't like nigs no how."

"No, Joe, nor nothing honest."

"Nice woman you be to tell your man he hain't honest."

"I ain't good at words, Joe, and I must say things as I see them. But if I was a niggah I think I would kill you, Joe."

A little color, a little shading, a little raging in the voice would have suited Joe.

The words of years had been running down into the hollow of his mind and dammed up.

If there was but an opportunity for them to work out.

But what chance was there against this dispassionate music?

None.

And Joe was afraid—he never said it to himself in words, but he was afraid of this woman.

Cowards always tremble in the presence of the unintelligible.

Without further words he turned away.

That night he rode with Captain Pelter.

He did every night.

But he found no entrance to his cabin late in the night.

The door was sealed against him.

When he rode late at night he was compelled to sleep in the corn crib.

But Joe rode and came to be recognized as one of the most devoted of his country's purifiers.

The second night after the Awk Trenhom affair they took a prominent young colored man from his cabin.

They charged him with being one of the murderers of Awk.

Yes!

They had positive evidence, so they said.

He protested his innocence—protested against the violence.

They took him to a grove and sat in mock judgment over him.

"You shall have a fair trial if that's what you want. Here, you can pick out twelve of us. Be tried if you will by a jury of twelve of your honest, intelligent countrymen."

The colored man picked the twelve.

Pelter, in mask, sat as judge.

Pelter called the witnesses, one two, three, four.

Each man answered to his number.

"Do you know anything about this charge?"

"Oh, yes! know all about it. Saw the prisoner take Awk away from home; heard his threats; followed him to the woods, heard the blows; became frightened; ran away; afterwards saw Awk dead."

Each witness told the same tale.

The black man questioned and pleaded.

Judge Pelter charged the jury.

The mock jury decided,

"Guilty."

Sentence of the court:

"One hundred lashes on the bare back, well laid on."

The sentence was executed promptly.

That was the biggest fun of all.

"Better ner a camp meetin'."

So said they, every one.

And they rode away from their torn and lacerated victim in high glee.

On the way home they met two colored men walking in the road.

"Niggers no business out that time of night."

"As we waltz by let's fire."

"Agreed!"

They plunged spurs into their horses' flanks.

As they galloped past the negroes they fired.

One, Jeff Gregory, was shot through the bowels, and died three days after in great agony.

The other, Hugh Gregory, had both legs broken.*

The moaning and agony lay in the road.

The "1900" disappeared in a cloud of dust, filling the air with their huzzahs and oaths.

"Oh! Cap'en, hole on!"

It was Joe that shouted from the middle of the column.

"Yan's the cabin of the niggah preachah; he swawrs he's gwan ter vote the rad ticket shoa'. Let's give him a histe."

Then the party whirled up the lane and paused before the cabin door.

"Hello! Hello!"

"Hello! Come out here!"

The door opened. An aged colored man stood in the gap.

"Does you want me, friends."

"Friends!"

"How mitey polite!"

"Bully for ole Hallelujah!"

"I say, daddy, are you goin' to vote the radical ticket?"

"That's my conscience, sah!"

"You've got to vote the Democrat ticket whole hog this time."

"I'd like to obleege white gentlemen, sah! But I can't do that."

"You're a drat fool!"

"I have only such sense, sah, as my Lord and Master gave me sah."

"If you vote the Radical ticket you're a dead man, sure!"

"If it's the Lord's will, I am satisfied, sah!"

"You'll go dead as sure as shootin'."

"I will have to die, then, for I must do my duty as I see it, sah, and vote the Republican ticket."

The last sentence had not passed his lips before there was a flash, and sharp report.

The old man staggered on to the beaten ground in front of his cabin.

It was Joe Ratley who did the dastardly act.

There was another flash and report.

*A fact.

An aged colored woman tottered to the door in her night dress.

"Keep back, there!" shouted one of the maskers, "or I'll blow your black head off!"

The woman saw her husband before her.

He had fallen to his knees.

His hands uplifted in devotion.

She, too, threw up her hands and lifted her voice.

"Oh! my blessed Lord! Oh! my blessed Jesus!

Flash! Flash! Flash! Bang! Bang! Bang!"

Slowly the kneeling man fell over on his side.

Fifteen shots were fired, and he still lay writhing, a tortured worm on the hard earth.

The woman's cries rose above the din, penetrating the heavens.

"Oh! my merciful Lord! My merciful Jesus!"

One of the men dismounted, and seeing that the colored man yet lived, he detached the powder horn from his side and pushed it under the dying preacher's head.

Then he placed a long strip of paper in the open mouth of the full powder horn.

He ignited the paper and sprang back from it.*

The paper burned slowly.

The blaze approached the nozzle of the horn.

It touched it.

There was a loud explosion.

Bones, flesh, and slime of brain were scattered upon the earth and the walls of the cabin.

The woman in the doorway had been held back from her husband.

As the explosion filled her horrified ears she threw up her hands, cried out in a voice of mortal agony, "Oh, my God!"

The men who held her released their clutch.

She tottered out of the doorway, and fell forward prostrate on her face.

On the morrow passers-by found the two, the aged preacher and his wife, lying prone on the earth before the cabin door.

And they were dead.

* A fact, as testified to by John Culpepper.

CHAPTER XXX.

THE TIDE OF PASSION.

Little pots boil quick.

Slimpton was in an uproar.

The outrages committed were known and magnified.

Then followed charge and counter charge.

Affirmation and denial.

" It was the whites who did it," said one.

" It was the blacks," said another.

Words are bellows to the coals of anger.

Strong words whirled through the town and fanned the excitement into a flame.

If any of the whites were shocked in the morning, at night the number who failed to approve were few

When Valore heard of the murder of the colored preacher, he was wrathful.

" Knew the old man ! Honest ! Inoffensive ! The perpetrators of the crime ought to be punished."

The knowing ones turned upon Valore.

Line upon line. Fact after fact. Coined for the purpose, of course. At first he doubted. Then he was shaken. Then convinced. He believed, as he was assured, that " the outrage was the work of masked negroes, who killed the old man to prevent him from voting the Democratic ticket."

He came into town fuming against white ruffians.

He went home raging against Republican brutality.

As the days rolled on the excitement grew.

In the furnace of words it intensified into passion.

Then came the Buzzer, charging all the outrages upon the Republicans, calling for organization and arms, denouncing Yankees, denouncing Southern renegades.

The conclusion of the article was this:

" Every man in this community, yea, every white man in the State, should be prepared for the emergency. You and your family's welfare demand this of you. It is too late when the hour arrives, to see if your guns and pistols and arms are in place. Is your powder dry? Are your caps sure to explode? A word to the wise is sufficient. Do not permit your energies to be repressed by well-meant appeals to what is called moderation. Moderation means apathy. And apathy means defeat and death. No victory was ever won by moderation. Don't be intimidated by talk of the Federal army. The man who talks of this army is a traitor. Spot him. They can not and dare not use it against us. We learn that some Yankees among us loudly talk of 'it ; that they threaten to call in the army for their protection. If they need an army, let them go where the army is. ' There have always been too many dogs in this country, and since the surrender we have had an influx of the Puritan breed that is very annoying. Shot-guns are best to use on this breed. Pimps, purps and Puritans had better hunt their holes if they don't want to be skinned alive.' " *

The article was exciting.

It was oil to fire.

But in another part of the paper were a few words in strong lines that created an even profounder agitation.

Advertisements are usually dry reading.

They lack the yeasting power for a ferment.

This advertisement was an exception.

The words were few and simple, but they were yeast in the Slimpton mind.

These were the words:

COTTON MILL FOR SALE.

THE SLIMPTON COTTON MILLS,
one of the
BEST APPOINTED IN THE STATE,
Will be positively closed on Saturday, and
WILL BE SOLD WITHIN THIRTY DAYS.

*Brandon, Miss., Republican.

If not sold then the machinery will be removed and the building and mill-site will be offered for sale.

Terms Cash or exchange for Northern property only.

JONATHAN SEEKPEACE, Proprietor.

Men read the advertisement and looked at each other.

"My Gawd! they hain't goin' to shet the mills be they?"

A committee was appointed.

The great American engine never moves without a committee on the fire-box.

The committee put their heads together, appointed a chairman and walked over to the office of the mills.

The proprietor saw them.

"Good morning, gentlemen."

"Mawnin'."

"How'de."

"Hum! Hum!" began Shootfast; he was the chairman.

"Mr. Seekpeace, we have seen an advertisement."

"Yes, want to buy?"

"We?"

"Yes, you say you saw the advertisement and called. Supposed you desired to purchase. Good property!"

"No! It is not quite in our way, Mr. Seekpeace, and I think perhaps if it was we would have some difficulty in raising the necessary money!"

"Ah! Then I hope you'll excuse me. I am very busy perfecting arrangements to close down on Saturday."

"That is what we came to talk about."

"There is nothing to talk about, gentlemen, unless you are prepared to purchase."

"But we don't want the mill to close."

"Ah! Is it my property, or yours?"

"Yours, of course! Yours, of course, sah!"

"Then, gentlemen, I claim the right to manage it as shall suit my own convenience and interests."

"But every gentleman owes something to the community in which he lives."

"And what may that be, sir?"

"Not needlessly to throw laborers out of employment, to

close a good market against producers, or to diminish the money the business puts in circulation."

"Why, judge, I thought you were opposed to mills and new fangled improvements."

"In the abstract, I am; for myself, yes; but this one is quite different; quite different, sah; it is of great value to the community."

"Then judge, I hope the community will buy it."

"You surely are not in earnest?"

"Yes, judge, I am!"

"And if not sold you will remove the machinery?"

"I positively will."

"I supposed it was a profitable investment."

"It has been so"

"And has it ceased?"

"Find me a purchaser and I will convince him in one hour it never was so profitable as it is to-day."

"Singular, sah! Singular! I think I express the sentiments of all the committee. We do not understand that." The committee nodded.

"I do not wish to be offensive, gentlemen, but I do not think it is necessary you should understand."

The committee opened their eyes. "But," continued the mill-owner, "as you are here I will say this to you: You, judge, said something of the duty a man owes to the community in which he lives."

Shootfast nodded. Mr. Seekpeace continued: "Did you ever consider the duty the community owes to a man and his family?"

"To protect! To protect them, of course!"

"Yes. More than that; to treat them as beings of feeling and affections."

"Have not you and your family always been treated with courtesy?"

"By you, judge, yes. By some others, yes. By the ladies of your family, no. By your ministers, no. My family attend church regularly. The adult members of my family belong to church. I have lived here eight years. During that time my

20

wife has been sick nigh unto death, and children have been born to me; and no minister of the gospel has ever crossed my threshold."

"I know! I know! Some of our ministers have not forgotten. The weak and non-combatants always cherish bitterness the longest. But surely our ladies have a right to select their own friendships."

"Undoubtedly they have. I only speak of it to show how far the community has had regard to our feelings and affections."

"And have you determined to sell because of this?"

"Not at all. I have jogged on eight years making money and content to wait for improvement. The articles in the Buzzer and the sentiment in the community convinces me they are striding backward instead of forward."

"Oh, that!"

"Yes, gentlemen, that!"

"Surprised! Surprised! Surely you do not take offence at that?"

"At the Buzzer articles and the applause that follows them?"

"Yes, my dear sah! They are not aimed at you. They don't mean you."

"Do you not see that we Northern people are called thieves and dogs?"

"Oh, yes; we read them, certainly."

"And approve?"

"In a general way. In a general way, of course. But, my dear sah, you surprise us. That don't mean you; not at all. Not at all, sah. We make an exception of you. Yes, sah; we make an exception of you."

"I am a Northern man and, during the war, a loyal man."

"Certainly, certainly, sah. But you are one of us now, and we have the more respect for you because you were true to your section. For myself, I say it openly, I despise traitors to their people, North or South."

"No, gentlemen; I am not one of you."

"Oh, yes, you are, sah. So are all Northern men who

come here to attend to their business. It is only the kiawpet-baggahs. Yes, sah, the kiawpet-baggahs who are not of us."

" Yet many of our own leading people are carpet-baggers."

" We refer to politicians."

" I mean them too. Some of your own leading politicians are from Georgia and Alabama.

" True, sah. But those are Southern States, and the people who come from them Southern men. Of course they are not kiawpet-baggahs. By kiawpet-baggahs, we mean the radicals from the Nawth, and we never have classed you with them, sah. You have taken no part in politics."

" But I claim the right to do so if I desire."

" Certainly, certainly; but with us."

" For you or against you, as shall satisfy my own sense of right."

" Certainly not against us! Not against us! "

" Yes, sir, against you if my opinions lead me that way."

" Oh! "

" Am I free? "

" Certainly, sah! "

" How can there be freedom if the right to exercise it is denied? "

" But it is not denied here. No, sah! We invite perfect freedom. Yes, sah! perfect freedom,—most perfect freedom, sah."

" But suppose I think you are wrong? "

" You can not think that, sah."

" Suppose I openly vote against you? "

" It would be an act of enmity, yes, enmity, sah! of open enmity to us. And you could not do that, sah! "

" Thus by declaring a vote against you an act of enmity you abridge the freedom of suffrage. Do you not see that? "

" Not at all, not at all, sah! the enmity is the other way, quite the other way. The man who votes against us is our enemy; yes, our enemy, and the ballot is his method of declaring it. Nothing can be clearer than that! No, sah, nothing clearer than that. No one who is not our enemy will do it."

"Well, gentlemen, I prefer to live where my vote will not be regarded as a declaration of war."

"It is not here, sah! No, sah! It is not here, unless a man is so lost to sense and honah as to vote the radical ticket."

With that the discussion ended.

On Saturday night the mill closed.

Forty days later the machinery was on the way north.

Slimpton missed the mill.

Missed the money it cast upon the town.

But it had its politics and its exclusiveness, and it was rapidly approaching the Elysium of unanimity.

The Buzzer had said: "If you want to see the Republican column move, apply the Democratic lash."

The lash was applied and the column was moving—the mill at the head of the column—and with it all improvements.

Mrs. Shootfast heard of the interview.

"Impertinent Yankee. Impudence unheard of. Presumption amazing. To expect Southern ladies to call on his Yankee wife."

"You did on Mrs. Huntley," retorted the judge.

"Ah, yes! That was exceptional; we did it for Dale. And that was a mistake. A great mistake. Some of our set never would do it, and now we who did call are affording amusement to them. I did it under protest, judge, as you know, and I could cry my eyes out about it."

"But I really do think the minister might have called. It seems to me it is his duty to visit both saints and sinners."

"But his wife is a Yankee."

"And yet I think if I was a minister of the Gospel——"

"You would have done as he has. Call indeed. Even if he had the disposition, which I am glad to say he has not, Mr. Purtense is a true Southern gentleman; he would have had an uncomfortable time; yes, indeed, a very uncomfortable time among his flock."

"Even the sheep would have butted him," said the judge, laughing.

"We would have suppressed him at all events."

"You have suppressed the mill at all events."

" I ? "

" You ladies."

" Suppressed, indeed. The fellow can't find meanness enough here to suit him, even among the negroes, and he goes North, where he can find nothing else."

" Whatever the reason, I fear it is gone."

" I am glad of it. Heartily glad of it."

"Oh, no ! "

" Yes, I am. I detested it from the first."

" It was a great advantage to the town."

" You never said it before."

" I never saw the danger of losing it before."

" For one I rejoice it is going. It was an unneeded inno-vation. The whir of machinery and the activity that sur-rounds it, puts ideas into people's heads."

" So much the better."

" So much the worse, judge, for a people who must be controlled. To control a people easily they must be ignor-ant. Not only ignorant of letters, but they must cease to think; and a machine, any active, stirring industry, even the new inventions for planters, excites the laborers' curiosity; sets them to thinking; and with that, ease of control disap-pears. Give me the good old days when there was no think-ing among the hands, and nothing to think about."

" You are going backward."

" Yes, to happiness ; to the times when gentlemen did the thinking and were the masters; when the negroes were slaves, and the brainless poor whites were being fitted for slaves. That is happiness. Take away your machinery and your tools, everything that can make poor people think. Then we will have a revival of the dear, good old times."

The arrival of guests ended the discussion.

A few days later a meeting was called to accelerate the movement northward.

It was in the night time, and the court-house was packed. Valore, Shootfast, Cartier, Bartdale and Lex were there.

A meeting without Lex, anywhere in America, would be a failure.

Whisper meeting and speech-making and Lex flings Blackstone to the dogs.

The word was whispered.

Blackstone was dumped.

Lex rushed to the fray, champing his quid as young colts do their bits.

Old heads and wise tongues.

Pshaw!

There is no head so wise, no tongue so waggy, as newly-hatched Lex, strutting in his pin-feathers.

Lex was at the meeting.

He was irrepressible.

He squirmed in between words.

He shook his mane in the tobacco-scented air, and hurled at the audience the Athenians, Parthenians, Carthagenians and Fenians, the fellow who plunged into the chasm, and Rome's geese.

Lex was confident and exhaustlessly voluble.

The crackers didn't understand, but they roared.

There is nothing like a dictionary flung 'round with vehemence.

Lex sat down in a lather.

Then came Bartdale, denouncing the Northern men who were candidates for office on the Republican ticket. "They ought," he said, bringing his cane down on the desk, "to be killed!" The cane was an exclamation point. "They must be got rid of. Every one of them. They poison the air. I couldn't lie in my grave with the breath of Yankees and niggahs ruling my beloved State over me. No, sah! They must be got rid of. We must carry this election at all hazards. At all hazards, gentlemen! Then! then! thank God! we will see the buzzards flying away to their Northern roosts. Yes, gentlemen, at all hazards — at all hazards! I say it, my suffering, down-trodden, oppressed countrymen. I, one of the sufferers, one of the oppressed, one of the down-trodden, I say it to you. We must carry the election at all hazards."

A tumult of applause followed Bartdale's address.

Then came resolutions.

A meeting without resolutions is an ocean without froth.

The resolutions were reported.

1. We will not employ or lease lands or rent houses to Republicans.

2. We will not recognize any person who does employ Republicans or rent them houses or lands.

3. We will not have social intercourse with any person who votes the Republican ticket, and will not recognize any such person as a gentleman.

4. Any person who makes or assists in making an official bond for a Radical office holder we will treat as a traitor and enemy to this community.

5. We will succeed in the coming election peaceably if we can, forcibly if we must.*

"Gentlemen, you have heard the resolutions. All in favor."

A tremendous " A-y-e ! " shook the building.

It was a roar.

It was Bull Run and Chickamauga rolled into one.

Now rivet it.

The Democratic candidate for the Legislature now opened his mouth.

There were several negro spectators.

The would-be law maker turned upon them.

"I tell you niggahs," he said, " I tell you now that the time has passed for Republicans to rule this county. We, the white men, offer you a ticket; and if you do not vote for us and we do not elect this ticket, the blood that was shed at Yazoo and Vicksburg will be as dew before the sun to the blood that will be shed in this county if we are not elected.†
We want you to understand once for all that our motto is:

" A white man in a white man's place."

" A black man in a black man's place."

" Each according ' to the eternal fitness of things.' And

---

* Adopted by many Democratic clubs.

† A fact, as sworn to.

rivers of blood will flow if you attempt to change the order."*

Then the meeting dispersed.

The tide of passion was rising.

It swelled over Slimpton.

It gathered about the Huntleys and the Trenhoms, and it surged out to the plantation of Jupiter Saltire.

* The utterer of this atrocious sentiment was elected.

CHAPTER XXXI.

ONLY A YANKEE.

After the meeting in the Shootfast parlors Slimpton became a polar sea to Mrs. Trenhom and Mrs. Huntley.

There is no stone harder than a woman solidified.

There are no eyes so blind as those of a woman who has determined to cut an acquaintance.

There is no chill like a flounced and gloved society iceberg.

They freeze.

They congeal.

Their eyes are zero.

Their mouths are twenty degrees below.

They are the pink snows of society.

These Slimpton ladies came and went.

Mrs. Erma Cartier was the solitary exception.

No inducements could bring her to the post-office, into the streets of the town, or any where that she might meet her old friends, Mrs. Huntley or Mrs. Trenhom.

Dale Cartier, her husband, expostulated; he urged upon his wife that she was punishing herself; that she could not pursue that course forever; sometime she must go; why not go at once?

To all this Erma could only answer:

"Don't ask it, Dale. Please do not. For you I forego the pleasures of their society. But I could not meet Kitty."

"Mrs. Huntley?" said her husband, with some sternness in his voice.

"Yes, Dale Mrs. Huntley; I could not meet her or her husband without speaking, not if all the world was pushing me forward. Indeed, indeed, I know I could not. If I should meet her—Kitty—"

"Mrs. Huntley." Her husband again interjected.

"Yes, Dale, Mrs. Huntley; I—I would kiss her if I perished for it."

"Erma! Erma!" replied her husband warmly, "you forget yourself—you forget yourself."

"No, Dale! No, dear! I remember. That's it, dear. When I draw near her I see only one thing, Dale; you, dear, lying prostrate on that awful hillside at Chickamauga with a smoking shell ready to explode by your side," and she shivered as she covered her eyes with her little white hands.

"Then—then, Dale," she added, "I see her noble husband standing up in a dreadful hail of bullets; I see him lift the shell; I see the shell rising in the air and rolling down the hill and exploding far away from you, dear, and I see her husband falling—wounded—wounded for you, Dale. Saving you to me, Dale. And now he is dying, Dale; dying, dear, for you; dying, that I might have you, Dale. Oh, I couldn't! I couldn't! I couldn't pass her in silence. Indeed I could not, Dale."

"That's sentiment, Erma."

"Oh, Dale!"

"Yes, mawkish sentiment!"

"Please don't, Dale."

"I would have done the same for him."

"I am sure you would, dear, and Kitty"—

"Mrs. Huntley!" interrupted Dale Cartier, with growing severity in his voice.

"Yes, Dale; Mrs. Huntley and her poor, suffering, dying husband would never forget. No, Dale, never; I am sure of it; and, dear Dale, you ought to remember them."

"I do remember."

"I am sure you do, dear, and, remembering, you should not ask this."

"But they are Yankees!"

"And they were our friends."

"Pshaw, Erma! It makes me sick to think of it."

"Dale, dear!"

There was a volume of reproach in the words. Her hands were clasped over her husband's left shoulder, and her wide-open eyes, full of entreaty, were looking up into his face.

"I mean it, Erma. The humiliation of receiving them in my home and calling on them is charge enough for any service. Yes, for even a greater service than that Yankee soldier did for me."

"Oh, Dale! Dale!"

Dale Cartier drew his shoulder from under his wife's hands and walked to the window. After a moment of silence he said, with his back to her:

"Avoid them if you will, Erma. But I insist that you do not again speak of what he did for me. In receiving him for a time as my guest and recognizing him I have returned him full value for his service. Much more than full value."

Erma walked after him to the window. Her eyes were full of tears and her voice tremulous with pain.

"If it had been a dog, dear Dale," she said, "who saved your life or the life of one of our precious children, we never would tire of petting him."

"Certainly not, Erma. But that is different. These are Yankees."

With this in his mind Dale Cartier walked out of the house and down into the town.

Erma buried her face in the lounge and wept. She grieved for her friends, and grieved more over the new light Dale's words had let in upon his character. She was beginning to understand that the human soul has secrets hidden even from itself.

Few men are what they seem.

Some are better, some are worse.

Far down in the depths of the earth are hidden streams.

Probed and penetrated, these streams rise to the surface.

And they rise up, some sweet, some bitter.

Events probe men in the same way.

They are all surprise boxes.

Touch the secret spring of their lives; from one springs a saint and a martyr; from another a devil.

After this no inducement could take Erma Cartier into Slimpton.

Not so the other ladies of her set.

They walked the streets.

They went to the post-office.

They encountered the tabooed ladies here and there.

Salute them?

Recognize them?

No! not once.

In the eyes of every one of the Slimpton ladies "I don't know you" was written in great frosty letters.

Among the first who came to the post-office after the gathering in the Shootfast parlors was Mrs. Shootfast.

She drove close up to the door.

The driver drew the reins. "See if that Yankee woman has any letters for me," exclaimed Mrs. Shootfast.

That was all.

But every word she uttered was audible in the remotest recess of the little office.

The driver entered.

There were no letters.

Then Mrs. Shootfast drove away, but her shrill notes were heard far beyond the post-office.

The passers in the street heard them.

Some stenches cling and spread.

Indignities are of this character.

These words did.

They were in every one's nostrils.

It was the correct thing to insult the postmistress.

The great Mrs. Shootfast had set the fashion. And the style of the great will be aped whether it be in furbelows, crimped hair or biting words.

An hour after Mrs. Shootfast left the post-office a huge "sand hiller" entered it.

He was one of the Pelter gang.

He stood before the delivery window.

"Say, Yank, be thah any lettahs fo' me?"

"What is your name, sir?"

"What? Don't know a Christian fellah-citizen's name? A bully post-woman you be. What yer heah fo', ef tain't to know yer bettahs when they comes?"

"If you will tell me your name I will look, sir."

The woman was all urbanity as she looked up at him through the small delivery window.

The man had never been there before.

She did not know him.

He never had received a letter from that office.

Never had received one from anywhere.

He could not read one if he had received it.

"Drat yo', I jist want yer to look."

"I will with pleasure, sir, if you will tell me what name to look for."

"Jist you rattle 'em over anyway. Does yer heah. Drat yer shackelty hide!"

Mrs. Huntley's earnest eyes were fixed on his face.

For an instant she was too full of amazement to speak. When she found words she said:

"I hope you have not come here to insult me!"

There was both courtesy and determination in her tones. For a moment the man was abashed.

"Insult you, you —— Yankee ——."

(The nastiness of the speech is omitted. It was slime of the brothel.)

Tears sprung into Kate's eyes.

A hot flush rushed to her cheeks.

She covered her ears with her hands.

And she shivered from head to foot.

It was dreadful. That she should listen to such foulness.

Then the beast turned away with a roar.

"Didn't I take that drat Yank down."

This, too, spread.

It ran from mouth to mouth.

The burly ruffian lounged down the street.

"An' did yer do that?"

"Yaas!"

"Dawg awn!"

He was the hero of the hour.

Men ran to the street doors to see him.

Bright eyes peeped out of windows to see the wonderful man who had insulted the Yankee postmistress.

Chuckling, laughter and laudation invited emulation.

Fools and blackguards are sheep.

Where one goes another will follow.

The next day the post-office was again invaded.

This invader the postmistress knew.

Time and again had Mrs. Huntley fed his wife and children when they were starving.

The dresses then on his little children's backs were her gift, the coinage of her nimble fingers.

This beast was Jim Gouge.

"Yaller Jim," he was called, and justly.

He was more swarthy than any mulatto in the town.

Gouge stood in the office before the delivery window.

"Say, whahs my lettah?"

"Have none for you, James."

"Mighty familiar, hain't yer! Jeemes! drat yer wrinkled hide!"

Kate was amazed.

Was the man drunk or crazy?

She bent down to the window and looked up at him.

She saw the broad grin on his jaws, and the wicked leer in his eyes. Then she said to him:

"Mr. Gouge, there is no letter for you."

"Look! Drat yo', look!"

"I remember every letter, Mr. Gouge."

The memory of some letter deliverers is wonderful and unerring.

"Dawg awn ef yer hain't got ter look."

"It is no use. I know."

"Drat yer low-lived Yankee, will yo' look! Jest yo' look, will yer!"

To avoid a repetition of the profanity, Kate looked. Let-

ter by letter she passed slowly from the left hand into the
right, carefully turning the superscription toward the window,
so that the man could see that she looked. When she reached
the last letter she said to him:

"You see, sir, as I told you, there is no letter."

"Ther hain't, hain't ther !"

"No, sir !"

"Waal, you jist look again."

At this time three or four of the Pelter crowd were gathered about the doorway laughing, and emphasizing their
merriment by poking each other in the ribs and bringing
their great hands down on their thighs.

Kate was full of suppressed wrath, but she lifted the letters and calmly went over them again.

"There is no letter, sir."

"Jist turn 'em over agin. Drat yo'."

"No, sir, I will not."

"You won't! Drat yer peekety hide! You won't! "

"No, I will not."

"You —— —— Yankee —— ——."

(His words, which were vile spume from a sink, were unfit
to be repeated.)

"I wish you would leave the office. You will oblige
me if you will. Go! Go at once!"

"I hain't going ter leave till yer look. Drat yo'."

"I will not look again. Go out! Go out at once!"

Then she turned away from the window and began
arranging papers with her back to Gouge.

"Yaller Jim " raved.

His mouth was a cesspool of nastiness.

Then he drew a pistol, leveled it through the window and
fired.

Kate screamed.

The gaping crowd at the door laughed and cheered.

Gouge roared again and in the cloud of smoke disappeared
from the office.

Kate was uninjured.

The ruffian possibly did not design to injure her.

The ball from his pistol imbedded itself in the wall three or four feet from her head, and Gouge was too good a marksman to fire so wide at muzzle range unless it was purposely done.

Kate was petrified with astonishment and overcome with indignation.

Her thoughts at first turned upon Gouge and his family—and what she had done for them.

She thought of the food and clothing she had given them; the nights she had sat by their sick bedsides administering the medicines she had purchased, and cooling the parchings of fever with draughts she supplied. And—for this! for this!

She thought of the flash, the shot, the bullet, and the danger. She did not know it was a scare, and not an escape.

Then an ague of fright took possession of her. "If he had killed her, what would become of Hal?"

With a pistol pointed at her head she would have been a rock.

Now that the danger was passed, she was a pebble shaken in the current, and thoughts of Hal brought a flood of tears.

Then she walked away into a back room to hide them.

Tears are hearts-ease.

Tears wash away pain.

In the flood of tears Kate found relief.

A footstep neared the door from the dwelling in the rear of the post-office.

Kate knew it.

It was her husband, Halmer Huntley, the sergeant of Chickamauga.

Her tears dried on the instant.

The torrent was dammed up.

The pause of weeping is a wonderful power of womanhood.

The door opened and Hal entered.

"Didn't I hear a shot, Kate?"

"Perhaps, dear. I believe there was one out there."

That might mean the front office, or the street, or beyond.

"Anyone shot?"

" Oh, no! only firing! "

" Ah! " That was a common thing.

And this is Sergeant Hal of Chickamauga.

But how changed.

Once he was tall and strong, and ruddy and erect.

Now he is thin and stooped and white.

Andersonville and the ball that penetrated his lungs when he stood up to hurl the shell away from the side of helpless Dale Cartier, have told on him.

His full, round tones are gone.

In place of the strong, eager voice, there is a strange grating sound, and a racking, hollow cough.

There is a hectic glow on his thin cheeks and an unnatural brilliancy in his eyes.

Kate hurried into the front office, gave some instructions to her assistant, and then came back to Hal.

" Come, dear, let us go out under the trees."

Then she led him out through the house in the rear, down in the garden, under the shelter of the fragrant magnolias.

There she read and sewed and sang, and so the morning passed away.

In the afternoon there were new troubles. Her female assistant in the post-office could not come any more.

" She needed the money, oh, so much! so much!" she said. " But what could she do?" The children in the streets derided her. They followed her, called her Yank, and traitor; one cried, "She im gwan to marry a nig." " Dear Mrs. Huntley, it is simply dreadful, and mother has put her foot down. She will not permit me to come."

" But, my dear, your mother begged me to take you. She said you were all literally starving."

" And it is true! so awfully true, Mrs. Huntley; we were, indeed we were."

" And have you saved any money?"

" Not one cent! Not one! Mother would buy ribbons and bonnets, everything to be up with her neighbors. She thought the river never would go dry, and now we have nothing. Boo-hoo-oo-oo ! "

21

"That's the way, dear. No cistern in the rain, no water in the drought."

"What we shall do I don't know." And the young lady wrung her hands and again wept hysterically.

"Why not continue, dear ; the duties are light and pleasant, and you know that I love you."

"Dear Mrs. Huntley, you have only been too good ! Too good ! I don't know how I can repay your kindness. I don't know how we shall live without the salary. But—but—oh, dear—dear—dear—boo-hoo-oo-ou ! "

"Is it quite impossible to remain?"

"Oh ! If I could ! If I could ! But there's mother—and —the—b-r-a-t-s—in the stre-e-eet ! Oh-ou-ou-u!"

"Well, my dear, I am sorry, very, very sorry to part with you ; but if you must go— "

"I must ! I must ! And I did so want to stay ! "

"Then let us see how much I owe you ! "

"I am afraid—noth-i-ing ! Noth-i-i-ing."

Kate looked.

She ran up a little column of figures. Then she ran them over again.

The assistant's account had been overdrawn more than fifty dollars.

"Do you know how the account stands, dear?" asked Kate.

"I know it is overdrawn, ever and ever so mu-u-ch ! aa-u-d I do-on't know how I shall pay-ay it. Boo-hoo-oo-ou ! "

Kate opened a little safe and counted over some bills. Then she approached the girl.

"Will you take this from me, dear ? "

She reached out the roll of bills.

The fair young hand stretched out for it, then drew back, and the young head with its wealth of soft curls dropped upon Mrs. Huntley's shoulder.

She spoke not a word. It was simply one prolonged "Oh-h-h-h ! "

And while she lay there moaning Mrs. Huntley pushed the roll of bills into her fingers. She kissed her forehead and her cheeks. And then they parted—parted forever in this world.

CHAPTER XXXII.

UNCHAINED TIGERS.

The following day brought a renewal of trouble to the post-office.

When a community uncages its tigers they will rend and crunch.

The tigers of Slimpton were unchained.

It was Joe Ratley who this day showed his teeth.

With him were three others, equally brutal.

They had been lounging at the grocery, whispering of the " fun " of the night preceding and laughing about the " skear Yaller Jim guv the Yankee critter."

" It would be a powah o' fun to gwo down ther' with a jug o' whisk an' play keards on the floa'."

It was Joe Ratley who suggested this.

It was a brilliant idea.

It was rolled over and applauded.

The doggery keeper was elated and agreed to loan the " papes " and furnish the " whisk."

It was the only gift of his vile " cawn-juice " he ever was known to make.

The whisky was drawn and jugged.

A greasy pack of cards was produced from a foul drawer.

Then the four started for the post-office, followed by a half-drunken crowd who had been advised of their purpose, to " see the fun."

When they entered the post-office they each demanded letters.

Mrs. Huntley told them there were none.

" Look again."

" No ! "

"Drat yer slattery hide, look !"

"No, sir; I have looked, and will not look again !"

"You won't ?"

"No, I will not. If you have come here to insult me, I have no way to prevent it, unfortunately ; none whatever. I have no protection. I am weak and at your mercy ; but I will not be an acquiescent and helping party to it by searching for letters when I have looked and satisfied myself there are none."

"Drat yer imperdence !"

It was Joe Ratley who spoke.

"Mr. Ratley, did it never occur to you that you are a coward ?"

Joe flushed to the roots of his red hair ; gawked a moment, then turned to the others:

"Come on boys, let's have a drink !"

He raised the jug and the hot fluid gurgled down his throat.

The others then drank and placed the jug on the floor.

Joe sat down beside the jug.

"Come on fellers, let's hev a game o' euchre."

The others sat down in a circle. The jug was in the center of the circle.

Joe shuffled the greasy pack of cards.

The doorway was blocked.

Any scoundrelism can find lookers on and applauders.

The lookers on in the door were compacted by the crowd extending far out on the walk.

Mrs. Huntley was looking with wide open eyes.

For a few moments she was petrified with astonishment.

"Surely, gentlemen, you do not intend to play cards there ?"

"Shet your gabblement."

"You bet we does."

"Shuffle, Joe."

"But this is a post-office, and the public must come here."

All four mouths opened and poured out upon Mrs. Huntley a flood of nastiness.

The crowd in the door laughed and shouted.

Kate was disgusted and shocked. Then she added :

" This office belongs to the government."

" Dawg awn your government."

" Hurrah fer Jeff Davis ! "

" Drat niggah government ! "

" Clubs are trumps."

" Play ! "

Kate walked quickly round from behind the delivery window.

She stood close beside the sitting bullies on the floor.

She stood facing the gaping, grinning, shouting bullies in the door.

" You must go out of here." Her voice was fine and clear. It rang out over the heads of the crowd.

" Go to ——, you —— Yankee ——."

It was a puttering of foulness.

It was horrible.

Mrs. Huntley reached down quickly over the shoulders of the group on the floor.

She seized the jug.

She lifted it up.

Then she hurled it over the heads of the mocking crowd in the door far out into the street.

As she did this Ratley and the others sprang to their feet.

Joe's cheeks were distended.

His mouth was full of saliva.

He ejected the filthy flood, tainted with tobacco, full at Mrs. Huntley's face.

Kate threw her head back.

The reeking stream missed her face, but struck her throat and rolled down upon her dress.

Instantly there was a cheer at the door.

Kate saw the cheering crowd at the door, and among them, a few feet away from the door, she saw one face that filled her with horror.

It was Major Dale Cartier.

Then she murmured, " Oh, oh, what a coward a brave man can be."

From this moment she abandoned hope.

If he—he, Dale Cartier, of all men in the world—if he can see Halmer Huntley's wife insulted, what must the rest be ? What would they not do ?

Before the thought was rounded in her mind there was a tumult in the door.

There was a rush.

Men jostled and crushed together.

Out of the melee one form became distinct.

He was within the door.

He was facing Joe Ratley and the others.

It was Colonel Walter Trenhom.

" Go out of here. Out of here, everyone of you ! "

" Scallawag ! " cried some one in the doorway.

Ratley was slinking away when he heard the word. Then he turned.

" Yaas," he stuttered, " whose gwine ter be ordered by traitors."

Trenhom took one step toward the man and halted " You ! You cowardly dog ! You dare to speak to me ! Miserable deserter ! I pardoned you once. The second time I secured your pardon after you were sentenced to be shot. The third time you escaped. And you—pshaw ! Go out ! "

The jam in the doorway bellowed " Stick ! Stick ! Don't yer git ! "

One of the ruffians drew a pistol.

The hands of the others went down into their pistol pockets.

But Trenhom was before them. He stood erect, facing the door, his eyes flashing with anger, his shoulders thrown back.

His revolver was elevated, pointing squarely at the head of the one who held the pistol in his hand.

The crowd in the door ran.

" Drop your pistol on the floor and walk out."

Trenhom's every word was like the crack of a rifle.

The bully dropped his pistol. The others withdrew their hands from their pistol pockets.

Then the four slunk out of the building.

The next morning when the post-office opened Mrs. Huntley found a letter in the drop box addressed to the postmaster.

She opened it and read :

" Take notis. We will only give you twenty days to leave this county. If you do not leave you may look out for about sixteen buckshot about whear your gallises crosses. We ain't going to have no more snekeing ignorant Yanks about hear. So git up and dust."

If Kate's husband had been in a condition to move, she would have gone away at once to the North, but he was not. He was fading away. The end she knew was not far off, and she had no fears of personal injury to him. He went nowhere ; the greater part of the time he was confined to bed or a sick chair. But she did forward her resignation to the postmaster general.

Days passed—twenty days. There had been petty annoyances, but no renewal of gross outrages.

Kate began to breathe freer.

On the night of the twentieth day, after she had retired for the night, there came a cry, "Fire ! Fire ! "

Kate drew the curtain, looked out.

The street about was as bright as mid-day.

She ran down stairs in her night-dress and opened the door leading into the garden.

Then she saw that the post-office was in a blaze.

The eager tongues of flame from the post-office building were already lapping the resin from the end of her dwelling.

A crowd had gathered in the street.

They were leaning against the fences, and standing with hands in pocket, looking on.

Kate cried out to them, "Oh! oh! Gentlemen, do help us!"

Not a foot or a hand moved.

Then Kate knew that the post-office and her home were doomed.

Again Kate cried out to the gaping crowd in the street:

"Oh, gentlemen! For God's sake help me out with my husband! He is helpless! Helpless, and will be burned to death!"

Joe Ratley was there. His voice was heard above the roar of the flames.

"Hear the Yank squall."

Then there was another voice.

It was "Yaller Jim."

"Hear the Yankee cat yow."

Several negroes started out of the crowd toward the door. Immediately there was a rush of white men, pistol in hand, after the negroes.

"Hiar, yeu! Git! Drat ye, git! Raise yer hands here and yer'l git yer heads blowed off."

"But, mawstah, the man in thah'll git burned."

"Let him burn!"

"Yaas, let the mizable Yank taste fiah!"

Kate turned from the crowd — turned to the door — with her hair streaming down over her night-dress and disappeared in the smoke.

Up the stairs!

She stood at her husband's bedside.

She raised him up.

She threw a blanket about him.

There was no time to think of dressing him.

There was no time to think of a covering for herself.

The flame was pursuing.

The roar was deafening.

The smoke was stifling.

She drew him upon her back.

She drew his wasted arms over her shoulder; then, with her burden, this frail, heroic woman staggered to the door.

A cloud of smoke rolled in upon her.

It filled her nostrils.

She found the hall.

She groped for the stairs.

The blinding suffocating smoke enveloped her.

She gasped.

She choked.

She stifled.

And the weight upon her back bore her down.

She was in an agony of terror.

When despair had almost clutched her, she found the head of the stairs.

" Ah, thank God ! "

Step by step.

Step by step.

Down, down.

The smoke filled her ears. It filled her eyes, filled her nostrils. It filled her throat.

Down amid the roar and crash.

The smoke was impenetrable.

Tongues of flame pursued her.

The heat was unbearable.

Down !

" Oh, are the stairs endless ? "

" Would she never escape ? "

Love nerved her.

Every fiber of her body was an intense struggle against despair.

Blindly she struggled on.

Feeling was gone.

The roar was unheard.

The heat and the flame were unfelt.

She only knew that she loved Hal, and that he was on her back.

Then a chill air swept over her face, and she fell forward with her burden.

As she fell forward, strong arms enveloped and held her up.

Trenhom had heard the cry of " fire," and Jupiter Saltire, who was with him at the time, in consultation, also heard it.

Together they ran out into the street.

Down toward the burning building.

From negroes they speedily learned the hostile attitude of the crowd, and of the door where Mrs. Huntley disappeared.

Reaching the front of the post-office, they broke through the human wall about it, and started for the door.

The crowd waved them back.

Infuriated men, pistol in hand, faced them.

Trenhom called to Jupe:

" Draw your pistol and face 'em."

Jupiter sprang to his side, pistol in hand.

With pistols raised, the two men fronted the crowd.

The crowd shrank from the muzzles of pistols in the hands of two determined men.

Then Trenhom and Jupiter walked backward in through the garden toward the door.

As they reached the door Mrs. Huntley emerged from the smoke, and as she was falling, Trenhom caught her and her husband in his strong arms.

Kate speedily revived.

Then she looked upon her husband and her heart stood still within her.

She knew it had come at last.

There was an ooze of blood upon his lips, and the red stream had dyed her night-dress upon the shoulder where her husband's head had lain and ebbed down upon its front.

From the excitement had come a hemorrhage.

Tenderly they bore him to the far rear of the grounds, away from the fire, smoke and roar.

Then they laid him down under the trees.   A moment he lay quiet.

Then he reached his thin white hands down upon his body.

His thumb and fingers came together.

Then they lifted and opened.

Again and again his thumb and fingers came together.

HIS HEAD WAS PILLOWED IN JUPITER'S LAP.

He was picking.

"Maggots!"

Halmer Huntley trembled as the word passed his lips.

His lips opened again.

"Worms!"

It was a murmur.

A gurgle.

For a moment he lay silent, his glazing, vacant eyes fixed upon the heavens above. Then he shivered again from head to foot.

He tried to rise up.

A fresh stream of blood burst from his lips.

A look of unutterable horror came into his eyes for a moment.

He moved his thin hands across his chest as if brushing away some loathsome object from his person.

Then again he murmured:

"Scrape them off—oh! oh! Kit! Kit! Scrape them away! Kit! Kit, come? I knew she would, Jack, old boy. S-c-c-h-h! Wirz will hear us. S-c-c-h-h! Kit! Kit! Escaped! Oh! Kit! Kit! S-c-c-h-h! It's Yankee Doodle. Free! Free! Kit! K-i-t!"

His head was pillowed in Jupiter's lap.

Trenhom was standing over him with a pistol in his hand.

Kate was sitting beside him holding one of his hands and wiping the bloody froth from his lips.

She felt the hand growing chill in her own.

Then she knew that by the torch of his own home he had passed away from the bellowing mob. Out of the Polar sea.

At last he was free—forever.

And her head sank slowly down upon his breast.

CHAPTER XXXIII.

MANSA'S FATE.

A few days after the catastrophe at the post office, Lindy Ratley saw " Yaller Jim " Gouge coming through the cornfield toward the cabin.

Joe had eaten his dinner and was lazily basking in the sun at the rear of his home, the direction from which Jim was approaching.

When Jim came into the opening between the corn and the cabin, he saw Joe stretched on the grass, with his shoulders supported by the cabin wall, half asleep and smoking.

After a mutual " Hallo ! " Jim prostrated himself beside his comrade.

Lindy was within, sewing.

The two men without were chuckling and plotting.

One word arrested Lindy's attention.

That word was " Jupe "

She drew near to the open window and listened to the low, grating sounds that rose up from the grass.

" Drat sassy niggah."

" Puts on heap o' airs."

" Ridin' on a hoss."

" An' a kerridge foh that black nig o' his'n."

" Makes me sick in the innards ter see ignurant nigs puttin' on sich airs."

" The boys ort to clean 'um out."

" Let's take 'em thar ter-night."

" Dawg awn ef we don't."

" Yaas; we've been skinnin' thar coons; dod rat ef they uns shan't skin our'n."

" Drat ef I don't take the bark off that niggah myself."

"Just think of him chucking inter the fiah longside that dratted traitah Trenhom."

"Pesky niggah."

"Makes my innards burn ter thinks of him."

"Drat ef we don't slug him ter-night arter the meetin'."

Then the two men stood up and walked around to the front of the house and shambled down the walk toward the gate and the road.

Lindy's light step was on the path behind them

When the men turned at the gate they saw her.

Then she spoke.

"Joe."

Joe paused irresolute; the other man shuffled up the road.

"Joe," continued Lindy, "you hed better leave Jupiter alone."

"Nothing but a niggah."

"Yes, he's black out, but he's white in, Joe, and you ain't white neither side; no, neither side, Joe; neither side."

Joe stood looking down in the road, pawing the dust with one of his huge feet, and he answered nothing.

"Mind, Joe," Lindy added, "you'd best leave him alone. Mind, I tell you, Joe; sure, Joe. You had best leave Jupiter Saltire alone."

She was looking straight in his face.

Her words came out very slow and soft.

"He ain't nothing but a niggah." That was the beginning and the end of Joe's argument before his wife. With any one else he would have been more voluble.

"Yes, Joe, he is a niggah; but he was good enough niggah, him and his wife, to nurse the children and me all one winter out of the scarlet fever. He was good enough for that, Joe, wasn't he? Yes, Joe, he was good enough for that; and you was a little afraid, Joe, wasn't you? Just a little afraid, Joe. You ran from the fever, didn't you, Joe, just as you ran from Yankee bullets, didn't you, Joe? Yes, Joe, you ran. You are good at running from danger, ain't you, Joe?"

Joe continued the restless pawing with his feet. He was really growing terribly afraid of this woman, who bit him with her relentless ironical words, without a shade of passion in them.

"And when you couldn't get anything to eat at home—afraid to come for it, wasn't you, Joe? Yes, afraid, Joe—Jupiter and his wife fed you. All winter, wasn't it, Joe? Yes, all winter. You wasn't too good to eat at the niggah table and to sleep in the niggah bed. All winter, Joe ; all winter when you wasn't drunk, and sometimes when you was, Joe. And when Jupiter plowed my fields in the spring, and wouldn't take pay for it, you wasn't too nice to eat the corn and sass that grew on it, was you, Joe?"

Joe was still silent.

"I hain't going to say no more, Joe, only you'd best leave Jupiter alone; mind you, Joe, you'd best. Yes, you had best. I know that, Joe. Yes, Joe, I am quite sure you had best."

Every word she uttered was in the same soft, coaxing notes that a child would use in saying: "Come, pussy, let's chase the butterflies."

Lindy said no more.

She turned away from Joe and walked up to the house.

Full half an hour Joe stood, thrusting his hands in his pockets, then passing them through his hair, and all the time pawing, pawing in the dust.

He was uneasy.

He dreaded. He did not know what, but he dreaded.

If "Yaller Jim" had not been waiting up the road, he would have turned back through the gate into the flowering garden.

But Jim was waiting, and he turned and walked away.

At the bend of the road Joe paused and looked back.

Look, Joe.

See the cabin to which you brought Lindy years ago.

See the changes she has wrought.

Think of what more she might have done if she had had a man for a husband.

Look !

Drink it in, Joe !

Now say farewell, Joe !

Never more ! never more !

When Joe disappeared, Lindy drew the children to her.

There were three at home now.

One, the oldest, was married.

A young farmer came down from the North. Bought a plantation. Married Lindy's daughter. Became disgusted with the South and went away North with his wife.

In the North they were prospering, and Lindy's oldest was happy.

The other three worked in the Slimpton cotton-mill until it closed.

Now they were home.

Lindy told the girls (they were all girls) she was going away. Might be gone all afternoon. Possibly all night. If she didn't come home early, leave the door unbolted and go to bed. No questions were asked. They were not chatterers. Lindy, as a mother, had few words. She never stormed or raged or threatened. If she disapproved, it was only " I think I wouldn't." But somehow that was enough.

Strong words are not government.

Storms are not control.

Without either Lindy controlled.

The children were pliant as putty under the touch of her soft words.

From her house Lindy proceeded to Jupiter Saltire's cottage.

Mansa was at home.

Mansa had changed since the morning she led Sherman's troops down through the streets of Savannah.

Then she was square and hard.

Now she was soft and round.

Time had dealt gently with her.

And the world — it usually treats people well who put it under the compulsion of sense, honesty and energy.

Her little home was bright as a new pin.

The surrounding ground was full of fragrance, of shading trees and trailing vines.

Mansa was a huge laugh.

22

Her days were prolonged fun.

It was so good to own yourself and have plenty to eat and to wear, and a horse and a carriage.

"I clah to goodness," she frequently said to Lindy, "when I see myself in a kerridge—ki—i—! I jiss think I buss, shoa! When Jupe fust git dat fo'-wheel behicle I look him all roun, an' tell him, look heah, Jupe, is I gwine ter tote dat, or is dat gwine ter tote me? Not as I didn't know. Laws, but jist think a'dat; dis yeah cottonfield niggah in a kerridge. Glory! What you think! When I done got in I tells Jupe: Now you look heah. You git a rope. Git one, Jupe. Laws man, quicker'n scat; ef yer don't I'll jist git wings and histe away. A kerridge! Ki—i—i! De Lawd. Ef ole Maws Titefist see dat! Glory!" and Mansa would bring her chubby hands down on her knees and laugh from the topmost kink of her hair down to the end of her toes. "Not dat I'ze proud, honey; you knows dat. Clah ter goodness, ef I don't want ter jist git spraddled on de hoss every time I sees it. But jist to think of this yeah chile in a kerridge, an' nuffin ter do all day long, an' all day long, but ter laugh an' git fat. It just makes me think, shoa 'nuff, of de day when we got out de kears on de Macon road, an' I got in the bush, and I heahs ole Maws Titefist. Guy! honey! I heahs him now! Deed I does. 'Whah the debil my she niggah!' 'Clah to goodness, honey, hain't de good Lawd done make change. Little yeah ago hidin' in de brush an' old Maws sloshing round fo' him she niggah, and now ridin' in my own kirridge and holdin' my sides to keep from bustin' at de fun! Mine you, honey! now you mine your eye. Some day you'll come here an' find I'ze just done bust and blow'd up wid ticklin' at de fun. Jupe says I ort to larn. Him done dat! 'Clah to goodness, honey, ef he hain't larned the laugh clar out of him. 'Deed he has, honey. Larned and larned till him got great big scrotches about the eyes and across him forehead. Reckon dat's whah de larnin goes in and pull de skin in arter it. But what's de use ob dat, honey? I'd rader hab one good laugh than fohty larnins. 'Deed I would. Ef I couldn't laugh I'd jist want the good Mawstah up yandah to say, " Now, you Mansa, you jist come heah whah dey's plenty laugh! "

This afternoon, when Mansa heard Lindy Ratley's story, the laugh died away from her lips.

" Good Lawd, honey, yer don't think they'd hurt Jupe ?"

" I am afraid they will."

" Why, honey, he 'um nebbah done nothin' to nobody. He 'um been honest and wucked hawrd, and got dis yeah stretch o' land, and he gives—"

Then Mansa remembered that even Mrs. Ratley had been a recipient of their bounty, and she paused. There was a current of delicacy running-through this woman's rudeness. Sweet flowers will grow among rocks, and spring out of the wilderness.

Mrs. Ratley took up and finished the sentence. " I know Jupiter has been generous, but I reckon that won't stop ' Yaller Jim' and them others. Maybe it's worse. I reckon they don't like to see a black man get on."

" In de good Lawd's name what's I gwine ter do ? "

Advising was not a forte of Lindy Ratley.

Then Mansa told her.

She knew she could trust Lindy.

The whites were to have a big meeting in town, day and night, and the blacks who had been waiting an opportunity when the attention of the white men would be diverted from them had secretly called a meeting for that night, in the country.

It was some miles away.

The colored people were to go to it avoiding the roads, and Jupiter had already gone.

When Mansa had told all she knew of the meeting she asked, " Does you think, honey, I'd best send to him?"

" I reckon! "

That was all Lindy could say. It was all she did say.

Mansa turned the matter over in her mind. She did so want to be advised. As a slave she was full of devices. She was fertile in plans for safety. She needed them then. As a free woman Jupiter did the thinking and Mansa enjoyed the fun. And now when she needed wit she had only trembling, and leaning on a reed that murmured back to her " I reckon."

One of the colored laborers on the place came in. Did he know where Jupiter had gone? No! But Jack did. Jack was in the town on an errand. Would return soon. With this Mansa was forced to be content.

In a little while Jack came. Mansa told the story to him. Yes, Jupiter had better be informed.

He would go. Didn't know exactly where the meeting place was. But he could find it.

Then he went away. It was a long afternoon.

Intolerably long.

A cloud was on Mansa's face.

A heavy weight was tugging at her heart.

She would stand, walk to the door, put her hands on her hips, draw a long breath, half a sigh, half a moan, and walk the floor in an aimless way.

During the afternoon she talked of the past. Of her mammy. When she was sold away from her. Her masters. Of Jupiter. His escape. Her escape. Every minute detail of her narrow life. And Lindy sat and listened.

Lindy was silent always.

This day she was unusually so.

She listened to Mansa's tale of sorrow and her note of triumph when she was finally united to her husband in Savannah.

" And youze had yer troubles too, honey."

But Lindy's tongue and face and eyes were dumb.

Night came.

Midnight.

Mansa began to hope the peril was past.

Then a sound reached their ears.

It was a muttering in the sky.

It grew distinct.

It was a beating of many hoofs on the road.

Then came voices.

They approached.

They were singing.

They reached the gate and halted.

The singing continued.

The gate was opened.

They entered the garden.   Then the words of the song became distinct.

> "We'll peel them off like taitahs,
>   We'll shuck them off like cawn,
> We'll tickle their backs with hick'ry
>   Till they cuss the day they's bawn."

Mansa cowered in the corner by the fire-place and shivered.

Lindy walked to the door and stood in the doorway.

Thirty or forty men were clustered before it, some in their saddles, others dismounted.

All wore black gowns reaching to their knees, and black hoods with eye holes over their faces.

The one who seemed to be the leader called out:

"Jupe, come out here."

Then Lindy spoke, "He isn't here."

The men without detected the voice of a white woman.

In the dark all faces were alike.

The men held a whispered consultation.

Then they drew nearer.

"See here, missus," said the leader, "you'd better go home."

"No, I reckon I will stay here."

"We've come for that niggah and we're goin' to have him."

"He hasn't been here since morning."

"He hain't?"

"No."

"Where is he?"

"He ain't coming here."

"He ain't?"

"I sent him word you were coming, and he will not come here."

"Oh, yer did, drat ye!   You're a nice white woman, goin' about hugger-muggin with niggahs."

Lindy was silent.

One of the invaders approached the open door.

Lindy stood firm in the gap.

" Git out of the way."

Lindy stood her ground.

A dozen men fronted her.

An arm was raised.

It came down with clinched fist.

Lindy saw it raise.

Saw it descending.

She never moved her head.

She never flinched.

She eyed the hand and the arm.

It came down.

Thud.

The blow struck her square in her face.

She neither moved nor cried.

She was a rock in the doorway.

Then the hand was raised again.

Another hand seized it.

" Hold on, Joe.   That's a white woman.   Dawg'd ef I'd
do that."

Then Lindy knew it was her husband who had struck her
a second time.

Joe was pushed back and a dozen hands stretched out and
seized the rock in the door.

Linda was dragged violently away.

The crowd ran in and struck a light.

Jupe was not there.

But they found Mansa.

" There ain't no one here but the she niggah."

" Where's Jupe? "

Mansa's lips were sealed.

" Where's Jupe? "

There was a blow for an interrogation point.

" Oh ! oh !   I doan know, sah."

" You're lying, you——."

Again Mansa's lips were closed.

" Ef you don't tell where he is you'll get skinned."

" I doan know, sah."

"Drag her out."

"Peel her."

"Drat her."

"Flay her."

"She'll answer hick'ry fast enough."

The hands drew her to the door.

They drew her out into the garden.

She looked about in terror.

Lindy was gone.

A half score of men had surrounded and pushed Lindy before them down the road.

Lindy walked on quietly until she heard a scream.

She knew it was Mansa in peril.

Then she burst through the wall of men and rushed back.

When Mansa was dragged out into the garden she was ordered to remove her clothes.

"Oh, good gentlemen, please, please. Ef you mus' whip me, leave my clofes."

"Off, off. Drat you."

"Shuck 'em quick."

Mansa clung to her garments.

They were not removed.

They were torn from her.

They were pulled away in shreds.

Mansa pleaded, prayed and wept.

She called on Heaven, on earth, on God, but piece by piece her garments were shredded away.

By the side of the graveled walk, a few yards from the door, was a rustic bench.

In the struggle to divest Mansa of her garments, she had been pushed down close to the bench.

Pelter, the leader, saw it.

"Ah! that's the place. Here, you nig! Bend over that!"

"Oh! oh! oh! Fo' de Lawd's sake, mawstah!" She shrank up with shame.

"Seize her arms and legs and drag her over it."

Four men seized Mansa.

One at each wrist.

One at each ankle.

Others pushed.

Mansa was bent down over the bench.

Her stomach lay upon it.

Two men sat on the earth on one side of the bench, grasping her wrists.

Two men sat on the other side of the bench, grasping her ankles.

Mansa was in a human vise.

She was in the clutches of four great hooded and venomous toads.

Then a hickory rod was raised.

It whizzed through the air.

It descended on Mansa's unprotected back.

Mansa shrieked.

It was the cry that reached Lindy.

With the fleetness of wind Lindy started up the road.

She tore through the thorny hedge and rushed into the path.

The rod was raised for the third blow.

The maskers were torturing deliberately.

Then Lindy stood by Mansa, and flung herself upon her nude black body.

Her action was so sudden there was no time to arrest the blow, and it fell with tremendous, biting energy upon her own back.

But Lindy was voiceless. She made no sign.

She simply clung to Mansa.

It was vain struggling.

What could one woman do against two-score infuriate men ?

Lindy was dragged away.

Strong men held her by the wrists until she was led far down the road.

When she recognized how powerless she was, Lindy spoke to her captors.

Even then there was neither excitement nor passion in her voice; not even a trace of emotion.

"'Tain't no use, is it?"

"No, course it ain't."

"Well, let me go and I'll go home."

"Shoa?"

"Yes."

"No fooling?"

"No."

The men released their hold and stood in the road watching her.

They saw her walk away slowly down the road, without once turning her face backward until she was swallowed up in the darkness.

When Lindy was borne away from the garden the beating was renewed.

Five blows were struck with brutal energy.

Five great welts lay across Mansa's back.

Then there was a suggestion.

Mansa heard it.

She shivered!

She renewed her struggles.

Then she cried out:

"Oh, good gen'lmen! Fo' God's sake! I'ze only a po' niggah, a po' black niggah! Beat me, mawstahs! Beat me, mawstahs! Scoa it hard, mawstahs! I won't cry no mo'— no, mawstahs! Please, mawstahs! So hard as you like, mawstahs! We'll go away, mawstahs! Jupe and me, mawstahs! Out de State, mawstahs! Out o' de wuld, mawstahs! 'Deed we will! 'Deed we will, mawstahs, Jupe and me! Lick me hawd, mawstahs! Hawd as yo' like, mawstahs! An' I'll git Jupe ter come an' take a lickin', mawstahs! 'Deed him will! 'Deed him will! But—oh! oh! mawstahs, deah, good mawstahs, I'ze been an honest woman. 'Deed I has! 'Deed I has! Fo' de Lawd sake, mawstahs! For Gawd A'mighty sake, mawstahs—don't—do-o-n-n-'t do dat! Don't! Don't! Don't! mawstahs!"

Vain pleading! Mansa was entreating tigers.

CHAPTER XXXIV.

PRAY QUICK, JOE!

When Lindy Ratley was relieved from the clutch of the men who dragged her forcibly from Mansa, she walked instantly away from them.

The shouts, the laughter, the profanity of the "1900" behind her, rioted on the calm air and assailed her ears; but she walked steadily on toward her home.

Only once she faltered. A shriek of Mansa's rose above the roar of the mob.

But the uselessness of resistance occurred to her.

She knew the men behind her.

They were violent as passion.

They were unrelenting as destiny.

She understood them thoroughly.

They were hungry wolves rending their prey.

They were a storm unloosed.

They were an ocean in fury.

And she knew that no entreaties of hers could shatter the rock of their will.

She knew that no force of hers could turn the current of their purpose.

She set her face resolutely forward and walked on.

The oaths grew fainter.

The roar became a hum.

Then a floating huskiness in the air.

Then died out.

The pendicle of plaint and moan and bellow no longer swept on her ears.

The pungent fragrance of the forest pines enveloped her.

The profound hush of night wrapped her in.

But her nostrils were sealed to the aroma of the pines, and her senses were dead to the solemn calm by which she was surrounded.

Walking down the road, she saw nothing, heard nothing, felt nothing, thought of nothing in the wide universe but Mansa, tortured and suffering, and — Joe, Joe scourging Mansa.

But her thoughts never laid hold of her limbs.

Her lips were dumb and motionless.

There was no blind striking out with her arms.

There was no halting for thought.

Many do that. In a maze their limbs refuse to move. Their muscles are in the grip of a dazed mind. They stand. Then move on again. Their progress is one of purposeless hurrying, faltering and halts.

But Melinda Ratley was not one of these.

No threats passed her lips.

She neither hurried forward nor halted.

The pace with which she started from her captors she maintained, a steady, unhurried, unfaltering pace to the end.

Her lips were not compressed.

There was not even a trace of anger in her eyes.

She was like one who had seen and forgotten.

A child could not have been more composed as she turned from the road into the path in front of her own gate.

She lifted the hook that held the gate, entered and pulled the gate softly after her.

Then as softly she latched it and walked toward the house.

Within a few feet of the front door there was a path, almost hidden with flowering shrubs, leading around the end of the house to the corn crib.

When Melinda reached this path she turned into it without an instant's hesitation, as if it had been her purpose from the beginning, and walked on, without halting, until she reached the corn crib. Then she unlatched the door and entered.

In a few moments she came out again and closed the door behind her.

When Melinda entered the crib her hands were empty.

When she stood out again in the moonlight they grasped a gun.

It was Joe's rifle.

From the corn crib, with the same deliberation of movement, Lindy Ratley walked along the path, through the cornfield in the rear of her cabin, toward the broad belt of timber that lay between her home and Slimpton.

It was this path Joe Ratley invariably followed on his return home.

Reaching the skirt of the forest, Melinda entered it and walked on until she came to a spot where the light of the moon penetrated the tree-tops and shone full upon the path.

Then she paused and drew herself behind a tree.

There she stood motionless.

Her eyes were riveted upon the path.

Her ears were alert for every sound.

Her body and limbs were immovable.

Hours passed away.

Her position was unchanged.

She had moved neither hand nor foot since she paused at the tree.

Her eyes had never moved from the path.

She was a molded purpose.

She was a statue.

A fate.

Long past the middle of the night Joe Ratley turned away from the "1900."

He entered the eastern skirt of the forest.

He stumbled into the path singing a ribald song.

His forward movement was not rapid.

He was more than half drunk.

The scenes of the night filled him with a devilish glee.

They unrolled like a charming panorama before his dull mind.

As scene after scene flashed through his brain he paused and slapped his thigh and roared, "Ha! ha! ha!"

Then he staggered on again.

When he entered the little spot of moonlight beyond the center of the forest he heard a voice.

It was soft, and low, and passionless.

"Joe Ratley, does you ever pray?"

It was the same voice that Joe heard long ago when he lay bound on his cabin floor under Lindy Ratley's vigorous scourging.

It entered Joe's ears.

His knees rocked under him.

He was smitten with terror.

"Pray Joe—yes, pray quick, Joe. You'd best, Joe. I am going to kill you, Joe."

The rifle in Melinda's hand was raised.

Its muzzle was but a few feet from Joe's head.

Joe might have sprung upon it.

But Joe was a coward.

He fell upon his knees. His teeth beat a horrible tattoo.

He writhed upon the ground.

He was a groveling worm.

Before a real danger he was the spume of abjectness.

"My Gawd, Lindy, you hain't?"

"Yes, Joe. I must, Joe. I'll give you till I count ten. Till I count ten, Joe."

"Lindy! Lindy!"

"Mansa helped me and the children, Joe, and you beat her; beat her, Joe."

"Lindy! Lindy!"

"And you ain't fit to live! No, Joe, you ain't fit to live. Pray, Joe! Pray! you best! Yes, you best."

"Lindy! Lindy."

"One!"

"Oh my Gawd!"

"Two."

"Spare me; spar——"

"Three."

" Oh ! oh ! oh ! "

" Four ! '

" I'll never agin——"

" Five ! "

" Hurt no one."

" Six."

" I swar it, Lin——"

" Seven ! "

" I'll give up the—"

" Eight ! "

" I'll be yer slave. I—"

" Nine ! "

" I swar it. I swa—"

" Ten ! "

There was a flash and a sharp report ; a little puff of smoke rose up between Melinda Ratley and Joe, and the Confederate deserter and member of the " 1900 " rolled over into the path.

For nearly a minute Melinda stood rigid and silent.

Then seeing that the body in the walk was motionless, she moved toward it, laid the rifle by its side, and instantly turned her face homeward and walked out through the silent forest and the field of corn, never once looking backward.

The broad green corn leaves, with their bedewed surface glistening in the moonlight, betrayed as much emotion as this woman walking deliberately away from the man who lay with his face turned up to the sky in the forest path.

She neither hurried nor dawdled.

A nighthawk burst away from a low lying limb close before her.

From a tall deadened pine in the midst of the cornfield, standing a blanched and solitary ghost of a forest, the " hoo ! hoo ! " of an owl startled the calm air.

But Lindy Ratley was dead to the rustling wings and the " hoo ! hoo ! "

If she heard, she made no sign.

She was a machine set with her face homeward, and with a perfect rhythm of motion she marched toward it.

Her hands, which hung listlessly by her side, moved but twice.

Then it was her right hand.

It lifted up and passed slowly across from right to left before her eyes, as if to brush something away. And fell slowly back again.

Thus she reached her cabin door and entered.

Lindy in her cabin was a new being.

She closed the door softly behind her.

A ray of moonlight stole in through the small window across the bed where her children lay.

One of the fair, young heads lay bathed in its glory.

Lindy drew up close to the bedside.

A gentle smile gathered about her lips.

Her chin dropped slowly down to her breast.

Her eyelids drooped.

A gentle light stole into her eyes.

She raised one hand and extended it, palm down, slowly over the sleeping innocence and its halo of golden light in the bed.

Then, when she had almost touched it, she drew her hand slowly back again, walked over to her own bed in another corner of the room, lay down without undressing and almost instantly she was sleeping. Sleeping as calmly as the children in the fading moonlight.

When the children prepared breakfast in the morning Melinda Ratley watched their every motion.

When the frugal breakfast was on the table she arose, bathed her hands and face and joined them.

When the children stood up from the table Lindy spoke for the first time:

"Children, how would you like to go North?"

"To sister?" And the three girls clapped their hands in chorus.

These three girls and the "sister" in the North were the Ratley family.

These and a babe, that had died long ago in infancy, that was all.

The three girls on the Ratley place were delighted with the prospect of seeing the sister from whom they had never before been separated for a day.

Hearing no response from their mother, one of the daughters repeated:

"To sister, mamma?"

"Anywhere North, children!"

"Oh, yes, mamma; but let us go to sister."

"I have money," said one.

"And I!" added the second.

"We have all money, saved from the mill," exclaimed the third.

"And you have some, mamma?" asked the oldest.

"Yes."

"When shall we go?"

"Now."

"This day?" exclaimed the surprised girl.

"Now."

"Immediately."

"Now."

Melinda spoke in torpid monosyllables, looking up from her seat at the table.

"This minute?" asked all of the wondering children in chorus.

"Yes."

It was but one word tranquilly uttered, but they all understood it. Perhaps they thought it was useless to ask questions. Perhaps in their joy at the prospect of seeing sister they forgot to ask. But they asked none. The oldest daughter moved toward one of the beds and began to roll it over. Her mother noticed the movement.

"You need not."

The daughter released her hold of the bed and looked up at her mother with some surprise.

"Not take this, mamma?" she asked.

"No."

"What shall we take, mamma?"

"What clothes we can carry in bundles."

The children picked out the best garments and hastily tied them up. Melinda took nothing but a change of undergarments. In less than ten minutes the four women stood in the cabin door with bundles in their hands. As the children stepped out into the path, Melinda spoke:

"You walk on down the road, children, I'll be up with you in a minute."

The girls faced down the path.

Melinda entered the house and went to the loft.

There before her was a rude, board cradle.

In it she had rocked the little babe of long ago. The lost link of her young wifehood. Night after night she saw it far away. Oh, ever so far. She reached out to it. It was a star. It was a fleecy cloud. It was a ray of moonlight. But it was there. And it was a babe yet. Not thin and wan as when she laid it away from sight. Not with a cold damp on its white brow as when it last lay on her breast, but bright and glorified. And last night she lost it. The moon hid it. The stars obscured it. The babe, the glory, where had it gone? Where? But it would come back. Yes. It would come back. And that was its cradle—when was it? Oh, so long; so long ago. And Melinda knelt down beside it; knelt reverently down and laid her face against it; laid her head where the baby's head had lain and kissed it softly and reverently. Then she chipped a little piece from the side of the cradle where the baby hands had touched, and wrapping it in her handkerchief she pushed it away in her bosom.

After this she pressed her lips to a little spot where the baby fingers had rested long ago, a little spot covered with dust, and stood up and went out of the loft, out of the house, down the walk, through the gate and joined her daughters in the road. And the four women, with bundles in their hands, faced the North star.

CHAPTER XXXV.

THROUGH BRAMBLE, BRIAR AND MORASS.

The blacks throughout the entire county were profoundly agitated. The articles in the Buzzer and the changed temper of the people had disturbed them. Still they had hoped—hoped it was a passing storm that would soon spend its fury. Now, suddenly, their meetings were broken up and a tempest of threatenings, whippings and deaths burst upon them.

What would they do?

What could they do? In every community there are men who are light-houses in a storm. There were there.

Jupiter Saltire was the light-house to whom all on the troubled sea looked.

The ignorant slave had grown into a tower of knowledge and judgment.

That is strength.

Negroes whispered it from one to another: " What do Jupitah Saltiah say?"

They soon heard and whispered that,

" We must meet and determine. There must be agreement and unity of action."

That was what he said.

But how meet?

The hawks were in the air, and every movement of the negroes noted.

There is a ford to every river, a bridge to every difficulty. It was found in this.

The whites were to have a great meeting at Slimpton, day and evening.

That was the colored man's opportunity.

Immediately that Jupiter knew of it he sent out runners to every part of the county.

The order for the negro meeting was but a whisper, yet it ran through the county. In twenty-four hours every prominent negro knew of it; the day, the place and the methods of reaching it.

Among the blacks it was an open secret.

Among the whites it was unsuspected.

On the appointed day the whites filled the roads with tumult, with rioting, shouting and song.

A crowd of blacks went too.

They were of the multitude who looked for guidance, and they went to the white meeting under direction of their leaders.

Their presence was a blind to turn away suspicion from the secret meeting of the blacks.

On one side of the county is a river.

It runs away from the county.

Then suddenly turns and rolls back upon it.

The river is a broad, silvery elbow, fringed with a thickset growth of cottonwood.

Back from the fringe is a dense growth of heavy-trunked, broad-spreading oaks, festooned with moss.

In the heart of this timber there was once a dwelling which disappeared in a cloud of smoke and flare of light, and the river closing in upon it the site was abandoned. One remnant of residence alone remained—a long, low warehouse, hid away, reeking with moisture, under broad branches and pendant moss, a home for bats and owls.

This was the old Moncore cotton house.

The whites headed toward Slimpton, courting the bright sun, and followed by clouds of dust.

All through the night before, throughout the entire county, dusky forms were gliding along the paths and by-roads, through bramble and briar and morass, and during the day, too, but with more caution, and seeking the depths of the forests, toward the elbow in the river.

They began arriving early in the morning.

All day long the tide rolled in steadily.

Men sprang out of trees; out of clumps of bushes; out of the earth; and still silently, stealthily, they came.

At night, between two and three hundred were gathered.

Men of every shade, from clear white to pure African—but all negroes.

Every crevice of the old building was stuffed with moss.

Four sticks were driven into the earth at one end of the building.

They were table posts.

On top of them a board was laid.

Thus a table was made.

That was the president's desk.

On this four candles were placed.

For candlesticks they had sweet potatoes.

When the candles were lighted men searched the building round and round on the outside to see if one ray of light penetrated the walls.

When they were satisfied a number of the least important of the blacks were sent far out into the woods, making a chain of vigilance across the neck of timber.

Then the meeting began.

It was a solemn-faced assemblage, scarcely speaking above its breath.

They began by calling upon the Lord to give them wisdom.

Then an old colored man stood up.

"Brethren, I don't know what's best. I don't know as any of us does. But we can talk it over, brethren. It's the multitude of sticks that make a cabin, brethren. [Dat's de ole man.] Let us put our sticks in the heap and the good Mawstah in heaven will tell us how to put them together. [Oh! oh! An' you hear him!] We know, brothers, what has done come to us. [O-h-h-h.] We was free. [Glory.] May be we was too put up with our freedom. [Oh! oh!] We thought the day of trouble was done passed. [Um-m-m.] We thought we had entered the promised land. [Laws! Laws! Does ye hear 'im.] And now, brethren, they tell us we must quit off the Republican party. [Oh! oh!] They have whipped some of our brethren most awful. [Dear Lawd.] They have shot, [dat dey has,] and they have beat, [O-h-o!] and they have killed, [deah Lawd!] and they tell we that is only the beginning; [um-m-m!] a little drop before the big storm. [Lawd! Lawd!] Oh, my brethren, if that is all these dreadful doings is, [O-h-o-o-o!] if this blood that has been spilled is only a little drop, what will be the big rain? [A prolonged oh, filled the building.] I am an ole man now, brethren. [Dat you is, daddy.] I've passed through the fiah of mo' than seventy year, [shoa! shoa!] a little mo' or a little less to the ole man [po' ole daddy] is nothing, brethren. [Moas' home! Deed he is.] I can stan' it. [Po' daddy.] I have suffered [dat you have daddy,] and I can suffer. [De Lawd!] But I think of the young. [O-h-h!] For myself I would submit. [S-c-c-c-ch!] I would lay done the vote [no! no! Nebah! nebah!] and say, ' White mawstahs [d'ain't no mawstahs] do as you will.' [No! no! no! no!] But, brethren, there is the young! [Dat's it, daddy.] There is the young! [Dat's it.] What will become of them if we give up the vote? [Now yer talking. Heah de man.] Brethren, I don't say fight, [oh!] I don't say give up, [oh!] but I do say whatever you agree upon, think of the young! [Glory!] Think of the young! [Glory!] I trembles. [Po' ole man.] I does, brethren, when I think of the past. [Po' ole daddy.] When I think of the lash [um-m-m!] and the dog, [um-m-m!] And I pray the Lawd to save these young people from going down into the same drefful jaws." [Dat's de ole man! Glory, daddy!]

On the motion of Jupiter Saltire a committee was appointed.

The committee acted promptly.

They reported a resolution.

" Resolved, That we stand by the Republican ticket. That we will vote it whenever we can without meeting certain death. That we will adhere to the Republican party at all hazards, and secure our lawful rights peaceably if we can, and failing that we will appeal to the conscience and humanity of the entire country, believing that public opinion will ultimately correct the abuses that threaten us, and secure us or our children full rights under the laws."

Several voices, some of them pitched in wrathful tones, called for the reading of the resolution again.

It was read.

Then a tall black man strode forward out of the gloom to the speaker's desk.

Behind was a sea of faces.

In the dim light it was a black wave with flashing eyes floating on its surface.

" Mr. Chairman, I don't like dat resolution of the brother's. [Dat's de word wid de bark on !] It's all coon squall. [Jis so ! Jis so !] Yes, sah ! [Youze right, Mistah Stoutah !] That's what it is [Dat's so ! Glory !], and mighty young coon at dat ! [Jiss heah de man.] Please good mawstah white man [Gui ! O, de Stoutah !], please let me [ugh !] ; if ye don't please, I'll sniffle a little [Jiss heah dat !] an' I'll grin and b'ar it [oh—O !], and call on the Lawd. [Did ye ebbah heah de likes o' dat !] Dat ain't no way. [Sure ! Sure !] When yer tells a tyrant you's gwine ter grin and b'ar it and call on the Lawd he'll crunch yer with his fist [Dat's so ! Dat's so !] and tell yer ter grin. [Does ye heah his horn !] An' he'll crunch yer under his heel [Dat de trumpet !] an' tell ye to bar it. [So, Bruddah Stoutah.] And dey'll blow yer head off wid a powdah hawn [Oh-h-h !] as dey did de odder night [U-m-m-m !], and den tell yer how yer gwine ter call on the Lawd den. [D a-a Lawd !] De Lawd ain't no fool, bredren. [Oh, heah de man !] Yer can't put chicken squall on de Lawd for de crow of gaffed roostah. [Ho ! Ho ! Hi !] No sahs ! Who you think the Lawd help ? Does yer think the Lawd's gwine ter hill up cotton, less some man handles the hoe ? [Dah's glory for ye.] Does yer think the Lawd's gwine ter fotch down the coon less some man holes the gun. [Dat's de Lawd's truth !] Ef yer does yer fool'd ! [Shoa ! Shoa !] Dat's it, sah, mighty fooled. [Dat's so !] De Lawd helps the men wid de hoe and de gun. [Shoa as you bawn !] De Lawd helps de man dat won't grin an' bar it. ['Clah. 'Clah ! dat man knows a power !] De Lawd hates a whine.

[Eh! Eh!] Dat's so! De Lawd nevah put legs under a snivel in de world. [What dat?] Nevah in de world, sah. [Oh-o.] An' I'm 'sposed! Yes, sah! most perfect composed to dat 'Please good mawstah white man.' I'ze had 'nuff o' dat. [Me, too ; me, too. Glory!] It nevah brought no answer but a lash. [Dat's Gawd's truth.] An' I ain't gwine to hab no mo' of it. [Dah's de music.] No, sah! Dey have no mo' right to deny we de suf. ferin' (suffrage) dan we hab to deny dem. [Oh, O, Glory.] Dey has no mo' right to break up ouah meetings dan we have to break up dey'as. [Oh! O, Glory!] Dey has no mo' right to hickory we uns dan we uns hab to hickory dem. [Ki-ki ki! Hear de man.] Dey hab no mo' right to shoot we dan we hab to shoot dem. [Fo' de Lawd.] Ain't dat so, sah? Ain't dat so, bruddahs?"

"Dat's so! Dat's so!" from all parts of the house.

"But," asked an aged colored man, "what are you going to do?"

"Do! Jist heah dat? Heah de bruddah! Dat's mo' please good mawstah white man! Do, sah! Dey ain't no tellin' how pudding tastes till ye put it in yer mouf, is dah? [No! no! no!] Yer can see 'em an' smell 'em, but dat ain't no taste. No, sah! [Oh-o!] Ef dey cook puddin for we, dey must eat it. [Um-m.] Dat's it, sah, make 'em eat it. [Oh-h-h!] Den sah dey'll know how it taste."

" Dat's de way."

" Dat's the trumpet."   "Oh-o!"

" Does the brother mean," asked the former interrupter, " to return lash for lash and bullet for bullet?"

"No, sah! No, sah! Not dat way, sah! I has a mo' general (generous) sperit dan dat, sah! I'ze fah bettah pay dan dat, sah! [What dat?] I'ze fo' gibbing dem two fo' one, sah, five fo' one, sah! I'ze fo' stuffin dey moufs chuck up full of dey own puddin, and let 'em see how dey likes de taste!"

The meeting was in instant uproar.

"Oh! oh!"

"That's it!"

"Glory!"

" No ! no ! "

" Never do in the world."

" Smite one cheek, turn the other."

" Bah ! "

" Cheek-turners are always getting cuffed."

" Hallelujah ! "

These were the sounds that came up from all quarters of the house.

The crowd was closely packed about the president's stand.

It was in upheaval.

It ejected a young mulatto.

The black sea turned its floating lights upon him.

His oiled locks clung close to his head.

A broad, white collar assailed and threatened his ears.

A huge breast-pin was spread out on his bosom.

He was crying out :

" Mistah President ! Mistah President ! "

The chairman noticed him

" Ah, brothers, ordah ! ordah ! Mistah Jackson has de floah ! "

A hush fell upon the wave.

" Mistah President, I rises in my place, sah, for the purpose to ax, sah ! of the distincwish cheerman of dis yeah meeting, sah, with the perfoundest respec, sah, where is de arms? Dat's de question of de occasion, sah ! Where is de arms ? "

" What you want o' guns ? " cried a voice out of the dark.

" Mistah Jackson " turned on the voice.

" I don't banty no words wid you, sah ! "

" Coase not," answered the voice. " Dey ain't no banty 'bout you 'cept the legs ! "

" Ordah, gentlemen ! " cried the chairman, " dat ain't de way to cherish one annudder."

Then turning to Jackson :

" What arms you ax for, Breeah Jackson ? "

" Mistah Cheerman, I rises with perfoundest respec, sah, to infaum you knowledge, sah, dat I reads de papahs, sah ! "

The chairman nodded.

" An' I see in de voracious Buzzer of Slimpton, sah, dat up Nawth dey has sole a pile of wooden hams, sah, and bought a stack of guns, sah, for dis yeah occasion, sah ! "

A low laugh ran round the room.

Then the chairman explained.

The Buzzer story was all fudge. Circulated to excite and rouse weak-kneed whites. It was entirely false.

A lie, manufactured out of whole cloth.

They had sent no arms and would send none.

The shirt-collar and oily head subsided.

In their place stood a short, stout black man.

" Mistah Chawman, I'ze bin heahin' dis. I'ze clah ter Gawd I wish I wus a slabe agin."

A prolonged groan rose out of the dark.

A score of angry faces were pushed close up to the speaker.

" Traitah ! "

" Cowa'd ! "

" Sneak ! "

" Misable niggah fool ! "

" I clah ter Gawd, I does ! I does ! "

" Ter be sole ! "

" Wife sole away ! "

" Lashed ! "

" Fool niggah ! "

" Lost him sense ! "

" Breeren, I wus a eighteen hunder dollah niggah, I wus. Yes, sah! Dey takes keer o' eighteen hunder dollah niggahs, they uns does. No one slash me den but mawstah. I ain't afeard o' slashin' den. I ain't afeard o' shootin' den. Dey uns ain't fools to burn eighteen hunder dollah niggahs in shot guns. Now I owns myself I ain't wuth nothin' ter no one. Dey slashes and dey shoots. Slabery's bad, yas, sah, mitey bad, pow'ful bad, an' I prayed de Lawd foh de freedom. Now, breeren, it am come, an' I'ze wus dan befo,' an' I pray tu God dat I wur a slabe again, wuth eighteen hunder dollah ter some white man."

Then he paused, amid hisses and groans.

Other speakers came.

They denounced the man who prayed for slavery.

Some advocated the resolution.

Some opposed it.

Then Jupiter Saltire was called.

All desired to know his views.

Jupiter was a shrewd politician.

Too shrewd to wear himself out on the picket line.

In legislative and all other deliberative assemblages, the men whose tongues are in the dish in all stages of preparation have no mouth for the rounding-up desert.

The honors go the men who wait and come in at the finish.

Jupiter could wait.

He had waited.

He waited this night until he was called.

Then he was listened to with breathless attention.

He went calmly over the ground.

He spoke of their rights and their wrongs.

He drew his audience slowly along with him.

Then he came to the remedies offered — patience and retaliation.

"Now, my brethren," he proceeded, "what can we gain by retaliation? We complain that they violate the law. While we stand there, stand demanding justice under the law, we have the conscience of being right, and faith that in God's time the wrong will fall in the wine-press of Divine wrath. But, brethren, if we take to retaliation, we are no longer in the right. We, too, become violators of the law. We become guilty of the crimes we charge against the whites. Can we ask God to bless us in this? [No! no! no!] No, my unfortunate, persecuted brethren, we can not! [Dat's so.] Can we ask the sympathy of our countrymen and of the civilized world? [Dahs de sense.] No, my crushed and despised friends, we can not [dat's so], and we will not receive it. Brethren, wrongs may be remedied by lawful resistance; but no wrong ever found its remedy in retaliation; never. [Oh,

heah de wise man.] But, my brethren, if we were so evil-
minded, what good would it do? What good would follow it?
The first blow we struck for revenge would only call in the
hawks; our first blow would be a signal that would call in
every white man from Alabama and Louisiana, and from all
the neighboring counties. [Shoa! shoa! shoa!] The railroads are in their hands [dat's so], and all the means of con-
veyance. They hold the telegraph, and all the means of rapid
communication. They own the arms. They have full control
of every engine of speed and force. [Shoa! shoa! shoa!]
They can come; they will come ['deed dey will], and we
alone, without means of securing aid — we, if we raise our
hands in retaliation, would be wiped out in blood ['deed we
would]; crushed from the face of the earth. [Oh-h-h!] And
our wrongs would not end with us; they would be hurled back
upon our inoffensive brethren in every part of the South.
[Lawd! Lawd! Lawd!] For these reasons, my brethren,
I hope we will pass the resolution and abide by it."

Jupiter paused.

A breathless silence followed.

Then the chairman asked:

"Brethren, are you ready for the question?"

The breathless silence continued.

"All in favor of the resolutions reported by the committee
will say 'Aye.'"

A low "Aye"—a murmur, no more—floated up on the
surface of the wave.

"All opposed say 'No!'"

There was no response.

"Is any brother opposed to the resolutions?"

Silence was the only answer.

Then there was a commotion in the back end of the
building.

It was a messenger for Jupiter Saltire.

The man came in.

It was Jack.

He told his story.

A few discreet friends heard it.

They advised Jupiter not to go home.

That was Mansa's request.

"Yes! He must go. They might beat Mansa."

The strong man shivered as he said it.

Volunteers to go with him were numerous.

"No! Numbers can do no good."

Saying this and thanking his friends he turned and hurried away with a thorn of anxiety probing his soul.

CHAPTER XXXVI.

PO' JUPE !

Jupiter strode away from the meeting in the forest with Jack hurrying at his side. For a few score yards he was followed by several of his prominent colored friends—followed in an aimless sort of a way. They had no intention of going on with him to his home. They knew that to do so would be entirely useless. They knew they could neither advise nor aid him, and yet they followed until Jupiter was lost to sight under the shadow of the broad spreading oaks. When he was no longer in view they paused, paused and gazed silently into the dark, paused and thought and wondered what would be the outcome of it all. Usually voluble of words, they stood silent and looked. They were dazed in the presence of the impending danger. Each felt for himself how entirely impotent and helpless he was.

The threat that assailed Jupiter reached them all.

It was him now.

It might be either of them to-morrow or to-night.

Where was there safety ?

Where was there a refuge ?

How could they escape ?

They looked and listened until the retreating feet of Jupiter ceased to disturb the stillness about them. Then, with audible sighs, and more than one exclaiming " Dear Lawd " and " Hebin presarb we," they turned and walked slowly back to the whispering, awe-struck crowd at the cotton house.

While they were looking and listening Jupiter was hurrying forward.

For the first mile Jack kept pace with him, running on by his side.

If Jupiter knew that he was there, he made no sign.

His wide open eyes penetrated the dark·before him.

He neither turned his head to the right nor the left.

He spoke not one word.

Some men would have asked questions.

Some would have kept up a running fire of interrogations: "Jack, do you think they will do this?" "Jack, do you think they will do that?"

But what response could Jack have made to any questioning.

He could only have answered nothing.

He could know no more than the questioner.

Jupiter knew this.

For facts he would have inquired.

But surmising was profitless.

And that is all Jack could have returned to volleys of questioning.

Hence Jupiter asked nothing but strode on in silence.

At the end of the second mile Jupiter was alone.

Jack was unequal to his vigorous pace.

It was not Jack's Mansa who was in danger.

It was Jupiter's Mansa, and Jupiter loved her.

She was black and ignorant, and had been a poor, toiling, driven slave, but Jupiter loved her.

For her he had entered the jaws of secessia.

For her he had risked capture and faced the torturing that would follow it.

And since they had become free Mansa had not kept pace with Jupiter's intellectual growth.

She had never shaken off the old plantation life as Jupiter had.

It was a scale on him and he had flung it away.

It was a part of her nature; it was imbedded in her life and it clung to her.

But Jupiter, if he had grown, he had not outgrown the old love.

He never looked down on or pitied Mansa.

He never felt himself unequally yoked, as many do when

one of a married pair develops and the other stands still.

Education and honors had widened no gulf between them. She was yet Mansa. The same Mansa whose glad song made his soul light when the burden of slavery sat heavy upon him.

His love lifted her up, and bore her along with himself.

She was a part of his life, and this part of his life was alone and in peril.

This thought set his jaws tightly together.

This thought nerved his limbs.

There is a wonderful momentum in love.

It drove him forward.

The low-lying limbs brushed against his face ; rank weeds and dank grass twined about his limbs ; thorns and briars tore his clothing and tore his person ; yet he dashed against the limbs, through the grass, and through the briars and thorns, ignorant of the rending and pain.

He only knew that Mansa was threatened, and that speed brought him nearer to her.

On and on this heart-sore man pressed.

On and on, through briar and thorn and morass.

Jack was left far behind.

At last Jupiter stood in the skirt of the forest looking down upon his cottage.

There was no sense of fatigue upon him.

He was possessed of but one emotion—an intense longing to know how it was with Mansa.

A thin veil of mist lay like a fleecy mantle upon the valley of Peeky Run, obscuring his garden and the road and all of his house except the roof and the chimney, which stood out in relief against the sky.

A moment Jupiter paused and listened.

No sound assailed his ears.

Then he bent down to the earth and listened again.

And there was no response but silence.

Had the " 1,900 " come ?

Oh, how he hoped they had not.

Or were they gone ?

Or were they in hiding awaiting his coming ?

These thoughts passed rapidly through his brain.

Then he hurried with more stealth than had previously marked his movements through the low brushes to the cornfield in the rear of his home.

Up to the skirt of the timber Jupiter had dashed impetuously over obstacles.   Now he moved about them.

His course had been resonant

It was the vociferousness of hurry.

Now it was soundless.

It was the muteness of caution.

He reached the edge of the corn and listened again.

He detected no sound.

Then he entered the cornfield.

He pushed aside the broad leaves with the hush of dew upon them and stealthily moved on to the garden about his home.

Here he dropped on his hands and knees and crawled through the shrubbery and along on its inner side under its shadow until he reached the front of the house.

From this point he had full view of the house and the road.

He saw that the garden and road were surrendered to silence and solitude.

His heart bounded within him for joy.

He whispered, " Thank God !   Thank God ! "

Then he stood up and hurried to the door. It was wide open.

But Mansa was safe.

Of course she was safe.

He never doubted that.

And he was so thankful, so anxious to clasp her in his arms and tell her so, that he never thought to wonder at the open door.

He thought of nothing but her—of Mansa.

He was too glad to think, and with this gladness in his heart and hurrying his footsteps, as anxiety hurried them before, he entered his home.

So opposite feelings produce like results.

Within the house was dark.

Jupiter called,

"Mansa?"

A voice answered him.

"Oh, Jupe! Jupe! I'ze so glad."

"Thank God!" Jupiter's whole soul was in the words.

"I did think you'ze nebbah gwine ter come."

"Dear Mansa?"

"You'ze so lang, so lang!"

Jupiter paused in the middle of the floor puzzled. He noticed that the voice came from before the fire-place instead of from the bed.

"Are you not in bed, Mansa?"

"No, Jupe; no, I'ze heah! I'ze heah, Jupe."

From the garden, when Mansa recovered consciousness after the departure of Pelter's gang, Mansa dragged herself to the house.

She partially clothed herself and sank upon a stool before the broad open fire-place.

Her mind was on Jupiter. "Would he escape?" Again and again she murmured "Po' Jupe!"

But she thought nothing beyond this.

Thought rarely grows out of great suffering.

Thinking is consumed in the furnace of pain.

There is sensation. No more.

She had that.

It poured itself out in low moans.

Thus she had sat during the waning hours — sat with crouched form on the stool, with her face buried in her hands and her tearless, straining eyes fixed upon the blackness of the yawning chimney.

When she heard Jupiter's voice, Mansa's first impulse was to spring into his arms.

Then the scene in the garden rose up before her—and she remembered her shame — she half rose and sank back upon her stool, bending lower and lower, until her face almost touched the floor.

24

In this position she spoke to Jupiter.

When Jupiter realized his wife was not in bed, he spoke to her in a voice of affectionate surprise.

" Waiting for me, Mansa ? "

" Oh, Jupe ! Jupe ! "

" You ought to have gone to bed, Mansa ! "

" Oh, Jupe ! an' dey didn't ketch yo' ? "

" No, Mansa.   I am quite safe."

" I'ze so glad !   So glad !   Po' Jupe ! "

" Poor chile, you oughtn't to worry for Jupe."

Jupiter had drawn to her side and placed his hand upon her shoulder. Mansa shivered under the touch and sobbed aloud.

" Don't worry, Mansa."

" Po' Jupe !   Po' Jupe ! "

Jupe knelt down beside her with his arm about her neck, and drew her to him.

Mansa's sobbing redoubled.

He tried to soothe her, and she only answered back, " Po' Jupe !   Po' Jupe ! "

Minutes they sat there.

Then a thought of the open door flashed through Jupiter's mind. Can it be possible the " 1900 " had visited his home in his absence ? Was this the cause of Mansa's unusual agitation ? Could it be possible they had ill-treated her, ill-used Mansa ?

Then he asked her.

He halted between words, as if fearing to know.

" Mansa, has-any-one-been-here ? "

" Dey has, Jupe.   Dey has !   Dey has ! "

" Masked-men, Mansa ? "

" Oh, Jupe !   Jupe !   Jupe ! "

" And they were here, Mansa ? "

" Oh, Jupe ! "

" Did they scare you, dear ? "

" Oh, Jupe ! "

" And—and did they—did they hurt you, Mansa ? "

"Lawd! Lawd! Lawd! How's I gwine to tell yo', Jupe?"

Then she told of the occurrences of the night; told it all.

Mansa, as her narrative progressed, broken with sobs and trembling, could feel the strong form by her side shivering. She could hear his teeth grinding together. And the bones of her broad hand were crunching together in his strong grasp. When she had done, her head was drawn close to his breast, and he was murmuring:

"Poor Mansa! Poor, suffering Mansa!"

Minutes they sat that way, Jupiter bolt upright on a stool beside his wife, her head pressed close against his breast, and looking down upon the dead ashes before him; looking down upon the dead ashes of his wife's honor.

Then Mansa shrank away from his embrace. Shrank down upon the floor by his side, and buried her face on his knees. Suddenly she seized one of Jupiter's hands in both of her own, and pressed her cold lips against it, pressed them upon it again, and again and again, all the time sobbing,

"Po' Jupe! Po' Jupe! Po' Jupe!"

After this, Mansa stood up and reeled to the door. There she paused an instant and looked back toward where Jupiter sat.

Her lips opened.

It was but a whisper.

"Po' Jupe! Po' Jupe!"

Then she staggered out upon the walk; out into the garden; out into the dark.

Jupiter sat. Minutes passed away. At last he spoke:

"Mansa, we must go away from this."

There was no answer.

"Yes, my poor, wronged girl, we will go North, North, Mansa; North, dear, where we can be free! Where we can be men and women."

Still there was no answer.

"Mansa!"

There was no response.

Jupiter reached out his hand.

There was only vacancy about him.

He stood up and called—

" Mansa ! "

He hurried to the door and called again—

" Mansa !   Mansa ! "

He hurried into the garden.

" Mansa !   Mansa ! "

He searched the bushes and the outhouses.

" Mansa ! Mansa ! Mansa ! "

From the top of a dead oak in the cornfield an owl cried "hoo ! hoo !" and the dew dropped silently down from the roses.

But Mansa never answered.

Jupiter searched all through the night. He scoured the fields and the woods. Searched everywhere until daybreak ; until sunrise ; everywhere calling, " Mansa ! Mansa ! Mansa !"

The bright sun mounted above the treetops, gilding the broad leaves and the lilies that lay in the pools of Peeky Run.

Jupiter was crossing the run.

To his right lay a cluster of reeds.

A bit of muslin floating idly on the surface of the water near them attracted his attention.

Jupiter approached it.

He stood beside it.

He drew it to him.

It came slowly and heavily.

He lifted it up.

Then his anguish burst forth anew.

" Mansa ! Mansa ! Mansa ! "

She was in his arms.

But Jupiter's wail fell upon ears that were dumb.

He laid the body down on the grass close by the floating lilies.   He devoured the cold lips with kisses, and he sat down beside it, one chill hand in his own, sat down and looked.

Hours passed away.

The sun had climbed to its azure height and was descending again.

Then two men came down to the Run.

They saw Jupiter, and one of them pointed toward him.

Both hurriedly crossed the run and stood beside him. In his arms was the body of his dead wife and his face lay upon her breast.

One of the men spoke.

There was no answer.

Then the man put his hand on Jupiter's shoulder and exclaimed:

"Jupiter Saltire, I arrest you for the murder of Joe Ratley."

But Jupiter never heard.

He had passed beyond the touch of earthly troubles and the judgment of human tribunals.

CHAPTER XXXVII.

A CHILD'S CRY LOUDER THAN THE STORM.

Joe Ratley was dead.

Col. Trenhom was in his parlor walking to and fro. He had returned a few moments before from a walk through the town ; on his way home he had met Jim Ratley, a brother of Joe's. Jim was with Joe in Trenhom's regiment. When they met Jim said to him :

"Kunnel, they be some durned fools as says you know something of Joe's killing."

"I ! " responded the colonel hotly. "I ! "

"Yas, kunnel, but it's all a dratted fetch, we all knows that. You was allers good to me in the regiment, kunnel, an' I ain't gwine ter forgit it.

"We boys is all yer friends, every one on us."

This was added to the rest as Trenhom strode through his rooms.

What did it all mean ? Even if Jupiter had anything to do with the killing of Ratley, could it be possible there was any plot to connect him with Jupiter.

Was it this way they intended to interrupt his meetings ?

Only the day before he had caused posters to be put up announcing a series of meetings through the country, at which he promised to address the people. And during the night a letter had been pushed under his door.

As he walked the floor the letter lay spread out on the center table staring him in the face.

It was a villainous letter :

"Kunnel Trenhom, you take notis. This Co. must have paece. We

have got to have it, if you die for it. So you just take warning and pull
down your meeting notises. If you don't you'll go dead sure."

1900

While looking at the notice and thinking of Jim Ratley
and his words, Trenhom heard hoofs on the graveled carriage
road, then laughter, and he knew that his children, Nellie and
Johnnie, were returning from a morning ride.

As he passed the window he caught a glimpse of Nellie
tripping up the front steps, shaking her long, golden curls in
the soft morning air.

He could hear his wife and children conversing and laughing on the broad porch.

He heard other voices.

He paused.

Who could that be ?

He stepped out on to the porch.

Then he saw the sheriff of the county and two other gentlemen.

"Ah ! good morning, gentlemen, good morning; will you
come up ?"

They advanced up the steps and stood on the porch.

"To what do I owe the honor of this early visit, gentlemen ?"

The sheriff grew red in the face, fumbled in his pockets.

"Hum ! "

Then he produced a paper and muttered : " I've been sent
to arrest you ! "

"To arrest me ! me ! "

"Yes, kunnel, to arrest you. I'm sorry, I swar I am ! "

"And for what do you presume to arrest me, sir ? "

"On the accusation of knowing something of Joe Ratley's death."

Mrs. Trenhom stepped instantly between the sheriff and her husband.

"Mr. Sheriff, you do not believe this?"

Mr. Senter, the sheriff, was an old man, with gray hair and flabby, wrinkled face. He looked down at the papers in his hands, turned them over, pulled them first one end, then the other—"I — I — hum!"

"You know you do not, sir. You know it, sir."

"Well, you see—"

"Pshaw, Mr. Senter. Talk like a man. You know, sir, that this is part of a plot to murder my husband; and you, an old man, you, who must soon face your Maker, are lending yourself to it. You know it. You know if my husband goes with you he will be killed."

"Oh, I hope not!"

Then Trenhom spoke.

He had one arm thrown about his wife's waist, his daughter Nellie was clinging to his other arm.

"I demand instant preliminary trial, and to remain in my house until the result is known."

"Certainly! Certainly!" responded the sheriff. "That is fair enough, with guards."

"Place what guards you please here. Remember, sir, they have not dared go far enough to charge me with murder, or with inciting or aiding it — only of knowing something about it."

"Yes, that is all."

"Even that is not true. No man who knows me will credit it, not for an instant, sir. But, sir, I shall not go tamely to a slaughter-pen."

While they were speaking, Pelter, Jim Gouge and several other members of the Pelter company of "1900" lounged into sight about the corner of the house nearest the road.

Almost at the same instant, Savage, Boozy, and a dozen others came through the grounds from the other side of the house.

Trenhom looked for his son.

He was gone.

A moment after he heard the boy whispering over his shoulder.

The boy had thrust a revolver into his father's pockets, and disappeared again.

The crowd about the house swelled.

The most of them rough, lank-jawed, shrunken-eyed, skulking creatures, the lean and hungry wolves of the country.

As they gathered, others came, a number of Republican friends of Col. Trenhom, and with them Col. Valore.

Johnnie, seeing the gathering crowd, had slipped out the back way and roused the known friends of his father.

Col. Valore heard rumors of the disturbance, and came voluntarily.

As Valore came upon the porch, he asked for an explanation.

It was given.

" Pshaw ! " he promptly exclaimed ; " this is an outrage— a shameful outrage.   I don't like the colonel's politics, but he had no more to do with the killing of that Ratley scoundrel than I had myself."

Mrs. Trenhom turned to the colonel, her eyes suffused with tears.   " Dear old friend, I thank you."

The words and the tone were a bomb-shell under the colonel.   He blushed like a school-girl.

" Ah ! ah ! madam ! I ! — I — ! The truth is, I am not — not — blameless.   But if I had been in the post-office, the other day, when that Ratley rascal insulted Mrs. Huntley, I would have shot him myself and saved them all this trouble. I tell you, madam, that is carrying politics too far. Dirty dog! Dirty dog ! There ought to be no questions asked about who killed him.   We ought to thank God for his taking off."

Mrs. Trenhom took Valore's wrinkled hands in her own and kissed them.

Noble old friend.

At this instant there was a clattering in the road.

The party on the porch looked.

Thirty or forty men armed with double-barreled shot guns were entering the gate.

Trenhom was among the first to notice the armed crowd.

He turned to the sheriff.

" For what have you brought this set of cowardly ku-klux scoundrels here with their guns ? "

The sheriff shuffled his feet on the porch and thrust his hands uneasily in his pockets.

" Have you brought them here to kill me " continued Trenhom. " I verily believe you have. I believe you will kill me before night. But, mark what I tell you ! I will go down with my colors flying, and some of you will bite the dust with me."

Valore laid his hand on Trenhom's shoulder. " That's it, colonel," he said, " and I will help you to dispose of some of the dirty dogs."

Pelter and Savage held a whispered consultation with the sheriff.

Then the officer turned to Trenhom.

" The citizens are afraid of a rescue."

" That is preposterous, and you know it."

" I cannot help it. They insist on your going to jail."

Mrs. Trenhom interposed herself between the sheriff and her husband.

" Do not go," she said, in a firm, clear voice. " Do not go, Walter ! if you have to be murdered, my husband, let it be in your own home." Her voice grew tremulous with emotion as she proceeded. " You will at least have your wife and children to help you."

" And me, madam, and me," spoke Colonel Valore. " I agree with you entirely. I say stay here and I will stand by him to the last. To the last, madam."

The crowd heard Valore and muttered.

They pressed up the steps, filled the porch, filled the hall, filled the rooms, and down in the gardens their numbers were not diminished.

The wolves smelt prey and they gathered.

With the house and porch and garden full of infuriate

men, the jail was more secure than home, if it could only be reached in safety.

This was the opinion of Trenhom's friends, Hilber and Maclarum.

Valore acceded. "Yes, and we'll take him there in safety."

The procession was formed.

The sheriff in advance, Johnnie Trenhom, aged fifteen, following ; close after the boy his father, with his wife and daughter on either side, not clinging to him, but leaving his arms free.

Close behind, Valore erect and stately, with a cocked pistol clasped in his right hand ; stern as honor, turning his face and flashing eyes backward on the mob.

Hilber and Maclarum flanked Valore on either side.

Down the steps.

Along the walk.

Under the shadow of scowling faces and bloodshot eyes.

Under the points of pistols, rifles and shotguns.

Across the street.

Across the green.

The murderous wave opened for their passage and followed on.

The door opened, swallowed them, and was closed again.

The party breathed freer.

Mrs. Trenhom cried out :

" Praise God from whom all blessings flow."

Then she turned to Valore :

" Dear, dear, old friend, how shall I ever thank you ? "

She knew that Valore's social position was worth a regiment of men in their passage through the " low down " mob.

Valore bowed.

" I have but done my duty, madam, as a citizen and a gentleman. No more than your husband or your noble father would have done for me."

Valore bowed again. He was a grand stately old man at that moment. Then he turned and walked out.

The mob rolled back on either side, and Valore passed on up the street through the town to his home beyond.

Trenhom, Johnnie and Nellie, following a deputy sheriff, passed up a stairs, through a long corridor and paused before a door.

It was an iron lattice.

The lattice opened.

Trenhom and his children entered.

Then the door closed.

The crowd waited without, scowling at the walls, waited singing, cursing and threatening, until Valore disappeared. Then they rushed at the jail door.

The door opened at a word, and before Mrs. Trenhom had realized there was danger the treachery was complete.

The hall was filled with the rushing, surging mass of armed, drunken and blood-thirsty wolves.

They filled the hall, the stairs and the corridor beyond.   A portion of the crowd saw Hilber.

" Ah ! here's one of them ! "

" Kill the black Republican ! "

" Kill him ! "

" Cut his throat ! "

In an instant Hilber was trampled under foot, seized by the hair and dragged down the stairs into the road.

There frantic exertion gave him a moment's freedom.

Then a bullet crushed through his arm.

He leaped into the air and ran.

A hail of bullets followed him.

He stumbled.

A bullet crushed through to his brain.

He fell to the earth.

The mob in its madness trampled him into the dust.

Then with renewed fury, they turned back to the jail.

As they were entering the door, one noticed Maclarum.

Maclarum was an aged man with silvery hair floating down his shoulders.

" Here is another Radical dog."

" Shoot him."

"Smash him."

"Pass him out!"

In the twinkling of an eye he was under their feet.

They kicked him!

They leaped on him.

They crushed him.

They dragged him by the hair into the street.

A dozen bullets penetrated his body as they drew him out.

When they hurled him upon the sidewalk he was dead.

And lying there dead as he was upon the walk a burly ruffian bent over the white head, dyed red in its own blood, placed a pistol close up against the bleached and wrinked forehead and—fired.

Back again to the jail the mob rushed.

The two friends were dead.

The wolves had a taste of blood.

Howling they rushed on to the catastrophe.

A portion of the mob already filled the corridor, Jim Ratley at their head.

Trenhom, Johnnie and Nellie were in the cell.

The wolves were gnashing their teeth and raging outside in the corridor.

Mrs. Trenhom was far back in the passage pressing her way through; pushing between bodies; crawling under legs, railed on, spit upon, cursed, but pushing on resistlessly toward her husband and her children.

At last she was crouched at the foot of the iron latticed cell door.

Nellie was standing within covering the door with her body.

It was a tender, heroic shield for a noble father.

She was crying to Jim Ratley.

"Go back! Go back! Don't kill my papa! Don't kill my papa! Think of what he has done for you! Oh! Have you no hearts? Have you no souls?"

It was a piteous wailing?

It rose above the oaths.

It rang down the corridor!

And the mad crowd roared back sneers and jeers and curses.

In the crush Mrs. Trenhom was pressed against the door on her knees and unable to rise.

A gun was thrust against the bars close down on top of her head

She seized it.

The upper end of it was held by a youth not more than twenty.

"Oh! oh!" she cried. "Don't! Don't; you are too young to stain your soul with blood!"

"Yer might as well hush wauling. I ain't no officer. I'm only a private and must obey orders."

The press from behind brushed the boy and the gun beyond the door.

One only of the crowd stood.

Whoever was brushed away, one was left before the door.

That one was Jim Ratley.

The crowd surged about him.

The men before the door changing with every upheaval, but always the same sallow, fierce face and blood-shot eyes, and Jim Ratley stood before the lattice.

His gun was thrust through the lattice.

Mrs. Trenhom reached up and seized it.

"Oh! oh! merciful heaven, have you not had blood enough for one day?"

"Go to ——."

Then a pistol was placed against Mrs. Trenhom's head.

Down on her knees as she was, she looked up firmly into the eyes of the man with the pistol, "Fire, if you have the heart to do it. If that will satisfy your thirst for blood."

A hand reached down and seized the barrel of the pistol.

"That's a woman!"

"Yaas."

"You wouldn't shoot a woman!"

"Yaas, —— her! I'd shoot anything that gets in my way!"

Within, Trenhom stood in the center of the cell, his son Johnnie clasping his arms about his neck.

Nellie was against the lattice.

Jim Ratley's gun was thrust through the bars over her shoulder.

There was a flash, a detonation.

The cell and the corridor were full of smoke.

When the smoke cleared away Nellie had recoiled from the door and Johnnie stood before it.

His arms were upraised.

One fair little hand was dropped over upon his arm hanging by a shred of skin, and the hot young blood spurting out of the stump.

The full charge of Ratley's gun had struck the tender wrist, torn away the flesh, torn away the bone, and the boy, weeping tears of blood from his veins, was crying to them.

"Oh! oh! don't hurt my pappy! Please! Please don't hurt my pappy!

And for an answer Jim Ratley thrust his gun through the jail door for the second time and fired.

Nellie seeing the gun, seeing Ratley holding it, seeing the devilish light in his eyes, pushed her father suddenly toward the side of the cell.

The flash was full in her beautiful face.

It scorched her golden hair.

It filled her lips and her cheeks with powder.

One of the slugs struck the bracelet on her arm, shattered the bone, and imbedded it deep in her flesh.

A portion of another slug penetrated her side.

Without were the raving wolves and the wife and mother down on her knees.

Her hands were lifted up in entreaty.

Her eyes were an invocation.

"Oh! Men! By the mothers that bore you! By the wives that love you! By the God above you, spare! Oh, spare! my husband and my children!"

And they answered her with tramp and crush and roar and smoke and flame.

Gun after gun was thrust through the bars.

Ratley again fired.

The ball crashing through Trenhom's side.

Within, near the bars, a faint voice was calling :

" Mamma ! "

A child's cry is louder than the storm.

Mrs. Trenhom heard it.

It was Nellie.

Faint from loss of blood, she had dropped to the floor, her face against the lattice.

A hurricane of passion and death was raging overhead.

These two women, the girl and the mother, were whispering love down below.

" Mamma ! "

Nellie's mouth was at the lattice.

" Yes, dear ! "

" Oh ! dear mamma ! "

" Are you hurt, dear ? "

" Yes, mamma ! "

" Very much, dear ? "

" Yes, mamma ! and I won't care, mamma, if they will only let papa alone."

There was a flash above, and the strong man within staggered.

" Can you stand, dear ? "

" No, mamma ! "

It was only a breath.

But no storm could drown it to a mother's ears.

Nellie was prostrate on the cell floor.

Her lips were against a little opening between the intersecting bars.

The mother lay prostrate without, in the corridor.

Her hair had been torn down.

Great feet trampled upon it, trampled upon her dress, trampled upon her person, and in the tramp and crush these two women pressed their lips together through the cold bars and kissed.

"Good bye, dear mamma ! Good bye, dear ——— ! "

A CHILD'S CRY IS LOUDER THAN THE STORM.

" Nellie ! "

The lips at the bars were silent.

" Nellie, dear ! "

The lips within were growing white and colder.

" Nellie !   Nellie !   Nellie, my darling ! "

Then the mother knew her Nellie was whispering her answer from a world where there were no mobs, or shot-guns, or political assassinations.

At that instant there was another flash and report.

Jim Ratley cried out, " By ——, he's dead, boys ! "

Mrs. Trenhom sprang to her feet.

" Oh, merciful heaven ! you have murdered my husband and my daughter ! "

The crowd surged close up to the door, pushing Mrs. Trenhom far up the corridor.

Two hundred infuriate faces pressed in through the bars as they passed.

" Yaas, the dratted scallawag is dead, sure enough."

" Reckon he won't hev no Republican meetings in this year county."

Then, with an accompaniment of oaths, laughter and huzzas, the wolves shuffled out of the corridor and out of the jail.

In a few moments the jailor came and opened the barred door.

The frantic mother entered.

Nellie lay across the opening.   A smile was yet upon her powder-burnt lips.   Johnnie lay crouched in a corner.

As Mrs. Trenhom entered, her husband raised his head.

" Oh, Lou !   How glad I am !   You are uninjured ? "

" Yes, dear ! "

" Thank God ! "

" And Nellie ? "

" Dead, Walter ! "

" Noble daughter.   And Johnnie ? "

" Here, papa ! "

It was a little voice piping from the corner of the cell.

" Hurt, Johnnie ? "

" Yes, papa ! "

" Does it pain ? "

" Not now, papa ! "

" Come to me, Johnnie ! "

The boy made an effort.

Then he sobbed :

" I can't, papa ! "

In an instant he was in his mother's arms,

Then she shuddered.

" Poor boy !   Dear boy !   Noble boy ! "

She laid him down by his father.

The two heads drew close together.

" Are you hurt, papa ? "

" To the death, dear boy ! "

"Oh ! papa ! "

" Brave boy ! "

" Kiss me, papa."

With painful efforts the father placed his chilling lips against the boy's.

And the boy murmured :

" Oh ! mamma ! mamma !   Kiss —— "

And his head dropped back upon the cold stones of the floor.

Johnnie had joined Nellie.

Trenhom was fearfully wounded, torn and shattered by a dozen bullets.

He knew it was only a question of hours until he would join his children.

His wife put away trembling and tears and staunched his wounds.

She did all that could be done, but he was beyond help.

He could only have quiet and affection.

Toward evening, Valore stood by the wounded man's bed. He had just heard.

" Colonel ! madam ! " he exclaimed, as he entered, "as God is my judge, I never dreamed of this.   Never ! never ! "

" Dear friend, we know it."

"Politics has estranged us, madam ; but this is horrible,

horrible ! If I had dreamed of it, I would have remained. My God, colonel, I never can forgive myself for going away."

The dying man reached out his hand.

" Take no blame to yourself. If I die, friends, with you I am content.

The brave old man grasped his hand.

" May God forgive me for ever being your enemy. I never can forgive myself. I never can. I feel my guilt. The social barrier we have raised around you; the public sentiment we have created, have caused this. Without that, these creatures never would have dared to commit this crime. I knew nothing of their purpose. I believed you were safe. But in the sentiment that prepared the way for it, that made it possible, I am guilty. May God forgive me, guilty ! "

" Dear old friend, do not take blame to yourself," said Mrs. Trenhom, kindly.

Valore turned to her with tears in his eyes.

" And you forgive me madam ? "

" Yes, dear friend."

" And you, Trenhom ? "

" From the bottom of my heart." Then he turned over on his back, breathing with difficulty, and he murmured, " Lou ! faithful wife; I can not — see — you.— Good-bye — Good-bye.— I die for my—country.—Good-bye, faithful love. —Kiss me ! Kiss ! Faithful love ! faith — ! "

Wrestling, struggling and beseeching, Mrs. Trenhom passed through the stormy day of horror and blood. Now she bowed over the white face and mutilated arm of her boy; bowed over the powder-burnt lips and golden hair of her daughter ; bowed over the torn and shattered form of her husband; bowed down over all that God had given to her to love, and baptized them with her agony.

CHAPTER XXXVIII.

A VOICE FROM THE NORTH.

The gathering in the Shootfast parlors was the beginning of what Major Dale Cartier then hoped was a mere temporary alienation between himself and Col. Trenhom. If any one had then suggested to him that he would ever come to hate Col. Trenhom he would have ridiculed the thought. Were they not fast friends in boyhood ? Was there not between them a bond of reciprocal kindnesses running all through the storms of war ? These things were strong in Carter's mind on the night the decree of social proscription went forth against all " scallawags," which of course included Trenhom, for he was a Southern man, holding office by the votes of Republicans. And every Southern born man who did that, no matter what his previous social position ; no matter how high his character ; how pure his life or how sterling his honor, was a " scallawag." Neither worth, nor intelligence, nor length, nor heroism of " Confederate " record could save them from that designation of reproach once they voted with the despised Republicans or held office at their hands.

But while Cartier lamented what he esteemed as the degeneracy of his former friend and old commander, his heart was yet warm toward him. He still thought of him as " Walt." The same " Walt." that he was in boyhood ; the same " Walt." whom he followed in the desperate charge at Chickamauga. And if he agreed, as he did with the others, to wall Trenhom and his family in with barriers of social ostracism it was more out of love than out of hate. Again and again on that night Cartier said to himself " Walt. won't stand it long. He can't desert his old friends. A few days or weeks of this and the old boy will be with us." But before three weeks passed

a change had begun in Cartier's mind. He was keeping pace
with his associates. Gradually all who were on the opposing
side of the barrier were regarded as enemies. Trenhom came
in for his share of public reproach and sneers. At first Cartier
listened impatiently to the gibes and oaths hurled at his friend
in public and private. Then under the constant dropping
of this foul flood his impatience wore away. He found himself smiling and then laughing at ribald jests uttered at
Trenhom's expense. The sentiment of friendship was weak-
ened. There was no internal prompting to champion his old
comrade when assailed. From sympathetic utterance he had
fallen back to unsympathetic neutrality. But beyond this he
had not gone. In his heart there was no personal bitterness
against Trenhom. This was the condition of his feeling on
the day of the cowardly card affair at the post-office.

On that day he stood on the skirt of the crowd looking
through the door.

He was a witness of the dastardly outrage upon Mrs.
Huntley.

It was the husband of this woman who had saved his life at
Chickamauga.

It was he and he alone who was responsible for their coming to Slimpton. And while he stood there in the skirt of the
gaping, jeering crowd, laughing with them at the unmanly
insults heaped upon their helpless Yankee post-mistress;
laughing at insults which would have instantly ceased with
a word or look from himself; he saw Trenhom breasting
through the crowd; he saw Trenhom's eyes fixed upon him
for an instant; he knew then that Trenhom had detected him
looking on and doing nothing to prevent the outrage, and
in that instant he felt that he hated Trenhom.

A hot flush grew up in his face and he turned away from
the crowd and walked off toward his home without awaiting
the result of Col. Trenhom's defense of Kate Huntley.

Yes, he positively hated Trenhom. He knew that now.
He was a miserable "scallawag." He blamed himself for not
interfering. He felt keenly that he ought to have done that;
but he never paused to tell himself that he hated Trenhom,

not because he was a " scallawag," but because Trenhom
had detected him in a cowardly act.   But that was the
fact.

There are men who will forgive an eye that directs a rifle
ball at them sooner than an eye that detects them in a meanness.

Cartier was one of these.

After this no mouth in Slimpton surpassed Cartier's in
railing at Trenhom.   Other men in his social circle took it up.
On the night of the post-office burning Cartier was looking on
without an effort to stay the ruin.   He heard Kate Huntley
appeal for help ; he.saw her despairing face as she rushed into
the burning building to save her husband ; and he saw her
when she fell into Trenhom's arms with her dying burden.
Then the curses he muttered against Trenhom took wings
among the Pelter gang and the other " low-downs," and they
then knew it was as safe to assault Trenhom as it was to
batter down the doors of negro cabins and outrage their helpless and defenseless inmates.

Out of this knowledge was born the crime and catastrophe
at the Slimpton jail.   Cartier saw the mob gathering ; saw the
heroic procession to the jail ; saw the passion charged cloud
that followed it, and from across the road he witnessed the
fury that burst upon the devoted inmates of the jail after the
departure of Valore.

If he regretted the assassination of Trenhom, his brave
young son, his. beautiful, heroic young daughter, and his aged
friends, he made no sign.

Except his Uncle Valore, none of his friends did.

If there were regrets there were no whisperings of it.

Col. Valore raged.

He was roused indignation.

He denounced it as a cowardly crime.

He denounced the actors as murderers.

He demanded the vengeance of the law.

All this Cartier was compelled to hear in his uncle's home
and in his own.

And he heard it without retort.

Other of Cartier's and Valore's mutual friends were as silent under Valore's breathings of indignation.

Several weeks passed away, then one evening as Dale Cartier walked through the town, he noticed that many people held newspapers in their hands, and as he passed they put their heads together and whispered.

Once when he turned his head he detected, or thought he detected persons running from the interior of a store to the door and windows, looking and pointing at him.

Could there be anything wrong about his dress ?

He looked but saw nothing.

At the post-office he received a newspaper.

As he walked toward home he opened it.

Then he saw it was the " Valley Star," published in an interior town of the State of New York.

Why send it to him ?

He was about dropping it in the street when he noticed heavy blue lines drawn around one of the columns.

This attracted his attention. He paused and looked.

He saw his own name.

Then he saw his wife's name.

He read a little.

His face flushed.

He ground his teeth together.

Then he crushed the paper in one hand, clasped the other over his forehead and reeled like a man who had been struck a tremendous blow.

He had been struck.

It was a terrible blow.

Pulling the broad brim of his hat down over his eyes he rushed toward his home.

Erma heard his footfall on the stoop.

His daughters heard too, and they ran to the door.

Dale entered, pale and trembling, with the crushed paper in his hand.

The children ran to him.

He waved them back.

His wife opened her arms.

He pushed her away.

He stood glaring at them.

The two daughters shrank away weeping.

They never had been treated so before, never.

"Papa must be tipsy," they thought. "Poor papa, how sorry he will be."

They were right, he was tipsy—with fury.

Erma was amazed, but she was the first to find words.

"What is it, dear Dale?"

Her husband started as if he had been stung.

He thrust the paper towards her.

"Is that true? Is that true?"

She glided toward him.

"Kiss me, dear."

She was the poetry of motion.

"Tell me! Tell me! Is that true? My God, I shall go mad—mad!"

He was beating his forehead with both hands.

Erma took the paper and glanced at it.

The hot blood rushed to her cheeks.

"Hear me, my husband!"

"By —— I will hear nothing—till you tell me it is a lie! A lie! An infernal lie!"

"One word, Dale!"

"Is it a lie? Is it a lie? Is it a lie?"

His eyes were blood-shot.

A white foam was gathered upon his lips.

Erma was standing near a lounge.

She sank down upon it.

Her white face was lifted toward her husband.

Her eyes were appealing to him.

He strode to her

He tore the paper from her hand.

He held it out in his left hand and with the first finger of his right hand he pointed to the blue lines, and in a voice hoarse with passion he shouted: "Tell me before I strike you down, is that a lie? Is that a lie? Is that a lie?"

"IS IT A LIE? IS IT A LIE?"

His wife folded her arms on the end of the lounge, bowed her head down upon them and sobbed :

" It is true—true ! "

For an instant Dale Cartier stood petrified.

Then he raised his clenched hand to strike.

His weeping daughters rushed upon him.

They seized his uplifted arm.

Cartier dashed them upon the floor.

Then he cried out : " My God !   My God ! " and rushed out of the door and away from the house.

CHAPTER XXXIX.

WHAT WILL THE PEOPLE SAY ?

When Major Dale Cartier rushed from the presence of his wife, prostrate on the lounge, and his children, prostrate upon the floor, he had no definite purpose except to fly. To be away from them.

He had been dealt a tremendous and unexpected blow.

He felt it.

Its bruise was upon him.

At first it crushed out purpose.

Purpose needs thought.

He had none.

His limbs moved.

They were impelled by a panic.

They carried him into the road in front of his house.

They carried him on up the road beyond the few isolated hovels that lay like rotting toadstools upon the decaying skirt of village.

Beyond that was the frayed edge of the forest.

He strode on into this.

He penetrated the shadow.

There the influence of silence and solitude fell upon him and he paused.

He clenched his hands.

With his clenched hands he smote his forehead.

Then he cried out in agony of spirit :

" My God ! My God ! '

They were the first words he uttered since leaving his home.   Yet all that time they had been glowing in his brain like super-heated gas seeking an outlet.

There is a lethargy of grief.

Bound up in this paralysis mortals feel without thinking.

They suffer without moaning.

That is coma.

When it passes some shiver under the pain and bind their tongues.

Others roar.

Cartier was not gifted with power of repression.

When he felt the thorn in his side he cried out.

Then he trembled.

He was a poor wind-shaken leaf.

Then he sat down between the uplifted roots of a great oak that stood removed from the path and pulled his hat down over his eyes.

He had sat down to pull his scattered wits together.

He tried it.

He thought aloud.

Some people in dilemma can only think when they speak.

Cartier was one of them.

His first thought was this:

"How can I ever face the people?"

His own voice startled him.

He looked about him.

Then for the first time he seemed to realize where he was and that he had spoken.

But he was but a poor creature after all.

He had faced glinting sabres, whistling bullets and hurtling shells. He had passed through hospitals and battle fields; he had marched and endured and hungered and charged; he had watched the blood flowing from his gaping wounds; he had felt the clutch of death upon him. He had passed through this as a man and a soldier; he had heard the "general orders" that announced his courage. Yet this man was a coward; only a poor coward after all.

The truly brave are self-forgetful.

This man was not.

He was wanting in chivalrous self-abnegation.

He thought in this hour, but he thought only of himself.

"What will people say?"

He writhed and shrank before thoughts that would never reach his ear.

He saw around him society, its tongue bristling with thorns, and he cowered before it.

Dale Cartier with all his dash and his wounds, was a coward.

Did he think once of how he could help the wife he had left in his parlor ?

No !

Or of the innocent children whose devoted love had always been his ?

No !

He thought only of miserable Dale Cartier. What will people think of him ?

Then came another thought : " What shall I do ? " At that moment he would have given worlds for an arm to rely on or a hand to trust in. But he had none. He was there alone in the solitude of the forest with the shades of night gathering about him, trying to work out the weightiest problem of his life !

Surely the horrible fetor of the lazaretto will fill his nostrils and he will think of the tender woman who walked calmly into its putrid stench to save his life !

He did.

But it was only to exclaim : " Why did she not let me die ? "

Surely he will think of the heroic woman searching among the mutilation and gaping wounds of that dreadful hillside at Chickamauga until she found him and gave him life.

He did.

He thought of it all.

The past whirled through his brain.

It is wonderful what a breadth of life can be encompassed in a moment's thought.

He saw Erma in the hospital.

He saw her on the battle-field.

But he thought only of himself.

He was still a coward.

" Why, my God, why did she not let me die ? "

Better if she had.

He would have been saved from man's worst enemy—himself.

He would have been saved from a madness and a crime.

He would have died a brave man.

That is better than to live a revealed coward.

He saw in all that Erma had done for him only that she had saved him to suffer.

Her heroism he forgot.

It was himself, always himself, that he thought of. He was an egotist.

Few men stand still.

But there is a downward as well an upward growth.

Men shrivel and dwarf as well as broaden.

Cartier had expanded during the war.

Most men who engaged in it did.

But on the night of the Shootfast parlor meeting his growth came to an end.

After that he began to contract.

To stunt and wizen a man's soul fling him into the narrow wine-press of bigotry.

Dale Cartier flung himself in.

The press was upon him.

His manhood grew pursed up and pinched.

He was never great.

Few men are.

The multitude are partly molded and unmolded by the plastic hand of circumstance.

He was only one of them.

Always surrounded by generous impulses he could always have been good and generous.

But once started on the slippery way of the unscrupulous he could be as paltry and scrubby as the meanest.

These were his possibilities.

His action during the disgraceful scene at the post-office and its burning and his subsequent conduct toward his old

26

friend and commander, Trenhom, showed that he was on the downward road.

This evening he was treading in the depths.

He waited in the forest until he saw the stars breaking through the leaves of the trees.

And he was always thinking, " What will they say ? What shall I do ? "

Then he thought of his aunt Valore.

" Yes, she will advise me."

With this in his mind he stood up, and pulling his hat further down over his eyes, he started forward through the trees toward the edges of the town, and avoiding the traveled paths, he turned off toward the house of his uncle. This he reached without meeting any of the dreaded public, and he stood in the parlor of Col. Valore.

When Cartier entered, the bruise of his wound was yet strong upon him.

It was not in swellings and contusions.

Such are not the severest wounds.

Dale Cartier's marks were white lips, deep lines, dazed eyes, and tremulous twitchings.

The moment Dale entered the room Mrs. Valore noticed it.

" Are you not well, dear ? "

Dale covered his face with his hands, dropped into a seat and moaned.

" Are you ill, Dale ? "

" Oh, that I were. If I were only sick."

" What is it, Dale ? "

" Oh, aunty, how can I tell you ! "

" Are you in trouble, dear ? "

" My God, my God ! I wish I were only dead ! dead ! dead ! "

His hands were still upon his face and his head bowed down almost to his knees. Mrs. Valore walked over to him and laid her right hand upon his head. She loved Cartier. For many years he had been nephew and son to her. She could not have loved him better if he had been her own child.

"No mere bodily injury could make you feel this way," she said.

Cartier only answered by his continued moaning.

" Is it an insult, dear ? "

" Insult ! Insult ! Would it were no more than that ! "

" Is it money, Dale ? "

" Oh, auntie, auntie, how can I tell you ! How can I tell you ! "

Mrs. Valore was deeply moved by the poignancy of his grief. She sat down beside him. Then she laid her arm over his neck and drew his head to her.

" Tell me, Dale ! " she cooed in his ear.

Without raising his head Dale began his story. He told of his visit to the post-office. The reception of the paper. The deep blue lines drawn about one of its columns. The discovery of his name and his wife's name in it. And then he rehearsed the narrative of the paper. It was a rambling narrative, broken and disjointed, often incoherent, and all along interlarded with moaning and exclamations of grief and shame, and the sentence " How shall I ever face the people? " As the story progressed, Mrs. Valore's face blanched, an unwomanly sternness gathered about her lips and crept into her steel blue eyes.

When Dale finished she was sitting bolt upright beside him.

She was an implacable woman at that moment.

" And she ? "

They were but two words. But they were doom for Dale Cartier's wife. Mrs. Valore did not yet know that the story was true. She had heard nothing but the article in the " Valley Star." And yet she was prepared to believe.

Why is it that women are so stern against their sex ?

Not all.

But so many.

What becomes of their tenderness when they become judges ?

What do they do with their mercy?

" Judge not."

But they will judge.

They will be sharp, severe, and bitter.

They might help.

They crush.

This woman, without knowing, was prepared to believe and prepared to crush.

A man would have had more mercy, at least for a woman.

But she—well, she was a woman judging a woman.

Dale evidently had not heard her. Then she repeated it.

"And she ? "

"Oh, auntie, that is not the worst of it. She admits all—all."

"Miserable creature ! Admits it ? "

"Yes, all ! all ! Admits that it is true. Oh, how shall I face the people ? "

"Vile, dreadful creature ! And she admits it, you say ? "

Dale was silent.

"Did you tell her the whole story ? "

"I showed her the paper."

"And she read it ? "

"She glanced at it."

"And then admitted it ? "

"And then admitted it was true. Oh, auntie, how shall I ever face my friends again ? "

"It is not your fault."

"To think, auntie, that my life is destroyed."

"My poor Dale ! "

"My home, happiness, good name, everything, everything that I valued, shattered and lying in ruins about me."

"Dear boy ! I do pity you."

"And the people ? "

"It is not your fault, Dale. Not your fault, dear boy."

"Good heavens, auntie, to think of it."

"It is dreadful, Dale ! Dreadful !"

"And to think of every low ruffian in the town with a paper in his hand."

"Can that be true ? Papers sent to so many? "

"To everyone. The whole town knows it."

"That is shameful !"

"And all looking at me ! pointing at me ! pitying me in my shame and disgrace."

"It is too bad ; too bad !"

"I could bear anything but that. To have my disgrace known. To be the butt and laughter of the low-down mob."

"Dear Dale, I am so sorry for you."

"To think of their gibes. To be the object of their merriment."

"But they must sympathize with you."

For the first time Dale raised his head. He stood up before his aunt. He raised his right arm. An imprecation was upon his lips. But it died out in the presence of the woman who stood looking into his eyes. His arm fell down again and he cried out :

"I could not endure it. I could not endure it."

"Dear boy."

"Auntie, I feel that if any man should express sympathy to me I will kill him."

"Dale !"

"I could not help it, auntie. To be laughed at or sympathized with in a matter of this kind. They are both alike. could not endure it. I tell you I could not endure it."

Mrs. Valore laid her arm about him.

"Sit down, dear."

Dale was a child under her words,

He sat down.

"Let me see the paper, Dale."

Dale looked dreamily into his hands.

He felt his pockets. "I—don't—know ! I must have left it with Er—with her—with that—Oh! my God!"

"The wretch ! The dreadful wretch !"

"Oh, aunt ! aunt !"

"She is a wretch ! A vile wretch to bring such ruin upon your life. My poor boy. It is shameful, disgraceful."

Dale covered his face again and moaned.

"And you left her, Dale ? You did that, did you not ?"

"Leave her ! Leave my—Er—that woman ?"

"Yes, did you not ? You cannot go back to her as your wife ? You cannot do that ?"

"Oh—h !" and he wiped the cold **moisture of** pain from his brow.

"You will not go back to that creature ?"

"No! no, aunt, I cannot do that—and—yet—we have been so happy ! Good heavens, what will the people say !"

"Did you not tell her so, that you had left her forever ?"

"Oh, my God ! what else could I do !"

Then he repeated the scene in his own parlor.

"You acted properly, sir, like the gentleman that you are, sir. The infamous creature, to deceive you so. You, my nephew, my almost son."

At this instant Valore hastily entered the room.

Seeing Dale he turned to him and spoke.

"Dale, what story is this I hear ?"

Mrs. Valore told him, down to the parting scene.

The old man listened with anger gathering in his eyes.

When his wife concluded with the exclamation, "He has parted from the deceitful wretch like the gentleman that he is," Col. Valore's cane dropped from his hand and a sternness settled upon his face such as his wife had not witnessed for years.

Without a word, leaving his cane lying upon the floor, he turned and walked out of the room and out of the house.

CHAPTER XL.

DAUGHTER OF A SLAVE.

For ten years Valore had not walked without the aid of a cane. But when he walked out of his own parlor he forgot it. He forgot his seventy years. He forgot his infirmity. He forgot everything but his indignation and his eagerness to see Erma.

Unannounced he entered her home and stood in the door looking into the room from which his nephew had fled.

He saw Erma.

She lay as Dale left her.

Her arms were resting on the end of the lounge.

Her face was plunged in them.

Her two daughters—her only children, bright, beautiful girls, knelt on the carpet, their arms wound about their mother.

The mother moaned.

The daughters baptized her moans with tears.

On the floor near the head of the lounge lay the thunderbolt that had shattered the happiness of this family.

It was a crumpled newspaper.

Valore was deeply moved.

He walked softly across the floor and stood by the lounge.

Grief is louder than sound.

Valore was unheard, unseen, until he laid his hand upon Erma's head.

She thought it was Dale come back again.

A tide of joy rushed to her heart.

It electrified her.

She sprung up.

Then she saw it was Col. Valore, and she fell back again upon the lounge.

She was lost.

So she thought.

If Dale had turned away from her what would not this stern old man do ?

"Erma ! Erma, dear, listen to me."

How soft and tender the words were.

But the bursting of clouds would not have reached her ears as surely as they did.

There was so much hope in their tenderness.

"And Dale has sent you ? He will forgive and come back to me ? "

Valore drew a chair by the side of the lounge and sat down, stroking the glossy head that lay on the lounge.

"Erma, can you hear me ? "

"Ye-s ! " she moaned.

"Yes, uncle. Say that, Erma." His hands were gently smoothing her disordered hair.

How sweet the words were to her then,

He did not fling her away.

But—did he—could he know.

Pain smote her again and crushed the hope out of her.

"Oh ! oh ! Do—you. Do you——know ? "

"Yes, my dear Erma—my dear niece, I know! "

"Oh-h-h ! " It was a profound sigh of relief. He knew and he—he—Dale's uncle—Dale's mother's brother called her his "dear Erma," his "dear niece."

Erma seized one of his hands, drew it to her, and laid her cheek upon it.

How good he was.

Wrinkles ?

No, he had none.

Tenderness is a magician.

He was the most beautiful being under the sun.

He was an angel.

"Can you talk to me, dear ? "

"Yes, sir ! "

"Say yes, uncle! Uncle Gersh! always your Uncle Gersh!"

"Yes, dear Uncle Gersh."

"Thank you, dear."

Her cheek was welding to his hand.

"You are so good, so good, dear, dear Uncle Gersh, always so good!"

"My dear, no goodness can equal your merits."

"Generous, noble friend. Dear, dear uncle!"

"Can you tell me the origin of this exposure?"

She pointed to the thunderbolt on the floor.

Valore lifted it and read it from beginning to end.

It was a long article.

More than a column of it.

A communication to the "Valley Star."

It was all about politics and people in Slimpton.

It referred to outrages committed on negroes and the people who approved them. No man in Slimpton, it charged, is more malignant than Dale Cartier, formerly a Confederate major.

"Every outrage and crime committed upon the blacks, every invasion of their rights as men and citizens is applauded by him. No one in all Slimpton is louder in his exclamations of approval. He is the commander of one of the military companies, organized avowedly to preserve the peace, but really to break up Republican meetings and grind the colored people into the dust. Yet this man's wife is a NEGRESS, and her mother was a slave."

The correspondent continued:

"I have it from unquestionable authority. My informant was a servant of her father and was with him when he purchased Mrs. Cartier's mother. He went with them to France and lived with them there. He was there when Mrs. Cartier was born."

There was much padding of details. But this was the substance of the letter.

After Valore read it he laid his hand upon Erma's head again.

"Is this true, dear child?"

"Yes!"

"Uncle Gersh!"

"Yes, dear Uncle Gersh."

How good he was. He said this to her to call him uncle. He asked her, a child of the despised race, to do this. She was amazed.

The surprise almost stupefied her.

"How long have you known it, dear?"

"This day. This day only."

"How did you discover it, my dear?"

"Dale desired an old deed, and in searching for it I discovered a package of papers addressed to myself."

"Will you permit me to see them, Erma?"

Erma stood up.

She would have fallen but for the aid of Colonel Valore.

He caught her.

Then he offered her his arm and led her to the library.

There she placed the papers in his hands.

He looked them over.

"Yes," he said, as he looked them over, "here is a bill of sale, made at New Orleans, of Erma, property of Gervaise Petillant, to General Chartrass, for $5,000.

"Here is a deed of manumission by General Chartrass, dated the day of the sale bill, manumitting Erma Petillant, purchased of Gervaise Petillant. ·

"Here is a marriage certificate, signed at Paris, France, of the marriage of Gerald Oliver Chartrass and Erma Petillant, with the name of officiating priest and witnesses."

When Valore saw this he turned to Erma.

"Ah, dear child, your noble father, my lamented friend, was an honorable gentleman, always, dear, always, dear."

The next paper was a certificate of the birth of Erma Petillant Chartrass, with a statement in General Chartrass's writing of Erma's identity.

Then followed a certificate of the death and burial of Erma Petillant Chartrass.

After Valore finished he turned to Erma.

" Yes, dear, there can be no doubt of it, none whatever."

" And," whispered Erma, " you—you do not—not cast me away."

She was trembling like wind-driven vapor when she asked this question.

" Erma ! niece ! " Valore was standing up before her, looking reproachfully down upon her. " What have I done to deserve this ? "

" Oh ! Forgive me ! Forgive me, dear Uncle Gersh."

" Dear child. How you must suffer to ask that question of me. Your noble father's and your friend, yours always, dear."

" You are so good, so good, Uncle Gersh."

He drew her to him and kissed her white forehead.

" And you will bring Dale to me ? " she whispered.

" Yes, dear, I will bring him to you. He must come to you."

He took the children in his arms.

He passed his hands over their innocent young heads.

He urged Erma to " be of good cheer."

Then he went away.

While Valore was with Erma, Major Dale Cartier was with Shootfast.

He had been urged by his aunt to consult the judge as to his position, and he went

What was that position. He had loved his beautiful, devoted wife.

He had loved the children who filled his home with sunshine.

They had been happy, very happy together.

But she was a negress, and her mother had been a slave, and he had lived with her as his wife. He—a Cartier—had done this—and he had introduced her to the world as his wife.

What humiliation !

How would he face the sneers of society ? How would he survive the behind-back chuckling of the low-downs ?

He thought of these things again as he walked to Shootfast's.

but—was she his wife ?

This was the question Mrs. Clarissa Valore suggested.

If she was not, then there was hope.

He could live and breathe again.

Desire to know was stronger than the pain.

In the roar and certain ruin of the breakers men will strain their ears to the leadsman in the chains.

If the leadsman's cry runs down "four" "a quarter less four !" "and a half three !" "By the mark three !" so much the worse.

But there is relief in knowing.

Shootfast listened to Cartier.   He heard him through.

Then he answered :

"If Erma's mother was a slave when Erma was born, Erma was a slave, was so at the time of the marriage ceremony, and the marriage was a nullity because a slave cannot enter into a contract.

"If Erma was born free but had the proportion of African blood in her veins which made her a negro by the statutes of the State, the marriage would be void, because prohibited by law.

"The fact that the law was afterward altered does not change the matter. Void in the beginning, void ever after.

"Now, what are the facts ?"

Dale did not know.

When he returned to Valore's the Colonel was there.

Seeing Dale enter he asked him,

"Have you been to Erma ?"

"I ! Heavens, no !" answered Cartier, looking at his uncle in amazement.

"She is perishing for one word from you, Dale."

"From me ! From me !"

"Yes, Dale, and you should go to her at once. Do not delay a moment, nephew. Do not permit that dear girl to suffer."

"Go to her as my wife ?"

"As your wife ! As your wife ! I do not understand you, Dale."

" Uncle Gersham ! "

" Go to her, my dear boy ! Go to her ! To see her suffer would melt a heart of steel ! "

" And live with her ! "

It was Mrs. Valore who asked the question.

She had at that moment entered the room and heard her husband appealing to Dale.

" Live with her ? What a question to ask," responded Valore.

" Impossible ! Absurd ! " returned his wife. " After this vile cheat of a marriage is out of the way, then if she wishes to live with Dale——"

" Clarissa ! Clarissa ! Stop ! Stop ! for heaven's sake ! "

" Stop, indeed ! Are you bewitched ? "

" Clarissa ! "

" Colonel Valore ! "

" You, a woman, make such a horrible suggestion ! "

" Horrible, indeed ! As if she is better than other negresses who occupy the same position."

Valore turned in his chair, facing his wife.

Great drops were gathered in his eyes.

" Oh, Clarissa ! " he said ; " that I should live to hear this— from you. Nearly half a century we have been married. I have believed in you. And now—Clarissa—my—cup—of— sorrow—is full, full ! "

" Huh ! Much ado, indeed, about a little negress."

" Yet she is the one woman that for twenty years past you have most admired, loved, fondled and kissed."

" And I could bite my lips off and my tongue out for it. To think that I have petted and loved and made much of a nasty little negress."

" She is whiter skinned than most of us."

" Huh ! Indeed ! " tossing her head.

" And the whitest souled woman in the State—the whitest souled woman in the country ! "

" I'm disgusted with you, Colonel ! Disgusted with you, sir. But Dale has more sense, I am glad to say. He will be guided by me in this matter, sir, and preserve the family honor, sir ; preserve its honor ! ”

Valore turned to Cartier.

“ Is that so, Dale ? ”

“ Yes.”

“ Dale, but for her you would have perished on the battle-field of Chickamauga before help reached you.”

“ Yes, but—”

“ And she faced the horrible stench of the room where you lay rotting with the small-pox. Faint and weak she marched into the loathsome pest-house, reeking with corruption, bristling with death, and dragged you out of the grave.”

“ God knows she was brave and true, but oh ! uncle, her mother was a sla—v—e ! A sla—v—e ! ”

“ Dale, listen to me. If it was me, if she braved perils for me as she has braved for you—if she had done for me one hundredth part of what she has done for you, I would not abandon her if she were a murderess.”

“ Nor would I ! Nor would I ! ” exclaimed Dale. “ But this is different. She is a negress ! ”

“ And you will not go to her ? ”

“ When this disgraceful marriage is out of the way, if she— ”

Valore sprung to his feet and drew a pistol from his pocket.

“ Stop! stop, sir ! By my soul, sir, if you make that vile suggestion about Erma Chartrass in my presence, I will shoot you down like a dog if you were one hundred times my sister’s son.”

Mrs. Valore ran in between her irate husband and Dale.

“ Colonel Valore, you forget yourself, sir. You forget yourself.”

“ Let us have no words, Clarissa. But my dear old friend’s daughter shall be respected in my presence.”

“ Indeed ! ”

Valore paid no attentien to the gadfly. He turned to Dale.

“ Do you intend to go to Erma ? ”

" No, he does not ! " exclaimed Mrs. Valore.

" I ask you, sir ! "

" No, uncle ! "

" Drop the uncle, if you please. Drop it now and here-after. Do you intend to have the marriage annulled ? "

" Yes, he does ! " snapped gadfly.

" I ask you again ? "

" I certainly do," answered Dale.

" Where are her bonds ? "

" What bonds ? "

" The government bonds left her by her father."

" Some I have used."

" And the others ? "

" I have them."

" How many ? "

" About $50,000."

" Give them to me, sir ? "

" To you ! For what ? "

" To deliver to Erma."

" Ah ! "

" What foolishness ! " cried the gadfly.

" Where are they—the bonds ? " persisted Valore.

" I must see about my right to them."

" You will not give them up ? You will not surrender them ? "

" If the law compels me."

" You turn Erma away from you ! You break her heart !——"

" Pish ! negress ! " sputtered the gadfly.

" And yet you keep her money. You are a scoun-drel "——

Dale made a step toward Valore, and raised his arm.

" If you were not my uncle——"

" Drop that word ! I am no uncle of yours, miserable cur ! No uncle of yours ! Out of my house ! Out this in-stant ! Out ! out ! out ! "

Under the pelting of the old man's wrath, Dale Cartier hurried away from the room and the house.

The husband and wife were alone.

The gadfly buzzed.

" Colonel Valore, have you lost your senses ? "

" Would to God, Clarissa, that I had."

" You act like it ! Indeed you do, defending that woman."

" My dear Chartrass's daughter."

" A negress ! "

" If she was twice a negress, she has been a pure woman, a devoted wife and an angelic mother."

" You make me sick."

" Clarissa ! "

" You must cease this, Gersham. It is intolerable."

" Cease defending and befriending Erma ! "

" Cease talking of that negress."

" Clarissa ! " He turned his face toward the ceiling, raised his open hand above his head, " May the good Father in Heaven desert me when I desert that poor, suffering, abused girl."

The gadfly walked up before him.

Her hands were on her hips.

Her elbows were bent.

Her cap frills were dancing in his eyes.

" Colonel Valore, if you ever open your mouth to that negress again, I will never speak to you afterward as long as I live. Never ! Never ! Never ! "

Valore leaned forward on his cane and looked earnestly into the face of his wife, and slowly answered :

" Clarissa, in one year more it will be half a century since we were married. I have loved you all these years, and—I love you now, Clarissa, as much as I did when we were first married. It would pain me, Clarissa—deeply—deeply, more than I can say, Clarissa, if you would pursue the course you threaten."

His lips were tremulous and his voice broken with emotion.

" I will ! I will, I will ! " screamed the gadfly.

"May God forgive you, as I will, for any suffering you cause to me."

"Pish!"

"But, Clarissa, I shall do my duty to Erma."

"Negress! Negress! Negress!"

"If all the world turned against me!"

"You will?"

"I will, Clarissa! Heaven help me, dear. I can do no other."

"Then we may as well begin now."

She turned and marched out of the room, and so they parted.

In the morning Valore saw Erma.

She had passed the night in her parlor sleepless.

She soon understood that it was decided Dale and she must part.

The moment she understood it she looked like one stricken with death.

She said she would go away.

"Yes. I will go away. It will be better for Dale. How can I endure it, to live here near him, a gulf between us? And how can he endure it? It must pain him so!"

Then she fell to sobbing.

Valore agreed it was better to go away.

But she could not go without seeing Dale.

"For one minute, only one minute! one look! one word!" So she pleaded.

Valore overcame his repugnance so far as to convey the request to Cartier.

Dale "hemm'd" and "haw'd" and finally consented.

"It would do no good, but he would go."

He came.

Erma was an eager furnace.

Dale was an iceberg, with his face wrapped in clouds.

Erma opened her arms.

No!

Dale would not embrace her.

27

She flung herself at his feet and twined her arms about his ankles.

"Oh, Dale, speak to me. One word, Dale, only one word. Not one! not one! never again! Oh, my God! my God! And shall I see you never more—never more! Ou-u! Ou-u!"

And she lay shivering and moaning on the floor kissing his feet.

His children twined their arms about him.

They looked up in his face.

They called him "papa," and begged for one kiss, "only one, papa!"

His denial was to tear himself away and rush from the house.

Erma lay inanimate and senseless behind him on the floor.

Valore was not present.

He said to Mrs. Trenhom afterwards:

"I dare not be there. I knew how it would be, and—I would have killed him. I know I would."

When Mrs. Trenhom turned her face away northward from the graves of her loved ones, Erma, her two children and Valore went with her.

It might do the sufferer good to be with Mrs. Trenhom. They were such old friends.

So thought Valore and he hastened the departure.

All the long journey from Slimpton to Washington Erma sat in the corner of the seat close in by the window.

Her eyes were never closed.

She never ceased trembling and moaning, "Ou-u! ou-u!" It was pitiful to hear.

The stoniest hearts in the car were melted to tears.

At Washington they bore her to a hotel and laid her in bed.

Through the long night the moaning continued, only broken with one word, "Dale! Dale! Dale!"

Valore, Mrs. Trenhom, and her two daughters watched by her bedside.

Toward morning the murmurs became fainter.

Mrs. Trenhom's fingers were on her pulse.

As the soft light of the new day crept into the sky Mrs. Trenhom stood up with a startled look in her eyes and whispered to Valore :

"She is dying !"

Valore quickly bent down over the sufferer in the bed.

"Erma ! Erma ! Can you hear me ?"

Her eyelids drooped.

"God helping me, I will be a father to your children."

Erma drew his hand to her lips and held it there.

CHAPTER XLI.

SOMETHING BETTER THAN PREJUDICE.

Mrs. Trenhom, looking down upon the glassy eyes and pallid face of Erma Cartier and feeling the chill that came into her hands, believed it was dissolution. In this belief she had whispered to Col. Valore, " She is dying ! " Happily the physician who had been attending her, entered the room at that moment and stood by the bedside.

While Erma's children and friends were abandoning themselves to despair, the man of science was investigating. That is the use of science. It examines and tests. The friends moaned and wrung their hands ; the man of science was much more practical. He used his ears and a looking-glass. By the aid of these, he was able to detect a cheat. It was not death. It was death's counterfeit, syncope. Then a struggle began, science against syncope, for a flickering, languid life.

When Erma's sense was restored, the man of science brought another element to his aid—that was the children.

One love was tearing down ; he put another love over against it to build up.

It was love against love.

Mother love against wife love.

If this was the teaching of his science then science is wise.

Mother love once roused fought valiantly on the side of the doctor and life.

It was a tedious contest, there was so little life in her when it began, but the doctor and mother love won.

A morning came when Erma could leave her bed. Kate Huntley was there with Mrs. Trenhom and the children to help her out, and then when she was comfortably placed in a chair, Col. Valore came. The old man was charming in his

delight. He laid his hands on Erma's head, then he kissed
her and said, " Thank God, dear." After that he snapped his
fingers, dropped his cane, and waltzed around the room with
Erma's children. Erma laughed, the children and Mrs. Huntley clapped their hands and vowed that Valore was as " nimble
as a cricket." Valore laughed too ; but they could see two
great drops in the corners of his eyes as he added, " Ah ! if
Clarissa were only here I would be the happiest old boy ! "

A few days later, Erma was able to travel. There was
a tender parting with Mrs. Trenhom, who, having found
employment in a government office, remained in Washington.
Then Kate Huntley carried Erma, her children and Col.
Valore away with her to her new home among the Berkshire
Hills. There three months passed away. Erma gathered
strength. Neighbors came to see them. New friendships
were formed ; new likings grew into their lives, and Valore,
in the church and the village, where he was soon known to
everyone, became a prime favorite. All this time, the Colonel
was sadly torn. He felt that his duty, for the present, at least,
was with Erma and her children ; but his heart was far away
with the wife of nearly half a century. Not a day passed
without his saying something to Kate Huntley, Erma and her
children about Clarissa. How she looked as a girl ; what she
wore when they were married, and the many, many happy
days they spent together. And every Monday he wrote.
They all soon came to know it. That was " Uncle Gersh's letter day." But in all these weeks there came no answer to his
letters—not a word. At first Valore hoped. Then he went
regularly to the little post-office. At last he gave it up. But
some one of the others went every day. Then they would
whisper to each other, " Oh ! if I were only Aunt Clarissa,
I would write to dear, dear Uncle Gersh ! "

At the end of three months a carriage drove up from the
depot and paused in front of the door. The girls heard it
stop. That may sound like a solecism, but it is a fact. The
carriage door opened and a lady stepped out. The children
saw her and cried " oh ! " Erma looked out of the window
and echoed "oh !" Then Valore looked, and he—he never

said a word, but dropped his cane and ran out of the door. In the garden, Valore threw his arms about the woman and cried " Clarissa," and she pulled down his face and kissed him as she answered " Gersham."

Then she took his arm. As she walked toward the house she said to him, " I tried to keep it up, Gersham, but I couldn't do it." Valore's tremulous lips were silent, but he pressed the arm resting in his own closer to his side.

" More than half of me," continued his wife, " was here, and I've brought the other half to stay with it." Valore found tongue to answer " Don't say another word about it, Clarissa, we have been separated but never apart." Then they entered the house.

To Kate Huntley, Erma and her children, Mrs. Valore extended the tips of her fingers. It was evidently Valore and not them she came to see. During the evening they were all uneasy ; they tried to define their relation to Mrs. Valore. The Colonel had but one word of advice, " Wait, fretting don't open flower buds ; spurring won't hasten to-morrow." Wise saws. His was the philosophy of contented happiness. Waiting had won for him, why not for them. But the same answering thought was in all the other minds, " She is not my wife."

Geese ! Wives are sometimes the most implacable haters.

The next morning Mrs. Valore was complaining. Then followed a low fever. It was not serious, but it confined her to her bed, and required care and attention.

It was then that Kate Huntley and Erma came out strong. They were a combination of prudence and devotion. Then came the neighbors, first to inquire, then to act. They brought little tid-bits, they robbed their conservatories of flowers for the sick-room, and they sat up nights with Mrs. Valore when she was at the worst. Afterwards, when she was convalescent, they came and amused her with gossip of the neighborhood, quite as entertaining to some women as the brightest of books.

One day after her visitors had departed, this conversation occurred.

"Gersham, they are a charming people."

"Of course they are."

"I think I could love them."

"I know I do."

"Ah! you truant!"

"Especially the pretty girl who brought you this," picking up a little basket of flowers and putting them to his lips.

"I must get well to look after you."

"And that white haired lady who has just departed."

"Ah, indeed!"

"She looks so much like you."

"You flatterer!"

Valore put his hand over his heart and bowed. After a few moments' silence Mrs. Valore spoke again.

"Gersham, sometimes I think if our friends at home knew these people better, it would be different."

"There is no doubt of it. For years we have been playing at misconceptions on both sides."

"And will it never end, Gersham?"

"Yes, Clarissa, when we know each other better. There is half a cure in commingling. With that comes better knowledge, and transfusion of ideas. For the other half, we must depend on ourselves. Our best people in the South must not shrink from looking squarely at the abuses we have suffered to grow rather than created, and must combine to compel their cessation."

"Since I have known these dear people, I begin to wish it could be."

"It will be, Clarissa, when we see the North as it is and ourselves as we are."

On the evening of this conversation, while Erma's oldest daughter was smoothing the invalid's pillows before she retired, Mrs. Valore drew the young head to her and whispered in her ear, "Rissy, sleep with your old aunty to-night!"

Rissy (her name was Clarissa, after Mrs. Valore) assented, then slipped away and told her mother. The news was too good to keep. Erma was in the seventh heaven of delight. She waltzed around the room on her tip-toes, and hugged everyone within reach. Valore pulled her little pink ears. Then she mounted a chair and waved her hands over her head, as much as to say "three cheers and a tiger," very silently of course.

The next morning, when Erma entered the bed room to wake her aunt, Mrs. Valore caught her hand, drew her face down to her and pressed a kiss upon her cheek, "Erma, forgive an old woman ?"

"Yes, Mrs. Valore."

"Oh! Mrs. Valore, indeed. Aunt Rissy; remember that, dear, your Aunty Rissy."

"Yes, dear Aunt Rissy."

And she pressed kiss after kiss upon her wrinkled lips and cheek. Just then Kate Huntley and Erma's youngest daughter entered the room and both came in for a share of the embracing. As Kate and Erma danced around, helping Mrs. Valore to dress, she looked on with glad tears in her eyes, and when they were through, Col. Valore entered the room to escort his wife to the breakfast-room. She whispered in his ears, "Gersham, there is something better than prejudice." Then she gave one arm to Erma and another to Kate and walked away between them. Col. Valore, with "Rissy" on one side and her sister on the other bringing up the rear. And they all assembled about the breakfast-table, with the echo of a thousand cheers in their hearts.

THE END.

Americans in Fiction

A series of reprints of 19th century American novels important to the study of American folklore, culture and literary history